Martyn Young trained as a Registered Nurse, working in Operating Theatres for 15 years. Following his NHS career, and a short career in business, he trained as a Pilot, going on to qualify as a Commercial Pilot and Flying Instructor and Examiner. He now works part time and is looking forward to a fulfilling retirement. His interests include Fine Art Photography, he is a self-confessed petrolhead with an interest in anything with wheels, wings or an engine and travelling.

Dedicated to my wife and my daughter—thank you for all your help and encouragement. I also dedicate this to all students, past and present, with whom I have shared a passion for flight.

Martyn Young

PETER

AUSTIN MACAULEY PUBLISHERS™
LONDON * CAMBRIDGE * NEW YORK * SHARJAH

A CIP catalogue record for this title is available from the British Library.

ISBN 9781398480520 (Paperback)
ISBN 9781398480537 (Hardback)
ISBN 9781398480544 (ePub e-book)

www.austinmacauley.com

First Published 2023
Austin Macauley Publishers Ltd®
1 Canada Square
Canary Wharf
London
E14 5AA

1

Peter slowly opened his eyes. It was early and the house was quiet. The room was dark with just the first vestiges of light creeping under the curtains. He switched the bedside lamp on and checked his wristwatch. *Good*, he thought to himself—*about 10 minutes until the first of the morning departures.* He continued to lay in the stillness as if disturbing the quiet of the morning was somehow a profanity.

Finally in the distance came the familiar sound of piston engines straining against the morning sky. Peter slid out of bed, gently opened the curtains and grabbed his binoculars. He saw the aircraft climbing ever higher as it passed over the house and he focused the binoculars in order to capture the details, noting the registration, time and date in his well-thumbed notebook. Once the aircraft had disappeared over the factory chimneys, he slid back between the sheets, satisfied.

He lay for a while in that delicious space between sleep and wakefulness, enjoying the solitude and the quiet which was only disturbed by the morning chatter of the birds in the garden.

Finally, movement jerked him into full wakefulness. His mother was pottering about in the kitchen, preparing the family breakfast, humming quietly to herself. She knew that Peter would be awake and will have noted the departure from the airport just a couple of miles away. She allowed herself a smile at the rigidity of his routines. She would leave him to come out of his room in his own time, knowing that to disturb those routines was sometimes a precursor to trouble.

Today, being a weekend, meant that there was no school and nothing was required of Peter's time. As was usual, Peter planned to jump onto his bicycle and cycle to the airport, getting to his favourite spot on the little mound next to the runway. This lofty perch afforded him a great view of aircraft both taking off and landing and he could fill the day jotting down the details. Rarely did he see any of his school friends at weekends, but this suited his solitary nature. He didn't care much for most of them anyway. He was comfortable with his own company and people found him difficult to relate to. He found social situations nearly impossible and kept away from them whenever possible.

Peter got out of bed and, rubbing the sleep from his eyes, wandered into the kitchen.

"Morning," came his mother's greeting.

"Morning. What's for breakfast?" he replied.

"The usual—what do you fancy?" asked Annie, his mother.

"Hmmm—some toast I think, please," Peter decided.

Annie smiled, knowing that this would be the answer—it was always the same.

Peter's dad Paul came into the kitchen, greeting Peter by ruffling his hair and grunting an unintelligible greeting.

"Morning, Dad," said Peter. "What are we doing today?"

"Let me see—fancy a ride to the airport?" asked Paul, knowing full well what the answer would be.

"Yeah, that'd be great," Peter replied, excited at the prospect of spending time with his father.

This was precious to Peter as Paul worked long shifts at the factory where he was an engineer and often Peter was in bed before his Paul arrived home. His dad knew all sorts about the aeroplanes, having worked on them during the war and was an endless source of information and facts.

"Don't forget that your brother is coming home on leave today," Paul reminded him.

Peter's heart sank—the bully was going to be back home for a while. Peter silently resolved to stay as far away from his older brother as possible and also reminded himself to hide as many of his model aircraft as he could, so that they couldn't be "accidentally" broken.

"It'll be nice to see Ben, won't it?" asked Annie.

Peter mumbled a reply and finished his breakfast. *No, it won't—he's just a thug and a bully*, he thought to himself.

Annie continued, "It'll be lovely to see you both together again—I do enjoy it when he's here."

I don't, thought Peter. "How long is he home for?" asked Peter, hoping that his Mum's reply would indicate the shortest time possible.

"Until next weekend—he goes back to his unit on the Monday," came the reply.

Great—a whole week of having to put up with him. Hopefully, Ben would be out most of the time with his old schoolmates—no doubt spending most of their time in the pub. It was a world that Peter wanted no part of. Most of Ben's friends had left school without qualifications—just like Ben—and were now in dead-end jobs or on the dole. Ben had chosen a career in the Army and had joined as a driver 2 years previously. It wasn't what Peter aspired to and he was looking forward to getting his GCE "O" Level exam results soon.

"Come on, Peter—let's get going," called Paul.

Peter raced downstairs after carefully putting his binoculars and notebook into his old army satchel, which he slung over his shoulder. He met his dad in the kitchen just as he was packing their lunch into a bag.

"I've seen in the local news that there are going to be new jet aircraft arriving soon and some of the old piston aircraft will be getting retired," Paul told him.

Peter grew excited at the prospect of seeing jets roar across the rooftops. "Wow—that'll be so cool," Peter said. "When are they being delivered?"

"Soon, I hope," came the reply.

Peter and his dad went out into the warm sunshine, unlocked the garage and got their bicycles out. They relocked the door and pushed the bikes down the front path and across the road which ran in front of the house, lifting them over the stile onto the old track which crossed the farmer's field.

"Come on—I'll race you," called his dad, charging off down the dusty lane.

Peter leapt onto his bike and set off at a furious pace to catch and try and pass, his dad. His dad was having none of it and whilst Peter's younger legs made catching Dad easy, Paul was a master tactician, swerving and blocking Peter's attempts to pass. They both raced along, enjoying the beautiful morning, laughing at each other's tactics as they tore towards the horizon. They eventually reached the old perimeter road which ran around the airport, which was an old World War 2 RAF base, hastily converted for civilian use.

A modern terminal building had recently been added and there were plans for further expansion. None of these details bothered Peter as they arrived at the mound and they dismounted, laying their bikes on the ground. Peter was first to climb the short way to the top and he quickly settled into his favourite place, unpacking his binoculars and notebook. *Ready for action*, he thought to himself. His dad joined him and settled onto the grass beside his son.

Shortly, Peter picked up his binoculars and watched intently at a faint image in the distance.

"One taxiing out," he said to his dad.

Paul squinted into the sunshine. "Let me know what it is," he said.

"Sure thing," came the excited reply.

Paul lay on the grass watching Peter intently. Aviation was an obsession with the young man and always had been ever since Paul had taken both boys to the local air shown when they were young. Over the years, Peter had lived and breathed aeroplanes and he had many completed notebooks of aircraft registrations, models, picture albums and photographs. When Peter wasn't watching aircraft and collecting registration numbers, he was building models, reading books about aircraft and it was usually his only topic of conversation.

Paul found this worrying to a degree, as was Peter's lack of confidence when in mixed company and his lack of friends. He was obviously intelligent and worked hard at his studies with a career in aviation his only goal. Peter hadn't started speaking until he was three years old and Paul and Annie had taken him to the doctor worrying that there was something seriously wrong, but the doctor had dismissed their worries.

"I'm sure he'll catch up," the doctor told them. Well, he'd certainly done that. "He'll grow out of it," Paul often told Annie, although there were no signs of that happening yet. Annie thought of Peter as a delicate child.

The aircraft, now airborne, roared past, tucking its wheels away in a smooth ballet of technology. Peter read off the type and registration to Paul and made careful notes in his book. Paul smiled—he enjoyed these times with Peter and felt that it was the only time that they managed to connect on a real basis. He lay back on the grass and listened to his son's excited chatter and continued to mull over just what made Peter so different to his elder brother.

Ben was very direct and although Paul was disappointed at Ben's lack of formal academic qualifications, he was proud of the fact that he had joined the military and was serving his country. The heavy goods licence that Ben had gained would stand him in good stead when his time in the Army came to an end. Quite where Peter would end up would remain to be seen.

The day wore on with Peter noting every arrival and departure. They broke for lunch and ate their sandwiches and drank tea from Paul's flask whilst Peter continued to tell Paul about each aircraft movement. Paul had heard it so many times before, but he listened intently to every word Peter said.

Experience had taught him that to not pay attention could lead to one of Peter's temper meltdowns. These happened rarely these days as Annie & Paul had learned how to manage, but they both still exercised caution. As the afternoon wore on and the sun began to sink lower in the sky, Paul suggested that perhaps it was time to head home. Peter responded by asking what time

Ben was expected home and seemed to suddenly become anxious. Paul did his best to calm him and eventually they climbed down the mound, mounted their bikes and set off towards home. Peter cycled slowly, obviously reluctant to get home, but wouldn't discuss why with his dad and despite Paul's encouragement, there was no racing on the return trip. By the time they arrived home, Pater had withdrawn into himself completely and they put their bikes away in silence.

When they got inside the house, Peter immediately ran up the stairs to his room without saying a word. Paul and Annie exchanged a knowing glance as they understood exactly why Peter's demeanour had changed so suddenly. They knew that there was little love lost between the two boys and there had been many problems with Ben bullying Peter, teasing him about his aviation hobby, breaking his models and tearing up his books. Paul had been forced on many occasions to have to discipline Ben and when these occasions arose it was always difficult.

2

Peter closed his bedroom door and sat on the edge on his bed, retreating into his dark private world. Thoughts crowded his head, filling the crevices of his mind with his darkest worries and he desperately thought of ways to try to avoid his brother and any ensuing conflict. As always, Peter's brain was hyperactive, charging off at tangents and filling his head with every possible scenario about what may happen whilst Ben was home.

He had hidden most of his models and notebooks and would try to remain as out of sight as possible. Ben was what was often described as a larger-than-life character and was loud and brash with it—altogether the antithesis of Peter. He shut his eyes and rocked gently backwards and forwards, which he found calmed him down. He felt like he was sitting in a dentist's waiting room, with the inevitable unpleasant ordeal before him and listened to the minutes ticking away on his bedside clock.

He could hear the sounds of his parent's muffled conversation in the kitchen below and he hoped that they were discussing ways of keeping Ben away from him and out of his room. The problem for Peter was that he felt that his parents just didn't understand him—nobody did—and he found it so difficult to relate to them and to open up to them to discuss his innermost and darkest thoughts.

It was the same for his fellow school colleagues—so many times Peter would sit in class listening to the teachers putting across the simplest of ideas, yet he found it frustrating that so many in his group just couldn't grasp these ideas or concepts without having them explained over and over again.

What was up with people? This was 1969 and Peter was in a Grammar school and not some Victorian poorhouse, so he expected that his fellows would be able to learn at the same rate as he —after all they had passed the same entrance exams. Perhaps, he thought to himself, I'm just better at learning technical subjects.

Luckily, Peter had two good friends at school—people who not only liked him, but whom Peter felt understood him and who tolerated his routines and ways of doing thing. It was good to have friends like Liam and Alex—both shared his interest in aviation and they were fast learners like Peter and good companions.

This musing allowed his mind to wander towards his goals—of learning to fly and becoming aircrew. It had always been his ambition, ever since Paul had treated him to a short pleasure flight on summer holiday and the visit to the air show and no amount of persuasion from his parents or teachers had swayed him from this path. Peter simply wasn't interested in doing anything else and everything he studied at school—especially maths and physics—was intended to achieve that goal.

The highlight of his summer holidays the previous year had been, along with his dad, to visit an open day with a local airline, where he had been shown around the offices and listened to a presentation about the airline and how it worked. However, the main highlight of the day was to be taken on board one of the aircraft and to be allowed to sit in the right-hand seat on the flightdeck.

Here, Peter was able to marvel at the bewildering array of dials, switches, levers and knobs used to control the aircraft in flight. One of the airline Captains was on hand to explain what things were and how they worked and Peter was enthralled. He felt like he had found his true place in the world and it strengthened his resolve to make this his chosen career.

His thoughts were interrupted by the sound of the front door opening and raised voices welcoming his brother home. He heard Ben's voice cutting through the chatter and his heart sank.

His mother called up the stairs, "Peter—Peter. Ben's here—are you coming down?"

Not if I can help it, he thought and he stayed on his bed.

Eventually, there was a gentle knock and his father poked his head around the half-open door. "Are you coming down? Ben's here," said his dad.

Peter slowly got up and reluctantly followed his dad downstairs—inside he was shaking and his mind raced with the prospect of what Ben may have in store for him in the coming week. Life had been so much more settled since Ben had left to join the Army, but things quickly returned to normal when Ben was home and Peter found it harder to cope with every visit.

They walked in to the kitchen, where Peter could hear Ben's loud voice explaining something to his mother. Peter tried to stay half-hidden behind his dad, but Ben saw him and jumped up to greet him.

"Hey—how are you little brother?" Ben slapped Peter on the arm in greeting, which made Peter recoil—he hated physical contact, especially with Ben.

Peter looked at Ben and as Peter was a good five inches taller, he thought to himself, *I'm not such a little brother anymore.* "Yeah, I'm OK," he muttered. "How are you? How's the Army?"

"Great thanks—you should join up, you'd love it," said Ben. "So what have you been up to?" Ben added.

"Oh, usual stuff really—been busy with school and have been sitting my GCE's, so I'm waiting for the results."

"Ahh, yes, of course." Ben went on, "You love being a swot."

"Ben—that's a little unfair," said Paul. "Peter enjoys his studies."

"Yeah, well, they never did me any favours," said Ben. "I have a great job and am earning money, so what's the point of books and studying?"

Yeah and you've no qualifications and will be stuck in a dead-end job for the rest of your life, thought Peter, but he kept this to himself.

"You still interested in your aeroplanes?" asked Ben. Peter nodded. "Thought you'd have grown out of building toy aircraft by now," Ben quipped.

"They're not toys, they're models," Peter said.

"Yeah whatever—still toys to me," Ben snapped.

"Come on, Ben—you can help me with dinner," said Annie, in an effort to defuse the conversation. She could see where it was headed.

"Yeah, OK," said Ben.

Peter turned around and went back upstairs to his room, gently closing the door. *He hasn't changed*, Peter thought. *Still the same idiot.* Peter closed his eyes and again rocked gently, drawing his privacy around him like a dark cloak. He'd go back down for dinner and, hopefully, Ben would be going out with his friends, so he wouldn't have to avoid him all evening.

He wasn't pleased to see Ben and, in fact, felt nothing at all. There was no affection or bond between them and Peter had spent a lifetime being the object of Ben's bullying, his teasing and being the butt of Ben's often obnoxious behaviour. Ben was another who didn't understand Peter and Peter was determined to keep Ben out of his world and his private space.

Annie's voice floated up the stairs, "Peter—dinner's ready."

Peter got up and slowly went downstairs. The air was filled with the heavy scent of boiled cabbage and potatoes. He took his place at the table between his dad and his mum and opposite Ben. Annie laid full plates in front of them all and Peter ate in silence. Ben was in animated conversation with Paul, but Peter just ate his food and listened in a half-hearted way.

After a while, Peter realised that Ben was speaking to him directly. "When do you get your exam results?" Ben asked.

"Next Saturday," Peter answered.

"Oh great, I'll be here to help you celebrate—or otherwise," said Ben, doing his best to bait Peter, but Peter didn't respond—he just hoped that he'd done well enough to move on to the next level.

"I'm sure Peter has done his best," said Annie. "He's worked so hard."

"Well, we'll see," answered Ben. "Being at his posh school doesn't mean that he'll automatically do well."

"I'm sure Peter has made an effort," Paul responded, thinking to himself, *He couldn't do any worse than you.*

Ben had attended the local Secondary Modern school after failing his 11 plus exams and had failed to shine academically. He just wasn't suited to the education environment and there had been many occasions, following parent's evenings, where there had been heated discussions regarding Ben's lack of effort and interest.

He had failed his mock GCE exams and had therefore not sat the proper exams, leaving school with just a general certificate of education and despite Paul's best efforts in obtaining Ben a place as an apprentice with the engineering company, they had refused Ben a place due to his lack of qualifications. The army, whilst an honourable career, had seemed like the only option for him.

All of this was now history. Ben seemed to be settled in his role and Paul's attention was on Peter's forthcoming results. He had high hopes for Peter and had a secret feeling that he would do very well indeed.

After dinner, Peter helped Annie clear away the dinner plates and he ran hot water into the washing-up bowl to wash the dishes. This was one of his routines and he actually enjoyed doing the dishes, as it gave him time alone with his mother. They would often chat about all sorts of things and Peter would sometimes open up to his mother if was in the mood. Today though, Peter washed in silence, the thoughts of his brother and the coming week filling his head.

Annie recognised the silence and didn't try to break the spell. She knew full well that there had been issues between the boys since they were small and Peter's introspective personality was completely opposite to Ben's and Ben seemed to resent the extra time Annie and Paul had spent with Peter when he was small, encouraging him to speak and helping him learn. Ben had been a normal, loud, brash and lively boy and had grown into much the same sort of an adult, but Peter was quiet, shy, a loner and very deep. Annie often felt that she would never know the real Peter and he gave out very little.

Washing-up completed, Peter wiped the dining table and helped Annie clear away the last items from the meal. He then started towards the stairs, but was stopped by Annie's question, "Peter—what are you worried about?"

Peter paused, turned slowly around and spoke quietly, "Oh you know—the usual stuff. Ben can't resist having a go at me whenever he gets the opportunity and you know he'll try to break my models—just like he did last time. He just loves to wind me up—why can't he just leave me alone?"

Tears pricked his eyes and Annie put her arms around him. "It'll be OK—your dad & I will be watching out for you," she reassured him.

Peter wiped away the tears and gave Annie a squeeze. "I know," he answered. "It's just that—I know he doesn't like me, although that's OK. It's just that he can't get used to the fact that we're both so different."

"We know," replied Annie. "We know."

Peter let go of his mother just as Ben came back into the kitchen.

"Ha! Getting your mummy's boy cuddles?" he sneered.

"Ben," barked his mother. "There's no need for that. Gosh, you've only been home for a couple of hours! I hope that we're not going to have all the usual nastiness all week," she added.

"Yeah, whatever," Ben responded. "Anyway, I'm off to the pub with my mates, so I'll see you all later."

"OK," Annie said. "Be careful and try not to wake us if you're home late."

"Yeah, OK," came Ben's response and he picked up his jacket, barged past Peter and went out of the door.

"Exactly like that," said Peter.

Annie nodded her head and Peter left the kitchen and returned to his room. He picked up his favourite book, which was an autobiography of a Test Pilot from the war and opened it to read. He was quickly lost in its pages, vicariously living the life of the man involved.

Downstairs, Paul and Annie were deep in conversation. "You know Peter's worried about Ben being home?" Annie said. "It's always difficult when they're together. It's actually been a relief whilst Ben's been away and it's been nice seeing Peter finally coming out of his shell a little bit. I just hope that there's no issues this week."

Paul listened in silence, nodding his head. "I agree," he replied. "The problem is that they're like chalk and cheese—so different and as the doctor once said, Peter may have developmental problems, although he seems very intelligent. I worry that he's setting his goals a bit too high and he'll be awfully disappointed if he can't get to where he wants to be. I just wish I knew how to help and understand him more."

Annie nodded her agreement. "Let's just see how this week goes and we'll have to manage the situation as things arise," she said and getting up, kissed Paul and said goodnight. "I'm off upstairs—I need an early night," and she left Paul picked up a book and began to read.

3

The banging of the front door made Peter wake up immediately. He sat up in bed, listening to the sounds of feet climbing the stairs. *Please go straight to bed*, he thought to himself, but this was not to be. His bedroom door was being pushed slowly open. He flicked his bedside light on and saw the face of his brother peering around the door, wearing a large stupid grin.

"Hey baby brother—you OK? Can I come in," Ben said.

"I'd rather you went straight to bed," Peter responded, but Ben came further into the room.

"What's up? Not pleased to see me?" Ben asked.

"Not really," Peter replied with his characteristic honesty. Peter always told it straight—he found no need for dressing it up.

"Well, tough—I'm here for the next week. We're going to have lots of fun," Ben said with a hint of menace in his voice.

"Well, would you mind getting out of my room and going to bed?" Peter asked.

Ben sat down on the edge of the bed, the stench of stale beer and cigarette smoke emanating from his every pore. "Why don't you want to talk to your big brother?" he asked.

Peter remained silent—he knew Ben was trying to provoke a response and was probably itching for an argument.

Ben continued, "What are we going to do tomorrow, little bro? Perhaps I should take you to the pub or maybe we could go out chasing girls. What do you think?" Peter didn't respond. "Cat got your tongue, Peter? We'll see about that," and Ben stood up.

Peter cowered in fear, but just then, Paul appeared in the doorway. "Ben—leave him alone and get to bed. You've woken the whole house up."

Ben sighed and turned away. As he did so, he muttered something about helping Peter grow up and he stomped out of the room.

"You OK?" asked Paul.

"Yes, I guess so," Peter replied.

"Goodnight."

"G'night," Paul said and softly closed the door.

Peter lay in the darkness for a long time, different scenarios playing out in his head. Why was his brother such a jerk? Why couldn't he just leave him alone? Eventually, Peter fell into a restless sleep, alone with his dark thoughts and dreams.

Peter woke early as was always the case. Today being a Sunday there would be no early departure for him to log, so he lay in silence. His mind was still in turmoil from the previous evening's events—what had Ben meant helping him to grow up? In what way? Peter felt he was growing up just fine and in his own time and he certainly had little interest in the things that seemed to consume his brother.

He hadn't really shown an interest in girls and like his parents, had no interest in visiting pubs and drinking. It all seemed like a waste of time and money to him and he wanted nothing that would interfere with his studies and ambitions. The daylight began to appear and the room gradually became lighter, allowing Peter to pick out the details. He got up and after visiting the bathroom, he went downstairs to get a drink.

He sat at the kitchen table enjoying his coffee and heard footsteps on the stairs. Annie appeared in the kitchen doorway and she smiled when she saw him.

"You're up early," she remarked.

"Yeah, I couldn't sleep," Peter responded.

Annie came up behind Peter and wrapped her arms around him, kissing him gently on the back of his neck. "It'll all be OK," she whispered.

Peter folded his arms across hers and nodded his head. "I know," he said quietly.

Annie went to the kettle, refilled it and switched it on. "More coffee?"

"No thanks, I'm full," Peter replied.

Annie sat down next to Peter. She had so many questions to ask and there was so much she wanted to know, but she knew that Peter was a very private person and that he wouldn't open up so easily. "What are your plans for today?" Annie asked.

"I'm not sure—I may go out for a ride later this morning," Peter responded.

Annie knew that he would want to keep as much distance between Ben and himself as possible. "Ben's OK you know—he doesn't really mean any harm," Annie suggested.

Peter stiffened. "Oh he does—he hates me, he thinks that I'm weird and he enjoys every opportunity to annoy me as he loves getting me to a point where I have a meltdown. You just don't understand how he's been with me and all the things that he's done to me over the years. Remember the time that I came home from school to find him sitting on my bed breaking one of my models apart bit-by-bit? Or the time that he pulled all the pages out of one of my notebooks? I won't forget—and you can hardly say that he doesn't mean any harm. He's a callous and nasty piece of work and you just can't see what he's like."

"Well, your dad and I will keep a close eye on him—but he does live here as well, this is still his family home so it'd be lovely if you could both get along."

"Maybe so," said Peter, "but you're not going to be here all week, so I just want to stay out of his way."

"I've taken the week off work," said Annie, "so I'll be here with you both all week."

Peter relaxed a little—he knew that his Mum's job as a receptionist at the local doctor's surgery was flexible and this news came as huge relief.

Peter stood up. "I'm going to get washed and get ready," he said.

"Are you having some breakfast?" Annie asked.

"Yes please, when I come back down," Peter replied.

He went back upstairs and met with his dad who was just coming out of the bathroom.

"Hi, buddy. What are we up to today?" his dad enquired.

"I think I may go for a ride," Peter responded.

"Do you fancy a visit to the museum in town?" asked Paul.

"Let me think about it," said Peter as he pushed past his dad and into the bathroom.

Peter dressed and went back downstairs, seating himself at his place at the kitchen table. His dad was helping Annie with the breakfast. After a minute or so, Annie placed Peter's toast in front of him.

"Thanks." He ate in silence, listening to his Mum & Dad's muted conversation.

They came and sat with him and Paul said, "we thought it would be nice to have a family day out. Do you fancy anywhere in particular?"

"No not really—as long as I'm not left alone with him," Peter said, gesturing upstairs.

"You won't be, so don't worry," said Paul.

Peter picked up his book and resumed his reading. After around an hour, they heard footsteps upstairs and heard Ben going into the bathroom. A while later, Ben appeared in the kitchen, looking pale with red rings around his eyes.

"Good morning," said Annie, but she was ignored.

Ben went to the kettle, switched it on and made coffee, sitting down at the table with a thump.

"Thought we might have a family day out together," Paul said to Ben, who was busy slurping his coffee.

Ben didn't offer any response, so Paul continued, "anywhere you particularly fancy, Ben?"

"Anywhere as long as it's nowhere near the airport and has nothing to do with planes," Ben growled.

Paul looked at Peter. "That's fine with me," said Peter. *Round one to me,* he thought to himself.

"I thought maybe the transport museum in town might be a good idea," Paul suggested.

"Yeah, whatever," came Ben's reply.

"Good—that's settled. We'll set off when everyone's finished breakfast," Paul added.

As Ben didn't feel like having any breakfast, they left the kitchen to get themselves ready. Annie had made sandwiches and a flask of tea and there was a cafe at the museum where they could get something hot to eat if they fancied. Peter finished getting dressed and slipped a notebook into his pocket. He could write down anything of interest that caught his eye. He went back downstairs, where mum & dad were ready.

Ben eventually appeared and they all got their jackets and left the house, locking the door carefully. It was just a short walk to the bus stop and Ben walked along in front of the rest of them, his hands thrust deep into his pockets. Peter walked alongside his mother, but there was no conversation. They got to the bus stop and within a couple of minutes the green and cream bus appeared around the bend.

Paul stepped forward and put out his hand, signalling the bus to stop. The bus slowed and turned into the bus stop and the doors opened with a creaking sound. They hopped on board and Ben disappeared upstairs, saying that he was going for a smoke. This surprised the rest of them, as they had no idea that Ben had taken up smoking.

"All part of growing up," said Paul, but he was disappointed at Ben for starting what he considered to be a filthy habit.

The bus rolled and wheezed its way into Westlea town centre, eventually coming to a halt within the terminus. Everyone on board stood up to disembark and Peter was temporarily parted from Annie. He began to feel panic rising within, but his mother quickly caught up and put a reassuring hand on his arm.

"I'm here, sweetie," she said quietly and Peter smiled and tried to relax. He hated crowds and couldn't cope with turmoil and lots of people buzzing around. They waited for Ben to appear and then set off towards the museum, Peter staying close to Annie, with Dad and Ben trailing along behind.

When they arrived at the museum, Paul purchased tickets and they went through the turnstile and inside. Immediately, Ben saw a display of Army trucks and he and Paul began to look them over. Peter turned a different way and walked briskly towards a different room, with Annie breathlessly catching him up.

"Are you in a race this morning?" she laughed.

"No, just doing my own thing," Peter replied, stopping in front of a display case containing aircraft instruments from old RAF bombers.

"What are these?" asked Annie.

"Cockpit instruments," Peter replied. "They give the pilot information on airspeed, altitude, that sort of thing," he went on.

"Ahh, OK," Annie responded. "I always wondered how the pilots steered the aeroplanes."

"They can give all sorts of information." Peter continued, "From direction of flight, information about how quickly they are going up or down and even if they are right side up or upside down."

"Amazing," muttered Annie, trying her best to take it all in. She did her best to understand, hoping that knowledge would act as a gateway into Peter's world.

Just then, Peter was tapped on the shoulder and he heard a voice say, "Hi, buddy."

He turned around and there was Alex from school. "Hi, Alex," said Peter. "What are you doing here?"

"Much the same as you I guess—family day out," Alex replied.

"Yeah, us as well. My brother is home on leave from the Army, so Dad bought us all here this morning. You know my Mum?" Peter asked, turning to his mother.

"Yes, of course—Hi," Alex said.

"Hi, Alex—nice to see you. I guess I'll leave you boys alone and go and find your father," Annie said, wandering off.

Peter was so pleased to see his friend—Alex was such a good guy and they usually had a lot of fun together. They continued to walk around the exhibits, chattering about the vehicles on show and pretty soon the conversation got around to the forthcoming exam results.

"I need to get at least 5 A Grades," said Alex. "I need really good grades to be able to go on to start my A-Levels. Dad wants me to follow him into medicine." Alex's father was a doctor at the local hospital. "It's a bit of a family tradition," he added.

"I'm hoping to get a few A's," Peter said. "Although I don't need specific grades for flight school, just a good general standard. Would be nice to beat my brother though," he added.

"That won't be difficult," quipped Alex and they both roared with laughter.

"When can you start flight school?" asked Alex, somewhat curious.

"At seventeen, although I can apply when I'm sixteen," Peter replied, adding, "I guess I'll stay on at school if my grades are OK, just to fill the time and better my chances."

Alex smiled to himself—he knew that whatever the outcome, Peter would probably get the highest grades in the year—he and all of the other pupils looked up to Peter as he was very bright.

The boys wandered around for quite a while longer and were interrupted by Annie finding them and telling Peter that they were going to the cafe for lunch.

"I guess I'd better go and find my folks. See you tomorrow," said Alex.

"Sure thing," said Peter, joining his mother.

They walked to the cafe, where Paul and Ben were waiting.

"Hi, son—what have you been up to?" asked Paul.

"I met my buddy Alex from school and we've been looking at stuff," Peter responded.

"Swapping serial numbers?" sneered Ben.

"Ben—there is no need for that," snapped Paul. "Just leave him be."

Annie arrived with a tray with their lunches. "Paul—will you go and collect the drinks please," she asked.

Paul stood up and walked towards the counter.

"That was your fault," hissed Ben through closed teeth. Peter didn't respond, but let it pass.

"What was Peter's fault?" asked Annie.

"Oh nothing," said Ben—"just having a joke."

"OK, well let's enjoy lunch in peace," said Annie. She was so tired of being the referee—she longed for the day that the two of them could just get along normally.

"What have you been looking at?" Peter asked his father.

"Oh, all sorts. Ben has been showing me the Army trucks and has been telling me how the trucks that they use nowadays are really just a development of the older stuff. Nothing much is really new. They really are quite interesting—you should come and have a look."

"Maybe after lunch," Peter said.

"I'll take you around," said Ben—"Show you some proper stuff."

"Oh that would be nice," said Annie. "It'll be good for you to spend some time together."

Hmmm maybe, maybe not, thought Peter. He consoled himself with the thought that in a public place he'd be safe from Ben's teasing and sniping.

When they had all finished, they stood up and walked back outside into the museum. "Come on then," said Peter. "Show me your Army trucks."

"Walk this way," replied Ben, who shot off at a fast pace towards the Army exhibits.

Peter followed, glancing back over his shoulder. Annie gave him a small wave before his parents disappeared in the crowd. Peter followed his brother into the hall where the trucks were. Ben had stopped beside a huge vehicle.

"This is a 10-ton 12-wheeler personnel carrier," he said. "It very similar to the type I drive, although ours now have mod cons such as bigger and more powerful engines and power steering."

"What is it like to drive?" asked Peter.

"Brilliant," came the reply. "I pulls like a train and will go anywhere and carry anything."

Peter regarded the sides of the truck. "Is it armour plated?" he asked, adding, "It doesn't look like it will stop an air rifle pellet let alone a bullet."

24

"No, they're not," explained Ben, getting into his stride. "The canvas back on won't stop anything, but the idea is to get personnel into the war zone before fighting starts. The squaddies are transferred to armoured personnel carriers or into tanks when the fun starts," he added.

Peter stood and read the information board pertaining to this particular truck. "It says here that it was designed in the 1930s," he said.

"Yeah, probably," came Ben's response, adding, "ours are a more modern design, but basically the same."

"Oh, OK," said Peter, unimpressed.

Ben continued to move from exhibit to exhibit, talking all the while, although Peter wasn't really paying attention. His earlier conversation with Alex was playing on his mind. *What if I've messed up*, he thought, worrying that inferior results or re-sits could jeopardise his chances. He began to play through the possible scenarios in his head, his mind racing with doubt and uncertainty.

He just kept hoping that things were OK, but his lack of confidence in his own abilities would not allow him any peace. Peter became aware that he was being called.

"Peter—Peter. For the last time, have you seen this?" Ben was trying to get his attention. Ben was standing in front of a small truck with huge wheels.

"Sorry—what is it?" Peter asked.

"It's what we call a scout car," said Ben. "Four wheel drive, armour plating and a massive engine, so it can go anywhere. Would be great fun to have one of these parked outside the house, don't you think?" he asked.

"Yeah, sure," agreed Peter, saying anything to keep the peace.

"You don't seem impressed," said Ben.

"Oh, I am," said Peter. "It's just that I don't know much about trucks or cars."

"You don't know much about anything except your damn aeroplanes," Ben spat.

"Whatever you say," Peter responded, anxious not to get into a fight. Ben continued to move through the exhibition hall and finally Peter spotted his parents a short distance away. "I'm going to join mum & dad," he said to Ben, moving away.

Ben ignored him and carried on looking over the tank which had now taken his interest. Peter reached his parents and took his mother's arm.

"Where is Ben?" Annie asked.

"Oh, he'll be along in a minute," said Peter, wishing that he wouldn't be.

"OK," she said quietly, knowing that Peter would speak when he was ready. After a while, Ben joined them. "Good time?" asked Annie.

"Yes—been broadening Peter's education with some proper vehicles and not an aeroplane in sight" Ben replied. "It was all very interesting," said Peter, adding, "I never knew that there was so much variety in military vehicles."

"We've only just scratched the surface," Ben replied. "Lots more to come."

Paul had been looking at his watch. "Probably time to head out for the bus," he said to them.

"Sure," said Ben, racing off to be first at the bus stop. Peter walked slowly with his mother, not saying anything.

They arrived home and Annie went straight to the kitchen to start preparing dinner. Paul and Ben sat on the sofa chatting, so Peter went to see if his mum needed any help.

"I'm OK thanks," she said. "Go and sit with your dad and your brother. I love it when my boys are all together." Peter went back into the living room and sat down in the armchair.

"Good day?" Paul asked.

"Yes, thanks it was OK," Peter replied. He sat listening to Paul and Ben's conversation, not joining in but taking in every word. He had gleaned a lot of information about the vehicles from both the museum information and from Ben, but it didn't interest him. Tomorrow was a school day and he was already focusing on that.

Shortly, Annie called them in for dinner. Peter took his usual seat and ate his meal in silence despite Annie's attempts to include him in the conversation. Once the meal was finished, he started helping with the washing up as usual. His mother helped in silence, as usual enjoying this private time with Peter. When all was done, Peter said that he was going to his room to prepare for school and went upstairs. Annie watched him climb the stairs in silence, deep in her own thoughts.

Later on, Peter heard the front door slam and looked out of the window to see Ben walking off down the street. *Probably off to the pub again*, he thought and went back to his book. Gradually, his eyes grew heavy and the words started to float on the page. *Time for bed*, he thought and he went to the bathroom to get ready, shortly afterwards slipping between the cool sheets and switching his bedside light off. He lay for a while enjoying the silence and drifted into a deep dreamless sleep.

4

After an undisturbed night, Peter was up early for school. He didn't have much to take with him as following the completion of the exams, there was little for pupils in his year to do before the end of term. He quickly ate breakfast and after saying goodbye to his mother, got his bicycle out of the garage and set off. He would call at Liam's house which was on his route so that they could ride together and chat about what the day may bring.

After a short ride, Peter arrived at Liam's, only to find him waiting for Peter outside. "Up early?" asked Peter.

"Yes—I couldn't sleep thinking about the results," replied Liam. They set off towards the school, which was about a 20-minute ride away.

"I've been thinking about those as well," said Peter. "I'm really worried."

"I don't think that you've anything to worry about," Liam responded.

He too held Peter's ability in awe and counted himself lucky to call Peter a true friend. Soon they were at the school gates and after locking their bikes away, they proceeded to their common room for registration. After a short while, Mr Adams, their form teacher, came in and started chatting. He seemed pretty relaxed and there seemed to be no urgency in his manner this morning.

"Right lads," he started. "There's nothing on the timetable this week. Suggest that you bring books to read or if you want you can play football or rugby. There won't be anybody available to supervise you, but think of this week as a pre-end of term holiday week."

This bought a murmur of approval from everyone and football teams quickly began to be formed and finalised. Peter felt safe, knowing that he wouldn't be picked. It was well known that he hated sports and that his skills with a ball were non-existent. He just smiled to himself and got his book out of his satchel—he had anticipated this being the case. Liam was an avid footballer, but Alex less so and he came and sat with Peter asking about the book he was reading.

"It's an autobiography of Squadron Leader David Mills, the test pilot," Peter explained.

Alex took the book and thumbed through the pages. "Interesting?" he asked, knowing what the answer would be.

"Yes, fascinating," Peter replied. "An amazing man and an amazing pilot—a true professional." Alex picked up a magazine from the common room table and they were quickly both lost in their reading.

The morning wore on and soon it was lunchtime. Their colleagues returned from the football pitch and breathlessly changed back into uniform and then it was the usual mad dash to the dining hall. They got their meals and sat in their usual places, noise filling the air. Peter sat between Alex and Liam, eating quietly, but soon joined in the conversation as it turned to discussing the forthcoming results.

"Who plans to stay on next year?" Peter asked. This bought a mixture of replies—some saying that it depended on the results and a few saying that they already had jobs or apprenticeships to go to.

"What about you?" asked another friend.

"Depends," Peter replied. "It's all about the results."

"Ahh, you'll be fine," his friend responded to a general murmur of agreement. This bought Peter back to his private deep thoughts. He was desperately trying to maintain his expectations, but didn't want to think that he had done well, as he couldn't stand the thought of disappointment.

After lunch, the boys returned to the common room and some immediately began to organise more football. When they left for the playing fields, the room was once again quiet, allowing those remaining to read in peace. At about 2pm, Mr Adams came in and told them all that they were free to leave for the day if they wanted.

This led to a mass exodus and soon they were out of the gate, racing along with the wind in their hair towards Liam's house. Both Peter and Alex had good racing bikes, so were able to maintain a fair speed, but Liam was getting left behind on his older bike. They slowed to allow Liam to catch up and arrived at Liam's at the same time.

"Coming in?" Liam asked.

"Yeah, sure," they both responded and they all piled into Liam's bedroom. He too was an avid modeller and Peter immediately began admiring the models that Liam had on show. They all chatted about the day and hoped that the rest of the week was as relaxed.

After a couple of relaxed hours, Peter and Alex stood up to leave. Peter made his way slowly home, reluctant to be there. He put his bike away in the garage and stepped into the kitchen, where he found his mother busy. Preparing dinner.

"Hi sweetie—good day?" she asked.

"Yes, great thanks," Peter replied. "No timetable, so spent the day reading my book and we were sent home early so we went to Liam's. Probably the same tomorrow."

"Oh, that's lovely—if you're early tomorrow, would you like to go to town? I'd like to get you some more summer clothes," Annie said.

"Yes, we can do," Peter replied. Secretly he hated shopping for clothes with his mum—their tastes were very different and he preferred to be on his own, but it would be nice to spend some time with her.

"Ben's in the living room," Annie said. "I'm not sure what he's up to."

Peter didn't move from where he was sitting. "OK," he said. "I guess I'll see him later on," and he stood up and went upstairs to his room. Thankfully, everything was still in place. Peter settled onto his bed and got his book out.

Just then, the door opened and Ben walked in. "Good day at your posh school?" he asked.

"Yes, thanks," Peter replied. "What do you want?"

"Just to spend some time with you," Ben responded. "It's time we got to know each other a bit more." Ben sat himself down on the end of the bed, taking a long hard look at Peter. "You know all my buddies think that you're weird?" Ben stated. Peter shrugged his shoulders and didn't respond, but his mind started to race. "Yeah, they think that you're really strange. No interest in sports, girls and obsessed with you own little world of your aeroplanes and notebooks. You're not queer are you?" Ben added.

"No," Peter said quietly.

"Good. Couldn't stand that. The guys in my barracks would take the piss relentlessly," Ben went on. "It's bad enough that you don't like the usual stuff. I've begun to think that you're just not normal."

"I don't really care what you think," Peter replied. "I really don't. You live in your world and I live in mine. Simple."

"Yeah, but you're my brother—we should be doing stuff together," Ben went on. Peter stayed quiet keeping himself as calm as possible. "We've never done stuff together. Let's go out somewhere," Ben continued.

"There's nowhere I want to go. I was reading my book," Peter said.

"Come on—let's go out," Ben repeated and he stood up, punching Peter on the leg playfully.

"No—you go. I'm OK here," Peter replied. He was getting fed up with Ben's over-friendly camaraderie and it was making him anxious.

"Suit yourself," Ben spat and he stomped out of the room.

Peter got up and closed the door and then went to the window to look outside and to try and clam himself down. *Only another 5 days*, he thought to himself, *and he'll be back to his beloved Army.*

He could hear Ben's raised voice downstairs, talking to his mother. Peter didn't want to listen. He just wanted life to return to normal. The voices subsided and shortly afterwards Peter heard Paul arrive home. He would usually go straight downstairs to see his dad as he enjoyed asking Paul about his day and Peter was interested in Paul's work, but today he stayed in his room. Plenty of time to catch up.

After dinner, Peter got his bike back out of the garage and set off towards the airport. He had arranged to meet Alex at the mound and hoped that they would have some fun together. When Peter arrived, Alex was already there. They climbed the mound together, sitting down to watch the arrivals and departures and chatting excitedly about the prospect of seeing the new jets when they arrived over the summer.

After a while, Peter heard his name being called. He turned to look and his heart sank. There was Ben with one of his buddies, cycling towards them. Peter stood up to leave, but thought better of it and he knew Ben would chase him. At least he had Alex there for support. Ben arrived and jumped off of Paul's bike, which he threw to the floor.

"What are you doing baby brother?" Ben called. Peter ignored him and as Ben began to climb the mound, Peter's heart started to race and he had a hollow feeling in the pit of his stomach. "I asked you what you were doing," Ben repeated, kicking dust and stones towards Peter.

"Please don't do that," Peter said.

"Why not?" Ben asked, kicking more dust.

"Because I asked you not too," Peter said, panic building within.

Ben then picked up a handful of stones and threw them at Peter. "There—I said we needed to do stuff together, didn't I, baby Bro?" he called, laughing at Peter's obvious distress. Ben's friend stood quietly, watching intently.

"Shall we show him some Army self-defence?" Ben's friend asked with a wicked grin.

"Yeah, let's," said Ben and he immediately jumped on Peter, punching and kicking him. Peter tried to throw Ben off, but Ben was heavy and had a tight hold on him. Alex tried to help, but Ben's companion stood in the way. "None of your business," he said menacingly. "Unless you want some?" Alex remained quiet.

Eventually, Ben tired of punching Peter and he stood up, breathless. Peter stayed curled up, his mind racing, loathing for his brother filling his heart. "Just go away," he said quietly.

"Sure—we'll go when I've had enough," Ben responded, administering a final heavy kick. "Why—what are you going to do? Run and tell mummy?" he sneered. "Because it will be worse next time if you do."

Peter knew from previous encounters that this was not the best thing. "No—just leave me alone," he said.

After a few tense moments, Ben went back down the mound and he and his friend cycled away, laughing.

"Are you OK?" asked Alex. "I'm sorry that I couldn't help."

"Yes, I'll be OK and it's alright—his mate was a lot bigger than you. No point us both getting hurt," Peter said, inspecting his injuries, the bitter iron taste of blood in his mouth. They both remained quiet for a few moments and then Alex suggested that they cycle to the maintenance hangars for a closer look. Peter agreed, but his heart wasn't in it, although he knew Alex meant well. After an hour or so, both Peter and Alex set off home. They got to the point where they would split up and Alex asked Peter if he would be OK.

"Sure—just another day with my bully boy brother. Wouldn't it be great if he was to suffer a nasty accident?" he said. "See you tomorrow," and they both cycled their separate ways.

Peter cycled slowly home, arriving just before dusk. He went into the house and Annie called to him. "Hi—you OK? Have a good time?"

Peter went into the living room where his mum and dad were sitting on the sofa and Ben was sitting in the armchair. Peter looked across at Ben who was ignoring him.

"Yes, it was alright," Peter said quietly. "Anyway, I'm off to bed—school tomorrow. Goodnight all."

"Goodnight," came the chorus of voices. Peter turned and climbed the stairs to the bathroom, where he removed any traces of injury and he splashed his face with cold water. He could feel himself retreating to his dark place, but tried desperately to remain calm. He finished and took himself to bed, closing his bedroom door securely.

He lay in bed watching the light fade and the shadows lengthen, his mind turning the evening's events over and over. His final thoughts as he drifted off to sleep were that it wasn't that he wasn't normal, but just different, although Ben's words stung to the core.

The rest of the week passed uneventfully, with shorter days at school and Peter continuing to avoid Ben when he was at home. It finally got to Friday afternoon, which was the last day of term and for Peter's class, school leaving day for some. They all spent the afternoon chatting and laughing about their times together and recalling all of the antics that they had been up to. Whilst there was a jovial atmosphere, it was tinged with sadness and the boys knew that this would be the last time they would all be together.

Mr Adams came in to join in the fun and for the first time allowed the boys to use his first name, which they felt was an honour. Those who were leaving had made an large poster on which they had all written messages of thanks. Mr Adams got quite choked up when he started saying his goodbyes and hands were shaken and backs were slapped.

"Now then," Mr Adams started. "Tomorrow is a big day for all of you. Whatever the outcome of your exams, I just want to say that it has been an honour and a privilege teaching you all. I know you have all done your best. To those leaving, I wish you the very best in your chosen careers. To those staying—" he paused. "I expect much harder work next year!" There was a roar of laughter and Mr Adams smiled. "Now, get out of my sight," he joked.

Peter shook hands with his colleagues and the boys drifted away slowly, reluctant to break the bonds that had been formed over so many years. For the first time in his life, Peter sensed an real change in his life and he felt like he was now growing up fast. The future now belonged to him.

5

As was usual, Peter awoke early listening for the sounds of aero engines. He hadn't slept well, anticipating what the day would bring. He got up and went to the window, awaiting the early morning departure. It was then that he noticed that his binoculars were missing.

"Damn you, Ben," he cursed, but he didn't want to start a fight so early in the morning. He would find them later on—or maybe mention their absence to Annie quietly. It was dark outside, with low grey cloud and the trees in the garden were whipping around in the wind. Peter loved this kind of weather—it made him feel more connected with nature.

Once the aircraft had flown overhead, Peter returned to bed, picking up his book. It was almost finished and Peter had relished every moment. He was immediately absorbed in the words on the page and he delighted in every single one, rolling them around in his mind, teasing all of the meaning out of them and treasuring every letter. Soon he reached the final page and he put the book down slowly, his mind turning over the experiences of the test pilot and he allowed himself to dream of a similar career.

He was disturbed by Annie peering around the bedroom door. "Hi," she whispered. "Ready for some breakfast?"

"Sure—I'll come down," he replied, sitting up straight.

Annie knew that Peter would be awake early—more so than usual. She had butterflies in her stomach awaiting Peter's results, but was trying to remain calm on the surface. Peter joined his mother in the kitchen where she was busy brewing coffee. She placed a steaming mug in front of him and busied herself making toast. Peter know that when his mother got so busy and was scurrying around it was because she was nervous or occupied with something. She placed Peter's toast in front of him and sat down.

"I was wondering—" she started, but Peter cut her short.

"With the postman. My results come with the postman," he said.

"Ahh, OK," she responded softly. She wanted to know, but didn't want to discuss it directly in fear of raising Peter's anxiety levels. Peter was actually quite calm. He had told himself yesterday that what was done couldn't be undone and that he's make the best of whatever transpired. He ate quietly and they were soon joined by Paul.

"Hi, buddy," he said to Peter. "How are you feeling about today?"

"OK, I guess," Peter answered.

"We shall see what we see," Paul smiled and squeezed Peter's shoulder.

After breakfast, Peter dressed and returned to the kitchen. It was the family meeting place and most family discussions took place to the kitchen table, usually over cups of coffee or tea and Peter loved it for its familiarity. After an hour or so, Ben appeared, looking as dishevelled as usual and with what appeared to be the start of a black eye.

"Good night?" Annie asked. She'd heard Ben returning from the pub after midnight. "What happened to your eye?" Annie went on.

Ben shrugged, saying nothing and filled the kettle. Peter got up and went upstairs to Ben's room to see if his binoculars could be found. He couldn't see them, so decided a direct approach was required. Heading back downstairs, he entered the kitchen and taking a deep breath said, "Ben, My binoculars are missing. Have you got them?"

There was a short awkward silence before Ben replied, "Yes. I borrowed them. So what?"

"Well, I'd like them back please," Peter insisted.

"Yeah, whatever," Ben mumbled before Paul intruded.

"Please give them back, Ben—you know how important they are to Peter."

Ben said nothing, but stomped out returning a few moments later with the binoculars, which he threw across the kitchen towards Peter. Luckily, Peter caught them mid-air.

"Thanks," he said cheerily. Ben sat down, glowering across the table at Peter.

"Right boys—what are we up to today?" Annie asked in an effort to break the tension. Ben said nothing and Peter replied that he was off out on his bike. "In this weather? Are you sure?" Annie asked, surprised.

"Yes—I love this kind of weather," said Peter with a smile.

Ben got up to go back upstairs and they heard the sound of the letterbox snapping shut. Peter exchanged a quick glance with Paul, who stood up and went to collect the post. Ben was already there. Ben passed his father a letter and went to climb the stairs.

"Is this all there was?" he asked.

"Yep," came Ben's response.

"Are you sure?" Paul asked again. "Nothing for Peter?"

"Nope," Ben laughed, running up the stairs. Paul shot up the stairs after Ben and Peter sat at the table, his eyes filling with tears. No Results? The school said that they were guaranteed for delivery today. Upstairs, Peter and his mother could hear shouting and raised voices. Eventually Ben reappeared holding a brown envelope.

"Here, you are weirdo," he called, screwing the letter into a tight ball and throwing it at Peter.

"Ben," Annie screamed. "How dare you?"

Ben shrugged and went back upstairs, leaving Peter holding the ball of paper. Peter could hear more raised voices. *No problem*, he thought to himself, smoothing the letter out as best he could and he stood up and gathering up his binoculars and his shoulder bag containing his notebooks and pen. He went to the back door, put on his waterproof over trousers and his jacket and left the house, unlocking the garage and getting his bike.

In a few moments, he was cycling like fury down the footpath against a vicious crosswind with the lashing rain stinging his face, the brooding clouds bearing down threatening all beneath, the storm ready to unleash it's fury on innocent souls below. Peter loved this kind of weather—it bought him back to nature and made him feel small and insignificant, which appealed to his personality.

He eventually reached the mound and Peter sought shelter under the lonely tree. He sat down, drawing his legs close and pulling his hood down as far as it would allow. After a while, the rain eased and Peter pulled the crumpled envelope from his bag.

He sat for a while staring at his name and address on the front. He was enjoying the anticipation. A new sound made him look up and he grabbed his binoculars, peering through the gloom. There was an aircraft that he hadn't seen before—a jet! It was taxying out for departure and Peter followed it's movements along the taxiway towards the runway. It slowly turned and sat for a moment.

Peter then saw black smoke appearing from the back of the plane and almost simultaneously heard the engines spooling up. It set off at a great pace and was soon airborne, screaming past Peter and into the sky. Peter noted the registration and went to get his notebook. His stomach sank—where was his letter? He looked frantically around and eventually spotted it blowing away in the wind. He jumped up and ran after it, laughing as he chased it all around, eventually having to dive upon it.

With the letter secure in his hand, Peter returned to the tree, sitting down at the base. Slowly he peeled the envelope open, pulling out the documents inside. He slowly read downwards. "Dear Mr Peter Marham," the letter began. "Please find enclosed the results of your General Certificate of Education (GCE) results. This is an important document and we strongly advise that you keep it in a safe place, as it will need to be shown to future employers or centres of Further Education. Please note that the Examination Board cannot issue replacement certificates."

Peter turned to the second page, his heart racing, his mouth dry. It said simply "Results" and listed each subject sat and the exam grade achieved. Peter read slowly down the list. 8 exams sat, 8 results listed. *Haven't failed any then,* Peter mused. Slowly a grin spread across his face. 8 passes—all Grade "A". Perfect.

He clutched the page to his chest and a tear ran slowly down his cheek. He sat quietly for a few minutes. What a perfect morning—except for Ben's antics. A new jet aircraft at the airport and straight "A" results. And the wind. And the rain.

He heard movement and opened his eyes. His dad was dismounting his bike and the bottom of the mound. He waved up at Peter.

"You took off like a scalded cat," he laughed.

Peter excitedly shouted back, "Did you see the jet? A Hawker Siddeley Trident. Amazing."

"Yes—well, I heard it at least," his dad called back, eventually joining Peter at the base of the tree. "Well—how have you done?" Paul asked, seeing the torn envelope and the letter clutched in Peter's hand.

"Oh, OK, I guess," Peter replied, offering his dad the letter. Paul put on his glasses and read slowly down the page. He didn't say anything but looked at Peter with tears in his eyes. He moved closer to Peter and put his arm around Peter's shoulders. "Well done, son. Well done—so proud of you."

"Thanks," Peter whispered.

"Best go and show your mother," Paul suggested, but Peter wasn't ready.

"In a while," he said quietly. He went on "Dad. Why is Ben like he is with me? Why doesn't he like me?"

Paul had been anticipating this for a while. He took a deep breath. "I don't think that it's a question of not liking you. I think it's because you're such different people. He can be difficult and he was always a handful. He certainly kept your mum and me busy when he was smaller—he still does in a way. You're much quieter and as your results show, much more clever. I think he resents that in a way. We've always tried to include you both, but I think that there may be a hint of jealousy from when you were small, from when you needed more help and support with your speaking for instance. He does love you as a brother though," Paul added.

"I'm not so sure," Peter went on. "I was here with Alex on Monday and Ben followed me here with his mate. He jumped on me and was kicking and punching me and seemed to enjoy it. Please don't say anything though as it will make it worse," Peter implored.

Paul's heart sank. Ben was such a bully and Peter was so—so fragile. "I'll not say anything if you don't want me too, but you should stand up to him," Paul responded.

"Maybe one day I'll surprise him, but it's not my way," Peter replied. They sat for a while and the rain eventually ceased altogether. Another departure and a couple of landings followed and Peter dutifully logged the details. Paul sat quietly, immensely proud but worried at the same time. He knew Peter would do well, but Ben's prospects didn't look anywhere near as bright.

Peter stood up. "Guess we'd better put mum out of her misery," he said, gathering his stuff and packing it into his bag.

"Good idea," said Paul. "Let's go."

They mounted their bikes and cycled slowly home, the rain turning the pathway into thick gloopy mud and the wind howling in their faces. The put their bikes away and went into the house through the back door, removing their wet outer clothes as they went. Annie was in the kitchen.

"You boys must be ready for a warm drink," she said, putting the kettle on. They sat themselves down at the table whilst Annie made the drinks. Ben was nowhere to be seen. Annie placed the drinks on the table and sat down next to Peter. She didn't say anything, leaving Peter to speak when he was ready. Peter took a few sips of his coffee and reached into his bag, pulling out the crumpled letter, which he passed to Annie.

She sat quietly reading the contents. After a few moments she stood up and put her arms around Peter's neck, drawing him close and kissing him gently on the forehead. "Well done—superb results," she said quietly.

"Thanks," muttered Peter—he hated being the centre of attention and he was feeling a little uncomfortable.

"Let me get Ben so you can tell him," said Annie, but Peter stopped her.

"Nothing to do with him. Let's enjoy the moment," he said. Annie smiled and sat down.

"So where do you go from here?" asked Paul.

Peter thought for a moment. "Well, I could start my A-Levels, but the airlines say that there's no need. They'd take me two years and I can apply for flight training in September when I'm sixteen and start at seventeen, so no point. I need to think of something to fill the next 12 months."

"Well, I could ask at work to see if they've something to tide you over for the next year," Paul suggested.

"Hmm maybe," Peter replied. "Let me think it over."

Ben walked in looking for food. He saw Peter and the crumpled letter laying on the table and thought it best to say nothing. Nobody spoke, until Annie finally broke the silence. "Peter has done so well with his exams. Top grades. Such a proud mother," she said, wanting Ben to know how well Peter had done. Ben remained silent. Trying to elicit a response, Annie went on "A-Levels next or maybe some work experience before flight school. Are you proud of your brother?" she asked Ben directly.

"Yeah, whatever," Ben muttered and walked out of the kitchen. Annie was disgusted and looked so embarrassed, but Peter shrugged it off. *Way better than you*, he thought to himself.

"Don't let him dampen your day, sweetie," Annie said to Peter. "This is your day so enjoy it."

Peter smiled at his parents. "Oh, I intend to," he said with a grin. Both Annie and Paul smiled. *Maybe dad was right—maybe I should stand up to Ben*, Peter mused. *I'm certainly going to rub this in.*

Peter returned to his room and looked for a safe place to hide his exam results letter. Once he had stashed it in a place that he was sure would be safe, he returned to the kitchen.

"I'm off to see Alex," Peter said and he looked outside to see if the rain had started again or whether it was dry. The sky was still leaden and the wind was blowing, but the path was dry, so Peter put his waterproofs back on and went out to get his bike out. He quickly rode to his Alex's and knocked at the back door.

Alex's mum opened the door. "Hi, Peter—come on in. Have you come to compare results?"

"Hi. Yes, I wanted to see how Alex had done," Peter replied.

"He upstairs in his bedroom, so just go up," Alex's mum said. Peter slipped off his shoes and waterproofs and climbed the stairs, knocking on Alex's bedroom door and pushing it open.

"Hi, buddy," Alex said.

"Hi—well, how did you do?" Peter asked. Alex handed over his results. Peter read down the list quickly. "Wow—seven A's and a B. Well done," he said, slapping Alex on the back.

"Cheers. How about you?" Alex asked.

Peter felt a little uncomfortable, as he hated talking about himself. "Oh, eight A's," he muttered.

"Brilliant," came Alex's response. "So what now?"

"I'm not sure," said Peter. "I'm going to write to the two airlines that I applied to for a cadetship, as they asked me to inform them of my results and I'll take it from there. A-Levels for you?" he asked.

"Yeah, I guess so," Alex answered, a little unsurely. "Dad's still wanting me to follow him into medicine and it would be a great career, but there's a part of me that's not sure. I'll start the A-Levels and see where they take me."

"Good plan," Peter responded and the boys continued to chatter about their plans and their futures for the rest of the afternoon.

At about 5pm Peter stood up to leave and Alex followed him downstairs. "Let's make some plans for the holidays," he said as Peter was putting his waterproofs on.

"Yeah, let's," Peter replied, excited at the prospect of the six week holiday before them.

"I'll see you tomorrow," said Alex. "Shall I come to yours?"

"Good idea—Ben goes back tomorrow so it'll be more peaceful," Peter replied and bidding Alex farewell, he jumped on his bike and rode quickly home.

Peter arrived home to find Annie in the midst of cooking dinner. "Have you had a good time? How did Alex do?" she asked.

"He did well—he's going to start his A-Levels when we go back," Peter replied, sitting down at the kitchen table so that he could chat. "Mum," Peter began, "I have to write to the airlines with my results. Would you mind helping me with the letters?" Peter asked.

"Of course, sweetie," Annie said. "Shall we do them on Monday when we can be undisturbed?"

"Good idea," Peter replied. He needed every word to be perfect and the letters needed to be polite but business-like and Peter knew that his mum had a gift for such things as her job was not just as a receptionist, but also as a secretary.

"If we write the letters together, I'll type them up at work," Annie added.

Peter's face lit up. "Yes, please—that would be awesome," he said.

"Dinner will be in five minutes—why don't you go and wash your hands and call you father and Ben?" Annie asked.

Peter did exactly as asked and soon they were joined by Paul, with Ben following a few minutes later. Annie served dinner and she chatted throughout the meal to Ben about Peter's prospects and of how proud she was. Ben sat silently giving Peter the occasional filthy look, but he said nothing.

Peter glanced at Annie before picking up on the same topic. "So, remind me how you did in your exams Ben," Peter asked. This was met with glowering silence. "No passes, wasn't it? Oh no, silly me, I forgot—you failed your mocks so didn't sit the proper exams—am I correct?"

Still Ben didn't respond, but the atmosphere was thick with hatred and venom. Peter smiled, "Well, I guess you don't need much to drive a truck."

Ben opened his mouth to say something, but Paul told both of the boys to finish squabbling. At the end of the meal as he stood up, but Annie pushed him back down into his chair.

"We haven't finished yet. I've made Peter's favourite cake as a way of saying well done," she said and placed a large chocolate sponge cake on the table. She had iced the top with the words "Well done Peter". Peter smiled, saying thank you, but Ben's face was furious. *Hmm, he's not happy*, thought Peter, enjoying the moment.

"Yes, well done, Peter," added Paul, passing Peter a knife. "You'd best cut the cake up," he added. Peter sliced the cake into equal segments, which Annie passed around on small plates.

Ben's slice went untouched. "I thought you liked chocolate cake?" Annie asked Ben.

"I'm full," he growled.

"OK," Annie responded, winking at Peter. Peter smiled to himself, thinking, *She's enjoying rubbing this in.*

After dinner, Peter started the washing up as always and Paul and Ben went into the living room. "Thanks for my cake, mum," Peter said.

"That's OK—just my small way of celebrating," said Annie, giving Peter a hug.

"I don't think that Ben was impressed," Peter went on.

"Nor do I," said Annie, adding, "but I'm very proud. Your Dad and I were often told that you might struggle with school work and you've always been so quiet about your achievements, but we've both always been behind you every step of the way. Passing your 11-plus exams came as a great surprise as we'd been told at primary school that you would probably not do well and then to get straight A's today is beyond our wildest expectations."

Peter was so fed up about hearing what others thought he couldn't do—he was more interested in showing people what he could achieve. "Yes, well, I learned a long time age to just keep my head down, work hard and say nothing just in case something stupid or inappropriate came out of my mouth," Peter replied. "It's sometimes so difficult to fit in to what's expected," he added.

"Well, you're doing just fine," said Annie, giving Peter a hug.

"I hope so," Peter muttered. They heard the front door slam. Annie went into the living room and Paul told her that Ben had gone out with his friend to the pub. Annie called Peter and they settled down for an evening together, discussing the future and what it might hold.

The opening of the bedroom door shook Peter into wakefulness. He switched on his light, heart racing. It was Ben.

"What do you want now?" Peter asked.

Ben stood before him, feet apart and hands on his hips. "You think that you're so clever don't you?" Ben started. "Well you smug little shit, I'm telling you this—if you ever get or stand in my way, I'll take you out." Peter absorbed every word, his mind painting dark painful scenarios. "Just because you've passed a few exams doesn't mean that you're clever." Ben went on, "It just means that you can study. It doesn't mean that you can do anything practical in life. Just remember, I'm the older one here and one day I'll be head of this family and I'm gonna make your life a misery."

Peter lay quietly, not giving Ben the courtesy of a response. "I leave around lunchtime tomorrow." Ben continued, "and next time I'm home you'd better watch out." Peter continued to lay without responding and eventually Ben turned to leave. "You're gonna achieve nothing," Ben spat as he left the room.

Peter got up and closed the door, returning to bed and switching the light off. His mind was filled with anxiety and dark hatred for Ben. *Achieve nothing? I'll show you, big brother*, he thought as he attempted to get back to sleep. *One day I might just take you out.* What had he meant?

Peter waited in the darkness for the house to fall silent whilst exploring every crevice of his mind for answers. With the remarkable clarity of his near photographic memory, he tried to think back as far as he could—deep back into his childhood. He had spent his life looking at people whilst wondering why they didn't care about being structured or organised, why they were not able to focus on a subject, had unreliable memories and just said things that they didn't mean—and try as he might, Peter couldn't remember a time when there weren't issues between Ben and himself.

There had been the constant teasing, bullying, disruption of Peter's careful routines, the breaking of his models and worse of all the unexplained and unexpected death of Peter's pet rabbit. Just four years old and healthy, yet found dead in his hutch the morning after. Peter just knew that Ben was to blame, but as usual he denied any wrong doing, although the nasty smirk on his face gave him away.

Peter had cried and cried and was inconsolable for weeks afterwards. It had taken a long time for his young mind to internalise what had happened and ever since he had shunned the idea of getting another pet. All his life he had cowered beneath Ben's swaggering and demeaning attitude, his laziness, his expectation of just getting everything he wanted and his exaggerated sense of entitlement.

Well, the time was now. Once he was satisfied that Ben would be asleep, he slipped out of bed, switching on the lamp on his desk and, pulling out his notepad, began to write.

"Ben. For years I have put up with and have been the butt of your jokes, insults, bullying, jealousy and violence. I understand that we are different people and that I live my life in the way that nature has chosen for me. I don't know what perverse pleasure you gain from being as obnoxious as possible towards me and so many times I have wished for a brother who would not only understand me, but one that would be a true brother and companion and indeed one who would look after me as a big brother should.

"Your latest drunken outbursts and your attitude and arrogance towards me is enough. I'm glad that you are going back to your regiment and that you're being posted as far away from me as possible. I really don't know what you meant tonight about standing in your way or taking me out, but I will live my life as I wish and choose the career I want.

"You obviously think that you're a hard man in your pathetic uniform, but as I get older, you may find that my tolerance for your boorish behaviour becomes less. Personally, I have no desire to see you again and you may find on your next visit that I'm a different person. If I never see you again, I can only say that it will be a pleasure. Rot in hell."

Peter then tiptoed downstairs as quietly as he could and finding Ben's rucksack packed and ready on the kitchen chair, he unzipped it and tucked the folded letter into the very bottom of a compartment containing some of Ben's clothing. He was satisfied that Ben wouldn't see it before he was back in barracks.

Peter was up early and checked that his exam results were still in their hiding place. He hesitated and went back upstairs, putting the results in his shoulder bag just in case. He didn't trust Ben not to look for them and if they were found he'd probably steal them or destroy them. At least he'd be gone once he got home. Ben was being posted to Cyprus for a 2-year posting, so hopefully he'd stay there for his leave periods and Peter felt that he'd get some peace.

After breakfast, he left to meet up with Alex and Liam, as they had arranged a trip into town. Peter knew that Ben would be gone when he got home and he could write his letters. Peter's mind began to wander on the bus ride into town, imagining what to say in the letters and how the airlines would respond. The bus eventually hissed to a stop and Peter jumped up to disembark. Liam and Alex were waiting outside and the three walked off together, chatting happily. There was a local coffee bar where students liked to gather and they took a table near the window.

"How did you get on, Liam?" Peter asked.

"OK—probably not as good as you though. A mixture of A's and B's. You?" Liam asked.

Peter felt a little embarrassed. "Straight A's," he said.

"Wow—well done," Liam responded, his eyes filled with wonder.

"A-Levels next year?" Liam asked.

"Not sure," Peter said. "I have to send my results to the airlines and I'll do whatever they ask. What about you?"

"I'm going to work for my dad—going to train as a plumber," Liam responded. "Should be fun."

"Yes—and you'll have a trade for life," Peter said, adding, "and some money!"

"Oh yes—looking forward to having a few quid in my pocket," Liam answered.

They finished their coffees and decided to spend some time window shopping and just looking around the town centre. Much of it had been recently redeveloped and there was lots to discover. Many new shops had moved in selling exciting new fashion clothing, records, books and there was a new shop selling the latest bikes and accessories. They stood outside this shop for ages looking at the new racing bikes in the window.

"If you earn enough, you can buy yourself a new bike and get rid of your old clunker," Peter teased Liam. "It's about time you had a good one."

"I won't bother," said Liam. "Dad says I can learn to drive and have use of his van when I'm seventeen."

"Cool," said Alex. "You can run us around."

"I will if you don't mind sharing the back with lead piping and old toilets," Liam laughed and they all laughed together.

Peter so enjoyed the company of his friends, but he was still preoccupied with home. He planned to get to the railway station for around 2 PM, as that was the time of Ben's train and Peter wanted to make sure that he got on it. He couldn't cope with the thought that Ben would still be at home.

After a pleasant morning, Peter looked again at his watch and decided that it was time to make his way to the train station. He bid goodbye to Liam and Alex and walked the mile or so to the main station, where he knew of a pathway which would take him alongside the platform behind a fence. From here, he could see the trains departing but could remain virtually hidden from view. He settled down to wait, guessing that Ben would leave it until the last minute before boarding. Punctuality had never been his strong point.

After a short while, Peter saw Ben coming through the ticket barrier, with his rucksack on his back. He walked down the platform until he found a smoking carriage and he opened the door, throwing his bag inside and settling down next to the window. *Good*, thought Peter—*You're finally out of my way.*

A whistle blew and the train began to move, clanking it's way forwards. As Ben's carriage passed Peter's vantage point, Ben saw him standing behind the fence. They made eye contact and Peter held Ben's gaze until he disappeared from view. There was no waving, no other gestures—just pure coldness. Peter felt a great sense of relief wash over him and a weight lift from his shoulders. *I hope I never see you again*, he thought to himself.

6

Watching the train vanish into the distance lifted Peter's spirits, so much so that he decided to walk the three miles home and to enjoy the afternoon sunshine. The roads were quiet and he could hear birdsong in the trees and hedgerows. It was now time to begin his applications in earnest and he would sit down and start writing as soon as he got home. He paused a short way from home to watch an aircraft climbing high into the sky and read it as a good omen for his own future.

Arriving home, he pushed open the back door and found Annie in the kitchen already preparing dinner.

"Hi, mum," he greeted her, although when she turned around he could see concern written on her face. "Everything OK?" he asked.

Annie took his hand. "Yes, but please don't be too upset. Ben has left you a parting gift in your room."

Peter let go and shot upstairs, throwing open his bedroom door. There on his bed was one of his best models. The engines, wheels and wings were broken off and scattered around. Peter stared at the wreckage, fury building inside him. "Ben. You just had to, didn't you? You just couldn't resist one last dig at me."

He heard his mother following him into the room. "I'm sorry Peter—I was at work this morning so I couldn't watch over him," Annie apologised.

Peter bit his bottom lip. "It's OK—it'll mend," he said. Annie stroked his arm, concerned and filled with dismay at Ben's actions. "I'm just so glad that he's going to be away for quite a while," Peter added.

"I know," Annie said quietly. "Don't forget, sweetie, the darker things seem, the easier it is to see the starlight." Peter squeezed her hand.

Despite the tension between the boys, she was going to miss Ben's home leave and was relieved that he hadn't been posted to an active zone. "You go carry on with dinner," Peter said quietly, "I'll sort this out." He sat down on the edge of the bed, turning the broken pieces over in his fingers. It would mend, but

46

it wouldn't be back to the standard that it had been before. His mind was once again filled with confused thoughts and Peter's enmity towards Ben know no bounds.

One day, he would stand up to Ben he promised himself and with his chosen career, Peter knew that he would always do better in life. If he was successful getting a cadetship, he would most likely have to live away from home so would be away from Ben, especially if he got the position with International Airways, as they were based at London airport, so commuting would be out of the question.

Peter gathered up the broken pieces, placing everything in his modelling box and got his other models out from their hiding places, relieved to see that nothing else was wrecked. After calming himself, he grabbed his schoolbag and went back downstairs.

"Are you OK, sweetie?" asked Annie.

"Yeah, guess so. Can we start on these letters?" Peter asked, sitting down at the kitchen table and pulling his writing pad from his bag.

"Yes of course," Annie smiled, sitting down next to him. "Where shall we start?" Peter started writing, referencing the letters from both airlines and with Annie's help, they soon had drafts completed. "Let's show them to your dad and he can read them through," Annie suggested, to which Peter murmured his agreement. "Come on—you can help with dinner," Annie said brightly, but Peter shook his head.

"I'd like to go back upstairs if that's OK," Peter said quietly.

"Yes, of course," Annie agreed, knowing that Peter would need some time alone to put his room back to normal. Peter walked slowly back upstairs, dreading inspecting the damage to his model. He sat down at his small desk and, getting all the broken pieces together, he spread them out on the desk top. His heart sank as he looked each piece over. He knew that he could just glue some pieces back on, but some other parts would need to be fabricated from scratch.

As he inspected the parts, his mind was turning over and over, constantly asking himself the same question—why? Why was he different? Why didn't Ben like him or treat him like a normal brother? Why couldn't he relate to people? If Ben stood in his way, then he'd see a different side of Peter—one which had always been kept under control in the deepest recesses of his soul. He would simply crush Ben—physically, if necessary.

Peter found himself heading for his dark place—the place he retreated to when everything got too much. His place of safety. He ended up just sitting and staring into space, black thoughts filling every part of him.

The sound of his father arriving home shook Peter back into reality. He pushed all the broken parts away from himself and went downstairs to greet Paul.

"Hi," he began, "good day at work?"

"Hello, son," Paul responded. "Oh, the usual Monday. How's things with you?"

"Oh, OK," Peter replied, adding, "Ben smashed one of my models this morning whilst I was out so I'm pretty fed up about that. I really do hate him at times."

Paul sighed—this wasn't what he wanted to hear and he knew how much this would have affected Peter. "Will it mend?" he asked.

"Yeah, I guess so, but it won't be the same," Peter replied with exasperation.

Annie, who had been listening, came across and said, "Peter and I have written some draft letters for his cadetship. Will you read them through with Peter and see if there's anything else you can think of to add?"

"Of course," Paul replied.

"Come on buddy—let's go into the living room and have a read."

Peter gathered up the letters and followed Paul, sitting next to him on the sofa. "I've had a word with the boss today—he says that if you want to come in to work for us in a junior role, he'll do his best to find you something to tide you over, but don't feel obliged. I know that you want to see what the airlines say, so let's look at these letters."

Paul started to read, making the occasional note but saying very little. Once he had finished, he sat pondering the contents before speaking. "OK—they are pretty good—positive, polite and factual. Just an idea—in the letter to the local airline, why don't you add a paragraph after where you've asked for their advice on what to do for the next 12 months, to see if they have a junior role that you could do, to help you get your feet under the table?"

"Brilliant idea!" Peter replied excitedly. "Can you help me with that?"

"Of course—let's have a think," Paul said and picked up a pencil.

Together they drafted a paragraph and once they were happy with both letters, Peter took them into the kitchen to give to his mother. "Here we are, all finished. Will you be able to type them tomorrow?" Peter asked.

"Of course," Annie replied. "C'mon—let's eat," and they all sat down to enjoy their meal.

The following day dawned wet, cold and miserable. Both Liam and Alex had things to do, so Peter decided to stay at home and start to repair his model. He loved to build these kits and it was a familiar ritual of setting everything he needed out on his desk in a very particular order—he loved the routine. He began to inspect each part and to repair and reassemble the aeroplane. He had music from the new pop station playing on his transistor radio and he was in better spirits that yesterday.

Hours passed and slowly the model was transformed back into the complete and finished article. Peter knew that there would some repainting to finish it completely, but he was happy with the result. He continued and was surprised by Annie knocking on his bedroom door and poking her head around, as he hadn't heard her arrive home.

"Hi," she said. "How are you getting on?"

"Well, I got it all stuck back together and just have some touch up painting to do, so I guess that it'll be OK," he replied.

Annie smiled—she knew that Peter was in his happy place. "I've done your letters—come and see," she said. Peter got up excitedly and followed his mother downstairs. "Be careful not to crease them," she said, handing them over for Peter to read.

Peter read every line carefully, looking for errors. Finally he looked up "Thanks, mum—they're perfect. Shall I sign them at the bottom?"

"Yes—just above where I typed your name," Annie told him, adding, "I even typed envelopes, so they will look professional." Peter was over the moon. He signed both letters with a flourish and Annie folded them carefully before sliding them into the correct envelope. "They have stamps on, so why don't you run to the post box and send them on their way," Annie suggested.

Peter grabbed his coat, slid into his outdoor shoes and was off like a rocket to the post box at the end of the road. He stood for a moment wishing both letters good luck on their journey and popped them into the box. The rain had finally ceased and he walked back towards home, content. *I wonder how long it will take to get replies*, he thought as he arrived at the back door.

Inside, Annie had started preparing dinner and was humming quietly to herself. She hadn't seen Peter this content for ages and had thought that maybe the disruption of Ben's visit would have unsettled Peter for a while, but clearly

Peter's results and getting his letters done had helped to lift him. She hoped beyond hope that something would come of them, as she knew that he didn't handle rejection well.

After dinner, Peter and his parents spent the evening discussing his future and Peter was in full flow, talking about his plans, the training required and his prospects. Annie tried to introduce a note of caution, but Peter was having none of it. Inside, he was determined and nothing was going to get in his way. After a lifetime of people doubting his abilities, it was time for him to prove himself and there would no distractions, no diversions, just sheer hard work.

The week went by uneventfully. Peter filled his time by completing the repairs to his model, going out with Alex and Liam and, of course, visiting the mound and the actual airport. At the airport, he made enquiries about the return of the jet that he'd seen the previous week, but nobody behind the check-in desks seemed to know anything about its return.

Outside, Peter was able to watch the aircraft being loaded and unloaded and being refuelled. Lines of passengers walked the short distance from the gate to the aircraft, queueing politely at the bottom of the steps to board. Once the doors were shut, the engines coughed into life in an explosion of noise and blue smoke. The noise from these old piston engines was deafening and the blast of wind from the propellors blew dust and smoke into Peter's face. He didn't mind though, it was all part of the experience and Peter loved it's familiarity—the smells and sounds made him feel comfortable and content.

He watched the aircraft taxi away, dreaming of what the destination might be and the reasons for the passenger's travel. Foreign holidays were only just becoming available, but the cost was outrageous, so Peter guessed that for most people, the flight would be for business or family reasons. It didn't matter to him though—the pilots at the front were getting paid to do an amazing job whatever the reason!

On Friday evening, Paul started chatting to Peter over dinner. "The boss says that if you want to come in three days a week, we could use a lad like yourself for basic duties if you fancy?"

"What sort of stuff?" Peter asked.

"Oh, helping in the workshop, loading stuff, sweeping up at the end of the day, that sort of thing. It's won't pay much, but it will be more than your pocket money and it will be valuable work experience. Have a think about it," Paul said.

"Hmm, OK," Peter replied.

He was so anxious to get replies to his letters and the more time wore on the darker his thoughts became. Annie kept telling him that "no news is good news" but Peter didn't share her positive outlook. To him, no news meant no cadetship, although he comforted himself with the fact that his letters were only posted 4 days ago. Peter asked Paul to tell him more about the job and the company, as he would be interested if there was anything that he could learn that would be useful to his aviation studies—after all aircraft were built by engineers, so there must be something that could be learnt.

Even if the airlines wanted Peter to start his A Levels, he could get 6 weeks experience during the holidays—and six weeks' pay. After listening to and questioning his dad for most of the evening, Peter agreed. Annie was delighted and then announced that they had some news.

Peter's ears pricked up. "Oh—what?" he asked.

"We're getting a telephone fitted. We both thought that with Ben being away for some time and you potentially going to London if you're successful with the airline there, that it would be a great way to keep in touch."

What Annie didn't mention was that she thought that there may be times where Peter would need to speak to either of them, especially if things weren't going well.

"Great idea," Peter replied. He was impressed. A telephone—only the kids from the best houses had telephones. "When is it coming?" Peter asked.

"Sometime next week," Annie answered. Peter nodded slowly—technology was becoming better and better.

Saturday dawned with the sun filling a cloudless sky. Peter as usual was awaiting the sound of the early departure, but nothing could be heard. He got up anyway, pulling back the curtains and looking out over the garden. Then he heard it—not the usual sound, but a muffled scream. A jet!

He quickly grabbed his binoculars and was just in time to focus on the aircraft as it roared overhead. Peter was just able to make out the registration, although it was moving quickly. The same aircraft as last week. Thinking quickly, he deduced that it would probably return around lunchtime, so he planned to be at the airport to watch it land. He'd never seen one close up and was excited by the prospect. He carefully filled in the aircraft details in his notebook and went downstairs only to find Annie already up and about.

She looked up. "What was that?" she asked.

"A jet," Peter replied breathlessly. "Looks like they will be a regular thing soon."

"Well, I hope that they're not all as noisy as that one," Annie laughed.

Peter sat down, accepting his mother's offer of coffee. "Do you think I might hear anything today?" Peter asked.

"It's still a bit early, love," Annie replied. "I think it may take a couple of weeks at least. It's summer season, so they will be busy."

Peter nodded. He knew his mother was talking sense, but it didn't stop his impatience. "Guess you're right. I just need to know that's all."

"I know," Annie said softly, placing her hand on his arm.

Paul appeared in the doorway. "I think those jets of yours are going to keep us awake," he joked.

"Yes, they're pretty noisy," Peter replied, smiling. He was happy—the future had arrived at Westlea Airport and he hoped to soon be part of it. "I'm going to go over to the airport around lunchtime to see if it's back by then," Peter added.

"Good plan," Paul said. "I may come with you."

"Great," Peter replied before taking himself back upstairs to get dressed.

Just before midday, Paul and Peter dragged their bikes out of the garage. Peter's bag was already over his shoulder and they set off in high spirits. The ride to the viewing area was quite a bit longer than to Peter's usual spot on top of the mound and they both rode along chatting happily. Paul was pleased to see Peter so excited for his future and felt that on days like this that they could really communicate.

In a short while, they arrived at the airport locking their bikes to the fence in the viewing area. The apron before them was empty, save for a couple of small training aircraft. "What are those?" Paul asked, pointing to the little planes.

"Cessna 150's," Peter replied. "Basic trainers—it's what I'll probably be starting on," he continued.

Paul nodded and smiled to himself. He knew full well what they were, but knew Peter would be eager to share his knowledge. After a short while, the sound of approaching engines made Peter put his binoculars to his eyes.

"What is it?" Paul asked.

"Oh, just one of the old airliners," Peter replied, disappointment in his voice. The aircraft landed and taxied in, blasting them both with the prop-wash as it turned around. Quickly the engines were shut down and then there was nothing but silence and the ticking of cooling metal. Doors opened and passengers descended the steps, filing into the building. Vehicles surrounded the plane, ready to offload baggage and cargo and to refuel for the next trip. Peter continued to scan the approach path, but could see nothing.

"Shall we get a drink?" Paul asked.

"Sure," said Peter, still scanning. He was about to put his binoculars down when something caught his eye. He looked harder. There was an aircraft turning onto the approach—and it was trailing two lines of faint black smoke. A jet. A Jet! "There dad look," Peter pointed, excitement building in his voice.

Paul looked. "Ahh, yes—I can see it," he said.

Peter's eyes were glued to the approaching aircraft, watching it grow in his binoculars. He watched as the wheels came down and it positioned itself for landing. Neither Peter nor Paul could hear anything.

"Isn't it quiet?" Paul remarked.

Peter nodded but didn't budge. The aircraft swooped low over the hedge at the end of the runway and touched down smoothly. This was instantly followed by a roar as the engines reversed, slowing the aircraft to taxi speed. "Wow," Peter murmured, his eyes glued. The aircraft taxied slowly in, turning to park almost in front of them. Peter was amazed by the size and sleek appearance of the aircraft—it was clearly factory-fresh and gleamed in the sunlight.

The three engines were shut down with a quiet whisper as they slowly spooled to a halt and then there was silence. Peter turned towards Paul, who could see the excitement on his face. "Amazing. Just amazing," he said quietly.

Paul smiled and patted Peter's back. "That'll be you one day," he said.

"Hope so," Peter responded.

"C'mon, let's get that drink," Paul suggested. "You can tell me all about it." They walked to the cafe just inside the terminal and sat down. Paul bought drinks and Peter began to tell him all about the aircraft—what it was, how many engines it had, what speeds it flew. Peter was chattering away like a chipmunk and Paul listened politely, happy to listen and to see Peter so animated.

Drinks finished, Peter went to the airline desk to enquire about when the jet was going out again. "Not today," came the response from the lady behind the glass. She could see the disappointment on Peter's face. "Hang on," she said, getting up and leaving the desk. After a few minutes, she came back. "Would you like to have a look inside it?" she asked.

"Yes, please," Peter said, as quick as a flash.

"Hang on here a moment," she said.

A couple of minutes later, a man in uniform approached them. "Hi—I'm Captain Andrews. Come with me."

Both Peter and Paul said hello and followed the Captain. They went through a door, through another and out into the sunshine. The aircraft sat before them. Captain Andrews ran up the front steps two at a time and Peter and Paul both followed.

"Welcome to our new aircraft," said the Captain.

"Wow," said Peter.

The Captain showed them around the cabin, then sat down on one of the seats, motioning Peter to take a seat opposite. "Are you interested in aircraft?" the Captain asked.

"Oh, yes," replied Peter. "I've been interested all my life. In fact, I applied for a cadetship here a while ago and have just sent in my GCE results and I'm waiting for a reply."

"Really? Good lad. How did you do with your exams?"

"I got eight straight A's," Peter replied.

"Good, man. I'd best show you the business end then," said the Captain, who got up and walked towards the front of the cabin. "This is where the fun happens," he said, smiling as they went into the flightdeck. Peter stood and stared, his eyes like saucers.

"Wow. Looks complicated," said Peter.

"It's not really once you get used to it. Let me explain. Sit yourself down and I'll take you through it," and the Captain began to show Peter the controls, instruments and switches.

Paul stood in the doorway, fascinated, but equally pleased to see Peter so interested. When the Captain had finished his explanation, he asked Peter his name, adding that he was on the selection committee and whilst he couldn't promise anything, that he would look out for Peter's application. Eventually the Captain stood up and they left the aircraft and walked back to the terminal.

"Thank you so much," Peter said, extending his hand.

"My pleasure, Peter. It was my wife that you spoke to on the desk, so I thought I better do as I was told," he joked. "Hope to see you soon," said Captain Andrews, shaking Peter's hand.

"Yes, thanks very much," said Paul. "Much appreciated."

"No problem—bye for now," said the Captain, turning and walking away.

Paul and Peter walked back outside slowly. Peter was silent, but Paul could tell that he was buzzing. "Wow—what do you think of that?" he asked.

Peter looked up. "Amazing. What a nice man—I hope he can help," Peter added.

"Let's see, but don't get your hopes up too high," cautioned Paul. "Let's see what happens." He didn't want Peter raising his expectations and then seeing them dashed. All the way home Peter chatted excitedly about the visit and about Captain Andrews and he ran into the house to tell his mother all about his day at the airport. Paul smiled and left them to it.

7

The house was silent, except for the rain falling on the patio outside. Peter lay silently, his head was still reliving the visit to the flightdeck the day before. As Paul had remarked, getting to know people in positions of influence was as important as getting his exam results. He just hoped that Captain Andrews would remember his name.

As Peter had no plans for the day and by the sound of the weather, he decided to just see what the day bought. Eventually nature called and then he wandered downstairs into the kitchen. He was alone. Kettle on, then he drew back the curtains in both the kitchen and living room. Looking outside, he could see the deluge battering the flowers and trees. He made coffee, stirring the granules thoroughly and took his usual seat at the table. He knew that his parents would appear, but that his dad liked a lay in on Sundays.

As always, Peter enjoyed his own company as it allowed him to think and prepare for the day ahead. Finally, he heard movement and Annie eventually appeared. "I didn't hear you get up," she said.

"I've been up about an hour. Couldn't sleep," Peter replied, getting up to refill the kettle. It was his turn to make Annie a drink.

"Thank you," she said as Peter placed the steaming mug in front of her. "Looks pretty grim out there. Do you fancy visiting your Gran today—I'm sure she'd love to hear about your results?"

"Hmmm—yeah I guess so," Peter replied. Gran's house was on the other side of town and often full of family. "I hope that there's not many people there."

"Oh I'm sure that it'll be OK. Not usually many people about on Sundays," his mum responded, knowing Peter's dislike of crowds.

After a short bus ride and a damp walk, the three of them arrived at Annie's mother's house. It was a small bungalow, ideally suited as Gran suffered with arthritis and couldn't manage stairs easily. The front door was always unlocked, so Annie knocked and they went straight in.

"Hi," she called and they heard Gran's voice answering from the small living room.

Coats were hung up and wet shoes removed—Gran was very house proud and shoe removal was a strict rule. They trooped in and there was Gran—sitting in her favourite chair, her usual shawl around her shoulders. Annie bent to kiss her mother and then Gran motioned for Peter to come and sit next to her. She looked at him over her glasses—"My, you're growing. How are you, young man?"

Peter usually felt a little awkward for the first hour or so, but he responded to the question in his usual minimal way. "I'm OK, thanks. How are you?"

"Me? I'm just fine, thank you—it's all the others that you have to watch out for," she joked, throwing her head back and laughing.

Peter smiled—Gran had a great sense of humour, although she could be steel-like when needed. She didn't let people push her around. Soon, Annie and her mum were engaged deep in conversation and Peter got up to stretch his legs. Paul sat quietly listening—his relationship with his Mother-in-Law had always been a little frosty. Gran had once confided to Peter that at the beginning she didn't think that Paul was good enough for her only daughter, although her opinion had mellowed over the years.

Peter wandered around the house, looking at the pictures and family photographs. Most of the photos were old black and white portraits of people he didn't know, although Gran had once told him all the names and relationships. Peter hadn't remembered as it wasn't something that interested him. After a while he heard his name being called and he wandered back into the living room.

"Gran wants to know about your exam results," said Annie.

Peter sighed—he really didn't want people making a fuss. He sat down. "I got my results through last weekend," he began.

"Yes—well that doesn't tell me much," scolded his Gran.

"I got eight passes at A grade," Peter said quietly.

Gran looked at him for a few moments, allowing the news to sink in. "Clever lad," she said with warmth in her voice and taking Peter's hand. "So where does this take you? Are you still thinking about aeroplanes or maybe getting a different career?"

"Oh, it's still aviation. I've applied to two airlines and I'm waiting to hear back from them. We went to the airport yesterday and met one of the pilots who is on the selection board, so I'm hoping that he's going to remember me."

Peter went on to tell Gran all about the visit to the flightdeck and how the new age of jets was coming to Westlea. Gran sat quietly listening, secretly amazed and proud—she had endured many worrying conversations with Annie and Paul when Peter was small about his differences and difficulties and she also thought that he may not amount to much, saying that he was exactly like his Grandad.

Well, she thought, *he's certainly surprised all of us.* When Peter finished, Gran stood up and walked out of the room, returning a few moments later. She sat down and opening her purse, withdrew two £1 notes. She pressed them into Peter's hand.

"There you are—a little something for doing so well."

"Gosh, thanks, Gran," said Peter, leaning over to kiss her cheek. He carefully folded the notes and put them in his pocket. *£2. That's four weeks pocket money*, he thought to himself. *That can go into my savings account.*

As the afternoon drew on, conversations gradually faltered and eventually Annie decided that it was time to head home. After goodbyes were said and Peter gave Gran a hug and thanked her again for the money, the three left the house. Finally the rain had stopped, but moisture hung heavily in the air and they avoided walking under trees as they were still laden with rain. Peter walked quietly and didn't say anything until after they had arrived home.

After dinner, Paul asked Peter if he was sure about going to work with him. Peter agreed, asking what it was exactly that they made.

"Hydraulic pumps, accumulators and valves," Paul said. "I do the machining for the pump bodies."

Peter's ears pricked up. Hydraulics was one of the subject that he knew he'd have to study at flight school, so he was immediately interested. "Will I be able to learn how they work?" he asked.

"Yes, of course—I can take you through the principles anytime," Paul answered. Peter nodded. Strangely, he hadn't shown much interest in what Paul's company made, he just knew that his dad was an engineer. It was all starting to come together.

Monday dawned, dull but dry. Peter planned to go to the post office to pay in the money from his Gran and he was excited to see if the postman would bring anything. He heard his dad leave for work and cycle off down the road whistling. He could also hear his mum pottering about getting ready, although he felt no inclination to get out of bed. Eventually, he threw on his dressing gown and went downstairs, just in time to see Annie leaving.

"I'll see you later," she smiled, closing the door.

"Sure," he called and went into the kitchen. Alone. Peter loved times like this. Nobody to answer to, nobody hassling him, just himself in his own world, doing his own thing. Perfect.

After breakfast, Peter got his savings book out of the drawer and after locking the door, set off to the Post Office on his bike. He queued patiently, paying the money in and then he left and cycled to see Alex. Alex opened the door looking slightly ruffled.

"Hi," said Peter. "You OK?"

"Come in," said Alex, opening the door wider.

Alex was still in his pyjamas and left Peter downstairs whilst he went to dress. He came back down yawning and stretching.

"Are you sure you're OK?" asked Peter again.

"Yes, thanks—just a late night," Alex replied.

"Why—what were you up to?" Peter enquired.

Alex looked at Peter for a few moments, taking a deep breath. "I've got a new girlfriend," he explained.

Peter was amazed. None of them had shown any interest in girls, so this came as a shock. "Wow—you kept that quiet," Peter said, clearly impressed.

"Yeah, well I didn't want to say too much at first, but we've been going out for a couple of weeks now."

"Wow," Peter said again. His mind was turning over, taking it all in. Eventually he went on, "Well, who is she then?"

"Her name's Anna and she's in the same year as us at St Georges," Alex explained, continuing, "She wants to do medicine. Her dad's a doctor at the hospital as well and we've known each other on and off for years."

Peter smiled to himself. What a dark horse—keeping this quiet. "You'll have to bring her to meet Liam and myself," Peter said.

He was suddenly curious—girls just hadn't ever been on the boy's radar and all of a sudden they were growing up fast. Alex continued to talk about Anna and Peter found himself suddenly interested—was she pretty? Was she funny? Was she tall? He was too polite to ask these questions of course, but his mind was racing.

"When are you going to get a girlfriend?" Alex teased.

"No room in my life for one at the moment," Peter replied. He couldn't let the thought of a relationship get in the way.

Alex laughed. "You'll find one when you least expect it," he said, laughing.

"I won't," Peter replied, determined. He was pleased for his friend though—although he hoped that it wouldn't get in the way of their friendship. They continued chatting for the rest of the day and Peter left mid-afternoon to cycle home to see if there was any post.

Annie was already home. "Hi," she called as Peter closed the back door.

"Hi—any post?" he asked.

"No, sorry," came Annie's response.

Peter sighed. Maybe tomorrow. He put his savings book on the table, as he wanted to know how much was in the account. Peter had always been frugal and a good saver, so it was no surprise to see that there was a little over £100 in there. Annie was impressed.

"What will you do with all that money?" she asked, smiling. She was proud of his careful ways—unlike Ben, who spent money as soon as he got it.

"It'll come in when I'm training," Peter said.

"Of course—spend it wisely," she advised.

After dinner, once Peter had finished with the washing up, Paul called him into the living room. "Right," he said. "I've had a word with my boss. He'd like you to do three days a week, starting this Wednesday. It'll be for right through the holidays and can continue if you decide to not return to school. Is that OK?"

"Sure," said Peter, excited.

"Good. We start at 07:30 and you can come in with me. Now then." Paul went on carefully, "This is an engineering shop. It's all blokes and there's lots of banter and teasing, especially out of the apprentices and younger workers. I know sometimes you find it difficult to spot jokes and that you're quite sensitive, but there's nothing nasty or malicious, just guys having a bit of fun. The more you give back, the more respect you'll earn—but the most important thing is to not take it seriously. Understand?"

"Err, yes, I guess so," Peter said uncertainly.

"Another thing—there's also a lot of profanity, so you'll learn some choice new words. We leave those at work," Paul said.

Peter nodded. He was excited at the prospect of working with his dad and of learning new skills.

8

On Tuesday evening, Peter set his alarm carefully for the same time as his dad. He tossed and turned, unable to get to sleep, his mind filled with all the possibilities of tomorrow. Eventually he drifted off.

The alarm rudely intruded upon his dreams and he sat bolt upright. Gathering himself, he jumped out of bed and dressed quickly, meeting his dad coming out of the bathroom.

"Morning," Peter said.

Paul grunted a response and took himself downstairs. Peter quickly followed and Paul had made drinks and toast.

"Thanks" said Peter, wolfing his breakfast.

Soon, they were on their bikes, cycling and chatting. After a short ride, they arrived, locking their bikes in the shed provided.

"Right," Paul started, "You stay close to me at first. There are a lot of dangerous machines and I need to show you the ropes and what to avoid."

"OK," Peter replied, desperate to see inside. He'd never been in an engineering shop before.

They went in through the main door and Paul then showed Peter how to clock in using his own punch card. "You need to do that every day, otherwise you don't get paid," Paul explained.

Peter saw his name stencilled on top of the card. From there, they walked to the locker room, where Paul unlocked a tall steel locker, putting their coats inside and pulling out a pair of overalls, into which he squeezed his six foot plus frame. "We'll get you some of these from the stores—keep your clothes clean," Paul said.

Peter just nodded, fascinated. "C'mon, I'll introduce you to the main man," Paul said, striding off. Peter followed and they walked into a glass-fronted office. "Morning, Dave," said Paul. "This is my lad Peter."

Peter held his hand up in greeting. "Hi," said Dave. "Come in and let's get a good look at you."

Peter moved shyly into the office. Dave eyed Peter up and down. "Hmmm—I guess we can probably do something with him," he said, winking at Peter. Peter smiled. "Paul, I've taken you off machining this morning for a couple of hours so you can show the lad around. Usual stuff—fire exits, canteen, stores, toilets, first aid box, danger areas and what to avoid. Also, get him some overalls and gloves from stores—tell them I sent you."

"Sure thing—come on," said Paul, gesturing for Peter to follow. They went straight to the stores and Peter was issued with everything he needed. They then went back to the locker room for Peter to get into his new work clothes. He suddenly felt inadequate.

"Right—let's show you around," Paul said, setting off a great pace. There followed a maze of corridors which led into different manufacturing areas, specialist machining rooms, assembly areas and the parts department. Peter was also shown the fire exits and, as Paul said, the most important room in the factory—the canteen.

"If you get a bit lost—just ask," Paul explained. "We're in machine shop B," Peter just nodded. He felt overwhelmed with the barrage on information, but told himself that he'd get used to it. Eventually, they arrived back at Dave's office. He was shouting into the telephone about some parts which were late for delivery. Finally, he slammed the receiver down and took a deep breath.

"Right, lad—come and sit down. You go and get on, Paul—I'll bring him over," Dave said. Peter sat quietly. "Right—you'll be doing mainly chores. Fetching parts from the stores—when we have them," he said, giving the telephone a filthy look. "You'll be helping to keep the place clean, clearing up engineering waste and what have you. Now, waste—or swarf as we call it is sharp and dangerous. You must use your gloves and keep it away from your face or it will cut you to ribbons as it's sharp and springy. There are special collection bags to put it in.

"At the end of the day we clean the machines—each machine has its own cleaning brush. Please try not to get them mixed up. You'll work the same hours as your dad and have your lunch at the same time. It's three days a week and the pay is £4 per week, paid a week in hand. Any questions?"

"No sir," Peter replied.

Dave's eyebrows immediately ascended. "Sir? Sir? I've not been knighted—well, not yet anyway," Dave laughed. "It's Dave."

"OK, Sir—err Dave," Peter replied. Inside he was mortified with the faux pas he had just committed.

"Right—come on," said Dave, getting up and striding out of the office. Peter followed, almost at a trot, thinking *Why does everybody move so quickly?*

They soon arrived at a huge machine where a massive block of steel was being lowered onto it. Paul was looking at some large sheets of paper. "Here he is," said Dave, slapping Peter on the back. "He's all yours. Be gentle with him," he winked.

Paul smiled. "Right Peter, we are just loading a blank billet of steel. There are the engineering drawings, which I use to beat this block into something useful."

Peter looked at the drawings that Paul was holding—they were covered with lines, symbols and numbers. He was fascinated. The billet finally stopped with a crash and Paul then started to make his way around it, locking arms in place to hold it in position. Once it was secured, Paul released the chains attached to the top and pressed a button on a box hanging on a thick wire and the chains moved up and away.

"What's that?" Peter asked.

"An overhead crane; it runs on tracks in the roof," Paul explained.

"Wow," Peter muttered. He'd never seen anything like it.

Paul then took Peter around the machine, pointing out various parts. He also showed Peter a long metal rod with a hook on the end and a big wooden brush hanging on hooks at the rear. "That's a swarf hook—you use it to drag the swarf off the machine bed," he explained. "The brush is to sweep out the nooks and crannies once you removed the waste. OK?"

"Yes," said Peter, "I think so."

"Don't worry—I'll show you the ropes," his dad said. "Right—let's make something," he continued and went to a large wooden chest on wheels, pulling open a drawer. "These are cutting tools," he explained. "There are straight ones, angled ones, curved ones. They cut the metal." Peter just nodded. "There are all shapes and sizes and I need to select the correct one for each stage of the process." Peter nodded again. He'd no idea that his dad was so clever.

Paul selected a tool and returned to the machine. He took a steel ruler from a pocket in the leg of his overalls and mounted the tool into a block, locking it in place with a spanner, after carefully measuring it's position. "Right—put your gloves and safety specs on. Always wear your safety specs—metal fragments can blind you and there's no jobs for blind pilots," Paul instructed.

Peter did as he was told and Paul pressed a green button on the control panel. The tool began to rotate and fluid spurted from a nozzle. "What's the fluid?" Peter asked.

"Cutting fluid—a mixture of light oil and water. It keeps the cutting tool cool and sharp," Paul explained. He then moved levers to bring it into contact with the metal. Slowly a groove appeared and long ribbons of metal spiralled up from the cutting head. Paul measured the depth of the groove after each cutting pass, finally announcing that he was satisfied. He pressed a red button and the machine stopped.

"Get the swarf hook please," he asked Peter, who grabbed if from the rear. "This is how you clear the machine face," Paul explained, dragging the waste with hook and dumping it into a tray at the bottom of the machine. "We do that after every cut," he explained, "and empty the waste when the tray is full. I'll show you later."

Peter nodded. Paul then moved the position of the cutting head and after careful measurement, began a second cut. Peter couldn't take his eyes off the machine it was amazing. He hadn't done metalwork at school and he was finding this a real education.

After a couple of hours watching and removing the swarf under Paul's supervision, Paul said that this part of the process was complete and it was time to move the billet to another machine. Peter looked with awe at the maze of grooves cut into the block. "What are they?" he asked.

"Oil galleries for the hydraulic fluid," Paul explained. "We're now going to drill them to connect them together. First though, we have to reattach the chains," and he grabbed the controller hanging from the roof. Chains reattached, Paul unlocked the billet from the machine and raised it up a small distance. "I need to make sure that it's fully attached," he explained. Once he was satisfied, He moved the billet over to another machine, again lowering it carefully and locking it in place.

"Right, before we start, let's clear the milling machine," he said to Peter. They walked back to the first machine and Paul showed Peter where the collection bags were stored. They opened one and Paul showed Peter how to use the hook to drag the waste into the bag. Peter took over and they cleared the machine. "Good," said Paul. "Put the bag down there and we'll carry on."

They returned to the second machine. "What is it?" Peter asked.

"Drilling machine," Paul said, opening yet another drawer and selecting the correct size drill bits, which he again mounted after taking careful measurements. Paul then stood back and pressed the green button. "This is our newest machine," he said. "It's automatic. There's a punched card and it's read by a reader and that passes the information via a computer to the drill head. All we do it sit and watch," Paul explained with a smile.

Peter was amazed. He'd never heard of anything like it. He stood next to Paul watching the drill head moving back and forth, cutting fluid squirting from nozzles. Eventually, the machine beeped and the heads stopped spinning. "All finished," Paul said, looking at his watch. "C'mon, it's lunchtime."

Peter couldn't believe what he'd just seen. Science was moving on at such a pace.

Peter followed his dad to the rest room where they washed their hands thoroughly and then to the canteen. Paul joined the queue after asking Peter what he wanted to eat and Peter found a table. Paul soon joined him, passing Peter his lunch and other workers took the empty seats. They nodded at Paul as they sat down.

"Who's this then?" one asked.

"This is my lad Peter—here for a bit of work experience," Paul replied.

"He's only a baby," the man said, laughing. Peter blushed. "How old are you?" the man asked.

"Nearly sixteen," Peter mumbled.

"Sixteen? Jeez—I can't bloody well remember being sixteen." The man laughed.

"You never were sixteen—you were born at fifty," Paul laughed.

The man roared with laughter. "Aye—fifty and bloody poor," he joked. Paul smiled. "Are you going to be an engineer?" the man asked.

"No—I want to be a pilot," Peter replied.

"A pilot? You mean flying aeroplanes?"

"Yes," said Peter.

"Ha! No doubt wanting to go around chasing all those hostesses," the man quipped.

"C'mon, Frank—play nicely. It's his first day," Paul cut in.

Peter blushed furiously—he'd never heard anything like it. "Well, that's what I'd be doing if I were his age," Frank continued. "Good luck to you, lad. I'm going for a fag," and he got up, pushing his plate away.

Paul shook his head. "I told you what it was like—ignore him," he said. Peter just smiled—he was beginning to understand the banter and camaraderie and he found it amusing.

In the afternoon, Paul continued to work on the valve body that he was making and Peter was sent to various areas around the factory. He had parts to collect from stores and take to the assembly area, a couple of machines to clean and finally, he was sent back to his dad's shop to begin cleaning the machines there. Gloves and safety specs on, he began to feel part of the team as long as was near to Paul.

Peter realised that until now, he hadn't actually spoken to anybody else in the plant. No worry—he'd find his tongue in a day or two. He pulled swarf from the catchment tray on the bottom of the milling machine, bagging it as he went. Once the swarf was clear, Peter got the brush and swept up the smaller pieces which he also bagged. "What do I do about all this oil?" he asked Paul.

"Oh that? It will drain back into the tanks and is reused," Paul explained. "C'mon—I'll help you get rid of the swarf bags." They picked up two bags apiece and Paul led them outside to some large bins. "Swarf or anything metal goes in the yellow bin," Paul explained. "It goes for recycling."

"OK," Peter replied, throwing his bags into the open container. "What are the other bins for?"

"Red is for oil or cutting fluid containers, blue is for general waste. It's important not to get them mixed up," Paul said. "Let's go and get washed and back into our civvies."

Peter followed his dad to the locker room where there were lots of men getting changed and washing their hands at the basins. Peter and Paul did the same and on the stroke of 16:30, they queued up to clock out. They then walked outside to get their bikes for the ride home. Paul put his arm around Peter's shoulders. "How did you enjoy your first day at work?" he asked.

"It was great—very eye-opening. I still can't believe what Frank said to me at lunchtime."

Paul laughed. "There's lots of them like that here—as I said to you, it's all part of the banter. Don't take it to heart."

"I won't," said Peter.

Annie was waiting excitedly for them. "How was your first day?" she asked.

"Great, thanks. Everyone was so friendly and helpful," Peter answered. "Any post for me?" he asked.

"No, not today, sweetie," Annie responded. She was also desperate for Peter to get replies.

"OK, no problem, what's for dinner?" Peter asked.

"Your favourite—sausages," she said.

"Be ready in a little while." Peter followed Paul into the living room, collapsing in a chair.

"Tired?" asked Paul.

"Yes, but I don't know why," Peter answered.

"Well, you've been busy today—for you it's a lot of walking around the factory and lifting stuff which you won't be used to. You'll grow some muscles," Paul said, laughing. Peter smiled—it had been a great day with his dad and it had been an education watching Paul at work. He was clearly a very skilled man— more so than Peter had ever appreciated.

After dinner, during which Annie questioned Peter endlessly about his work day, they all chatted for a while, but Peter felt tired, so he took himself off to bed early, making sure that his alarm was set. He slid into bed and was asleep in an instant.

Downstairs, Annie asked Paul how Peter had fared. "He was fine—very shy as expected, but he'll be OK. I think he found the day fascinating—may make an engineer of him if the airlines don't want him," Paul replied.

Annie put her hand on Paul's—this was what she had wanted to hear and was pleased that it had been a good first day.

9

At Alex's house, Alex was enjoying an evening with Anna. They sat on his bed, the record player quietly playing their favourite songs from the charts—Alex was an avid collector—and Anna was quizzing Alex about his school and friends. "My best buddies are Liam and Peter," Alex explained. "We were at primary together and have been friends since, like forever," he told Anna.

"What are they like?" she asked.

"Liam is a great guy, very loud and full of himself, but he's got a good heart. Loves sport and follows the local team loyally. Peter is—well, he's a quiet guy. You have to get to know him really. He's a very private person, but very clever—he was top in our year in the exams. He doesn't say much until you get to know him, but he's OK," Alex answered.

"You'll have to introduce me," Anna said. "I'd love to meet them."

"Sure—maybe we could do something this weekend?" Alex suggested.

"That would be nice—maybe I could introduce them to some of my friends," she said playfully, snuggling up to Alex.

Alex laughed. "I think Liam would be up for that, but not Peter. He's far too private and not interested in girls—or boys for that matter," he quickly added. Anna smiled to herself—she just loved playing matchmaker and a few of her friends were desperate for a boyfriend.

Peter spent another two hectic days working with Paul and finally it was Friday afternoon. Paul had completed the valve body that he'd been working on and was inspecting it for measurement and accuracy. Peter stood watching, fascinated. "Is this how they would make aircraft parts?" he asked.

"Absolutely," Paul answered. "Engineering is engineering and it is all basically the same. We actually make some small components for the aerospace industry—some hydraulic components for Vickers. Tolerances are super-accurate as you'd expect," Paul went on.

"Really?" Peter asked in astonishment. He'd had no idea. Peter was amazed that what had started as a blank block of steel had been transformed into such a complex and beautiful component. He was really seeing his dad in a new light.

"Yep—I'm happy with that. Need to get an inspector to sign it off now," Paul said, straightening up. "Let's clean up." They both started on the machines, sweeping, wiping and bagging. Soon Paul was happy and they took the waste bags outside and then headed to the locker room. Paul looked down at Peter. "Don't you just love Friday afternoons?" he asked, laughing. Peter nodded, drying his hands.

In a few moments they were on their bikes, wind in their hair, pelting along the street, Peter's first week at work complete.

Arriving home, Peter could hear Annie's voice in the kitchen. Who could she be talking to? Neighbours rarely called and then Peter's heart sank—Ben. He hoped beyond hope that Ben hadn't returned. He followed Paul cautiously into the house and they could hear Annie chatting and laughing in the living room.

"We're home," Paul called out, but he didn't get a response. Paul opened the living room door and there was Annie, curled up on the sofa, chatting on the phone. It had been installed! Peter was once again amazed—he suddenly felt that they as a family had gone up socially. Eventually she said goodbye and turned to face them both.

"Hi. As you can see, we're connected to the outside world," she said laughing. The new telephone sat on a small table next to the sofa, bright and shiny. "I was just chatting to your Gran," Annie explained. "It will be so much easier to keep in touch, especially as she's not getting any younger" she added.

"Great," said Paul. "That'll make life easier."

Peter continued to stare at the new addition. "Can I give our number to my friends?" he asked.

"Yes, of course—they can call you anytime," said Annie, getting up and giving him a hug. "How are my two working men?" she asked.

"Tired," said Paul.

"Hungry," added Peter.

"Well, dinner's in the oven and it won't be long," Annie said.

"Good. I'm famished," said Peter, rubbing his abdomen.

"Well, in that case you can come and peel some vegetables and tell me all about your week," Annie told him, heading for the kitchen.

Once Peter had finished preparing the veg, he casually enquired if there was any post. "Not today," came Annie's reply. "Don't worry—I'm sure you'll hear soon." Peter smiled thinly. He was sure he would as well, but impatience was beginning to eat at him. Annie could see this and quickly changed the subject. "How's it been, working with your dad?" she asked, sitting down.

"Great. I've learned and seen loads of stuff. I never realised what skills he had as an engineer," Peter told her. "I was amazed that he could take a blank block of metal and turn it into something so beautiful and useful," he added.

"Oh, your dad's a very clever man," Annie answered. "Why do you think I married him?" she laughed.

Peter smiled. He loved being with his parents—they were his rock, his anchor, his port in a storm. He knew that they had always looked out for him and had helped him through difficult times. Peter knew that he still had issues socialising and meeting new people, but he felt hat he was improving, as long as his routines weren't disturbed.

After dinner, Peter cycled to see Alex and to tell him about his week at work. Alex was pleased to see him and they chatted for most of the evening about their respective weeks. Alex was fascinated to hear all about the engineering company and what Peter had been doing. Alex had spent a quiet week, reading some pre-course material for his A-Levels and had of course seen Anna.

"Do you fancy meeting up tomorrow at the coffee bar?" he asked.

"Yeah sure," Peter replied.

"I may bring Anna along as she's anxious to meet both you and Liam," Alex said casually.

Peter sat and thought for a while, finally agreeing. "Oh, I forgot to tell you, we're now on the phone," Peter told Alex. "Our number is Westlea 4818."

"Brill," said Alex. "Let me write that down. When did you get that?"

"It came today—mum was chatting on it when we got home from work," Peter replied.

"Ha! If she's anything like my mum, she'll spend all day on it," Alex replied and they both roared. They spent the rest of the evening chatting, laughing and listening to Alex's records and Peter finally rode home just before dark, going straight to bed.

For the first time in years, Peter slept so well he missed the usual Saturday morning departure. His first three days at work had taken their toll.

He rose slowly, stretching and yawning, his muscles aching from the unaccustomed exercise of lifting heavy objects. Paul and Annie were already up and having breakfast. "Good morning, sleepy head," said Annie, smiling. "The usual?"

"Morning," Peter replied. "Yes please."

"What's on your agenda?" Paul asked.

"I'm meeting Alex in town around midday, so I'll cycle in and spend some time with him. He may be bringing his new girlfriend along," Peter said in a matter-of-fact way.

Annie's ears pricked up. "Alex has a girlfriend? Good for him—your turn next," she teased.

"I don't think so," Peter muttered. He always found it difficult meeting new people and there certainly wasn't room for anybody in his life at the moment. Girls could wait. His life was well organised and to his liking at the moment.

The bang of the letterbox snapping shut caught Peter's attention. Annie wandered towards the front door, returning a few moments later.

"For you," she said, handing Peter a long white envelope. Peter studied it carefully, noting the crest of Channel Ferry Airlines in the corner. With butterflies in his stomach, he peeled the envelope open and began to read.

"Dear Mr Marham, Thank you for informing us of your GCE results. These are outstanding—well done. With regards to the Cadetship programme, this is on hold until September of 1970 and we suggest that for the next twelve months, you might wish to gain some work experience in industry. At the moment, we have no vacancies for a junior to assist in the administration side of our business, but should such a vacancy occur, we would be happy to inform you. We will be in touch again when formal applications for the Cadet programme are open. Kind regards."

The letter was signed Captain Andrews. So he had remembered Peter. Both Peter's parents were on tenterhooks wanting to know what the letter said, so Peter passed it to his dad, who read it aloud. Annie put her hand on Peter's arm— "That's positive, isn't it?" she asked.

Peter was silent for a few moments. "Yes—I guess so," he answered. "I can't start until I'm sixteen anyway, which will be September, so I guess you may have to put up with me for a while," he said turning towards Paul.

"I think we can manage that—I can at least teach you some basic engineering and all about hydraulics. I'll speak to Dave on Monday," Paul said. Peter smiled and got up to get ready.

As Peter cycled along, he went over the contents of the letter in his head and his spirits began to lift. At least he hadn't been turned down flat—that would have finished him. Despite the dull grey overcast, by the time he got into town, he was happy. Locking his bike to a railing, he walked the short distance to the coffee bar, seeing Liam in the distance heading the same way. He broke into a run, catching Liam and startling him.

"You silly sod," Liam shouted. "Nearly gave me a seizure."

"Sorry," Peter replied, laughing. They walked in through the door seeing Alex in the corner—with a very pretty girl.

"Hey up," Liam said quietly. "She's pretty tidy." Peter didn't respond and he let Liam walk in front. Alex greeted them in the usual way and introduced Anna. Liam was all over her, asking where she lived, where she went to school and was almost trying to get her life history.

"Easy tiger," Alex said "Give the poor girl a chance." Peter smiled to himself—typical Liam. After ordering a coffee, Peter sat quietly listening and watching. After a while, he realised that Anna was speaking to him.

"Sorry—miles away. What did you say?" he asked.

"I was asking what you were planning over the summer holidays," Anna replied.

"Oh, I'm working with my dad at his engineering company. It may carry on for the next year," Peter explained. As he spoke, he studied Anna carefully. Long dark hair, slim build, dark eyes and about the same height as himself. *Alex has done well*, he thought.

Anna broke the silence. "We must all meet up more often—Alex told me that you were top of year with the exam results," she asked.

"Well, I'm not sure—I don't know everyone's results. We all did OK though. How about you?" he asked.

"Yes I think I did OK—enough to start my A-levels next term," Anna explained. "I want to do medicine like Alex," she went on, adding, "What do you want to do?"

"I want to train as aircrew and fly jets," Peter said.

"And meet all the pretty hostesses?" Anna teased. Peter blushed. "Sounds like a great job though—I love travelling. Do you?"

"I haven't been many places, but It will hopefully allow me to see foreign parts," Peter replied.

After they finished their drinks, Anna suggested they had a look around the new shops. She and Alex set off at a pace, holding hands. Liam seemed to find this amusing and he kept making jokes to Peter, but they fell on deaf ears. Peter was, as usual, uncomfortable with strangers and he wore his privacy like a dark cloak gathered around him. He and Liam followed along like two obedient dogs, whilst Alex was treated to every shop window in the new arcade.

Most of the time, Liam kept up his ceaseless chatter and Peter remained silent, taking it all in. Anna and Alex had disappeared into a boutique and the two of them waited outside. Liam was talking excitedly about starting his apprenticeship and was looking forward to earning some money.

"I wonder if Anna has any single friends—what do you think?" he asked Peter. Peter shrugged—he wasn't interested. "Do you think that they're having sex?" Liam continued.

Peter didn't know what to say it was something that just hadn't crossed his mind. "Dunno—none of my business," he mumbled.

"C'mon—you must have an idea," Liam continued, enjoying Peter's discomfort. Peter shrugged, wanting Liam to change the subject. "Well if they're not, I'd be happy to stand in," Liam laughed.

Sex was something that Peter had never thought about—he knew the basics from education at school and from what other boys in their year had talked about, but it all seemed a mystery to him and was not something that was on his radar. He just wasn't interested.

Anna and Alex reappeared and the afternoon wore on with more shop visits and Liam continuing to make jokes and not taking his eyes off Anna. Eventually, Peter was tired of window shopping and began to make his leave.

"It's been lovely to meet you," Anna said, extending her hand. Peter took the proffered hand gently and muttered a few words. "Let's do this again," Anna went on, adding, "I'll bring some friends next time."

"Yes please," Liam said emphatically. Peter shook his head, smiling. Liam was certainly one of the lads.

The rest of the weekend was quiet and Peter spent his time reading and rereading his letter. On Sunday afternoon, he sat down with Paul and was shown the basics of a hydraulic system and how they worked. The physics appealed to

Peter's inquisitive mind and he understood what Paul was showing him very quickly.

After bombarding his dad with questions, he spent the rest of the day in his room, thinking about what he'd just been shown, but also remembering Anna's words about bringing a friend along. Inside, he was intrigued, but he was also certain that he wanted to remain single, in his own orderly world.

10

Monday morning saw the start of the normal working week. On Wednesday morning, Paul and Peter dropped into see Dave in the office and Dave agreed that Peter could stay on as a labourer for the foreseeable future. Peter was happy with this as it afforded him the training "in industry" as the airline had suggested and also meant that he'd be able to save some money for the future.

As the weeks went on, he got more used to the job and even started speaking to his co-workers around the factory. There was plenty of teasing at first and a few played practical jokes on Peter, but he learned to take it in his stride. He also started to go out cycling after work, as he was keen to build his fitness and after the initial aches in his muscles, his arms and chest began to grow and tighten. His appetite increased enormously as well and his mother commented that he was beginning to eat like a horse.

"He's a growing lad," Paul said, defending him. A few weeks had gone by since the letter from the local airline and Peter had begun to give up hope of hearing from International Airlines in London, but to his surprise one Thursday evening, there was a letter awaiting his arrival at home. Annie had propped it up on the table in Peter's normal place and he hadn't seen it until he was called for his evening meal. He picked up the envelope, reading the outside and again noting the airline crest on the back.

"Are you going to open it?" his mother asked, but Peter said that as it had taken so long to get a reply, another few minutes wouldn't make a difference and he tucked into his meal.

After had finished, he took the letter upstairs to his room and settled down on his bed to read it. It was beautifully typewritten on luxury headed paper and began:

Dear Mr Marham, thank you for your recent communication regarding your examination results, which we have duly noted. Interviews for the Pilot Cadet course will commence in October 1969 and we enclose an application form, which we would like you to complete and return to us, to reach us no later than 30/09/1969. If we wish to interview you, we will contact you again in due course, giving you full details. As it is our policy not to contact unsuccessful applicants, if you have not heard from us by mid-December then please consider that you have been unsuccessful at this stage. We look forward to receiving your application form.

Kind regards.

Peter read and reread the letter and then turned his attention to the form, which looked daunting. In addition to the letter and application form, there was a reading list of books to study prior to interview. *I'll get dad to help me with this*, he thought and he walked back downstairs. Both parents looked up eagerly as Peter entered the room.

"Well?" asked Annie.

"Here—have a read," Peter said, handing over the letter and form.

"Oh Peter, that's great news. You must get on to it straight away," she added.

"Yes, I was going to ask dad to help," Peter replied, handing the letter over to Paul, who quickly read it through.

"Shall we do it this weekend when we're not as tired and have more time?" Paul suggested and Peter agreed. Inside, Peter was excited but also apprehensive. His whole future depended on a paper form and the willingness of somebody somewhere to give him a chance.

The next day, being Friday, was pay day and Peter duly collected the small brown packet from the office behind his dad, signing his name in the box. They both cycled home together and this evening Peter decided that he wouldn't go out for a ride as he'd arranged to meet Alex and Anna.

Dinner was a rushed affair, then Peter washed and changed. The three of them were meeting at a new soft-drinks bar in town, which was becoming very popular with teenagers. He was uncertain on the bus into town, turning the application form over and over in his head, anxious to get it absolutely perfect. He'd keep it to himself for the time being, as he couldn't stand the thought of being asked questions over and over again.

He arrived first, getting a drink and finding a seat near the door. After a few minutes Alex and Anna walked in—followed by a slim dark-haired girl. Peter took no notice until they came to join him.

"Hi, Peter—this is my friend Sally," Anna said, sitting down beside him. "This is Peter."

"Oh, hi," Peter mumbled, retreating into himself, suddenly feeling awkward.

"Hi," said Sally, also taking a seat.

Alex shortly joined them carrying bottles and straws. "Hi buddy—you OK?" he asked.

"Yeah good, thanks," Peter replied.

His head was whirring with different thoughts and permutations—he just didn't know how to talk to or deal with strangers. He was cross with Alex—he could have warned him. Alex spoke first.

"Sally is a school friend of Anna's. Same year, so like us she's at a loose end and looking for things to do in the holiday." Peter didn't respond.

"So, how are you filling your time during the holidays?" Sally asked.

Peter waited before replying—he could feel his face burning and he was desperate not to say the wrong or inappropriate thing. "Erm—I'm working with my dad. Three days a week at the moment, so I'm off on Monday and Tuesdays."

He stopped himself—damnation. He'd just told Sally when he'd be around. He didn't like people to know his routine.

"What are you doing to fill your time?" Alex asked.

"I'm helping my mum in her shop—she runs a grocery store. Just filling shelves and so on," Sally replied. "Like you guys, I'm starting my A's in September."

"What are you planning as a career?" Alex asked.

"Hmm not sure," Sally responded. "Something to do with finance I think. What about you, Peter? What are you going to do?"

Peter took a deep breath. "I want to fly jets," he said quietly.

"Oh wow! That must be an awesome job," Sally replied. "Just think—jetting off to faraway lands and staying in beautiful hotels. It must be amazing." She went on.

Peter got up, excusing himself and headed for the rest room. Sally watched him turn the corner and disappear from view and then turning to her friends said quietly, "Isn't he shy? So quiet. Does he say much at school?" she asked.

"Yes, but as we said, it takes him ages to come out of his shell and to be honest, he's never had anything to do with girls," Alex explained. "Well, if he wants to get to know me better, he'll have to at least say something," Sally added.

"Give him time," Alex said.

Peter stood before the mirror drying his hands. How could Alex do this to him? To just appear with Sally without saying anything was bad enough, but it was obvious that Alex and Anna were trying to make up a foursome. "I'm not ready for this," he said to himself, yet there was something inside him that was curious—he could feel Sally pulling at him like a great black magnet buried deep within his soul. He was at a loss to know what to do. He didn't want to appear rude and leave, but he really didn't feel up to making conversation. He decided to just go back to their table and see how things went.

He sat down in the same seat to find the girls talking about films that they wanted to see and Alex seemed glad to see him. "Right buddy, what are we doing this weekend?"

Peter looked at his friend, his eyes imploring Alex to help him out of this situation. "Not sure," he replied. "Just take it as it comes, I guess."

"OK buddy," came the response.

Alex then started talking to Peter about the new jet aircraft, as he knew that Peter would be happier on familiar territory. They chatted for about an hour, with Anna and Sally still in animated conversation about their favourite pop stars. At about nine thirty, Sally said that she'd have to leave and catch her bus home and asked Peter if he'd like to walk her to the bus stop. Peter mumbled his agreement as he had to go the same way and they left Anna and Alex and walked outside into the warm summer evening.

"I love evenings like this," Sally said, waving her arms around and twirling on her feet. "I just love the summer—don't you?" she asked Peter.

"Yes, it's nice when it's warm and it's still light," Peter replied. They walked slowly along, with Sally chatting happily and asking lots of questions, most of which Peter didn't have time to answer.

They were soon at the bus station and Sally turned to Peter and said, "I like you. Can we see each other again?"

"Hmm, I guess so," came Peter's non-committal reply.

"Good," she replied. "There's my bus—must dash," and as quick as a flash, she gave Peter a kiss on the cheek and turned and ran for her bus.

Peter blushed furiously, not knowing what to do or how to respond. He just stood with his arms dangling by his side watching her bus vanish into the night, his head exploding. After a few moments, he turned and walked towards where his bus would stop, his mind in turmoil.

Saturday morning and Peter was awake very early. He sat at his desk, going over the application form very carefully, writing draft answers on his notepad to discuss with his dad. His concentration was, as always, broken by the sound of aero engines. Jet ones again today and Peter watched the new aircraft climb overhead. *To think that I was sitting in that a while ago*, he mused, returning to the form.

Eventually, he put the form down and went downstairs for his drink. Annie was already busy in the kitchen. "Morning, mum," Peter said, kissing her on the back of the neck.

"Morning, sweetie," she replied. "Are you doing your application with your dad this morning?"

"Yes, just as soon as we've had breakfast," Peter replied, sitting down.

Soon, Paul appeared and took his seat next to Peter. "Let's get your form done and get it in the post," he said to Peter, turning to Annie and asking, "Is there a postal collection on Saturday morning?"

"Yes, but I think you'd be best taking it to the post office and getting it sent Recorded Delivery. That way, it will need to be signed for and delivery is guaranteed. No chance of it getting lost in the post." "Good idea" Paul replied. "I've done some draft answers to some of the questions" Peter said, showing Paul his notepad. "Good man" Paul said. "Let's get to it after breakfast."

Breakfast finished, Peter cleared and wiped the table and then they both sat down to attack the paperwork. Paul read it through carefully. "You need to fill it in with a black pen," he said, getting up and going to the drawer.

Together, they started and wrote answers to the questions on blank paper, changing and improving things before committing them to the application form. After an hour they were done and Peter was happy. He then set about copying his answers so that he could refer to them if he was lucky enough to be offered an interview.

Once this was completed, they both got their bikes and rode up the hill to the post office. Peter had also bought his savings book and he paid in his wages for the previous two weeks, keeping just enough in his pocket for the weekend. The letter was marked as special delivery and the man behind the glass put it into a special sack, winking at Peter.

When they arrived home, Annie was waiting for them both. "I think we need to get you some new clothes young man," she said, adding, "You're outgrowing everything—you must have grown two inches since you started working with your dad and you're getting so muscular. You'll be as tall as him soon."

Peter sighed—he hated clothes shopping, but Annie had suggested it a few weeks ago and was making some sense. So off they went and soon Peter was being dragged around the arcade, trying on all manner of clothing. Annie kept making suggestions, which Peter usually rejected and Paul tried to act as referee. Eventually, they settled on some summer shirts, some of the new fashion jeans which were becoming popular and some tee shirts.

Shopping completed, Paul pleaded with Annie, saying that he needed a drink, so they took themselves to Peter's favourite coffee bar. It was fairly crowded, but they managed to find a table. Paul fetched the coffee and after a short while, Peter heard his name being called. He looked up and there was Sally across the room waving at him. His heart sank, but he raised his hand in acknowledgement.

Annie looked across the room and smiled. "Friend of yours?" she asked.

"No not really. Friend of Anna's—Alex's girlfriend," Peter explained. "Met her last night."

Annie smiled to herself, but didn't pursue the conversation, as Peter looked uncomfortable enough. "I walked her to the bus station as I was going that way." Peter went on, "But I don't think that I'm interested in her."

"Well, you'll no doubt find somebody when the time comes," Annie said, sparing his embarrassment.

It was obvious that Sally was leaving, but she made her way to Peter's table, saying, "Nice to see you again. I enjoyed last night. Perhaps we can see each other again?"

Peter smiled thinly and muttered, "Yeah maybe," and Sally then turned to go.

Annie was about to ask Peter all about Sally but Paul interjected. "Leave him be," he said quietly. Annie just smiled. Her boy was really growing up.

Arriving home, they were barely inside the door when the phone began to ring. Annie lifted the receiver and quickly answered, "Yes, hang on please— Peter, it's for you."

Peter took the phone and said hello. "Hi, buddy—it's Alex. Wondered if you wanted to come to the pictures this evening? We're going to see the new film *The Italian Job*."

Peter thought for a moment. "Will Sally be coming?" he asked cautiously.

"She can do if you want—I'll get Anna to call her—meet us at six-thirty outside the cinema. See you there," Alex replied and the phone went dead. This wasn't the outcome Peter wanted—he was going to say that if Sally was coming, then he wouldn't. Too late now.

Annie saw the dejected look on Peter's face. "What's up?" she asked.

"Oh, nothing. Alex has invited me to the pictures and I did ask if Sally was going. I wasn't going to go if she was, but I didn't manage to get a word in edgeways," Peter replied.

"Oh, it'll be fine I'm sure," Annie said. "It'll be good to expand your circle of friends."

Peter wasn't sure about this and he climbed the stairs to his room slowly, his head in turmoil as always.

"What time are you meeting up?" Annie called after him.

"6:30," Peter called back.

"OK—I'll get dinner ready early," Annie replied and she disappeared into the kitchen.

Peter washed and changed into his new jeans and a shirt, coming downstairs about ten minutes before the bus was due. Annie looked him over, nodding her head in approval. "Very smart—you're growing into a good-looking lad," she said.

Peter blushed and making sure that he had his house key and money, said his goodbyes and left to catch the bus. After a short ride into town, Peter walked to the cinema, checking his watch to see that he was on time. After waiting for just a few moments, Alex arrived with Anna and Sally.

"Hi," they all said at the same time and Peter responded with a nod of his head. "Shall we go straight in?" Alex asked and they all agreed.

"I'm so excited to see this film—I just love Michael Caine," Sally said, walking beside Peter.

Peter didn't know who Michael Caine was, but kept quiet just in case he made himself look dumb by asking a stupid question. They queued for tickets and made their way inside. It was brightly lit and they found seats directly in front of the screen, but a good way back from the front. Alex and Anna snuggled up, holding hands and began chatting together. Sally asked Peter how his week had been.

"Oh, OK, I guess," Peter answered. "Just been at work with my dad and going out on my bike to get a bit fitter—it's a physical job with lots of heavy lifting. How about you?"

"Like you, been at work with my mum and not doing much in the evenings. Do you do much after work?" Sally asked.

"No, not really," Peter answered.

"Well, maybe we could meet up?" Sally said hopefully.

Peter thought desperately for an answer, but thankfully the lights began to dim and images flickered onto the screen in front of them. As was always the case, there were a few adverts before the film started, saving Peter from answering Sally. Peter was more comfortable in the darkness and he could finally relax. After a few more adverts, the film began.

The whole cinema fell silent, eyes turned expectantly to the front. Peter didn't quite know what to expect—Alex had told him that the film was a bit of a criminal caper, but a comedy with a great car chase. Slowly the plot began to unfold and Peter found himself following the saga intently, which surprised him, as he'd never really been interested in the movies. He found himself laughing at the jokes and the absurdity of the story and after one scene the whole audience erupted into laughter and Peter felt Sally's hand on his arm.

"I love this actor," she whispered and gripped Peter's arm more tightly. This unsettled him, but he didn't move or brush Sally's hand away. Sally continued to whisper to Peter throughout the rest of the film and eventually it reached it's dramatic, cliff-hanger ending. Peter sat silently until the lights went up and the film was finished.

He turned towards his friends—Sally was looking at him intently and was asking if he'd enjoyed the film. "Yes—it was great," Peter replied, adding "How about you guys?"

There was much nodding of heads and agreement that the film had been great and Alex suggested that they get soft drinks at the new bar.

After they had made their way outside, Sally again fell into place beside Peter and took his hand gingerly and they all made their way to the bar, finding seats quickly. The girls immediately began chattering saying how much they had enjoyed the film and Alex asked Peter if he was OK. "Yes, I guess so," Peter answered. "Great film—I actually enjoyed it," he added.

"Good—glad you did," Alex replied. "Good to see you out having some fun. It's about time you started to live a little."

Peter smiled—yes, it was time he left the sanctuary of his bedroom and begin to stretch his legs. He could feel the changes from adolescence to becoming a young man within him and he had begun to feel that it was finally time to spread his wings. He still didn't really feel ready for a relationship, but he'd always known that one day he would have to take the plunge into what, for him, were uncharted waters.

He began to think about this new period in his life, but was disturbed by hearing his name. Sally was asking him if he'd enjoyed himself. "Yes, thanks—have you?" he answered.

"Yes, thanks—it's been so nice to meet up again," Sally said, looking directly into Peter's eyes. He felt himself blushing once again, but tried to continue the conversation as if nothing had happened.

"Yes, same here," he said quietly, continuing, "What time do you have to be home?"

"Oh, by 10 o'clock at the latest or my mum will fry me," Sally joked and they all laughed.

"Well, perhaps I can walk you to the bus?" Peter asked and Sally agreed.

After a short while, they all left and walked to get their buses and Peter took a deep breath, taking Sally's hand in his own. She squeezed his fingers and they chatted happily following Alex and Anna. Once they arrived, all of them except Peter took the same bus, so Peter said goodnight to Alex and Anna, giving her a quick hug, before turning to Sally. Without knowing why, he put his arms around her, drawing her close and feeling her soft body nestle against him.

"Thank you for coming," he said softly. "When can we see each other again?"

"Give me your number and I'll call you," she answered, taking a small diary out of her bag and quickly noting Peter's phone number. She then put her arms back around Peter's waist and raised her face towards his. Without thinking, Peter bent slightly forwards and kissed her softly on the lips.

"Look forward to hearing from you," he said, letting Sally slip out of his arms.

"So do I," she answered and she turned for the bus which was waiting with Alex and Anna already on board. Peter grinned all the way home, going straight upstairs to bed.

11

After a fairly lazy Sunday morning, Peter decided to go for a long ride on his bike—he felt the need to expend some energy. His route took him way out of town into the countryside, where he enjoyed the fresh air and the relative silence. Twice he stopped to sit and absorb the peace and solitude and drink from his water bottle, listening to the sounds of nature.

When he arrived home after a gruelling twenty miles, his mother told him that he'd had a phone call and that he could ring the person back. It was Alex. Peter washed and changed and then dialled Alex's number and shortly they were making arrangements to meet in the park that afternoon. A quick lunch and Peter set off at a brisk pace to meet up with his friend—who was already there with Anna and Sally.

Peter raised his hand in greeting and settled onto the grass beside Sally. It was another beautiful day and she was dressed in denim shorts and a light patterned camisole top. Peter remarked on how lovely she looked and she smiled, taking his hand. "How are you today?" she asked.

"I'm great, thanks—been out for a long ride this morning and it felt good being out of town," he replied.

Sally smiled—she was thinking that this may be the start of something. She'd wanted a serious boyfriend for a while and felt that she was the right age—after all she'd be sixteen in November. All the girls in her year had boyfriends, so it seemed the natural progression. After a short while, she folded the cardigan she had been carrying into a pillow and stretched out onto the grass, motioning Peter to lay beside her.

Peter hesitated at first, but quickly lay down taking her hand and they watched the occasional cloud float effortlessly across the sky. "Isn't it beautiful?" she remarked and all three agreed.

Alex was the first to speak. "Where did you get to on your ride?" he asked.

"Oh, out of the town along all the country lanes north of the airport to Wisleigh, then to Amberforth and back here," Peter explained.

"Wow—that's quite a ride," Alex said, impressed.

"Yeah—I felt the need to push myself," Peter said.

"Gosh—you must have some big leg muscles," Sally quipped, squeezing Peter's thigh. This made Peter jump, as he was quite ticklish and they all found this very funny.

"You should join, Peter," Anna said to Alex. "It'd do you good instead of just sitting listening to records and reading all day."

"No, I'm just happy exercising this muscle," Alex replied, pointing to his head. They all laughed again.

Peter found himself relaxing and his head clearing. He squeezed Sally's hand playfully and she rolled over onto her front, bringing her face close to his. "It's so nice seeing you again," she said quietly.

Peter smiled and pulled her closer, kissing her gently. "Sure is," he replied and she settled into his arms.

"Well, you guys seem to be getting along just fine," Anna quipped before pushing Alex down onto the grass and snuggling up. They lay quietly for what seemed like hours, making the occasional comment, but reluctant to disturb the peace of the afternoon before Anna announced that it was time that she had to go. It seemed a shame to break the spell of the afternoon, but they all got up and began to get ready to go their separate ways.

"Can I walk you home?" Peter asked.

"Well, it's in the opposite direction from your house," Sally replied, but Peter insisted. They all set off together, with Alex and Anna leaving them a few streets later. As Sally and Peter set off, she said, "You were very shy at first—I didn't think that you were interested in me."

Peter thought for a moment. "It's not that I wasn't interested, it's just that—" he hesitated. "Just that I'm quite insular, quite a loner. Some people don't understand me and think that I'm a bit weird. I don't find meeting people easy and I've always been happy in my own company, doing the stuff that interests me. I find a lot of people very superficial and I find it difficult to understand why some of them just don't get the simplest of things. I guess you'll have to get to know me slowly."

Sally listened carefully, taking it all in. It tied in with what others had said about Peter, but she liked him and didn't care—he was a tall, good looking guy and she planned to make him all hers.

Eventually they arrived at the end of the street where Sally lived. "I'll leave you here if that's OK?" Peter asked.

"Yes, sure," Sally replied, turning to him and folding her arms around his neck. "I'll call you if that's OK?" she asked.

"Yes, of course," Peter replied and he again pulled her in close for a kiss. She then turned to walk the short distance to her house and Peter set off for the long walk home.

Annie called him as soon as she heard the door close. Peter walked into the kitchen and was met with a barrage of questions. "Have you had a nice time? Where have you been? Did you meet your friends?"

Peter stopped dead in his tracks.

"Whoa—give the lad a chance," laughed Paul who was sitting at the table.

Peter sat down and began to tell them about his day, but skipping the part about who he'd met up with. Annie was having none of it.

"So, did you meet up with Alex?" she asked, tilting her head to one side.

"Yes," Peter replied matter-of-factly.

"Anyone else?" Annie pressed on.

"Yeah, just a couple more friends," Peter said, now enjoying the game.

"Anyone I know?" Annie continued.

Peter smiled—he was in control of this conversation, so he decided to carry on playing. "No, I don't think so," he replied truthfully.

Annie gave him a long look, her eyes bright and a big smile on her face. "Hmmm—male or female?" Annie pressed.

"Oh—you wouldn't be interested," Peter laughed.

Paul slapped him on his back, roaring with laughter. "Leave the lad alone— he's entitled to meet his friends you know," he scolded.

Annie gave Peter a quizzical look and turned back to her cooking. Peter smiled to himself—*it will do her good to wonder*, he thought. After a few minutes, he decided to put his mother out of her misery. "Met up with Alex's girlfriend Anna and her friend," he said carefully, hopefully giving nothing away.

Annie nodded but remained silent. Peter turned to look at his dad, who was sitting with a huge smirk on his face. He winked at Peter and said to Annie, "Why? you're not interested are you?"

Annie spun around looking at them both before replying. "Interested? Of course not. Peter is entitled to see who he wants and of course to keep his poor mother in the dark."

They all laughed and she ruffled Peter's hair. "I also met up with Sally," Peter explained. "I think that she's really nice."

"Good," Annie said. "It's about time you got some more friends." Annie continued with cooking, but her head was a whirl. She was concerned that Peter just wasn't ready for a relationship and that it would cause him to become very anxious if it didn't work out, yet it was something that she'd hoped would one day happen, helping to bring Peter closer to the normal world which people inhabited.

On Monday morning, Peter had breakfast with his mother, then left for the local library to see if any of the books on International Airlines' list were available. The librarian was very helpful, noting down the book reference numbers and pointing Peter to the correct section in the library. After a search, Peter had located two of the three books he needed. As he checked them out, he was also able to order the third volume which was currently out on loan.

Excited, he put the books in his bag and cycled home. When he arrived, he raced upstairs, opening the first book *The Principles of Flight* and he immediately began to read and take notes. Such was his interest that lunch was forgotten and it wasn't until his mother arrived home that he looked up at his bedside clock. He had been reading for almost six hours non-stop and had taken a lot of notes.

Annie called up to him and shortly appeared with a cold drink and some biscuits. "Thanks, mum," he mumbled.

Annie picked up the second book on Peter's desk, thumbing through a few pages. "Wow—you have to learn all this stuff?" she asked.

"Yes—that and loads more," he laughed. Annie smiled and left him to it. She was delighted that he was taking his application so seriously.

Peter continued until dinner time and over dinner began to tell Paul all about what he'd been studying. Paul listened patiently, very interested and when they'd finished and Peter had helped with the washing up, he called Peter into the living room. "What are the three main subjects you have to study?" he asked.

"Principles of flight, weather and air law," Peter replied. "I just need a basic understanding, as they may question me on anything during the interview."

Paul listened intently. "If you're called for interview, what is the process?" Paul went on.

"Well from my understanding, if I'm successful at interview, I then get invited back for a formal assessment in an aircraft simulator—a sort of aircraft cockpit on wheels," Peter explained, continuing, "Just to see if I have the basic understanding of how the controls work and to perform a couple of simple manoeuvres. Hopefully, it will be quite easy," he added.

Paul sat silently, thinking. He knew just how important this was and had been making enquiries behind Peter's back, but he decided not to say anything just yet and wait for the outcome of the application.

Peter continued to study late into the evening, closing the book as his eyes became heavy. He was asleep almost as soon as he slipped between the sheets. The following morning, he was awake before Paul left for work, determined to finish the first book before going to work the day after.

He was disturbed by the incessant ringing of the telephone at lunchtime. Peter raced downstairs, picking up the receiver and hearing a familiar voice. It was Sally. "Hi," she started. "How are you? I was just wondering what you were doing today?" she asked hopefully.

"I'm studying for my interview," Peter explained. Sally sounded disappointed. "I've got three books to read as they'll question me about them if I get called for interview," Peter went on, adding, "I've nearly finished the first book, but it's pretty hard with lots of different formulas to remember."

There was a short silence and then Sally asked, "Could we see each other this evening?"

Peter thought for a moment and then agreed to meet in the park after dinner. This seemed to please Sally and they said goodbye and Peter went back to his book, again not noticing the time. The next thing Peter heard was mum calling him down for dinner. During the meal, Paul continued to question Peter about his studies and seemed interested in some of the formulas used. "They sound very similar to what we use in engineering," he told Peter. "We mainly use calculus, but as the new machines are coming on stream, it's more like programming a computer."

Peter was, as ever, fascinated with the maths and physics behind both flight and engineering and he resolved to learn as much as he could at work with his dad as well as studying the books as hard as he could. After dinner, Peter began to ask more questions about engineering, but suddenly looked at his watch and realised that he had just ten minutes to get to the park to meet Sally. He quickly got his bike out of the garage and set off at a furious pace, determined not to be late, arriving at the park gates at the same time as Sally. She looked around, startled, as Peter skidded to a halt beside her.

"You made me jump," she scolded, laughing and taking his hand. Peter got off his bike, breathless and walked alongside Sally and they sat down on the grass. "How was your day?" Sally asked.

"Oh, I've been studying since early this morning. Just a couple of chapters to go, then I can get on to the second book. What have you been up to?" Peter asked.

"Working this morning with my mum, but it's half day closing which is why I rang you," Sally explained.

Peter nodded in understanding. "I'll try and remember that for next week. I work with my dad Wednesday to Friday, so Tuesday afternoon could be a good time," he said. Sally smiled—this was just what she wanted to hear.

She was keen to know more about the books that Peter was reading and began to question him. Peter explained the basics of what he was doing, but didn't go into too much detail. He was more interested in hearing about her. "Tell me all about yourself," Peter asked, laughing.

"Hmm—well, my mum works in the grocer's, running the shop, ordering, doing the cash and accounts. I fill shelves and help with customers. My dad is a lorry driver for the big transport company near the airport. I've no brothers or sisters—they obviously gave up when they achieved perfection!" she laughed.

Peter laughed at the joke. She seemed perfect to him. For the first time, he really looked at her. In fact, this was the first time that he had really studied a woman in detail—so far in Peter's short life the only women he'd had anything to do with were his mother and grandma. Shorter than himself, probably about five feet nine, slim waist, medium length dark hair, nice breasts and a pretty face with a cute turned-up button nose.

"What are you doing?" Sally asked.

"Oh, just taking in the view," Peter explained.

"Well, I hope you like what you see," Sally responded, laughing.

"I sure do," Peter replied, pulling her down and putting his arm around her. She snuggled against him, taking in his scent and the feel of his lithe strong body.

They lay together on the grass until the sun started to reach the horizon, the golden embers of the day signalling that it was time to part and Sally said that it was time for her to leave. Peter walked her home, giving her a quick kiss goodnight and they agreed to see each other again at the weekend. He then cycled home as quickly as he could as it was getting quite dark by now.

The next three days flew by, with Peter finding more questions for his dad at work and there was an endless cycle of work, out for his ride, dinner and study until Friday evening was reached.

When Peter got home, there was a card from the library telling him that the third book had been returned and was available for him to collect. Peter was delighted and resolved to collect the book the following day. After dinner, Annie asked him what his plans were for the weekend. "Well, I need to collect that book and I'm going to meet up with some friends. What have you got planned?" he asked, dreading some family event or visit.

"Oh, nothing," Annie replied. "I just wondered what you were up to. It's your birthday next week and we wondered if there was anything special you wanted?"

Peter was stunned—he hadn't realised that August had given way to September already. Where had the weeks gone? "I hadn't realised," he answered truthfully. "Erm, there's nothing really," he added.

"OK—if you think of anything, let us know," Annie replied. Buying presents for Peter was always difficult and she often ended up taking things back to shops to be changed or refunded.

"Yeah, sure," he replied and he took himself off to his room to continue his reading. He wasn't finding the second book—the one about weather—as easy as the first. He was, however, determined to learn what he needed to know.

12

After a rushed breakfast, Peter was on his bike pedalling furiously towards the library. He needed to get the remaining book so he could continue with his reading—although he hadn't yet finished the second one and had still to hear if he'd been successful in obtaining an interview. After chaining his bike to the railings outside, Peter rushed in to the library and made straight for the help desk.

The lady behind the desk looked up and smiled. "What can I do for you young man?" she enquired.

Peter thrust the card towards her without saying a word. The librarian's eyebrows raised momentarily and she then got up and walked to a filing cabinet, opening a drawer. She quickly returned with a book in her hand. "Library card please," she asked Peter, who again thrust his library card towards her. "Thank you. In a rush this morning?" she chided.

"Oh, er, sorry, yes in a bit of a rush. Need to get this book read as soon as possible," Peter explained, adding, "Sorry if I was a little hasty."

The lady smiled, handing over Peter's library card and the book. "No problem. Enjoy"

"Thanks—and sorry again," Peter said, turning for the door.

Arriving home, Peter found his parents in the kitchen, deep in discussion. Paul looked up, seeing the book in Peter's hand. "More reading?" he enquired.

"Yes," Peter replied. "Air Law this time," he explained.

Paul shook his head. "Sounds dreary," he said.

"Well, I hope not, but we'll see," Peter said, turning for the stairs. He quickly settled at his desk, opening the weather book and continuing where he'd left off. As he read, he made copious notes for revision purposes—it was just like studying again for his exams.

After a while, he could hear the phone ringing in the distance, but he ignored it. He then realised that Annie was calling him. "Peter—phone," she yelled up the stairs.

Peter rushed downstairs, wondering who could be calling him and picking up the receiver, he heard Sally's voice. "Hi," she said. "What are you up to today—as if I need to ask?" she laughed.

Peter laughed as well, replying "Studying. Lots to read."

"Well, how do you fancy meeting up for a few hours? I need to shop for some stuff for school," Sally asked. Without hesitation, Peter agreed and they arranged to meet in the afternoon in town.

After a rushed lunch and a change of clothes, Peter got ready to catch the bus into town. Paul was pottering about in the garden and Peter watched in amazement as his dad got his bike out of the garage—he never used it at weekends unless they were out together. He saw Paul cycle off towards the footpath across the fields. *I wonder where he's going?* he thought to himself before kissing his mum goodbye and walking to the bus stop.

After a while standing outside the bookshop where they'd arranged to meet, Peter looked at his watch for the hundredth time and started to become uneasy. Being late just didn't fit his routine, but a few moments later he heard Sally calling his name. She ran up to him, breathlessly. "Sorry—the bus was ever so late," she explained.

Peter smiled "No problem—you're here now," he said, taking her hand. "What do you need to get?" he asked as they set off.

"Oh, usual new term stuff—a notepad and I want to get one of those new electronic calculators for my maths," Sally replied.

"Wow—they are expensive," Peter said, but Sally explained that her parents had agreed to pay for it as it was important for her studies. They strolled slowly towards the main shopping area where there was a large stationery shop who stocked everything Sally needed. As they were unsure of what features the calculators had and what they could do, Sally asked the shop assistant for some help in choosing the correct one.

Peter paid a lot of attention, as he realised that some of them were able to do the complicated type of maths that he would need to be able to do and could calculate sine and cosine easily—something which was not easy using a pencil and paper. One Sally had chosen one, Peter asked the assistant to show him these complex types and he made his mind up that he'd buy one for his studies if he was offered a training position, although at £4, they were a week's wages, so were very expensive.

Once Sally had bought all she needed, they walked to the coffee bar for refreshment. There, sitting by himself, was Liam. Peter snuck up behind him and made him jump. "Bloody hell," he shouted. "Are you trying to give me a heart attack?"

Peter laughed and slapped Liam hard on the back. "Gotcha," he said.

Sally laughed, shaking her head. "You boys—always up to no good," she said, adding that she'd like a coffee. Peter dutifully went to order drinks and came back to the table with two brimming cups of steaming hot coffee.

"So, what are you up to?" Peter asked Liam.

"Not much," Liam replied. "I was supposed to be meeting someone, but I guess I've been stood up," he laughed.

"Really?" Sally asked. "A lady friend?"

"Well, a lady, but obviously not a friend," came Liam's reply. This seemed to open the floodgates and they all chatted for ages, with Liam taking lots of interest in Sally and what she was doing.

After a while, Sally got up to use the restroom and as soon as she was out of earshot, Liam turned to Peter. "Well—are you two going out then? Are you an item?" he asked.

"Well, it's early days, but we've seen each other a few times," Peter replied, maintaining his usual guarded manner.

"Does she kiss nicely?" Liam asked, winking.

"None of your business," Peter replied, laughing.

"Oh, so you've kissed then. Anything else?" Liam went on.

Peter blushed furiously. "Not at all," he said, adding "She's only fifteen— same as me."

"Ha! As if that matters," Liam responded.

"Well, it does to me. I'm just not thinking about anything like that yet," Peter replied.

"I bloody am," Liam answered. "Thinking about it all the time. Suppose I'll get a girlfriend eventually, but she'll have to be one that will do it," he said in a matter-of-fact way.

Peter shook his head—there had to be more to having a girlfriend than just sex. He didn't know much about it anyway—just what he'd learned in biology, so he was in no rush. Liam seemed to be though—Peter could see him getting himself into trouble—or even worse getting a girl into trouble and the stigma from that was huge.

Sally returned with her usual big smile. "OK boys, what's next?" she asked.

"Dunno—what are you guys up to this evening?" Liam asked.

Sally and Peter exchanged glances. "Nothing planned," Sally answered.

"Well, why don't we get together with Alex and Anna and meet back here?" Liam suggested. "I could give them a call."

"Good idea—what do you think, Peter?" Sally asked. Peter nodded his head in agreement.

"Good. I'll get on to it," Liam said decisively.

Sally and Peter strolled back towards the bus terminus, hand in hand, making small talk. Once they arrived, they had to split up for their separate buses home, so Peter pulled Sally against him and gave her a quick kiss on the lips before turning away—but Sally was having none of it. "Just a little kiss—don't you want to kiss me properly?" she asked.

Peter blushed and his eyes darted around, afraid that someone would see. "Well, yes," he stuttered, "but isn't it a bit public?"

"Nonsense," Sally said quickly, anxious not to lose the moment. She pulled Peter's face towards hers and their lips met for a longer, more sustained kiss. Peter eventually broke away, breathless.

"Wow," he muttered. "That was amazing."

"Plenty more where that came from," she said and patting Peter on the bottom, she turned and walked to her bus stop.

Peter stood silently, his head in a whirl and a tightening feeling in his groin. "I need to think about this," he said to himself and walking with his hands in front of him, he caught the bus home.

"Have you had a nice afternoon?" Annie asked over dinner.

"Yes, thanks," Peter replied and he told his parents about Sally buying her new calculator and how one might be of use if he got the trainee's job with International.

Paul questioned him about it, saying that they were still using slide rules at work and that electronic calculators were only just coming into engineering. Peter was convinced that one would be useful, but he would wait until the interview—if he was lucky enough to be invited. Annie mentioned his birthday once again, but Peter was still at a loss for anything that he wanted and he couldn't ask for the calculator as they cost so much. "I'll think about it," was the best response Annie got.

Peter washed and changed and prepared to leave, but he first asked if he could come home a bit later seeing as it was Saturday. "Of course," said Paul, "but no later than ten thirty."

Peter smiled and promised to be punctual.

Sally's bus arrived just a few short minutes after Peter's and they walked towards the coffee bar together. Sally had changed into a blue summer dress with white flowers around the neckline and Peter remarked that she looked beautiful. "Thank you—and you look good as well. That shirt enhances your physique."

"Thanks—I've been riding my bike a lot and my mum says that I'm growing taller by the day. She thinks that I'll be as tall as my dad soon and he's six feet three."

Sally sighed and squeezed Peter's hand and shortly they arrived to meet their friends. Alex was the first to see them and he called them over to where he was sat with Anna. Greetings were exchanged and after Peter ordered drinks, he came and took his place between Sally and Anna. After five minutes, Liam arrived and he squeezed himself into the corner next to Anna. Sally and Anna immediately started talking about the return to school in a week's time and they began to discuss studying for their A-Levels.

Alex listened politely, but after a short while Liam announced that he was having none of this school talk. "Let's talk about us and where we'll be in ten tears time," he suggested.

There was a long period of silence, then Anna began to speak. "Well, by then I should be a junior doctor somewhere," she started. "I'd like to do children's medicine if possible. How about you Liam?"

Liam closed his eyes for a moment. "Well, by then I'll be a qualified plumber, but I really want to be a pop star," he giggled.

"You?" exclaimed Peter. "You can't sing a note nor play an instrument. How are you going to be a pop star?"

"Who needs to be able to sing and play—half the people in the charts can't sing or play," Liam reasoned, "and if they can do it, so can I."

This comment bought a roar of laughter from them all, Liam included and then Sally asked, "Well, how will you convince somebody to let you cut a record?"

"Simple," Liam replied. "Pure charm and charisma."

This bought another roar of laughter before Peter said, "Why don't you become a comedian? You've obviously got a talent for that at least."

This bought more laughter and so the evening wore on with everyone teasing Liam. By ten o'clock, the coffee bar was closing and the five of them walked outside into the cool evening air to make their way towards the bus terminus. When they reached the terminus, Liam said goodnight to everyone, as he didn't want to hang around whilst the two couples were saying their goodbyes.

As Sally, Anna and Alex were all catching the same bus, Peter and Sally wandered off on their own to say their private goodbyes. Peter was starting to feel much more relaxed in Sally's company and he was becoming intrigued by the physical pleasures that may await him. Clearly, his earlier conversation with Liam had made him think and he would be sixteen next week, with Sally following in November and he felt that perhaps it was time he started thinking about such things.

He pulled Sally in close, his arms around her waist and kissed her long and hard on the lips. She responded by squeezing his bottom and he allowed his hands to explore her back and her sides. After a few breathless minutes, he said that he had to go and with a last kiss, walked Sally to her stop, saying goodnight to Anna and Alex at the same time. A shout from the conductor caught Peter's attention and he had to run for his bus, jumping onto the rear platform as it set off and we waved to his friends as they disappeared behind him. Peter smiled all the way home.

13

Peter was, as always, up early and after a quick cup of coffee, was engrossed in his book. After an hour or so, his reading was interrupted by Annie coming into his room with more coffee and toast, which he wolfed down. His mother sat watching in silence—she just couldn't believe how much Peter was eating and how fast he seemed to be growing. With all the extra exercise he was doing, he seemed to be suddenly much more lean and muscular.

Annie wanted to speak but knew that she'd have to tread carefully—it was going to be a tricky discussion. "Sweetie—hope you don't mind me asking, but are you seeing Sally seriously?"

Peter froze. He'd been half expecting this, but hadn't prepared for it. "What do you mean?" he asked.

Annie took a deep breath before continuing. "Well, I guess I mean is it a bit more than just having some fun and going out for coffee?" Annie was floundering, but she tried to carry on "I mean—well, do you understand the physical aspects of a boy—girl relationship?"

Peter sat in silence—he'd never had this kind of discussion with anyone before, let alone his mother and he was feeling very uncomfortable. He mind raced through possible answers before he asked Annie quietly, "Do you mean like kissing and that leading on to other things?"

Annie nodded. "I just want you to know that you have to be very careful if you get too—too involved," Peter nodded.

"Mum, I'm not quite sixteen and Sally's not sixteen until November and I don't think it's something that interests me yet. I'm too focused on all this reading and my application and I don't need any distractions. Yes, we have a little cuddle at the end of the evening and she's a good friend, but I couldn't handle anything serious," Annie sighed and squeezed Peter's arm.

"Just as long as you understand," Annie whispered.

Peter looked at his mother and smiled. He knew that she was only looking out for him. "You've nothing to worry about," he smiled and he returned to his book.

After a couple more hours study, Peter got up to stretch his legs and wandered downstairs. Outside, the rain was coming down in torrents, so he had no plans other than reading for the rest of the day. He found Annie curled up on the sofa, book in hand and asked her where his dad was. "He's in the garage," Annie responded without looking up.

Peter went to the back door, opening it and dashing across the yard to the garage, quickly opening the door and hopping inside. Paul was at the workbench. He'd been slowly restoring an old motorbike for some time and was working on the engine. Peter went to have a look.

"What are you up to?" he asked.

"I'm stripping the engine," Paul explained. "It doesn't turn over very well and I think it's got a bent con-rod."

Peter looked in amazement at the engine parts on the bench—all arranged in order for reassembly. "What's a con-rod?" he asked.

Paul pointed to the stripped engine, pointing out the various parts. "This part here which connects the piston to the crankshaft—it translates the up and down motion of the piston to rotary motion which eventually drives the wheels."

Peter stood and watched as Paul undid more bolts and removed them carefully and he slid the piston out of the engine before splitting the piston and rod, explaining everything as he went on. "Is this how piston engines in aircraft work?" Peter asked.

"Yes—exactly the same, although there are different designs and, of course, aircraft engines have many more cylinders," Paul opened a drawer, taking out a steel ruler and a gauge. He held the rod up to the light and put the ruler against it. "It's bent can you see how the light comes through?" he asked.

Peter looked carefully—"Yes—just there," he said, pointing to the spot.

Paul then took the gauge, making various measurements and said, "It's about three thousands of an inch out of true. It's scrap. No wonder it wouldn't turn over."

Peter was amazed. "Three thousands? That's a tiny amount."

Paul smiled. "Not in engineering terms it isn't. It has to be perfectly straight. Three thou is massive." Paul put the bent part to one side and continued to strip the engine. Once he'd finished, Paul explained the various parts and how they worked. Peter was fascinated—looking at an assembly of metal parts which, when assembled correctly, could drive a motorbike, a car, even an aeroplane.

"What will you have to do now?" Peter asked.

"I'll have to get a new rod—I'll probably get a pair and replace the other one just to be sure and new bearings and then we can reassemble the engine," Paul answered, wiping his hands on an old towel.

"What are you up to today?" he asked Peter.

"Still reading the weather book—almost finished," Peter answered.

Paul nodded. He knew that his son would be throwing himself at his studies once again and knew what they meant to him. "Is it interesting?" Paul asked.

Peter shrugged his shoulders. "It is, but it's not something that I've ever looked at before, so it's all new. I guess that if I'm accepted, then I'll need to be able to read and interpret weather charts and to be able to spot potential problem areas to ensure safe flight."

Paul nodded his agreement. "Ready for some lunch?" Paul asked. Peter nodded, so they quickly ran across to the back door and went inside.

Paul went to the kitchen sink to wash his hands and Annie appeared in the doorway. "You boys ready for some lunch?" she asked.

"Yes please," said Peter, rubbing his stomach. Annie smiled and started to prepare some food. She loved these family times and loved looking after her "boys."

Paul came and sat at the table. "Explain what the simulator check is all about," he asked.

"Well, the sim is like an aircraft cockpit set on a stand and it can reproduce the basic movements of flight. The advanced ones even have a television screen which can show you how the aircraft acts in the air. It does everything a real aircraft can do, so if you pull back on the controls it climbs and the instruments show a climb. The airlines use it for advanced training and you can stop it mid-flight to correct mistakes," Peter explained.

Paul nodded, asking, "and you'll have to do some basic manoeuvres in it if you're successful in the interview?"

"Yes, but nothing too advanced," Peter answered. "Just the basic stuff. I think that they want to see if we have a basic understanding of flight."

Paul smiled. "With all the reading you've done over the years, I'm surprised you're not an Apollo Astronaut ready for the next moon landing," he laughed, ruffling Peter's hair. Peter laughed.

"I wish—that would be amazing," he said.

Paul carried on, "So you understand all the basic controls and movements?"

"Yes of course—even some of the theory and formulae now," Peter replied

"Just in case it comes up at interview," Paul was impressed—Peter was giving it one hundred percent as expected, but Paul was always worrying how Peter would react if he was unsuccessful. They'd have to cross that bridge if it came to it.

Annie placed plates of sizzling bacon and eggs in front of them both. "Thanks mum," Peter said, full of enthusiasm. His favourite weekend lunch was always a winner and Peter attacked it with gusto, quickly clearing his plate.

"Wow—hungry?" Annie asked.

Peter nodded. "Always these days," he said.

"Well, you're a growing lad doing a physical job so I'm not surprised," Paul said.

Peter smiled and getting up announced that he was going to continue with his reading and he climbed the stairs to his room, quickly picking up where he left off. Downstairs he could hear the murmur of voices but couldn't make out what was being said and he was soon lost in his book.

Annie sat at the table, finishing her coffee. She told Paul to shut the kitchen door before asking him about his visit to the airport the day before. Paul explained, "I went to the flight school and spoke with one of the instructors. He's ex RAF like me, so we got on well. He said that if Peter is offered an interview, he can take him up for a one hour flight in a small aircraft and show him the basics to prepare him for the simulator check. He'll let Peter fly the plane and he'll just do the take-off and landing. It's not too expensive and I'm happy to pay for it if it increases Peter's chances and I'm sure he'll love it."

Annie nodded her agreement. "I bet he will—he'll be smiling for days. Are those little aeroplanes safe?" she asked.

"Yes of course—they are maintained to the same standards as any other aircraft, so it'll be fine. It will be a great experience for him seeing as he's never flown one before," Paul replied.

"Let's keep it to ourselves for the time being though—I don't want to get his hopes up too high—you know he doesn't handle failure well." Annie agreed, remembering the school sports day where Peter failed to win his race—he was devastated and it almost prompted a full scale meltdown, although he was older now and these events were now rare.

"What are we going to do about his birthday?" Annie asked.

Paul sat silently for a few moments before replying, "Let's do nothing. We'll just get him a few small presents, but I see no point getting him stuff for his course at this stage—I feel like we may be tempting fate."

Annie agreed. "I could make him a birthday tea and he could invite some of his friends," she suggested, but Paul disagreed.

"He's getting a bit old don't you think? Why don't we let him arrange something with his friends—maybe go to the pictures—and we'll pay for it. I think he'll enjoy that more."

Annie again nodded her agreement. "I'll ask him what he wants to do," she said, clearing away the plates and cups.

14

Peter spent the next two days continuing with his reading and eventually started the third book on Aviation Law. He started to find it hard going initially, but quickly got into the subject. It all seemed to be a case of remembering facts and figures, dates and Acts of Parliament. As usual, he made many notes in his own style.

Wednesday finally came and he set off to the factory with Paul, chatting as they rode along. Paul was, as usual, happy to just listen and try to remember a few points to ask questions about later on. After arriving and clocking in, they made their way to the locker room to change and found Dave getting into his overalls. He looked up and saw Peter. "Just the chap I'm looking for—come to my office when you've got changed," he instructed Peter.

Peter's heart sank—what had he done wrong? Perhaps he wasn't needed anymore? With his mind in turmoil, he slowly approached Dave's office, knocking on the door. "Come in," Dave called out and he motioned Peter to take a seat. "Now then young man—how are you enjoying your job here?" he asked.

Peter was totally unprepared for this. "Yeah, it's great—interesting," he mumbled.

"Good," Dave responded. "Paul tells me that it's your sixteenth birthday on Saturday and we could do with you starting full time if you're interested. The hourly rate of pay will be the same but for five days it will go up to six pounds fifteen shillings. Interested?" Peter nodded enthusiastically. "Good. Now, I know that you've got your sights set on an aviation career, but we'll be opening apprenticeships in the New Year if the airline thing doesn't work out. Have a think about it. Engineering is a skilled profession as I'm sure you realise and you've done so well since you've been here that I'd be happy to take you straight on."

"Thanks," Peter replied. "I'll let you know but aviation will still be my first choice if that's OK."

Dave smiled. "Of course—now go and get some bloody work done," he laughed and Peter left the office. He felt so relieved—he certainly hadn't seen that coming.

He found Paul loading the milling machine. "What did Dave want?" he asked.

"He's made me full time from next Monday after my birthday. He's also offered me an apprenticeship in the New Year if the airlines don't want me," Peter explained.

Paul nodded. "Yeah, he said something to me last week about all that—must have forgotten to tell you," he smiled.

Peter looked at his dad before bursting out laughing. "So, you knew?"

"Yes, of course, but it needed to come straight from the boss," Paul said.

Peter just shook his head. He'd never understand people.

Riding home, Paul and Peter discussed his full time employment. "You'll have to learn to manage your time in a different way and make time for studying in the evening," Paul said. "You'll find yourself more tired to begin with so you may need to take it easy on the extra cycling as well."

Peter nodded agreement, but he never felt tired at the end of the day anymore. He loved the rush that the physical work gave him and the rides after work cleared his head. Arriving at the end of their street, Peter set straight off for his exercise ride and resolved to ride as quickly as he could manage for as long as possible. He covered the usual twenty miles in exactly an hour—a new personal best, arriving home breathless and covered in sweat.

Annie took one look at him and pointed straight upstairs. Peter smiled and went to wash and change, arriving back downstairs just as dinner was being served. "Good day?" Annie asked.

"Yes—not sure if Dad's told you, but I'm going full time from Monday. They've also offered me an apprenticeship in the New Year if I want it," Peter explained.

"That's lovely," Annie exclaimed. "What will you do?"

"Oh, I'll continue down the airline pathway because that's what I really want," Peter answered.

Annie nodded, smiling. *At least he's got an offer for his future now*, she thought to herself.

Peter spent the next two evenings finishing the law book and, on Saturday morning came downstairs with the intention of setting off early to the library.

However, having completely forgotten that was his birthday, he spent some time with Annie and Paul. After opening birthday cards and his presents from his parents, he set off to the library to return the books.

On Paul's suggestion, he looked for anything that the library had on the history of International Airways. Paul thought it a good idea to have some knowledge of the airline, just in case questions came up in the interview and for Peter to slip comments in regarding the history. After a search, he found exactly what he was looking for—a book about the development of commercial aviation in the UK and the book had a whole chapter dedicated to International.

He had the book stamped out—remembering his manners this time, as it was the same lady as the week before. Slipping the book into his army satchel, he strode into town to meet Sally and his friends at the coffee bar.

Sally, Anna and Alex were already seated by the window. Peter walked over and squeezed Sally's hand, asking if anyone wanted anything. "Could I have another coffee please, sweetheart?" Sally asked.

Both Anna and Alex shook their heads, so Peter went to the counter to order coffees, returning with steaming cups and sitting down next to Sally.

"How's it going buddy?" Alex asked.

"Good, thanks," Peter replied and before he could say anything else, they all shouted "Happy birthday" in unison. Peter blushed furiously—he hated being the centre of attention. "Thanks, guys," he mumbled, not sure where to look. Anna passed him a birthday card, which Peter tore open reading the message inside. "Thanks," he said.

Sally then gave Peter a huge card and she helped him to open it. It had a big teddy bear on the front and lots of kisses inside from Sally. "Thanks," he said, squeezing her thigh.

She smiled—"Happy birthday, handsome," she whispered.

"What shall we do today?" Alex asked.

Peter asked if they wanted to see a movie later as his parents were paying and they all agreed. The girls immediately started discussing which film to see and Alex and Peter chatted about their week. Peter explained about starting full time work from Monday and the offer of the apprenticeship and Alex asked if he was going to take it. "No—not until I see where my application ends up," Peter replied.

"Sounds like a good plan. Back to 6th form for me on Monday—the dreaded A Levels," Alex laughed.

"Rather you than me," Peter replied. As much as he enjoyed studying, he preferred to do it at his own pace, in his own way.

"Gotta be done—under lots of pressure from the old man to follow him into the profession," Alex went on.

"I suppose I'm lucky that way," Peter replied. "No pressure and my folks letting me do exactly what I want."

Alex nodded in agreement—he was happy to pursue a medical career, but would have liked a bit more choice. That was the problem with being an only child.

Anna bought them back down to earth. "Right—we've decided that we're off to see *True Grit*. It's a western with John Wayne." Alex and Peter looked at each other before nodding their agreement. "Good—that's settled then," Anna said with a flourish.

"What time?" Peter asked.

The evening shadows were lengthening and the days becoming shorter as summer began to give way to autumn and the reds and golds on the trees were announcing that the leaves were getting ready to fall. "Shall we do the 6 o'clock?" Sally suggested and they all agreed to meet at five-thirty outside the cinema.

Anna and Alex left after an hour, leaving Peter and Sally alone. She bought her chair closer, snuggling up to Peter and taking his arm. "What were you boys talking about?" she asked.

"Oh, I was telling Alex that I'm starting working full-time from Monday and the engineering company have offered me an apprenticeship if I want it," Peter explained.

"Full-time? That means that you'll have less time to spend with me," Sally pouted.

Peter thought for a moment. "But aren't you starting your A Levels on Monday?" he asked.

"Yes, but I thought we could see each other after school on Monday and Tuesday—my mum doesn't get home until six and my dad is often out until late evening."

"Well, we finish at half past four, so we could still see each other in the evening while it's still light," Peter replied.

This didn't seem to satisfy Sally—"But we need some time alone," she went on.

"Well, we'll get time alone in the park," Peter said, but immediately Sally said, "No silly—I mean private time alone."

Peter was still unsure what she meant but decided not to pursue it. After a few minutes, they left the coffee bar and walked towards the bus terminus where, after a quick cuddle, they boarded their separate buses.

As soon as he got home, Peter rushed upstairs to get ready. His parents had bought him some new slacks and a shirt which he put on and he went downstairs to tell them what he was doing that evening. Annie looked him up and down, squeezing his bicep and saying that he was "developing into a hunk". Peter had no idea what this meant, but he felt embarrassed.

Paul opened his wallet and gave Peter three one pound notes. "That should take care of your evening," he said.

"Gosh, thanks dad, thanks mum," Peter said.

"What time are you going out?" Annie asked.

"Catching the 5 o'clock bus," Peter said.

"OK, I'll get dinner sorted out," Annie said, going to the kitchen. Peter sat down and he talked to Paul about the stripped engine—Peter wanted to learn as much as possible.

For once, the bus was on time. Peter strolled the short distance to the cinema, arriving first. Shortly after, he heard his name being called and he saw his friends coming towards him. Sally walked straight up to him asking, "Well—what do you think?"

She was dressed in a blue short sleeved dress with a low neckline and was carrying a white cardigan. Peter was speechless.

"Wow—you look—you look amazing," he said. He couldn't take his eyes from her breasts which were very visible in the vee of the neckline.

"Like it?" Sally asked.

"Err yes—isn't it a bit low at the front?" Peter asked, still staring.

"No, of course not, you silly boy. If you've got it then show it," she laughed and leaning forwards whispered, "They're all for you."

Peter shook his head. Alex winked at him smiling. "Shall we?" asked Anna and they went inside, where Peter paid for the tickets.

Shortly afterwards, they took their seats, with Sally snuggling up to Peter and taking his arm. "Gosh," she whispered. "You're getting so muscular. I hope that this is all for me."

Peter was unsure of what she meant, so said nothing. The lights soon dimmed and the film started.

It was almost dark when the film finished and they walked back outside. It was also much cooler, so Sally put her cardigan on and Peter put on his jacket. Anna suggested the soft drinks bar and they made their way there, with Sally holding Peter's hand tightly. They quickly found a table and ordered drinks. Sally and Anna were immediately engaged in discussing the film, leaving Alex and Peter to talk amongst themselves.

"What did you think of the film?" Alex asked.

"Hmmm—I didn't really follow the plot and found the main character not very believable."

"Not really your thing?" Alex asked.

"Well, you know that I find it difficult to follow abstract themes and I often don't see jokes," Peter explained, "and I guess that if I have it explained to me then it's fine, but I didn't really get this."

Alex knew what his friend was saying. So many times over the years he'd had to take Peter to one side to explain random or abstract concepts and he knew that Peter couldn't really read people's facial expressions very well. He was beginning to think that Peter was going to find Sally a real handful. Anna had described Sally as a bit of a wild child—she'd not had much parental supervision and had often been left to do her own thing. There could be trouble ahead.

They all made their way towards the terminus after, what Sally described as "A beautiful evening" They split into couples to allow Sally and Peter time to say goodnight. Sally hugged Peter tightly, affording him another view of her cleavage as he looked down at her.

"So do you like what you see?" she asked.

Peter, unsure of the correct response just mumbled, "Yes, beautiful."

She looked up at him smiling. "Well, if you're a good boy, you'll get to see a lot more," she whispered, pulling Peter's face towards her for a kiss. Peter kissed her firmly, but his brain was in turmoil. More?

More of what? What was she on about? His hands were clasping her waist, but Sally put her hands over Peter's and moved them upwards towards her breasts. He waited until he was nearly touching them, then froze.

"What's the matter?" she whispered.

"Sorry—I'm just not ready for this yet," Peter whispered back.

Sally pulled away slightly. "You will be soon," she said and turning away walked towards her bus stop. Peter quickly followed behind, hoping he hadn't upset or offended her.

She turned back towards him saying, "Thanks for a lovely evening," and kissing him once more, hopped on board the bus. Peter turned and was forced once again to run for his bus as it was already backing out. He sat morosely all the way home, his head in a spin.

15

Peter went straight to bed, but try as he might, he just couldn't sleep. Sally's remarks had really unsettled him and he was at a loss of what to do. He tossed and turned, eventually slipping into a fitful rest. He dreamt and in the dream he was floating above the earth, looking down on a road which seemed to be his life pathway. Tossed by the boiling turmoil of his emotions, he could see Sally trying to tug him to one side, away from his chosen future. She kept coming towards him with more and more urgent demands and he could feel his control slipping away. She kept repeating, "Peter, I want you now. NOW."

He woke suddenly, sitting straight up in bed, covered in sweat. Whilst he waited for his heart rate to subside, he looked around in the familiar blackness.

This was who he was, he knew his destiny and he resolved that nothing was going to make him give up on his dreams. He decided that he'd try to tell Sally that he wasn't interested in seeing her again, but was not looking forward to the prospect of upsetting her.

Peter was up early despite the lack of sleep. He picked his book up and tried to read, but without success. His mind kept returning to the evening before. Sally was a nice girl, but he just wasn't ready for anything physical—which she clearly was. Sex was something so outside Peter's frame of reference that it just didn't figure in his thoughts. He'd listened to both Liam and Alex discussing girls and the things that they'd like to get up to, but he rarely took part in such nonsense. He'd have to go and see her and tell her—a prospect which he dreaded.

After an early breakfast, Peter set off for a ride to clear his head. It was a lightly overcast morning, but the wind was strong and he struggled against it, trying to maintain a good average speed.

The extra effort pleased him, as he'd always enjoyed the difficult rather than the easy and he eventually arrived home in good spirits. Annie was in the kitchen and she smiled at him as he came through the door. "Early start?" she asked.

"Yes—couldn't sleep so went out early," Peter replied.

"Did you have a good night with your friends?" Annie asked, her head on one side.

Peter said nothing, sitting down at the table. After a short silence he asked, "Mum, we spoke the other day about—you know—physical stuff between boys and girls." Annie sat down, fixing her eyes on Peter. He went on, "I think Sally wants to get sort of physical, but I really don't. I'm so wrapped up in my application and starting full-time with Dad tomorrow that I don't want the distraction. What do I do? How can I tell her?"

Annie thought for a moment. "Well, you must let her down gently. Tell her that she's a lovely person and that you like her as a friend, but be honest and just say that you're not interested. She knows about your ambitions I presume, so hopefully she'll understand. She probably won't take it well though," Annie's voice trailed off.

Peter sat looking downwards, shaking his head. Annie eventually broke the silence, "I think you need to shower and change young man—you're covered in sweat and grit. I also think you need to start shaving—you're getting quite a shadow. Get your dad to show you how."

Peter nodded and walked slowly upstairs towards the bathroom, carefully digesting every word his mum had said.

Around lunchtime, Peter was helping Paul with the motorbike in the garage when Annie called him. "Peter—phone call."

Peter wiped his hands on a rag and made his way into the front room. Picking up the phone, he heard Sally's voice. "Hi," she said. "Fancy meeting up later on?"

"Err yeah sure—I'd like to have a talk with you anyway," Peter replied.

"Really? What about," Sally asked.

"Oh, nothing really, just a chat. Shall we meet in the park at 2 o'clock?" Peter asked. Sally agreed and Peter put the phone down. With a heavy heart, he returned to the garage.

Paul looked at him, asking, "Everything OK?"

"Yeah, guess so," Peter replied without elucidating.

Paul nodded and went back to the bike. "So everything's fine?" Paul asked again without looking up. "Just that you're a bit distant today," he added.

"Oh, it's just the girl I've seen a couple of times. She's coming on to me a bit thick and I'm not interested," Peter explained. "Not whilst I've got all this stuff going on."

Paul listened carefully. "Take it real easy with girls. You have your dreams and you mustn't let anybody spoil that. There will be plenty of girls when you're qualified."

Peter nodded. "Yeah, I guess so."

"Don't get me wrong." Paul went on, "Girls are lovely and all that, but they can be a massive distraction and drain on your time and resources. Just take it easy." Peter nodded again and looking at his watch, decided that it was time to set off.

Arriving at the park, Peter settled on to his usual bench and a short time later saw Sally coming towards him. She waved saying "Hi" at the top of her voice. Peter waved back and she shortly sat down next to him. "How's my big man?" she asked.

"I'm OK, thanks," Peter replied.

Sally smiled and took Peter's hand. "What did you want to talk about?" she asked.

Peter withdrew his hand and took a deep breath. "Sally, I think that you're a lovely person and last night was great fun, but I'm not really ready for anything physical—not yet. It was great being with you but you have to understand that I'm so wrapped up in my application and my job right now that I just can't think of anything else at the moment. Perhaps we could leave the physical stuff for later?"

Sally sat silently for a while, tears welling up in her eyes. "Don't you find me attractive?" she asked quietly.

"Yes, of course, it's just that I don't feel ready to go to the next level yet," Peter explained.

"So, you find me attractive, but don't want to have sex with me, is that it?" Sally asked. "Well, let me tell you Peter Marham, there's plenty of boys out there who would love to and I think that I'm quite a catch, so you'd better think carefully. You'll never get another opportunity I can tell you."

Peter sat quietly, unsure of how to respond. He was careful not to reply with his usual bluntness and was trying his best to read the situation, but felt at a loss.

Sally sat for a while before spurting out, "OK, that's it then. You've obviously got nothing to say, so I guess you really aren't interested. Thanks for last night and thanks again—for nothing," she spat, standing up and walking away.

"Sally, wait," Peter called after her, but she didn't stop. He sat quietly, thinking, *That went well then*—and he finally mounted his bike and rode slowly home.

Monday morning arrived and Peter was up early, eager to start full time work. Paul didn't ask about Sally and neither had Annie and they both knew it was best not to enquire. Peter buried himself in the work and two weeks had flown by before he knew it. He was happy with the work, was exercising every evening and had regained his sense of purpose, seeing both Alex and Anna and also enjoying a night out with Liam—who had seemed interested in the fact that Peter was no longer seeing Sally.

One afternoon early in October, Peter arrived home with Paul after work and there was a long white envelope waiting for him on the kitchen table. Peter picked it up, noting the International Airways crest on the back and he took himself upstairs to read it. With his heart racing, he tore the letter open and began to read. Slowly a big smile crossed his face. He'd been invited for an interview later in the month. He raced back downstairs and gave the letter to Paul to read.

Paul carefully noted the contents before passing the letter to Annie. "Well done, son," he said. "Guess we'd better make some arrangements."

Peter had been invited to an interview and to attend an "Open day" with the airline with one of his parents. It would take place on a Saturday, at the London Airport headquarters, with an informal open day and presentation in the morning and interviews in the afternoon. Peter was beside himself with excitement.

After a while, Paul spoke. "I guess as it's starting at 9 o'clock in the morning, we'd best travel there on Friday evening and stay over. What do you think?" he asked Annie.

"Yes, perfect idea. The trains to London run until late evening and the Tube runs until midnight. We'll have to find you a guest house," she replied, being practical. "There's a lady at work who has a travel guide for London and I'll ask to borrow it as it lists guest houses and hotels," she added. Looking at Peter, she added "I guess you'll need a new suit as you'll have outgrown your old one. We'll get you one this weekend." Peter nodded.

Now, he could start rereading his notes and to try and think of some intelligent relevant questions to ask.

After dinner on Friday evening, Peter was talking about the interview and he asked his parents if he had to start paying board as he was now working full-time. They looked at each other before Annie said, "No. It's something we've discussed and seeing as we never took anything from Ben, we're not going to expect anything from you. You're a good saver and you'll need your savings if you get this cadetship, so just keep putting it in the Post Office."

Peter nodded his thanks, realising how fortunate he was. "We're off to town to get you a new smart suit for this interview in the morning, along with a new shirt and tie. What colour do you fancy?"

"I don't know," Peter replied. "Blue is the airline colour, so a blue tie would be a nice touch I guess," he mused.

Annie nodded, "Blue it is then."

The shops were crowded with people enjoying the October sales, but Annie made a bee line towards the tailor's shop on the High Street. As soon as they were inside, she found a sales assistant and asked for Peter to be measured and to see some suits. The young man busied himself with his tape measure whilst Peter stood cringing with embarrassment. Finally, he finished writing on his clipboard and came over to Annie, showing her a rack of suits of a suitable size.

"Which do you like Peter?" she asked. Peter looked and shrugged.

"What is the suit for?" the salesman enquired.

"A job interview," Annie replied.

The man pulled out a few suits for Annie to look at. "I'd recommend these for a formal interview," he said.

Annie took each one, holding it beneath Peter's chin before choosing one for him to try on. Peter took it into the changing room and undressed, pulling the suit on and opening the curtain. Annie shook her head and handed over another for Peter to try. Eventually, after much dressing and undressing, Annie had made her mind up.

"This one," she said. "Charcoal grey—very smart. He'll need a white shirt and a blue tie to go with it," she said to the tailor, who scurried off to find what she required, returning with a choice of ties. Annie opened her shopping bag and pulled out the International Airways envelope. "It has to match that blue," she said pointing to the crest and the man went over to the window to compare colours before returning.

"That's the closest," he said.

"Good," said Annie. "We'll take that one."

Peter was impressed that his mother had saved the envelope to get the correct colour. Paul paid for their purchases and they walked outside, with Annie asking whether Peter's best shoes still fitted him.

"Probably not," he replied. "It's been two years since I last wore them at the wedding."

She set off towards her favourite shoe shop at a great pace, leaving Peter trotting in her wake and with Paul following on laden with bags. Once inside, feet were measured and shoes were chosen and paid for. Paul whispered to Peter, "She's certainly on a mission this morning" This made Peter smile and he nodded his agreement.

"Right," said Annie. "Is that everything?"

"Nope," Paul said. "I need coffee—lots of coffee."

Annie smiled, "OK—I concede." She laughed and they set off towards the coffee bar.

Inside, they quickly found a seat and Paul ordered drinks and sat down feigning exhaustion. Annie was telling Peter how smart he'd look and how she'd have to wash and iron the shirt before he wore it, but Peter's attention was elsewhere.

Across the room, he could see Sally and Liam—holding hands and laughing. He didn't feel anything, just watched in detached amusement, thinking to himself, *Well, Liam old boy, you wanted a girlfriend who'd do it—and she wants to so guess you've got it made.* He was relieved that Sally was obviously OK— he hadn't wanted to hurt her. He just hoped that everything worked out for them both.

The next two weeks at work seemed to drag—Peter was so excited and eager to attend the interview, it was as if time had slowed down just to spite him and he filled his evenings reading and rereading his notes. Finally, Friday arrived and Paul and Peter cycled home together. When they arrived, they found Annie charging around the house, packing bags and putting Peter's suit and shirt into a special carrier which would keep it flat.

She had packed slacks and a sports jacket for Paul, insisting that he should be smart as well and had also typed out train and tube times and the address of the guest house. She seemed to be in quite a flap, but Paul's laid-back attitude seemed to calm her.

After dinner, as they prepared to set off for the train, she came to Peter and gave him a huge hug, wishing him the best of luck. She had called them a taxi and they were soon on their way. Paul got their tickets and they were soon speeding their way across the countryside, with Peter nervously talking non-stop. A short walk and a tube train ride later, they arrived at the airport and found their accommodation. Peter felt too excited to want to sleep, but they both went to bed early in order to be up in plenty of time the day after.

16

In the morning, Paul suggested that they dress in their normal clothes for breakfast, as "Egg on your tie wouldn't create a good impression." This made Peter smile, although he was feeling very nervous. Paul was doing his best to calm him down and tried to appear as casual as possible, although he could see the roller-coaster that Peter was on.

After breakfast, Peter showered and shaved and got ready carefully. Paul looked him over and nodded his approval. "You look great, lad—very smart. Now remember—listen carefully to questions, try to not be too hasty or blunt with your answers and remember your manners."

Peter nodded—he was well aware of how he needed to come across and felt as well prepared as he could be.

Leaving their bags at the guest house, they set off in plenty of time for the short walk to the airline offices. Peter was amazed by the huge building and the beautifully furnished reception area. They made their way to the desk where the receptionist took Peter's name and pointed out where the Open Day and Presentation were being held. They both followed the arrows along the corridor to a big room filled with display boards and long tables covered with brochures and books.

There were quite a number of people milling around, parents with sons and even daughters, like Peter there for interview and some in airline uniform, who were there to answer questions and to talk about the airline. Hating the crowd, Peter looked around the room with his eyes wide and immediately stayed as close to Paul as possible. They wandered slowly along some of the tables looking at the books and brochures and Peter then stopped next to a display board which was showing the history of the airline.

Conversation seemed to be being kept at a low level, like a muted hum, when all of a sudden a deep male voice rang out, "Marham? Paul Marham—is that you?"

Paul's head spun around to see a tall man in a Captain's uniform striding towards him, holding his hand out. There was a moment of silence before Paul replied, "Fozzy? Fosdyke? Dear Lord, what are you doing here?"

The man laughed, clasping Paul's hand and shaking it vigorously. "More to the point, what are you doing here? Fancying a career change?" and he threw his head back and roared with laughter.

Paul laughed. "No—not me. I'm here with my lad. Peter, come over here," and he waved to Peter to join them. Peter walked over and Paul said, "Peter— meet Flying Officer Fosdyke. Well, he was a Flying Officer—what are you now?" he asked.

"Captain—but still the same Fozzy," the man replied and he shook Peter's hand warmly.

"Fozzy was one of our FO's on the squadron—utterly fearless and loved taking pot shots at Jerries—almost as much as chasing the girls in the local pub!" Paul explained. "So good to see you again. So, you're a Captain here?" Paul asked.

"Yes. I joined them after I left the RAF in 1950 and have been here ever since. I'm now a training Captain for my sins, but still loving every minute of it. So, you want to join us?" he asked Peter.

"Yes, Sir—always wanted to fly and applied earlier in the year," Peter replied nervously.

Captain Fosdyke nodded. "Did you do well in your exams?" he asked.

"Yes, Sir—I got eight straight A's," Peter said.

The captain's eyebrows shot upwards. "Eight A's? Good for you. Yes. Well done—outstanding." Peter blushed—he hated self-praise. "Well, with results like that, we may just be able to do something with you," the Captain joked. "Always like to get bright people on the course—makes my life so much easier."

Peter said nothing, but immediately liked the man. Fozzy looked at his watch and said, "Look, old boy—will you excuse me for a few moments? Back in a minute," and he turned and left the room. He walked into one of the interview rooms, picking up a schedule and ran his finger down the page. Turning to one of the staff, he asked if they could swap 2 interviewees over so that he could interview Peter.

This was done and he returned to the presentation room a few moments later. "Right, that's sorted," he said to Paul quietly. "I have to mingle, but shall we catch up later on? Would love to hear what you've been up to."

Paul agreed and he and Peter walked off together. "Wow. What a stroke of luck seeing him," Paul said. "He's a lovely man. He bought a Hurricane back once from a dogfight with most of the rear end shot away. I still don't know to this day how he kept it flying—he just brushed it off and was back up the day after. Incredible pilot."

Peter listened, impressed. These guys from the war and the Test Pilots were his heroes and he'd never actually met any of them before, so he felt honoured.

A bell rang and a voice called out for people to take seats and that there would be a short presentation. Peter and Paul sat down and a man in a pilot's uniform stood up and welcomed everybody before going to tell them all about International Airways and the training programme. Peter sat enthralled. This was what he wanted so badly—he felt he belonged already. Paul sat quietly, thinking about the chance meeting with Fozzy and hoping that he might be on Peter's interview panel.

After the presentation, most of which Peter already knew from his library book, they were again free to look around the displays before lunch was served. Peter was too nervous to eat, but Paul persuaded him to have something just in case it was a long afternoon.

After the lunch, the bell sounded again and a lady stood up and announced that the schedule for the interviews had been pinned to the notice board and reminded people that lateness would not be acceptable. Paul and Peter joined the other parents and candidates and Peter quickly found his name, which was second on the list in room 12. *Not too long to wait,* he thought to himself, looking at his watch.

Five minutes before the appointed time, they both made their way to room 12 and sat down on the seats outside the door. Peter was beginning to feel very nervous and Paul did his best to calm him and after a short wait the door opened and a lady stepped out. "Mr Peter Marham?" she asked. Peter nodded. "Please come in," she said and turned and disappeared back into the room.

"Good luck," whispered Paul and Peter followed the lady inside. In front of him was a long desk with three people sitting behind it and a single chair in front.

"Welcome. Please sit down," Peter looked at the source of the voice—it was Captain Fosdyke, who winked at him and motioned to the chair. Peter felt relieved. Captain Fosdyke started to speak. "Welcome, Mr Marham. May we call you Peter?" Peter said "Yes" quietly. "Jolly good. This is a fellow training skipper Captain Edwards and on the end is Mrs Johnson from personnel. We'll be asking you questions in turn and then we'll have an informal chat if that's OK?" Peter again said yes and Captain Fosdyke took a deep breath.

Outside, Paul began to pace up and down nervously. He hadn't felt like this since being at the maternity hospital when Peter was born! He knew just how much was riding on this interview and he hoped that Peter wouldn't be too blunt or say anything inappropriate. Much as he tried, Paul could not tear his mind away from how he'd have to deal with Peter if he was unsuccessful, but knew he'd have a huge battle on his hands.

In the interview, the questions came thick and fast, but Peter answered each to his satisfaction and thought about his answers carefully before committing himself. The two Captains alternated with general questions about the job and technical questions, which Peter had prepared himself for. Captain Edwards asked a very difficult technical question about lift equations, but it was one that Peter had memorised and on giving the answer the Captain smiled and nodded his head slightly.

Towards the end came the one question Peter had been expecting. Captain Fosdyke leaned forwards and said, "So, why do you want to fly aeroplanes for a living?"

Peter took a deep breath and answered, "Well, Sir, I've always had a love and a fascination for aviation and I want a career where I'm challenged every day, not just by technical things, but also by Mother Nature. I'm sure she'll throw lots of things at me during my time aloft and meeting those challenges is something I look forward to, not just from a pilot's point of view, but challenging me to deliver my passengers safely and on time will be the goal."

All three interviewers nodded their agreement and Peter felt a sense of satisfaction inside. He'd done his best—it was up to the three people opposite to decide his fate.

After what seemed like an eternity, the door opened and Peter walked out into the corridor. Paul took him by the arm. "Well—how did it go?"

Peter smiled. "Your friend Captain Fosdyke was on the interview panel and it went swimmingly. No difficult questions, I got to ask my pre-prepared questions and they seemed happy enough. The rules have changed and we can start training at sixteen now, but can't get our basic licence until we're seventeen, so I could start immediately if I get in," Peter replied excitedly.

Paul let out a long breath that he felt that he'd been holding for a very long time—about a hundred years. "Good," he said quietly. "What now?"

"Captain Fosdyke asked us to wait in the presentation room for a few minutes," Peter replied and they made their way back.

After a short wait, Captain Fosdyke appeared and came up to Paul. "Are you needing to get away quickly?" he asked.

"No, not really," Paul replied.

"Good. There's a lovely little restaurant nearby if you fancy a bite to eat afterwards. Would be lovely to catch up."

"Hmm, yes, OK. Shall we wait here?" Paul asked.

"Yes, grab a coffee and I'll be with you shortly. Just one more to do," Fozzy replied and he walked off. Paul and Peter smiled at each other. This was going rather well.

About an hour later, Fozzy reappeared in civilian clothes and motioned for Paul and Peter to follow him. Once outside, he turned to Paul, saying, "Sorry for all the formality, but we have to follow protocol. Let's go eat—I'm famished," and he strode off down the street towards a small Bistro.

Once inside, he seemed to relax and began to chat with Paul. Fozzy told them about his flying career and bought them up to present and began to talk about his post as Training Captain. "I'm one of the crusty old codgers who'll put you to work and worry you like a terrier," he said, winking at Peter. "In seriousness though, we're there to guide you from training through to being a fully-fledged and reliable First Officer who occasionally knows what he's doing," he said laughing.

Peter smiled—he was warming to Fozzy. Paul interrupted. "There has been a question in my mind for a very long time. May I ask it?"

"Go ahead," Fozzy replied.

Paul continued, "Do you remember bringing back a very badly shot up Hurricane? Just how in heaven's name did you get it back to the squadron? It was shot to pieces."

Fozzy smiled and replied, "Do you know, I often think about that and I haven't the faintest idea, dear boy. I knew it was shot up pretty badly, but the shells had missed me thankfully and also missed most of the aircraft's vitals. My only real worry was, once I saw the field, was about putting the landing gear down. I honestly didn't think that it'd come down, but my worst fear was one wheel coming down and one staying up. I debated making a belly landing, but then thought what the hell and pulled the lever. To my amazement and to my huge relief, both green lights came on and I made a normal landing. She was a bit of a mess though."

Paul laughed. "A bit? It took us two months to get her back into service and it was lost three days later. What a waste."

Fozzy nodded. They continued to talk about the squadron until their meals arrived.

Following a thoroughly pleasant meal, Paul paid the bill and they left, saying their goodbyes outside. "Lovely to meet you," Fozzy said, shaking Peter's hand. "Of course I can't say anything about today, but leave it with me," and he winked and tapped the side of his nose with his forefinger. He then shook Paul's hand. "So lovely to see you again—you really must come to one of the squadron reunions."

"Yes, I should. Thank you so much for today—really appreciate your time," Paul replied.

"Ahh no problem—happy to help an old squadron comrade out. However, if you're called back, we mustn't let on that you know me—understood? That'll be bad form. We'll both have to be on our best behaviour."

Peter smiled and nodded and they walked their separate ways, with Paul and Peter returning to the guest house to collect their bags and for Peter to change out of his suit.

The journey home was a quiet affair and Peter fell asleep on the train. Once they walked into the house, Annie was all over Peter. "Well? How did it go? Was it really difficult?"

Peter smiled and sat down to tell his mother all about the day. She listened intently, but Peter missed out the part about meeting Paul's old squadron buddy—he knew Paul would fill in the gaps. He went to bed a short while later, daring to hope, but exhausted.

17

Following the adrenaline-filled day of the interview, Peter slept late and didn't appear until nearly lunchtime. He felt strangely deflated, as though he'd been training for a race and that it was finally over. His parents left him along to just come round in his own time. Eventually he joined them and Annie asked what his plans were for the rest of the day. Peter shrugged his shoulders—he really didn't know what to do with himself.

Outside, the rain was hammering down, precluding a bike ride and he had no reading or other prep to do. Paul suggested helping with the motorbike in the garage and Peter nodded his head, but his heart wasn't in it. Inside, he was already running through scenarios where he'd not been successful and wondered where to go from there. He'd never felt as helpless before, with no purpose.

In the garage, Paul had started to dismantle the motorbike's gearbox and was showing Peter how it worked. Peter did his best to take notice and eventually managed to pluck up some interest, asking a few questions and helping where he could. Paul however was intently aware of his discomfort and decided not to say anything else about the interview the day before.

It was Peter who broke the silence, asking, "Tell me all about Fozzy—what kind of a character he is, what he's into?"

Paul sighed and said, "He was one of our best. During the war, you often didn't have time to get to know people, as they were posted to the squadron and often weren't there very long. War is a terrible waste of life and Fozzy knew this and lived it to the full. A great pilot, a real gentleman if you like, very caring and supportive of the new guys, always teaching them how to watch their backs, how to defend themselves. He got shot up a few times, but seemed to lead a charmed life, never getting injured, always bringing the aircraft—or what was left of it— back home.

"Most evenings you'd find him in the local tavern, chatting to the girls and having a great time. Guess he was living each day as though it'd be his last—

which for some of the poor buggers, it was. He was always ready with a joke and has a great sense of humour which you've already tasted. He didn't seem to have many interests back then—none of us did really—and I'm not sure of what his interests are. We haven't seen each other for over twenty years."

Peter nodded. "So were you great friends?" Peter asked.

"Well, yes and no. I was part of his groundcrew and he always included us as part of his team. There was one occasion where the local paper sent a reporter and photographer to chat to him and he refused to have his picture taken unless we were in it as well. That's just the kind of chap that he is. I would imagine that as a training captain, he'll be brilliant."

"I'm hoping so," Peter replied, hopeful.

Paul placed his hand on Peter's shoulder. "Now that you've been interviewed, I'm sure you'll hear pretty quickly if you've got through to the next stage," he said reassuringly.

Peter nodded his head. "Guess that'll mean another trip to London," he said.

"Guess so," Paul replied, adding, "Now, let's get this gearbox stripped and examined."

Peter just smiled and shook his head—his dad was always so intent on finishing the job in hand.

At the factory, Peter threw himself into the work, running errands, tidying, cleaning and challenging himself to lift heavier bags of waste and swarf. Fitness was becoming an obsession and he was becoming proud of his physique. The after-work rides, the physical nature of the job and his desire to look his best all drove him on. He still listened out for the early departures and was usually on the mound near the airport on a Saturday morning, but he looked at the world through different eyes. Merely collecting registration numbers and times was no longer enough.

His obsession with aviation drove him on, making him hungrier than ever to fulfil those dreams. He continued to meet up with Alex and their friendship was as strong as ever. Alex was now studying hard for his A Levels and seemed to busy most evenings, but Saturday visits to the coffee shop remained an almost religious part of their collective routines. He hadn't seen much of Liam, but guessed he was keeping a low profile now that he was going out with Sally.

Alex quizzed Peter about this over coffee. "How do you feel about Liam seeing Sally?" he asked.

Peter just shrugged his shoulders. "None of my business," he replied.

"You know, she really liked you?" Alex went on.

Peter, again shrugged, "Yes I know, but I'm just not ready for all that physical stuff. You might find that weird, but I just wasn't interested. I guess I will be one day, but not right now. Aviation first, girls later."

"Well, you should be—it's great fun," Alex replied with a smirk.

Peter looked at his friend long and hard. "None of my business, but by that I guess you two are—you know—doing it?" Peter asked. Alex smiled and nodded his head. "I Hope you're being careful—remember what Mr Batchelor in biology taught us," Peter replied, genuinely worried.

"Don't worry—we've got it covered," Alex laughed.

"Gosh, I hope so. That would be the end of things for you otherwise," Peter chided, laughing. "Can't see you as a daddy yet."

Alex roared with laughter. "Nor can I mate; last thing I need," he said.

"So, what's happened to Liam these days?" Peter asked. "Is he keeping a low profile?"

"No, not really. We were out with them last Saturday. Think they just wanted to avoid you so's not to upset you," Alex replied.

"Ahh—that doesn't bother me. I'd quite like to keep in touch with Liam, as we've been friends forever and I'd be happy to see Sally. No hard feelings there," Peter responded. "It'll still be nice to all go out together."

Alex agreed and promised to make arrangements to meet at the soft drinks bar or the cinema.

Early one Saturday, exactly two weeks after the interview, Annie bought coffee and toast into Peter, whom she'd heard moving around. She also bought a long white envelope. She placed the tray on the table in Peter's bedroom, smiled and left the room, knowing he'd need some private time. Peter looked at the envelope and decided to wait until he'd finished his breakfast—no point being let down on an empty stomach he reasoned. Finally, he picked the envelope up and tore it open. Unfolding the letter within, he began to read:

"Dear Mr Marham, Thank you for attending the Open Day and Interview on 15 October. I am pleased to inform you that you have been recommended to proceed to the second stage. This will consist of a fifteen minute assessment in one of our aircraft simulators and will take place on Saturday, 6 November 1969. I would be grateful if you could telephone the above number to confirm your attendance. Kind regards."

Peter read and reread the letter before leaping up and dashing downstairs. Both his parents were sitting at the kitchen table as usual. They looked up and seeing the joy on Peter's face, realised that he'd been successful. Peter handed the letter to Paul to read and Annie gave him a big hug. Paul slapped him on the back, saying, "Well done. So remind me again what's with this simulator check?"

Peter sat down and explained, "Well, like I told you, it's an aircraft cockpit with all the instruments and controls just like a real aircraft. We have to demonstrate that we can do some very basic manoeuvres and that we don't crash."

Paul nodded, agreeing that crashing wasn't a good idea and got up and left the room. Annie was excited for her son and started asking all sorts of questions, but Peter didn't hear them—he was on another level and could only think of the next stage.

Paul returned and sat down. "Right, son," he started. "A few weeks ago I went over to the airport and to the flight school there. I was worried about this Sim check, seeing as you've never held the controls of an aircraft before. I've just phoned the flight school. This afternoon, we're going over and I've booked you a short introductory lesson—just to let you get a feel. Ex RAF chap runs the place and he said he'll look after you. What do you think?"

Peter stared at his father, speechless. "You mean—in a real plane?" he asked.

"Yep—a real one. Just don't crash it," Paul laughed.

Peter hugged his dad, saying, "Thanks, dad—thanks, mum. That's awesome—now I'll know what to do."

"Well, that was the idea," Paul said, ruffling Peter's hair.

Peter then said, "6 November—that's next weekend."

Paul nodded. "Guess we'd better make some arrangements," he said looking at Annie, who smiled and nodded.

Early afternoon and they were on the way to the airport. Peter knew the route like the back of his hand, although he'd never strayed as far as the flight school. They arrived and locking their bikes to the railings, went inside the hut. Behind the desk was sitting a man about Paul's age, with thinning hair and a huge moustache. He looked up, saying, "Ahh, hello again. So this is the young man for the first lesson?"

"Hello," said Paul.

"Yes, this is Peter. As I explained, he's been for interview and has been offered a sim check—whatever that is. So he just needs to be able to do some basic stuff to impress the airline I guess."

The man got up and came across, extending his hand towards Peter. "I'm John—ex Group Captain, owner of this fine establishment and chief instructor," he said with a smile.

Peter shook the offered hand warmly. "I'm Peter," he said shyly.

"Jolly good—so you want to be a jet jockey do you?" he asked. Peter nodded his head. "Well, we'd best see what you're made of then," he added and turning, he picked up the telephone and had a quick muted conversation. "Right then—let's get going. You can wait here or outside," he said to Paul.

Paul followed them out to a small aircraft sitting on the grass. "Right," said John. "This is one of our little training aircraft—this is Bessie. She's an American Cessna. Typical trainer, dead easy to fly and she's got no bad manners—in fact, she's a perfect lady," he added with a wink.

Peter stared wide-eyed. The instructor opened the door and motioned for Peter to climb inside. "Mind your head—she's a bit cramped and you're a big lad," he said, helping Peter into the seat and to fasten his safety belt. Turning to Paul, he said, "You can wait on the bench there if you like—just stay clear when I start the engine," and he went around to the other door and got in.

Once strapped in, John turned to Peter, saying, "Right. Probably looks a bit complicated, but believe me it's dead easy. Once we're upstairs, we do all our flying looking out of the window, not at the instruments—that's to prevent us bumping into anybody else," he laughed and switching on a big red switch and turning a key, he bought the engine to life. Peter just sat and stared, mesmerised.

He was given some headphones to put on and then he heard John asking Air Traffic for clearance to taxi. Soon, they were bouncing over the grass towards the runway. After a short wait they lined up and Peter saw the long ribbon of black tarmac stretching out towards infinity before him. John turned to Peter saying, "A wonderful view. Just remember—a mile of road will take you a mile, but a mile of runway will take you anywhere in the world. Ready?" he asked.

"Yes," Peter replied.

"Good. Put your hands on the controls lightly—enough to feel what I'm doing but not hard enough to impede my movements," John instructed. Peter did as he was told and John pushed a black lever forwards, making the aeroplane leap towards the horizon, gathering speed. "Here we go" John said, pulling back on the controls slightly.

The nose of the aircraft came up and the bumps stopped. They were flying! Peter looked out of the side window and watched the ground fall away. John turned to him, smiling. "That was easy wasn't it?" Peter nodded.

Here he was at last—up in his element, up where he belonged. He then felt the controls twist to the right, like a car steering wheel and outside he saw the horizon tilt to the left. "Whoa," he gasped, clutching the controls tightly.

"Relax," John laughed. "See how we're turning to the right?" Peter again nodded, relaxing his grip. Soon, they were away from the airport and John said, "OK. Take the controls and look out of the window."

Peter did as he was told and John pointed out the horizon sitting just above the instrument panel and told Peter that this was level flight. He then told Peter to pull back slightly on the controls, which he did and the nose came up, the horizon disappeared and they started to climb. They then went back to level flight and Peter was shown how to push the controls forwards, making the horizon go up and the plane go down.

Back to level flight once more and then John showed Peter how to turn the controls like a steering wheel, making the aircraft roll and turn. Peter soon got the hang of it all and they spent the next forty minutes rolling, swooping and dancing amongst the clouds, enjoying the freedom of defying gravity and being weightless amongst the heavens.

Soon—far too soon—it was time to return to the airport. John instructed Peter to keep his hands lightly on the controls and lined the aircraft up with the runway. "Err—how do you actually land a plane?" Peter asked.

John smiled—it was a familiar question. "See that long strip of tarmac?" he asked. Peter nodded. "Well, point the aircraft at it and try not to miss," he laughed, allowing Peter to continue to fly. Lower and lower they came, until they slid over the runway and John reduced power on the engine, settling the aircraft gently onto the ground. John continued to tease Peter, "You don't really land an aeroplane—did you know that?"

Peter looked at him questioningly. "No not at all—it's actually a mid-air collision between an aeroplane and a planet," John explained and roared with laughter. *I must think of some new jokes one day*, he thought to himself as they taxied towards the school. Peter laughed. He was beyond excited—he had just flown an aeroplane! He couldn't believe it. John cut the engine and they both climbed out.

Paul was waiting with a huge grin on his face. "Well—how was that?" he asked.

Peter could hardly speak. "Amazing. Brilliant. Awesome. Pure freedom," was all he could think of to say.

"Right—come inside for a chat," John said and they all trooped inside the school. John motioned them to sit down and he sat next to Peter. "Right young fella—did you enjoy that?" he asked.

Peter nodded enthusiastically saying, "Yeah—it was amazing."

"Good. You did well and I can't see why we couldn't make a pilot of you. That's probably all the airline will expect of you and just don't forget to look over your shoulder when you turn. I wish you luck—will you come back and tell me how you got on?" he asked.

"Yes, of course—and thanks very much. That was truly an amazing experience," Peter said breathlessly.

On the ride home, Peter chatted constantly, reliving the flight and telling Paul each and every detail. Paul just smiled as they rode along—happy to see Peter so excited and animated. It had truly been a good day.

18

Monday morning, Annie telephoned the airline offices to confirm Peter's attendance for the Sim check and was told to be there for 2 PM. This came as a relief, as it world save the trouble—and expense—of another stay in the guest house. Paul would accompany him for the journey. Peter spent the week reliving and memorising the control inputs he'd been shown and riding further afield in an attempt to control his nerves.

During the week, he called to see Alex and they spent the evening discussing Peter's interview and generally chatting and enjoying each other's company. Alex had arranged to meet up with Liam and Sally on Saturday evening, but Peter doubted he'd be back from London in time. "If you do see them, just tell them that I've gone for the second part of the interview—I'd still like to see them," he said to Alex.

Peter was ready very early on Saturday morning and after a rushed breakfast, he and his dad waited for the bus into town. It was a grey dull morning, but nothing could hide Peter's excitement. He knew that he was potentially one step away from being offered a training place and despite Paul trying to remain cautious, he was totally focussed on what was to come.

He remained very quiet on the journey and didn't speak until they arrived at the airline offices. Once they had been shown where to go, they sat down and he finally broke his silence. "Dad—do you think I can do this?" he asked with characteristic self-doubt.

Paul smiled and said "Of course. Just listen carefully to what you're being asked to do and take your time. If you're unsure of what they want, ask them to explain it again. You're going to be fine—remember what John taught you last weekend."

Peter nodded but remained silent. Paul could see how nervous he was, so continued, "This is the easy part—the hard part was the interview and they must be impressed with you or they wouldn't have called you back."

Peter again nodded and shortly afterwards a lady appeared and asked his name. "Ahh yes, Mr Marham. Please come with me. You may come as well if you wish," she said to Paul. Peter stood up and looked at Paul, who just smiled and nodded and he then turned and followed the lady through a door with Paul trailing behind.

Inside the room was dark and there was a faint hum from the simulator. They were shown where to sit and shortly afterwards they heard a familiar voice. "Mr Marham? You'll probably remember me from your interview—Captain Nigel Fosdyke." Peter stood up and shook hands. "Right, let's get started. Dad, you can remain seated just there and you'll get a good view. Now then Peter, sit yourself down there in the right-hand seat. No need to put your seatbelts on as we're not going anywhere. I'll show you how to adjust your seat to the right position."

Peter did as directed and was helped to adjust the seat so that he could reach the controls comfortably. Once Peter was happy, the Captain sat down in the left seat. "Right. My colleague behind us will be driving the Sim, but just pay attention to what I ask you to do. All we're going to do is to have you fly the aircraft straight and level, then we'll try a climb, then a descent and finally we'll try some turns. OK?" Peter nodded.

"Good. Now all I want you to do is use the control column—I'll work the thrust levers so you don't need to worry about power settings. No pressure today—if you're not happy with what you've done we'll have another go. Understand?" Peter nodded.

"Good—off we go. We'll start with straight and level flight. Charlie, set us up at 3000 feet please." There was a whooshing noise and Peter watched fascinated as the instruments jumped to show them at the set height. "Right—when I say start, just take the controls gently and try to keep us flying straight and on heading, shown on this instrument here and watch your height on the altimeter here," and the Captain pointed to two dials on the panel.

"Ready?" Peter quietly said yes and the captain continued, "OK Charlie, release us into the wild blue if you'd be so kind." There was another electronic noise and Peter felt the controls come alive in his hands. He gripped them but in a relaxed fashion as he'd been shown the week before and alternated his gaze between the horizon outside the window and the two instruments showing height and heading.

After a few minutes Peter felt himself relaxing a little more and the aircraft continued straight ahead. "Good," said Captain Fosdyke. "Now, let's try a climb—not too steep though—mustn't spill the passenger's gin and tonics." Peter smiled and pulled gently back on the controls. He saw the horizon vanish under the nose and the altimeter began to register an increase. "Try to level off at 4000 feet if you can—but don't worry if you over-cook it," the captain said.

Peter again nodded and waited until the needles almost registered 4000 and then he gently pushed the controls forwards, levelling off just above 4000 feet. "Good man. Now, let's go back down to 3000—but level off a bit before as Mr Newton's gravity will pull us down," the captain instructed. Peter pushed forwards gently and watched the horizon move up in the window and the altimeter begin to unwind. Peter pulled back on the controls and levelled the aircraft—and saw exactly 3000 feet!

"Good effort. Now let's try some turns. You can see that we're on a heading of South. Turn us to the left onto East," Peter remembered to glance over his left shoulder and turned the controls to the left. The horizon immediately tilted and round they went. Peter found himself looking outside so much that he forgot to look at the compass and when he remembered saw that they had turned too far. He immediately levelled the wings. "Made a mess of that—can I try again?" he asked meekly.

Captain Fosdyke laughed. "Of course—easy beginner's mistake. Take us right, back onto South." Peter rolled the aircraft to the right and remembered to look at the compass as well as the horizon and he rolled level as the compass approached the required heading. As the aircraft settled, the compass stopped floating and settled on South. "Very good. Happy?" Captain Fosdyke asked.

"Yes, I think so—just missed that first turn a bit," Peter replied.

"Ahh no worries—at least you haven't tried to kill us all," Captain Fosdyke laughed. "Let's have a bit of fun—fancy trying a landing? I know that it's not in the requirements for today, but let's see what you're made of."

Peter looked across at the Captain. "It's not something that I've planned for," he said quietly.

"No problem—this is just for a bit of fun and won't affect your score and I'll help you out," came the reply.

Peter thought for a minute and then said, "Yes OK, why not?"

"Good. Charlie, set us up on approach at five miles if you please." There was another whooshing noise and the controls jumped in Peter's hands. "Right—let's brief you. We're five miles out with the gear and flaps down all I want you to do is to stay on the runway centreline if you can using roll and a bit of rudder from the pedals and at the bottom when I say, raise the nose a little bit and bring the thrust levers all the way to the back and wait for the ground to arrive. OK?"

Peter nodded, but felt very nervous. "Right, off we go Charlie if you would." Peter placed his right hand on the controls and the captain showed him where to hold the thrust levers with his left hand. Again the controls came alive and the ground started to get closer. Peter did his best to relax and made small control inputs to stay pointing towards the white lines on the runway. Lower and lower they flew until finally the fence around the airport flashed past beneath the nose.

"OK, raise the nose slightly and close the thrust levers," the captain commanded. Peter did as he was told and waited—and waited. After what seemed like an eternity, he felt a bump as the aircraft settled onto the ground. "Jolly good—nice landing," the Captain said. "Happy?"

Peter nodded his head, beaming. "Yes, thanks—hope that was all OK," he said quietly.

"OK? No it wasn't OK—it was superb," Captain Fosdyke replied. "Really good effort. You're a natural—what did you think Dad?" he asked turning to Paul.

"Yes it looked really good from here—not that I'd know any different," Paul replied.

"That was very good for a beginner believe me," Fosdyke replied.

"Right my lad, let's get you out and you can relax. There's a waiting area outside—help yourself to coffee or tea and we'll come and see you all shortly. Just one more victim to terrorise," Captain Fosdyke again threw his head back and laughed. Peter smiled and pushed his seat back and clambered out of the cockpit.

Peter and Paul walked outside to the waiting area. Peter flopped into a chair looking exhausted. Paul bought coffee over and sat beside him. "You OK?" he asked.

"Yes—just drained. I hope missing that turn won't affect my score," Peter replied with a worried look on his face.

"I don't think so—Fozzy didn't seem too bothered. How did it feel to land the aircraft?"

"Scary but strangely satisfying. I'm sure it won't always be so easy though," Peter said, adding, "I'm glad he was there to stop me crashing."

"I didn't see any evidence of that—it was impressive watching you," Paul went on. "Made me very proud."

"Thanks, Dad," Peter said quietly. "Wonder why we've been asked to wait?"

Glancing around the room there were a number of people about Peter's age with parents also waiting. Paul shrugged. "Not sure—perhaps they'll need to debrief you today," he said.

They sat for about an hour with Peter fidgeting nervously, until they heard a lady's voice from the end of the room. "Will everyone whose names are on this list please go into the room at the end marked Training Room 1 with whoever is accompanying them. Everybody else is free to leave and thank you for your attendance today."

She then pinned a typed list onto a notice board and disappeared into the training room. Peter and Paul stood up and slowly took their place in the queue to read the list. When they got to the front, Peter quickly scanned down the short list of names. His name was there just above the bottom name. He turned to Paul with a worried look and shrugged. "Come on," Paul said and walked towards the training room.

"But Dad—what does it mean?" Peter whispered.

"Good news, I hope," Paul replied and they found some seats and sat down.

After what seemed like a very long time, the door opened and in walked Captain Fosdyke with another Captain and the lady. Captain Fosdyke coughed slightly and began.

"Right—thank you all for attending today. After careful consideration we're happy to say that all of you in here have been successful and we're happy to offer each of you a training place on the cadet scheme. The next intake will be in January and we will write to you with details of everything that you need to know.

"All we ask in the meantime is that you arrange to have your Civil Aviation medical carried out before you start. Details of how to do this will be in the information that we will be sending you. There will be forms to fill in and return, as well as all details of the training programme and everything else that you need to know. Any questions?"

Nobody had anything to ask, so he went on, "Right—you can all make you ways home and we look forward to seeing you again very soon."

Peter turned to Paul with tears in his eyes. "I've done it. Dad—I've done it."

Paul also had tears. He stood up and gave Peter a big hug. "I never doubted you—well done, son. We'd best call your mother," he said, turning towards the door.

Peter followed with his feet hardly touching the ground. Once outside, Peter took a huge gulp of fresh air—relief swept over him. Paul saw a telephone box outside the Tube station and after rummaging in his pockets for some change, stepped in and dialled their home number. Peter heard a voice and Paul shoved pennies into the slot.

"Annie—hi it's me. We've just finished—I'll put Peter on."

Peter took the receiver. "Mum. Hi—guess what. I've done it. I'm in—starting in January."

Annie shrieked down the phone. "Oh, well done, Peter—well done. That's so exciting. I'm so proud of you—are you excited?"

"You bet," Peter replied and they continued to chat whilst Paul stood and listened and could hear Annie's excited voice as she spoke to Peter. Finally they said goodbye as the money ran out.

"C'mon—let's get home," Paul said and they descended into the Tube station. Peter again fell asleep on the train on the way home and Paul just sat looking at him with a huge sense of both relief and pride. Peter had certainly defied his critics.

19

It was cold and dark when the train finally clanged to a halt and Paul and Peter both quickly walked down the platform as they could see a bus waiting outside. Once through the turnstile, they ran for the bus, just making it on board before it pulled out. Outside, they could see flashes of light as people were enjoying bonfire night. Peter had completely forgotten about it and suddenly remembered that he was supposed to meet his friends—but he felt too drained and, in reality, all he wanted to do was to get home, change out of his smart clothes and relax.

The bus slowly rattled its way through the dark damp streets until they were nearly at their stop. Peter stood up and rang the bell once, telling the driver to stop. As the bus creaked to a halt, Peter jumped off and Paul followed and they walked the short distance to their house. Peter opened the door and heard a voice yell out his name and then saw Annie running down the hallway towards him before throwing herself at him and clinging onto him tightly. He put his arms around her and could feel her shaking.

Finally, she looked up at him, tears rolling down her face and said very quietly, "I'm so proud. So proud." Peter too had tears in his eyes as he muttered his thanks. Annie finally relinquished her grip and turned to Paul, putting her arms around him. "What do you think of our boy? Actually, I should say our young man really?"

Paul gave her a squeeze, replying, "I'm also very proud of him. To think that he's going to be flying jets is amazing—he's done very well."

Peter stood for a few moments feeling awkward and uncomfortable. "OK— what's for dinner?" he asked with characteristic bluntness.

Annie let out a burst of laughter, wiping her eyes. "OK—bring me back down to earth. We're having lamb—which will be ready very soon. Go and get changed," she smiled and started back towards the kitchen.

After dinner, they all sat together in the living room, where Annie grilled Peter for a blow-by-blow account of how the day had gone. He ran through the whole day almost minute by minute and said that he thought that he'd blown it by missing the turn in the aircraft, at which point Paul butted in, "Not at all. As you turned back the other way, Fozzy looked at me and winked so I knew you were alright, although I obviously couldn't say anything."

"I'm so glad I flew with him." Peter went on, adding, "He was so helpful and letting me fly the approach and landing was awesome."

"Yes—as I said, he's quite a guy and meeting him again has been really fortuitous. I hope he's going to be doing a lot of your training."

"So do I," Peter replied.

Annie butted in, "So tell me more—were there lots of you? How many got through?"

"I think that there were about twenty of us, but only six got through—including a girl," Peter replied.

Annie nodded. "Good for her—I'm sure that she'll be as good a pilot as all the young men," she said and Peter nodded. "So what's next?" Annie asked.

"Well, we start in January and they will be sending me details of everything. I have to get my medical before I can start and once that's done, I'll carry on working with Dad until Christmas I guess," Peter explained. Annie nodded, but inside she felt a pang of emptiness. Her boy would soon be gone and the nest would be empty. She wondered how Peter would cope on his own and if his strict adherence to routine would fit in with his new working life. Time will tell she said to herself.

Peter arose very early the following morning—it was still dark outside and was cold. He'd already decided to go for a ride after breakfast as the adrenaline was still surging around his system and he needed to burn it off. He ate and finished his coffee quickly and was just getting ready to leave when Annie appeared. "You off out already?" she asked.

"Yes—I need to burn off some energy," Peter replied. "Why don't you go back to bed?"

"You know—I might just do that," Annie replied, adding, "Be careful out there."

Peter smiled and kissed her forehead. "Won't be long," he said, unlocking the door. Outside, the smell of bonfires and fireworks hung in the damp autumn air, urging Peter to get out into the countryside. He was quickly on his way, enjoying the familiarity of the route and the fresher air outside the town. Harder and harder he pushed, trying to get up to a high average speed and he pushed himself as hard as he could go.

Along the lanes he rode as fast as he dared, eventually reaching the half-way point. He climbed off the bike and sat down on his usual bench beside the old church. Waiting for his breathing and heart rate to subside, he looked around him. He loved the familiarity and routine, but realised that if he was serious about his fitness, he'd have to go further afield. He know that his future career would be fairly sedentary and that maintaining fitness would be paramount. With this in mind, he remounted and set off for home at a furious pace, just missing a reversing tractor on the way.

Peter arrived home in a new record time—he was really pleased with himself and wondered if he could better this new time. As soon as he entered the house, Annie took one look at him and – in her usual way—pointed straight upstairs. Peter smiled and instead of going straight to the bathroom, walked over and threw his arms around her.

She fought against him, beating her fists on his chest saying, "Get off—you stink of sweat and dust. Get upstairs," but Peter laughed and held her tighter. Finally, he let go and Annie looked at his smirk before bursting into laughter. "OK big lad—you win. Now, I'll stink of sweat all day," and she shook her head. Peter laughed again and then took himself upstairs—he really did stink and he couldn't stand the smell either.

Downstairs, Annie allowed herself a smile—she hadn't seen Peter so relaxed in a very long time. All was good in her world.

Peter was just getting dressed when he heard the phone ringing. Almost immediately Annie called up the stairs telling him that Alex was on the phone. Peter ran downstairs and picked up the receiver. "Hi, buddy," he started.

"Hi, mate," came Alex's reply. "How did you get on yesterday?"

"Yeah, OK, thanks—I passed and start in January," Peter replied.

There was a short silence before Peter heard a loud yelp of glee down the phone. "That's awesome—well done. We need to meet up to celebrate."

Peter agreed and was then subject to endless questions about the day. Finally Alex said, "Why don't we meet up this evening about six? You can tell us all about it." Peter agreed and put the phone down.

Annie asked him what his plans were for the day and he told her about arranging to meet up with Alex at six that evening and she promised an early dinner. "Where's dad?" Peter asked.

Annie pointed her thumb towards the garage. "With his mistress," she laughed and Peter laughed as well before joining Paul in the garage.

Paul looked up as the door opened. "Hi" he said. "Come to learn more about engineering?"

"Yes, please—I want to learn as much as I can before January," Peter replied.

"Good, man. Let's start with the engine rebuild. I got two new con-rods, bearing shells and a gasket set and it's time to put everything back together if you want to help."

Peter nodded. Paul, in his logical engineer's way, had laid everything out in order on the workbench and had de-greased every part with paraffin. "Right, let's start at the bottom," and Paul started to explain what each part of the engine was, what it did and how it fitted together. Peter followed what his dad was saying and it all seemed to make sense. Paul allowed Peter to fit the parts together, to attach the bolts and showed him how to tighten them to the correct torque.

For Peter, it all went together logically and because everything was so clean and new, the engine was soon assembled without any dirt or grease on Peter's hands. "Old grease and dirt can destroy a new engine which is why we put it together in a clean environment," Paul explained. "Just like on aircraft, everything was assembled cleanly and with new grease or oil. If our engine fails because we've been careless and put it together dirty, it's no big deal, but when we serviced the fighters, if we put them together dirty, things could jam and fail—and that could cost somebody their life."

Peter nodded his head in understanding. "Same on your jets" Paul went on. Peter again nodded in agreement, asking, "What happens to the old parts they take off?"

"Well, it depends," Paul explained. "Some parts such as pumps can be stripped and rebuilt, but some parts can't and have to be replaced with new. In the aircraft technical log, everything that's done to the aircraft is recorded and new serial numbers added so that there's a way of tracing who did what and when. Very important document and one which you'll get to know intimately I'm sure."

Peter again nodded. He loved working with Paul whether at home or in the factory and he learned so much. They carried on through the afternoon and Annie finally appeared in the garage doorway, telling them that dinner would shortly be ready. "Great—I'm famished," Peter said and Paul and Annie looked at each other, smiling.

Once inside, Peter and Paul were stood next to each other, still discussing engines, when Annie said, "Take your slippers off and stand back to back. I want to see something." Peter and his dad looked at each other quizzically and did as they were told. Annie went to the drawer, taking out a wooden ruler and then stood on a chair, placing the ruler on their heads. "I thought to," she said. "You two are exactly the same height. When will you stop growing?" she said to Peter, punching him playfully on the arm.

Peter looked at Paul, smiling and said, "Well I will if you don't feed me," and Paul roared with laughter. Annie sighed, saying that dinner would be five minutes, which was just enough time for them both to wash their hands. During dinner, Annie continued to tease Peter about his size and how much he was growing. Peter let it all wash over him, taking it on board but not really listening.

After dinner, he went upstairs to change and came back down ready to meet up with Alex and his friends. Annie took one look at him and said, "Is that the new shirt I bought you in the summer?" Peter nodded his head. Annie pulled at the buttons on the front saying, "Look—you've already outgrown it. These buttons are straining to stay fastened and the sleeves are tight around your arms. You can't go out in that. Paul, have you seen? What are we going to do with him?"

Paul smiled, shaking his head and went back to his book. "It's fine," Peter muttered. "Probably shrunk in the wash."

"I don't think so," Annie chided.

"Well, I promise to stop growing by the time I'm seventeen," Peter laughed and picking up his jacket left to catch the bus.

Once in town, Peter headed straight for the soft drinks bar. He quickly spotted Alex and Anna and, after getting a drink, joined them. Alex held out his hand and shook Peter's vigorously. "Congratulations buddy—well done. Really chuffed for you."

"Thanks," Peter muttered.

Anna stood up and put her arms around his waist, giving him a squeeze. "Yes, well done. When do you start," she asked, sitting back down.

"Sometime in January, but have to get my medical first—just to prove I'm still alive I guess," Peter joked.

Just then, Anna heard her name being called and they looked up to see Sally arriving with Liam. They soon joined Alex, Anna and Peter and Sally seemed a little distant at first, ignoring Peter. Liam was having none of it though and arrived at the table, putting their drinks down and slapping Peter heartily on the back. "Well done, old boy," he said.

Peter smiled. "Thanks, buddy," he said.

"Well done? Well done for what?" Sally asked.

"Sorry—didn't I tell you? Peter's got his airline job," Liam explained. Sally looked directly at Peter and then smiled and added her congratulations. This seemed to break the ice and everyone started firing questions at Peter. How did the day go, what did he have to do, was it difficult, when do you start?

Peter took a deep breath and ran through the whole day, talking about flying the Sim, doing a landing and mentioning that only six out of about twenty got through. They all listened intently and seemed genuinely pleased. The conversation then turned to normal topics, with Alex and Liam talking about football and with Anna joining in talking about their A Levels.

Sally sat quietly so Peter took a deep breath and asked her, "So, how are you? Everything OK?"

Sally looked at Peter for a minute and then replied, "Yes, thanks—I'm good. We wondered if it would be a bit awkward for us to see you that's all."

Peter shook his head. "No not at all. I'm sure that you're right for each other and I'm quite happy to see you together." Sally smiled and said thanks. "What have you been up to—going out much?" Peter asked.

"Yes, quite a bit, especially now that Liam's doing his apprenticeship and has a bit of money to spend. I'm going to be a kept woman," Sally laughed and ran her hands through her hair in a false show of vanity. Peter laughed and said that Liam should be earning a lot more once he was a pop star—or a full time comedian. This made Sally laugh and it seemed that they were friends again.

Sally then looked at Peter directly, asking, "So—are you seeing anyone?"

Peter shook his head. "Nope—and I don't plan to until I'm fully qualified in about eighteen months," he answered.

Sally nodded and said quietly, "Good. I thought it was just me that you didn't like."

"Not at all—just that the timing wasn't right for me that's all. I still think that you great and a lovely person—but you'll have so much more fun with Liam—he totally bonkers."

Sally smiled. "Oh, don't I know it," she said. Anna then joined back into the general conversation and they moved onto the subject of winter fashion, so Peter sat and listened politely.

Back at home, Annie and Paul watched Peter getting on the bus and saw it disappear into the distance. "Do you think he'll be able to cope living away from us?" Annie asked nervously.

Paul put his book down and thought for a few moments. "Well, I hope so—he's going to have to. The thing is, we've had to shelter and help him a great deal—especially when he was younger and often against Ben's bullying, but he's older now and if he can find his own space and routines, he'll be fine, I think. Look at him today—full of happiness and confidence.

"I know he'll be mixing with strangers and that he won't find that easy at first, but he'll get used to it I'm sure. I honestly don't think that we've anything to worry about. I was really worried at first when he started working with me—the guys at the factory can be pretty cruel when they want to be, but Peter's taken it all on board—even the teasing and practical jokes, so let's not worry too much."

"I hope you're right," Annie answered, "Because he could end up in a very lonely and dark place."

Paul put his arm around Annie and pulled her close. "He's given us so many surprises over the past few months—years in fact—that he'll surprise us again I'm sure."

Annie snuggled into Paul hoping he was right, but she was a natural worrier and Peter's childhood had been one of many unexpected hurdles and challenges, which added to her fears.

20

The working week passed quickly, with Peter back into his routine of work, cycle ride and dinner. The evenings were getting darker now and this put an idea into Peter's head. One evening after dinner, he said to Paul, "Dad. Would it be possible to build a frame to attach my bike to so that I can cycle throughout the winter without getting wet every day?"

Paul thought for a few moments and then told Peter to fetch his notebook and a ruler. They sat down at the kitchen table and between them they started sketching ideas, finally coming up with a rough drawing of two triangles attached by crossmembers which would act as feet. Peter seemed pleased with the idea, but Paul said, "That will attach your bike and allow you to turn the pedals, but there will be no resistance like there is on the road, so we'll have to come up with something to provide something for you to push against. Let me think about how we can do that."

Peter nodded and tried to think of a solution. The next day at work, whilst Peter was delivering parts, he was asked to help to remove a rolling machine which was being taken out of service and was being scrapped. After some struggling, Peter and four others managed to get the machine loaded onto a trailer and it was pushed outside to be dismantled. Peter took little notice and went back inside to carry on with his deliveries and he just casually mentioned it to Paul on the ride home.

When they arrived, Peter found a large brown envelope waiting for him. It bore the crest of International Airlines. Peter looked at Paul who suggested opening it and looking at the contents after dinner and Peter agreed. Meal finished, Peter and Paul went into the living room and Peter ripped the package open. Inside there was a letter, some forms and a book.

The letter began: "Dear Mr Marham, This letter is to formally offer you the position of Pilot Cadet commencing 2 January 1970. Please find enclosed—"

142

Peter read on and was soon lost in the abundance of forms for him to complete and return and he finally came across the important letter and details regarding getting his medical examination completed. This would have to be done in London during weekday hours which meant taking a day off work. Paul read through the other forms and said that there were to do with personal details, salary, uniform and accommodation and that they wouldn't take long to fill in and complete.

Annie volunteered to call the medical office to arrange an appointment and would endeavour to get Peter seen as soon as possible. Peter and Paul set to work completing what forms they could and Paul then started to read the information regarding accommodation.

"Right Peter, it says here that you will be staying in a crew house very close to the airport, in a single room. The cost for the room is included in your salary, but you are expected to pay for all your own meals and everything else you need. It says that you'll all be collected by bus every morning to be taken to the training airfield which is about fifteen miles away from the main airport. The good thing is that there is a payphone in the house so you can keep in touch with us if you need to."

"That sounds good," said Peter. "I'll need that"

"Good," Paul replied. "The only form that we can't really complete is the one for your uniform, as you have to be measured by the company tailor."

Peter nodded his head and carried on writing. Once they had done all they could, Peter picked up the book and thumbed through a few pages. It was entitled "Flight Training" and the note attached to the front asked cadets to read chapters 1-6 before taking up their post. *No problem—a little light reading*, Peter thought to himself.

The following day was Thursday and as Peter and Paul cycled to work, Paul asked Peter more about the machine which they had pulled out of the factory the day before. "It's an old rolling machine I think they called it. Don't know what it's for," Peter explained.

Paul nodded but said nothing. As Thursday was a very busy day for Peter, with deliveries arriving from suppliers, he didn't see Paul until lunchtime and after a quick break, he returned to the stores and next saw Paul in the locker room at the end of the day. Paul was about ten minutes late and quickly washed and changed and they set off together.

As they cycled home, Paul said, "Sorry, I was a bit late—I went to look at that old machine. It's got rollers on bearings and I think that if we could attach those to a frame, the back wheel of your bike could rest on the roller and it could provide resistance. I'll have a chat to Dave in the morning to see if I can salvage any parts—what do you think?" Peter just nodded his agreement—he was too focused on whether Annie had got his medical appointment made.

Arriving home, Peter set off for his evening ride as usual, after remembering to get his bike lights out of the garage as it would be almost dark by the time he returned. After a gruelling twenty miles, Peter arrived home tired but refreshed. He ran inside and immediately started quizzing his mum.

Annie smiled at him. "It's all sorted, sweetie—Friday of next week at midday. You can get the morning train and be home in time for dinner."

"Thanks mum," Peter said, giving her a quick hug. She immediately stepped back and looked at him with her head tilted to one side. "I know—upstairs," Peter laughed and he went to clean up.

The following morning, once Peter had changed into his overalls, he went to Dave's office and knocked on the door. Dave was on the phone, but waved Peter inside. Dave was, as usual, shouting at some poor unfortunate about parts deliveries. Peter had begun to think that this was all Dave did all day, but didn't say anything.

Finally, Dave replaced the receiver and with a final profanity, told Peter to sit down and asked him what he wanted. "Err well, I have my aviation medical arranged for next Friday. Mum made the appointment yesterday and it's in London so I'll need the day off if that's OK?"

"Yes, of course, no problem," Dave answered. "So I understand from your Dad that you've been offered a cadetship—correct?" Peter nodded his head. "Well congratulations—I'll be sorry to lose you as you're a hard worker. When do you start?"

"Second of January," Peter replied.

Dave nodded. "OK. We close just before Christmas for two weeks, so I'll expect that to be your last week. If you need a reference, I'll be happy to give you one," Dave continued.

"Thanks—and thanks for the offer of a reference—although they haven't asked for any," Peter replied.

"OK—you know what I'm going to say now, don't you?" Dave said.

Peter laughed. "Yes. Go and get some bloody work done." Dave roared with laughter and returned to the telephone.

Cycling home that evening, Paul asked Peter if he could give him a hand at the factory the next morning. "But it's Saturday," Peter replied.

"I know. I asked Dave about salvaging some parts off the old rolling machine today and he told me to take whatever I wanted, but not during work time. Want to help?"

"Yes, sure," Peter said, intrigued by what his dad had in mind.

That evening, Peter opened the flight training book and began at chapter one. He thought that reading six chapters would be a breeze, but the detail the first chapter went into and the copious notes Peter made, meant that he was only halfway through when he felt too tired to continue and he switched off the light and was immediately asleep.

Peter was woken by Paul, as he'd slept late. They quickly got organised and were soon on their way back to the factory. As soon as they arrived, Paul was let in by security staff and he went to his machine room to get tools, joining Peter in the yard by the old machine. Paul looked over it carefully and then began to loosen the bolts which attached the rollers to the machine bed. They were stiff with age and required both Paul and Peter to heave on them after attaching a long bar over the spanner to provide extra leverage.

Eventually, the bolts were free and Paul carefully levered the roller from the machine, He inspected the bearings carefully and seemed satisfied and then turned his attention to the frame, taking out a tape measure. Peter stood and watched in silence, fascinated. He could see that his dad was assessing how to construct a frame and thought that he probably had it already drawn and measured in his head.

Eventually, more bolts were removed and the frame supporting the rollers was teased from the machine. "Good—that'll do us," Paul said and motioned Peter to pick up the roller which Paul attached to the top tube on his bike.

The frame was tied to Peter's bike with strong twine and Paul disappeared to return his tools to the shop. They then rode carefully home, depositing their spoils in the garage. "Right, I need to get on with my reading," Peter said, leaving Paul to put their bikes away.

"Sure, no problem, let your mum know we're home—I'm famished," Paul replied with a smile.

Peter returned to his book and continued with his reading. Outside he could hear the sound of an electric drill and a hammer being wielded and he guessed that his dad was already hard at work. Late in the afternoon, Paul popped his round Peter's bedroom door. "Got a minute? Come and see if this will work." And he disappeared downstairs.

Peter finished the paragraph and put a note in the margin and then followed Paul outside. In the garage, Paul had constructed a frame exactly like they had designed and had the roller attached. "Hold your bike so the back wheel sits on the roller." Peter did as requested and Paul took more careful measurements before going to his workbench and pulling out boxes of bolts.

He attached two bolts to the rear wheel spindle and tightened them to the frame to hold the bike in place and then took his tape measure and made more measurements and then sat back. "OK. The wheel is not quite sitting on the roller—I'll need to add some packing beneath the bearing carriers. Leave it with me and I'll call you if I need you." Peter looked at his bike strapped to the frame—it was exactly what he'd imagined but could have never built it himself. It was so useful having a father who was an engineer!

After dinner, Peter was going to return to his reading, but a phone call from Liam made him change his mind. They agreed to meet up so Peter quickly washed and changed and was soon waiting for the bus. He arrived at the soft drinks bar to see all his friends in their usual spot.

Buying a drink, he joined them and was soon in animated conversation with Alex and Liam about the bike stand they were building. "What exactly is it for?" asked Alex.

"For winter. I want to be able to continue cycling throughout the winter months and if it works, I can do loads of miles in the garage without getting wet," Peter explained.

"Sounds like a good idea," Alex replied, but Liam scoffed.

"I'll be learning to drive next year so my bike will getting pushed to the back of the shed at home where it can gather dust. I'll be getting all the exercise I need," he said, winking at them.

Alex smiled and Peter said nothing—it took him a few minutes to realise what Liam was talking about. "Whose idea was it?" Alex asked.

"Well, mine really and then Dad and I sat down to draw up some ideas. There was a machine at work being decommissioned and we were allowed to salvage some parts and Dad got busy with his tools. He's a clever guy," Peter explained.

"Wish mine was practical," Alex answered. "He's obviously very clever as a doctor, but he can't boil a kettle of water." This bought laughter from them all and Alex continued, "I don't know what we'd do really if all the work people went on strike. Starve probably."

"Well, you'll be alright babe as you'll have me to look after you," Sally said, looking at Liam. Liam smiled and nodded his head.

"How will you get on when you start your cadetship and you're living in London?" Anna asked Peter.

"Dunno really. Guess I'll be living on beans on toast and cold coffee," Peter replied laughing before adding "My Mum mentioned it the other day so I be leaning to cook some basic meals I suppose. Hope that there's a fish and chip shop nearby."

This bought more laughter from the group and then Alex started listing all his favourite meals which, he said, he expected Anna to be able to cook to perfection. "You've no chance buddy," she responded immediately. "I'll be studying as hard as you as medical school, so if you want to eat, you can cook— for me as well."

This made them all laugh out loud and they continued the laughter and banter until it was time to leave.

Peter arose on Sunday with the intention of spending the day reading, but Annie had other ideas. After breakfast, she called Peter down to the kitchen. "Right, young man. I have written you a book of basic meals and recipes here, which should be easy for you to follow. I've even done a list of how long to cook vegetables, so you shouldn't have any problems. I don't want you starving or living off just toast and coffee so I thought that you could cook dinner today under my supervision if that's OK?"

Peter nodded his head without enthusiasm. "Good. You're going to cook Sunday dinner—chicken, roast potatoes and cabbage—dead easy." Peter again nodded his head and opened his mouth to say something, but quickly thought better of it. "Right, that's sorted. Go go and get on with your studying and I'll call you when we're ready to start." Peter took himself back upstairs and picked up the book and was soon lost in its secrets.

Annie called up the stairs and Peter put down his book, slowly descending to the kitchen. Annie was bursting with enthusiasm—"First thing is we wash our hands," she said, pointing to the kitchen sink.

Peter ran water and soaped his hands, asking, "Mum, why do I need to cook? I'll be OK I'm sure."

Annie looked at him for a few moments as he dried his hands. "Think about it, Peter. You're pretty much a loner and you're happy to isolate yourself from everybody else—you know how you don't like crowds, having people around you and you find it so hard to meet new people and make new friends. Nobody there is going to look after you and many of them will be in the same boat as you, living apart from parents for the first time.

"You need to be able to look after yourself—you'll have so much to learn and I'm sure that there will be lots of studying to do and you can't do that on an empty stomach. Let's get started," and with that she proceeded to show Peter how to prepare the chicken and how to cut and prepare the vegetables.

Eventually all was done and dinner was under way, so Peter went back to his book, returning to the kitchen when called to complete the meal. When it was ready, Annie called Paul and they took their seats and Peter served the meal. Paul made a great show of pretending to choke and feigned being poisoned, but Peter took in good spirits and they enjoyed the meal, with Peter once again going back to his studies once they had finished.

21

Peter attended for his medical examination accompanied by Annie, who wanted to ensure that he could travel and find the office without any problem. Peter was in the building for less than an hour and they emerged with his new medical certificate and Annie was relieved of fifteen pounds for the privilege. They were given two copies of the certificate and Annie had bought an envelope with a covering letter for the airline and they posted a copy off straight away. That was one less thing to worry about.

November quickly passed into December and Peter spent his time as usual, splitting it between working, exercising and studying and cultivating his cooking skills. He eventually finished the six chapters of the book and was reasonably comfortable with their content. He saw less and less of his friends, but Alex and Anna were busy with their own studies and Liam was learning on the job, so this was to be expected.

As they got towards Christmas, Dave called Peter into the office. "Now then, young man. You've been with us for quite a few months now. How have you enjoyed you time here?"

Peter thought for a moment before replying. "It's been great thanks. The guys have been very helpful, although they love to tease and play their jokes, but I've got used to that. I think I've learned some useful skills such as time management and self-motivation and I've certainly increased my vocabulary!"

Dave roared with laughter as this. "Yes, I bet you have—just remember not to use that sort of language where you're going."

Peter smiled and promised to leave those new words in the factory. Dave continued, "Well, I want to thank you for your hard work and just to wish you all the luck for your future. You've a steep mountain to climb I'm sure, but you're a grafter so you'll get there. Don't forget, with determination and hard work, you can achieve anything. Now, as you don't officially finish with us until the 31st, I'll be paying you the same Christmas bonus as the rest of the guys here—I hope that it helps you through. I'll make sure that it's in your final pay packet—is that OK?"

Peter didn't really know what to say, but mumbled his thanks and thanked Dave for the opportunity that he'd given him and stood up and shook Dave's hand. Dave smiled and said what he always said, "You know what I'm going to say next?" Peter laughed and went back to work.

The week before Christmas, Peter was in town buying small gifts for his parents, when he bumped into Liam. They immediately made their way to the coffee bar and Peter asked Liam how he was and what he'd been up to. Liam seemed a little distant, but chatted about how his work was going and what he was learning. He didn't mention Sally at all, so Peter thought it best not to enquire. Peter could sense that all was not well and in his usual blunt direct manner asked Liam if everything was OK.

"Oh, yes sure, just been busy and I'm a little tired. This working lark isn't all it's cracked up to be is it? The pay is nice and will be much better once I'm qualified, but I'm just bloody knackered all the time and fed up of putting my hands down people's toilets."

Peter nodded. "Yeah, that can't be much fun—but there must be an interesting side?"

Liam nodded. "Yes there is—learning to solder and join pipework is difficult, but it's good fun and learning how a boiler works is also interesting, but it's just not lighting my fires if you know what I mean?"

"Yes—I couldn't think of doing a job that I didn't love. Why not look for something else?" Peter asked.

"No I couldn't—not when it's Dad's business. He's already spent loads on my training and he's always expected me to follow him into the job. I just hope it gets better. It's OK for you—you're going to be doing something that you've always wanted to do, so you'll be OK." Liam shook his head and looked forlorn. "There's some other stuff going on which I can't talk about but that's not helping either," he said.

Peter looked at his friend—he had known Liam for years and hated seeing him like this. They sat in silence for a while whilst they finished their coffee and, wishing each other a happy Christmas, parted company.

The day before Christmas Eve, Paul and Peter cycled through the bitter cold to the factory—for Peter it would be his last day. The morning was the usual mixture of making deliveries and helping some of the engineers and when it came to lunchtime, Paul took Peter to the locker room and they changed back into their civilian clothes. Peter asked why and Paul just smiled and, putting his finger across his lips to indicate silence, told Peter to follow him to the canteen.

They took their usual seats and to Peter's amazement, he saw that a full Christmas dinner had been laid on at the factory's expense. Wasting no time and with his usual voracious appetite, he quickly got stuck in. The usual factory chatter permeated the conversation and after everyone had finished, Dave stood up and cleared his throat.

"Right—Here we are at the end of another year and what a successful year it's been. We've grown the business by about twenty percent this year, which is unheard of and it's all thanks to all of you. You've all worked so hard this year and have put in lots of extra effort, for which I'm eternally grateful. In the New Year, we will be updating some of the older machinery and will be able to increase productivity further."

This bought a collective groan from everyone. "Shut up you lot," Dave laughed and continued, "We've also seen the introduction of computer control this year and as the technology improves, we'll be investing heavily in that. We also start the apprenticeship programme in January," at which somebody shouted, "More lambs to the slaughter," which bought a huge roar of laughter and Dave struggled to continue.

"Yes yes. I wanted to finish today by letting you know that we're in a strong financial position and continuing to grow. I want you all to enjoy the Xmas break, put your feet up and don't spend your bonuses all at once. I'll see you rested and raring to go in January."

Somebody shouted, "No you bloody won't," and this made Dave laugh.

"Correction—I'll see everyone except Tom—who's retiring and of course Peter, Paul's lad, who moves on to pastures new. Happy retirement Tom and thanks for your service and all the best to Peter and a very happy Christmas to you all. Now, if you've all finished, stop making the place look untidy and bugger off."

This bought a cheer and everyone clapped and then Paul and Peter made their way outside. Peter turned round and said, "I've not been here long but I'm going to miss this place."

Paul slapped him on the back and replied, "It's been good fun having you around and good to get you amongst people. You've coped better than I hoped." They unlocked their bikes and cycled slowly home.

Christmas quickly came and went in the usual blur of opening presents, dinner, visiting family and throughout all of it, Peter tried his best but still felt uncomfortable when around others or in big gatherings. He was focussed on starting in January and as the date came closer, he began to feel more and more nervous.

The thought of meeting new people, living in an unfamiliar environment and being on his own filled him with dread. He was so looking forward to commencing the flight training and the studying held no issues for him at all, but the transition into adulthood was not a prospect that he relished. He hoped that people would leave him to be himself and that he didn't say anything inappropriate or stupid. The only good thing about the whole Christmas period was the absence of Ben.

The day after Boxing day Peter found Annie in a whirl, wondering what clothes and essentials to pack for him. Peter read the paperwork from the airline and then sat down with his mum to make a plan. "It says that we're expected to dress smartly until we're issued with uniforms etc, so let's pack my slacks, a shirt for every day and a couple of ties, my sports jacket and my new shoes. For the evenings I'll just wear my jeans and a jumper," Peter suggested.

"Oh, I'll also need my alarm clock and my notebook, the flight training book, my binoculars just in case I get any free time and my riding gear. I want to get some running shoes in the sales as I won't be able to ride so I thought I could start running instead."

Annie looked at the list and agreed that the minimum would be best. Although the course didn't start until the second of January, the accommodation was available two days beforehand so everyone could settle in. Once Peter and Annie had agreed the final list, Peter suggested a quick trip into town to get the running shoes he was after and so after lunch, off they went.

On arriving, Peter made straight for the sports shop where he'd seen the new racing bikes a few months previously and between them they found a decent pair of running shoes which were reduced in the sales. Not satisfied, as soon as they left the shop, Annie took them both to the men's fashion shop and chose a couple of new shirts, some casual tops and some more slacks to complete the picture.

Satisfied, they made their way home where they found Paul waiting for them in the kitchen. "Hi—we've been shopping," Annie announced and they put bags down onto the table.

Paul surveyed the pile of bags and shook his head. "What have you been buying?" he asked.

"Well, I wanted some running shoes as I'm not taking my bike to London and then mum decided to have a splurge," Peter explained with a grin on his face.

"So I see," Paul muttered.

"Well, he'll need spare clothes as I won't be there to wash them," Annie explained.

Paul just gave her a tired look and said, "Come on, son, let's start getting stuff together."

That evening, Peter had arranged to meet with Alex and Anna and they met at Alex's house. There was the usual chatter about Christmas and then Peter told them that he'd seen Liam and that he didn't appear too happy. "Really?" Alex asked. "I haven't seen him lately. What's up?"

"Well, he seemed a bit disappointed with work—not what he was expecting I think and I don't think he's enjoying it at the moment. He also said something about some other stuff going on which he couldn't talk about so I have no idea what that's all about," Peter explained.

Both Alex and Anna shook their heads. "No idea," Alex said. "Is he OK though?" he asked with concern in his voice.

"I think so—probably just a bad week. Said he was fed up putting his hands down people's toilets so I can understand," Peter replied.

"Well, who wouldn't be?" Anna asked.

Peter smiled—"It'll be as bad for you guys when you're both doctors. You be putting your fingers everywhere," he laughed.

Both Alex and Anna laughed. "I hadn't thought of that too much," Anna responded with a disgusted look on her face.

"Well, you'll have to think of a specialty where you don't have to, won't you? I thought you wanted to do children's medicine? Won't they throw up all over you when they're ill?" Peter asked playfully.

"I hope not," Anna said quickly. "I really can't stand the smell."

Alex laughed out, saying, "Well, my dear, you'll have to get used to lots of nasty smells and substances in our chosen profession." Anna just shook her head and fell silent. "When do you leave for the big city?" Alex asked.

"We can get our rooms on the 31st, which will give us a couple of days to get to know each other," Peter said.

"Two days? Jeez—you need two years to come out of your shell," Alex joked, roaring with laughter.

"Thanks, buddy—with friends like you, what's a fellow supposed to do?" Peter asked, rolling his eyes.

"Will you be home at weekends?" Alex asked.

"I think for at the beginning, but the training schedule is a bit vague once we start the flying programme. I hope I can though—I'll need my washing doing," Peter joked which provoked a rebuke from Anna and the more she told Peter off, the more Alex and Peter laughed. Eventually it was time for Peter to leave. "Well you two, it may be a while before we see each other again. Hope your studies go well," Peter said, standing up.

Anna stood up quickly and came over and put her arms around Peter. "You take care," she said quietly. "You know where we are if you need us."

"I will, thanks," Peter replied, giving Anna a final squeeze.

Alex seized Peter's hand, shaking it warmly. "Best of luck, buddy—hope it all goes well. It'll be strange you not being around—we've been mates a long time."

Peter clasped his friend's hand saying, "Cheers, old mate. We have and hopefully we'll be friends forever. Time for the next adventure for both of us." Alex murmured his agreement and Peter finally left, walking home in the crisp winter moonlight.

The following day, Peter organised his clothing into piles and his other necessities into a small bag ready to be packed. Both his parents had decided to accompany him into London to check his room and see him settled. They had decided to go early to allow themselves time to explore the area and to find shops and placed to get food and other supplies.

For the next three days, Peter divided his time between reading, riding, practicing his cooking with his mother and helping Paul in the garage with the cycle frame. Paul had made packing strips which allowed the back wheel to contact the roller, but the roller still spun too freely, so Paul had devised a screw system with a felt pad to slow the roller down and to provide resistance.

Peter tried it out, but there was still more work to do and Paul was clearly enjoying finding solutions to the problems that they had encountered. He promised to have it finished by the time Peter came home in January and Peter was delighted with what his dad had managed to design and make.

22

The morning of the 31st dawned cold, grey but dry with little wind. Peter was out of bed very early, going over his packing for what seemed like the millionth time. He was nervous and felt pretty anxious but was excited at the same time. Both his parents appeared in the kitchen soon afterwards and Annie started making breakfast. "A cooked breakfast will set us up nicely boys," she said, laying bacon in the pan and cracking eggs.

Peter spread butter on bread and Paul was assigned to make drinks. Once they had eaten, they decided to set off for an early train and to get Peter into London in plenty of time. Peter went back upstairs and placed the piles of clothes in his case neatly, ticking each item off a checklist which he had written. Once packed, he sat on his bed and looked around him.

This was his room, his haven, his place of safety, his sanctuary. He loved it for its familiarity, it's warmth, it's security. He was about to lose that for the first time in his life and the prospect filled him with dread. He closed and locked the case and with a last wistful look around him, carried it downstairs. Paul was waiting in the kitchen and he asked Peter to sit down. Annie sat alongside him and Paul began to speak.

"Right, buddy—here we are. Today marks the proper start of your working life and you're taking the first steps towards your chosen career. I know that you struggle with people and crowds and that you get frustrated with those less capable as you, but you will have to accept these things as best you can. The best advice I can give you is to keep your head down, work hard as you've proved so many times that you can, try to keep to yourself and try not to say anything out of place. You're going to be fine and I've a feeling that you're going to do really well. Understand?"

Peter nodded in agreement. "Remember, we're always here for you, so if you need to speak to us, just call us anytime," Annie said, squeezing his arm.

"I will, mum, don't worry. I'm going to be OK—I know my issues and have in the past couple of years learned how to manage them a lot better, so I'll be alright. I'm nervous of course, but more about the course rather than anything else."

Annie nodded and smiled. "I know sweetie—it's just so strange for us that you're growing up and flying the nest."

Peter smiled. "That's an appropriate analogy for somebody about to become a pilot," Peter laughed and Paul and Annie both laughed as well.

"Right—let's get going," Paul said, standing up.

The train was almost empty and they had managed to catch a fast train with just two stops between Westlea and London Central and the arrived late morning. The Tube ride across to the airport took around thirty minutes and they were soon out of the station and following the map which the airline had provided to the crew house. After a short walk, they found a tall detached house in a leafy street with a small garden to the front.

Paul knocked on the door, which was opened quickly by the same lady that they had met at the interview. "Hello. Can I take your name please?" she asked.

"Peter Marham," Peter said quietly and the lady looked down a sheet of paper.

"Ahh, yes—here you are," she said smiling. "Come on in."

They all went inside and the lady continued, "I'm Mrs Johnson from personnel. We met at your interview. I take you are both Peter's parents?" she asked, looking at Annie and Paul.

"Yes," said Annie.

"You're the first to arrive, so you can actually have a choice of rooms—let's go and have a look shall we? You can leave your case here for the moment if you want."

They climbed the stairs and were shown around four bedrooms, two at the front and two at the back, with a further two on the second floor with an additional bathroom. Peter said that he'd prefer a room at the back away from the traffic on the first floor and his parents agreed. Mrs Johnson then took a name strip out of her bag and slid it into a holder on the door. "There we are—all yours," she smiled. "Let's show you around."

They toured the house, with the bathrooms, kitchen and common rooms being pointed out. It was a large old house with central heating and a payphone in the hallway. Annie seemed pleased with everything and Mrs Johnson suggested that Peter could go upstairs and unpack if he wished.

Once this was done to Peter's satisfaction, they went back downstairs and Paul asked Mrs Johnson the whereabouts of shops and local amenities. "Of course," she said and pulled some papers from her bag. There was a map of the local area with shops and launderette, bus stops and food outlets clearly marked. Paul thanked her and suggested that they take a walk to familiarise themselves and they left the house and walked down the street.

After an hour or so, Peter and his parents were satisfied that they had a good idea of where things were and they had purchased some basic food for Peter for the first week and they returned to the house. As they were let in, Mrs Johnson produced two keys on a keyring, which she asked Peter to sign for.

"The gold-coloured one is for the front door and the long silver one is your room key. Remember to lock your room door whenever you're out as the company won't accept responsibility for any losses," she advised. "You can put your food shopping in the kitchen—you'll see a cupboard with your room number on and anything you put in the fridge I suggest you put your name on"

She then gave Peter a timetable for the first week, all of which would be at the main airline office around the corner. Peter thanked her and he and his parents then went back up to his room and as they opened the door, they heard a knock at the front door. "One of your colleagues, I would imagine," Annie said, glancing over her shoulder.

Peter stood looking out of the window and Annie came to his side and took his arm. "You OK?" she asked.

Peter nodded. "It's just becoming real—is this really happening?" he asked.

"It sure is, son," Paul said from behind. "It all starts here."

Outside they could hear voices and footsteps on the stairs. "I think Mrs Johnson is going to have a busy day," Paul remarked.

Peter continued to look out of the window—he was wondering where the flightpath was into and out of the airport. He was hoping that it would be a great viewing spot. "Anything to see?" Paul asked.

"Not yet," Peter replied. "I was wondering about the flightpath, but it will probably be best if they don't fly past the window as it'll be far too distracting."

Paul nodded in agreement. "Yep—no time for spotting now—time to learn to fly them."

Peter smiled to himself, relishing the prospect. Annie quickly bought them both back to reality. "Shall we find somewhere to eat? I want to make sure Peter has a warm meal before we set off home," she said.

Paul and Peter nodded in agreement and Peter suggested finding the Bistro where they'd eaten with Captain Fosdyke as it couldn't be too far away. A quick look at the street map and there it was clearly marked. A quick walk in the setting winter sunshine found them taking their places at a table and studying the menu. They ordered and whilst they were waiting for the meals to arrive, Annie pulled out the papers given to her and started to leaf through.

"There's all the information you need about the crew house, useful phone numbers and details of the housekeeping. It says that the cleaner comes in once a week, cleans the common room, kitchen, bathrooms and your bedrooms, changing the bed. She doesn't do washing up or tidy your room, but you'll be OK with that I guess?" Annie asked.

Peter nodded. It was all becoming a bit too much to take in and he was starting to feel very uneasy. Annie continued with her reading, which was soon interrupted by the appearance of food. Annie continued to chatter throughout the meal, which Peter knew to be a sign of nervousness, but he knew to let her be. Paul ate quietly for the same reason.

Once they had finished, they made their way back to the house and Annie and Paul followed Peter upstairs. Peter had never been in this position before, but he felt like he needed to be on his own, so he quickly turned to his parents and said, "OK. Thanks for bringing me here and thanks for the meal and everything, but I think it's now time for me to have some time alone to try and get used to all this."

Paul nodded and came over and embraced Peter. "You're going to be fine—it'll take you a few days, but they will be busy days so you'll be OK," he said reassuringly. Peter nodded and smiled. Annie gave him a huge hug without saying anything and quickly turned away

Peter had spotted the tears in her eyes already. "I'll see you both out," Peter said and followed them both down the stairs where he held the front door open for them.

"Bye, son," Paul said stiffly, slapping Peter on the arm. Peter smiled.

Annie gave him another hug, whispering, "Goodbye—keep in touch. You're going to be OK," and she kissed him on the cheek. Peter again smiled and watched them both make their way slowly up the street before returning upstairs.

He closed the door behind him and looked around the room. It seemed so bare compared to his room at home, so alien. He sat down on the bed and started to rock backwards and forwards, closing his eyes as he did so. He could hear voices outside, but couldn't make out what was being said and soon the sounds diminished to a murmur. The room was becoming dark and Peter stayed rocking gently for quite some time.

Eventually, he was awoken from his reverie by a knock on the door. He got up and switched on the light before opening the door. Standing before him was a young man about the same age with dark skin and a huge smile. "Hi—I'm Sanjay—Sanj to my friends," he said, holding out his hand.

Peter thought for a moment before remembering his manners. "Hi. I'm Peter," he said, shaking the proffered hand.

"Good to meet you—I guess you're starting the same course on the second?" Sanjay asked.

"Well, I'm starting the pilot cadet course, so if that's the same as you, then yes," Peter replied. Sanjay nodded. "Come in," Peter said, opening the door wide. Sanjay did so and sat down on the chair by the window. Peter sat back down on the bed and Sanjay started to introduce himself properly.

"I live south of London with my parents and little sister. Always wanted to be a pilot and was really pleased to get in on my first attempt, as I was worried that my exam results weren't really the best. What about you?" he asked.

Peter couldn't think of what to say at first, but eventually muttered a few details about his home town and about his parents and brother. "Sorry—I'm always really shy at first with new people," he explained.

"No worries—I used to be but don't worry about it these days," Sanjay explained.

"I'm in the room opposite, so I guess we'll be getting to know each other pretty well," he went on. Peter again just nodded.

"Well, guess I'd better unpack—maybe catch you later," Sanjay said with a smile and he left the room.

Peter closed the door behind him, sitting back down on the bed. "Well, that's one of my colleagues—wonder who the others will be," he mused to himself. He stood up, drawing the curtains and unpacking his flight training book, was quickly immersed in its pages.

On the train home, Annie sat quietly holding Paul's hand. Her head was in a spin and she was so worried about how Peter would cope on his own. Eventually she spoke up. "How do you think he'll be?" she asked.

Paul squeezed her hand before replying, "I think he'll be just fine—you watch, he'll surprise us both. This is everything he's ever dreamed of and I'm sure he'll find a way to make it work," he said.

She nodded, murmuring her agreement. "I'm not worried about his course or how he'll do at that, it's him fitting in and coping with strangers and new situations," she said quietly, but Paul again reassured her.

"He's got to face it sometime and I think he'll be fine," he repeated, although inside he was concerned about exactly the same.

After a restless night in the unfamiliar bed, Peter was up very early and after freshening up, he made his way quietly to the kitchen to make coffee, sitting at the table to drink. After an hour or so, he heard movement and Sanjay appeared. "Good morning," he said.

"Morning," Peter replied.

"Good night?" Sanjay asked.

"No not really" Peter muttered.

"No nor me—strange bed, strange room. Guess we'll get used to it—gonna have to," Sanjay said cheerily, flicking the kettle on.

"Fancy a refill?"

"Mmm, yes please," Peter said, getting up and putting his mug on the worktop.

Sanjay poured the drinks and they both sat down. "Is it still just the two of us?" Peter asked.

"No—the rest of the guys on the course arrived—Tom and Arnold, who likes to be called Arnie, along with Paula and Mark who are on the top floor," Sanjay replied. "We'll see them soon I'm sure," he added. Peter nodded. "What are you up to today?" Sanjay asked.

"Oh, I'll probably carry on reading the training book—I've read the first six chapters as they suggested, but I want to be well up to speed," Peter replied. "I may go for a walk if it stops raining and I'll probably ring my parents to let them know I survived the first night," he joked.

Sanjay nodded his agreement. "Yeah—good plan. My first night away from home as well, so I'll do the same—my mum is such as worrier," he said.

"Yeah—mine too," Peter smiled. More footsteps on the stairs and the opening of the kitchen door announced the arrival of another of their colleagues—a slim young man who looked a few years older than Peter and Sanjay.

"Hi," he said.

"I'm Tom."

"I'm Sanjay—Sanj," Sanjay replied, shaking hands.

"Peter," Peter muttered, extending his hand.

"Pilot cadets?" Tom asked and they both nodded their heads in agreement. "Same here—guess we'll all be on the same course," Tom went on. "Third attempt for me. Already been rejected by two other airlines—if I hadn't made it this time, it was back to the bank job sadly. How many of us are there?" Tom asked.

"Six, I think," Sanjay replied. "Including a girl," he went on, impressed.

Tom looked at him for a few moments. "A girl? Training to fly jets? Whatever is the world coming to?" he said, shaking his head before heading over to the kettle.

Peter left him to make a drink and headed back upstairs. It was still quite early and the street outside was deserted. He'd heard no aircraft at all, so deduced that it was either because of the holiday or that the flightpath ran in a different direction. After a final look out of the window, he picked up his book and opened it at the marked page.

A knock on the door woke Peter. He must have fallen asleep and the book had fallen onto the floor. He got up and opened the door—it was Sanjay. "I'm going to get some fresh air—fancy a walk?" he asked.

Peter stood for a moment before nodding his head and turning he grabbed his coat and keys. Outside, the rain had stopped and the sky was clearing.

"Which way?" Sanjay asked.

"Let's find the airline offices so we know where we're headed tomorrow," Peter suggested and after consulting their map, they walked off in the general direction of the airport. As they walked, Sanjay kept up a ceaseless chatter.

"I'm so excited about tomorrow. Just think that this time next year we'll be qualified pilots and well on the way to joining the airline for real. That's so exciting. Tell me—have you always wanted to fly?" he asked.

Peter nodded, replying, "Yes—Dad took us to an air show when I was little and we got a quick pleasure flight. I was hooked immediately and I've wanted nothing else. I worked with Dad after I finished school—he's an engineer and ex-RAF and a really clever guy. I was nearly tempted by an offer of an engineering apprenticeship and the offer's still open, but it's this or nothing for me."

"Yeah, me too. My folks have been great letting me choose my own career and I'm very lucky and grateful for that. In Indian culture its traditional that your career is chosen for you and you're not allowed to defy your parents, but mine have been so cool about it. Dad runs an import business, but I'm glad I haven't been forced to work for him."

Peter was impressed—he found learning about different cultures enjoyable and they had done a lot of lessons on cultures at school. He began to like Sanjay and hoped that they would become friends.

At the end of the road, they both turned right and shortly arrived at International's offices. Peter looked at his watch. "Seven minutes," he said.

Sanjay nodded. "That's pretty easy," he said. "Let's see what's up this way," and he strode off.

Peter quickly caught up and they carried on for another mile before the unmistakable sound of jet engines caught their attention. Looking around as the sound got louder, Peter spotted the aircraft climbing away over the trees about half a mile ahead.

"There, Sanj," he said, pointing.

"Yep—got it," Sanjay replied.

Peter figured that it was too far away to be seen from the crew house, which was probably a good thing. At least he knew where to come during his free time. They walked for a short distance more before Sanjay said that he needed to pick up some supplies and they found the closest shop on their map. However, they found it closed.

"Of course—it's New Year's day," Peter exclaimed. "What did you need?"

"Oh, just some basic stuff—bread, tea that sort of thing."

"You can share mine until the shops are open if you want," Peter replied.

"You sure—thanks," Sanjay said, relieved.

They walked slowly back towards the house, with Sanjay still chattering non-stop. Peter just listened politely, trying to take some of it in, but not really making much sense of what he was talking about. When they arrived, they headed straight for the kitchen—Peter was hungry and needed his breakfast. In the

162

kitchen they found Tom talking to a short tubby lad with bright red cheeks, who looked up as they entered.

"I'm Arnold—or Arnie," he said.

Sanjay and Peter introduced themselves and Peter unlocked his cupboard and pulled out a load of bread. "Do you want toast, Sanj?" he asked.

"Please—you want coffee?" came the reply.

"Yes please," Peter replied and put slices of bread into the toaster. They both sat down to eat and Tom and Arnie began to chat about the year ahead.

"I thought there were six of us," Tom commented.

"There are but I haven't seen the other two yet," Sanjay answered.

Tom nodded. After they had eaten, Peter returned to his room to be on his own as usual, thinking that it was certainly going to be an interesting year.

Later in the afternoon, Peter tired of reading and decided to ring his parents, as he knew his mum would be worrying about him. He's been given a big bag of change by his dad for the phone, so he took it and descended the stairs and picked up the telephone, dialling his home number. He heard his mum's voice and pushed pennies into the slot.

"Mum—hi, it's Peter," he said.

"Hi, sweetie—everything OK?" Annie asked.

"Yes, good, thanks—I've been meeting the other guys staying here who are on the course and having a look around the area. How are you both?" Peter said.

"We're fine—who else is on the course?" Annie asked.

"Oh there's Sanjay, Tom and Arnold—he likes to be called Arnie and Paula and Mark who are on the top floor," Peter explained. "All on my course."

Annie sounded relieved. "Good," she said. "Have you eaten today?"

"Yes, of course—you know my usual routine," Peter replied, laughing.

"I certainly do," Annie replied. "What time do you start in the morning?"

"We have to be there for half past eight, so I'll leave here at about a quarter past as it's only a seven minute walk," Peter explained.

"Good," came the reply. "Don't be late whatever you do"

"I won't, mum, don't worry. Anyway, I'm going to go now and see what we're doing about our evening meal. Speak to you tomorrow."

"OK," Annie replied. "Speak tomorrow—love you."

Peter smiled and put the phone down—his mum was always the same.

23

Peter spent a sleepless and restless night. The coming induction day was playing on his mind, as was the thought of being with a load of strangers in an unfamiliar setting. He was up very early and managed to get to the bathroom for a shave and shower before anybody else had stirred.

Once finished, he dressed in his casual clothes from the day before making himself coffee and some toast. He sat at the table staring into his cup for what seemed ages, thinking and re-thinking his strategy for the day. *Stay towards the back of the room—don't say anything stupid or inappropriate—try and stay below the radar* went through his mind again and again. He was nervous and it was beginning to show.

The appearance of Arnie shook him into action. "Morning," Arnie grunted, making a bee line for the kettle.

"Morning," Peter mumbled in reply before standing up and heading for the stairs.

"What time shall we set off," Arnie asked, just as Peter was leaving the room.

"I walked it with Sanj yesterday and it takes seven minutes, so I was thinking of setting off at about ten past eight to give myself plenty of time to get there for half-past," Peter replied.

Arnie nodded. "See you down here at ten past," he said, returning to the business of his breakfast.

Peter nodded and went back upstairs to his room to change.

Peter sat on the bed, eyes closed and rocked gently, knowing it would calm him and kept a close eye on the time. Eventually, he stood up to change into his day clothes, quickly donning his smart slacks, a shirt and the blue tie and his new shoes. Satisfied, he made his way downstairs where he found two other people that he hadn't met before.

One of them said, "Hi—I'm Mark and this is Paula—we're up on the top floor. Guess you must be on the same course?"

"Yes—I'm Peter," Peter replied quietly, shaking hands.

"Isn't this exciting?" Paula said in a hurry. "I wonder what today is all about?"

"Induction and admin is my guess," Mark said with a sigh.

Soon they were joined by the others and they set off en masse to the offices, arriving just before half-past. Mark led the way and was first through the door. Inside they found a large notice welcoming the 1970 intake and the receptionist asked them all to take a seat. Very shortly, they were joined by Mrs Johnson, who motioned them to follow her. She led them down a corridor and into a medium sized room with six chairs arranged around a long desk and a single chair in front of a flipchart.

Peter made straight for the chair furthest away and quickly sat down, his heart pounding.

"Good morning and welcome," Mrs Johnson began. "You're our first intake, not only of the year, but of this new decade, which is exciting for us all. Today will be a bit tedious I'm afraid and we're going to start with introductions and filling in some forms. Have you all met at the crew house?" she asked.

There was a quiet murmur of agreement. "Good—that saves me the trouble. I'll be handing out your name badges in a moment—these must be worn at all times. Now then, in front of you, you'll find some forms to complete for us in personnel—usual stuff, name, address, next-of-kin etc. Once we're done with that, I've a quick presentation to go through—you can start on the forms now if you wish."

Peter picked up the first piece of paper and began filling in his details. He quickly finished and moved on to the second form, getting the details of his savings account from the book in his inside pocket. The others were busy doing the same and shortly everyone seemed to have finished. "All done? Good—let me introduce you to International Airlines."

Mrs Johnson then started telling them all about the history of the airline, drawing numbers and symbols on the chart. Peter paid scant attention as he'd made himself familiar with all this for the interview, but he listened politely. When the presentation was finished, Mrs Johnson then took them all for a quick tour of the ground floor of the offices, showing them where the rest rooms, the classrooms and most importantly, the staff restaurant were located.

Satisfied, she led them back to the presentation room and they were shown where to make coffee and tea and they sat down to relax. Peter chose this time to stand by the window, alone with his thoughts and coffee. Soon, the session continued.

"OK group, you're now going to have a talk with one of our flight instructors about the course and timetable. I'll go and tell Captain Woods that we're ready," and she disappeared from the room, returning a short time later with a slim middle-aged man in uniform. Peter sat forwards—this what he'd waited so long for and he gave it his full attention.

"This is Captain Woods, one of the instructors—I'll hand over to him," Mrs Johnson said and she sat down.

"Thanks Sandra," the man said, turning to the group. "Well, welcome all. Great to see bright eager faces. I'm Paul Woods, one of the instructors on this first level of the course and along with my two colleagues, we'll be taking you through the initial stages of training. We split you into three groups and there are three training aircraft, so you'll buddy up for each lesson. The aircraft are four-seaters, so you'll do each exercise with one in the front flying and one in the back observing. You'll then swap over to repeat the exercise.

"That way you'll get double the exposure to the instruction given. We'll swap you around on a daily basis so you're not always flying with the same co-student. The training airfield is about an hour from here and a minibus will take you and bring you back to here every day. On days where the weather dictates that we can't fly, we'll cover ground school to help you study for the exams, of which there are fourteen subjects.

"We expect you to complete both the exams and the basic flying within the first six months of training, so it's going to be pretty intense, with lots of study in the crew house in the evenings for the exams—so no partying every night," he laughed.

Peter was listening with all his soul, absorbing every word, every syllable as the instructor set out the course in detail and each of the flying exercises was explained. The instructor continued for some time, mapping out the rest of the course and ended with a warning.

"You get 3 attempts at each exam—pass mark is seventy-five percent. Fail on the third attempt and you're out. Same goes with the flying—if we feel you're not making the required progress we'll hand you over to a senior instructor. If he passes you, training continues, but if his opinion is that you're not making the grade, then training ceases. That may sound pretty tough, but as a company we're investing a huge amount of money in your training and expect you to put in one

166

hundred percent, but some people just don't make the grade which is why we have this policy. Any questions?"

The room remained silent. "Good—I think it must be lunchtime, Sandra—what do you think?"

Mrs Johnson stood up, thanking Captain Woods and told everyone to follow her and they were soon in the staff restaurant, where Peter decided to order a hot meal as there may not be time for cooking this evening. His colleagues each did the same and they sat down together to eat.

Tom was first to speak. "That sounds pretty hard going—what do you think guys?"

There was a general nodding of heads, but Peter stayed quiet. He didn't think it sounded too intense at all—provided that the flying exercises progressed normally. He was just itching to get started.

Paula spoke up quietly, "Six months. That seems an awfully short time to complete both the exams and the initial flying. I was hoping to be able to go home at weekends and maybe go into London to see a movie of do some shopping. What do you think?"

Arnie agreed, but Tom seemed to be anxious about it all. Peter sat quietly listening, until Sanj asked him what he thought. Peter sat thinking to himself and then said, "I don't think it's a problem. We're all in the same boat, so we could all study the same exam subject at the same time together in the evenings, helping each other out. Six brains must be better than one. As for the flying, it's down to each of us, but having read through the training book, it all seems pretty straightforward."

"Great idea," Sanj said and the group nodded their agreement. Peter went on, "It's how I studied with my buddies for my GCE's and it all worked out fine, so guess we'll be working together in more ways than one."

"Sounds like a good plan," Mark added, finishing his lunch. Shortly, they were called back to the presentation room.

"OK everyone, more boring stuff I'm afraid," Mrs Johnson began. "We're going to get you all measured for your dress uniforms and then we'll go to stores to get your training uniforms. Shall we start ladies first? Paula, if you'd like to follow me—the rest of you can read or talk amongst yourselves," and she got up and led Paula out of the room.

Soon everyone was chatting away furiously—with the exception of Peter who chose to read a brochure he'd found about the airline and it's various destinations. Paula returned after about twenty minutes and then the males were led away in turn—Peter being last. In an adjoining room there was a man with a tape measure around his neck and a clipboard.

He looked at Peter. "Gosh—you're tall," he quipped and asked Peter his name. The man then proceeded to measure just about everything he could think of in Peter's opinion and finally finished. "I'll add some extra in the length of the leg just in case you're not finished growing yet," he said, winking at Peter.

Peter felt himself blush and he then returned to the presentation room. Mrs Johnson summoned the group telling them to follow her. In her hand she carried copies of the tailor's measurements and they made their way down into what Peter assumed was the basement of the building. They came to a plain wooden door and went inside. There were racks of boxes and garment hanging rails everywhere and a small man appeared.

"Hello, John—here's our first intake. We're here to collect training uniforms," said Mrs Johnson, handing over the papers she'd been carrying.

The man nodded silently and scurried away. After what seemed an age, he returned with a box laden with clothing. "The first one on the list," he said and disappeared.

Mrs Johnson looked at the name on the sheet of paper and called Paula over. "Here we are, my dear," she said, giving Paula the box.

Paula's eyes nearly popped out of her head when she lifted the box up. "Wow—that's heavy," she said.

"Yes—but don't worry. We don't expect you to carry it back to the house. We'll get a driver to put all the boxes in a van and he'll deliver them for you all," Mrs Johnson explained.

Eventually, there were six boxes and they carried them back upstairs, where Mrs Johnson took one of the boxes and started to explain the contents. "Right— you should all have five white shirts, two pairs of black trousers, a black jumper, a jacket, a company tie and a pair of epaulettes. You will wear a clean shirt with your epaulettes every day and keep you uniform clean and pressed. There is an iron at the house. You're responsible—or your mothers are—for washing and ironing your shirts. Any losses or damage must be reported to me. Understood?"

Everyone nodded their heads. "Good. Tomorrow, we're taking you out to the training airfield to look at the aircraft and facilities and you'll be issued course books for the first exam. The minibus leaves from here at eight forty-five, so be on time. Any questions?"

Again, there was silence. "OK—you may leave and the driver will be at the house at about five o'clock. See you all tomorrow." With that, they all stood up and trooped out of the door in single file.

As soon as they were outside, they began to chatter intensely. "I'm exhausted," said Tom.

"Me too," Sanj agreed.

"There seems to be a lot to remember," Mark commented and Paula added "There is—and don't all think that I'll be ironing your shirts just because I'm female, because you can get lost," and everyone laughed.

They walked slowly in the fading light, with Peter following the group a short distance behind. He felt relieved that this first day—the first of many he hoped—was over. He planned to call his mother when they got back to the house as he knew that she would be worrying about him. After the call, Peter wanted to go for a run to continue with his fitness programme—he feared that he may get behind with all that was expected of them and he didn't want that to happen.

24

The following morning, they were all gathered in the reception area waiting for the minibus. Peter's new uniform shirt was itchy with newness and he felt self-conscious and awkward. Chatter was being kept to a minimum and he sensed that everyone was as nervous as he was. After a short wait, the minibus appeared and the receptionist motioned them to go outside—Paula led them out in single file and they clambered on board with Peter going to the very back before sitting down.

There was plenty of space and everyone found a seat on their own.

"Is this everyone?" the driver asked and following confirmation, he put the bus into gear and they set off. They drove through a maze of streets, eventually coming to a main road which, Peter guessed from the position of the sun, was heading west. Slowly the silence gave way to excited chatter with everyone pointing out features on the journey and they gradually left the suburbs for open country.

Peter sat silently watching the countryside pass by and kept looking at his watch to time the journey—he felt like he was back on a geography field trip from school. After about an hour, they turned off the main road onto a country road surrounded by fields and trees and quickly came to a large steel gate which swung open automatically. There were some buildings and a large shed, which made it obvious that it was an ex-RAF airfield and the large shed Peter guessed was the hangar where the aircraft were stored.

The bus came to a halt and the driver opened the door. "Here we are, boys and girls—welcome to Longley Airfield."

They jumped off the bus to see a man walking towards them. "Good morning—follow me," he said and turned back towards a long single-storey building.

Once inside, they were taken straight to a classroom and were told to sit down. The man cleared his throat to speak. "Good morning, once again. I'm

Brian Jackson, one of the instructors—Brian to you. You've already met my colleague Paul Woods and the other instructor Mike Thompson will be joining us after this quick session. Firstly, just to make our lives easier, there is a piece of paper and a pen on your desks—please fold it into a triangle like this and write your name on and place it on the front of your desk so we know who we're speaking to until we learn your names."

They all did as they were shown and the instructor continued, "OK—my first task is to show you around so you know where everything is, so please follow me."

There followed a quick tour of the building, the student kitchen, the library and finally they were taken outside and over to the hangar. Brian continued, "Let me introduce you to three very special ladies—these are our training aircraft. They are Piper PA-28's and are what we use for the basic and intermediate training. You'll get to know them well," and with that, he opened the door of the nearest aircraft and invited them all to sit inside in turn and get a feel of the cockpit.

Once they had all sat inside the aircraft, Brian led them back to the classroom and they all took their seats. Shortly, they were joined by Captain Woods and another man. "Right—you've already met Paul Woods and this is our third instructor Mike Thompson. We're all going to get to know each other very well over the next few months I would imagine. We're happy to use first names as we like the informality which we think helps you relax a bit more in the air."

Brian went on before asking each of the group to introduce themselves and say why they chose an aviation career. Peter immediately froze—he hated this kind of thing and usually just mumbled a few words. One by one the group spoke and it quickly came to Peter's turn. "Err—I'm Peter Marham and I've wanted to be a pilot ever since I was taken to an air show and had a short flight as a kid," he stumbled.

He hoped that he wouldn't be asked questions and to his relief the instructors just nodded and moved onto Sanjay.

Once the introductions had been done, Brian moved on to outlining the training programme in detail, handing out copies of the timetables—one for the flying programme and one for the ground school study and exams. Peter gave them a cursory glance, knowing he could study them in detail later on the journey back to the crew house. Whilst Brian was speaking Peter noticed both Mike and

Paul looking intently out of the window before Mike left the room, returning a short while later and having a quiet word with both other instructors.

"OK—it would appear that mother nature in her wisdom has cancelled flying this morning, so let's go next door and get the first of the books and we'll start some ground school," Brian said before leading them to the library. "There are six copies of each study book—take one each and I'll give you a notepad," Brian said and they were soon back at their seats.

"All ready?" he continued. "Good—let's start at page one," and he began reading from the book and writing on the board. Peter found himself back in familiar territory—*Just like being back at school but in a different uniform*, he thought.

The morning wore on with Brian leading them through the first few chapters of Air Law—which Peter was well acquainted with from his pre-interview reading. The morning soon gave way to lunchtime and they found sandwiches and drinks in the kitchen provided for them and then they were into the afternoon session. Outside, it had begun to rain heavily and flying was cancelled for the rest of the day. Mike took them for the first afternoon session, with Paul finishing off the day at about four-thirty.

"OK—tomorrow looks decent," he said. "So this is the flying programme for the morning," and he pinned a sheet of paper to the noticeboard. "You'll each be flying two lessons tomorrow, so read exercises four and six in your books. Paula you'll be with Tom and me. Arnie with Mark with Brian and Sanjay and Peter with Mike in the morning. We'll swap you around for the afternoon— understood?"

They all nodded in agreement and they then heard a car horn. Paul swung around to the window—"The bus is here, so thank you and see you tomorrow," he said and they all ran outside towards the open door on the bus through the driving rain.

The mood was subdued at the crew house that evening. The group gathered around the table in the common room and discussed the day's events. Tom seemed to be pretty daunted by the mountain that they had to climb. "14 exams in 6 months—that's less than two weeks per subject and they all look pretty intense and then there's the flying on top. I think I'll be staying here every weekend just to get the study done" he said morosely. There was a general murmur of agreement. "I'm not a natural academic," Paula said.

"Nor me," Arnie added. "Not in the slightest."

Mark and Sanjay kept quiet, but Peter could tell that they were in general agreement. Peter stayed quiet and listened to the continuing discussion, but finally broke his silence. "I agree that it's a lot to expect, but we've just got to make sure that we support each other and get through. Why don't we have a look at the Law books from today, seeing as the exam is scheduled for the end of next week?"

Slowly, his colleagues got themselves together and Peter began. "Why don't we read and make notes for the first six chapters or so and then discuss it to make sure we all understand?"

Everyone nodded and they began to read and make notes. As the evening wore on it became a general discussion rather than formal learning and Peter did his best to guide everyone along.

He'd read the exact same book for his pre-interview reading and had found it rather dull but easy to extract the facts from and felt in a good position to help. As the evening wore on, the mood began to lift and by the time people began to think of getting to bed they had covered nearly half of the book.

The following morning dawned bright and cold and the group were soon at the offices awaiting the bus. Once on board, Peter reread the day's flying exercises and to his surprise saw that Tom had fallen asleep. This caused some amusement amongst the rest of them, so much so that they waited until they were pulling through the gate before shaking him into wakefulness. The mood was one of excitement at the forthcoming flying—and they were quickly briefed and out at the aircraft.

Brian spoke to the group before they started. "OK, group, first flying lessons today. Jim our ground handler has already pulled the aircraft out and fuelled them. You'll work with him closely regarding fuelling and checking oil etc. It looks like a great day, so let's get up into the sky."

Peter and Sanjay quickly found Mike, their instructor for the day and made their way towards the waiting plane. "Who wants to go first?" he asked.

They both shrugged. "OK—Sanj, you jump into the left seat, Peter you get in the back. You'll find headsets already plugged in. Put your seatbelts on and I'll explain how we run through the checklist before we start—OK?"

They both did as instructed and Mike sat down in the right hand seat, ran through the checklist and within a few short minutes, they were lining up on the grass runway. "All set?" Mike asked.

Peter said yes and heard Sanj say the same through the earphones. "OK—off we go," and Mike pushed the throttle forwards. Soon, they were climbing up towards the high thin cloud. Peter sat on the right so that he could look across and watch Sanjay's movements and try to learn by observation, whilst listening to what Mike had to say.

It all seemed to make sense and in a short hour, they were descending back towards the field, where Mike settled the aircraft onto the grass. Once they had come to a halt and the engine had been shut down, Mike debriefed Sanjay and then he and Peter exchanged places. Peter was nervous but so excited—finally his dream was coming true.

Up into the sky once more and under Mike's expert tuition, Peter soon got the hang of the basic controls. In no time they were again descending to a smooth landing and after a quick chat, Mike announced that it was lunchtime.

The afternoon session followed the same pattern—briefing for the lesson and then a flight each to fly the exercise. When they landed after Peter's afternoon session, he was surprised at how tired he felt—it had been a day of intense concentration, but so enjoyable.

Before they finished, all the group were shown how to complete their flying logbooks and were assigned partners for the following day. Peter would be flying with Paula and their instructor would be Brian. The bus ride home was a lively discussion of the day's flying and the exercises for tomorrow. Peter desperately wanted to go for a run when they got back, get something to eat and then to study some more.

Over the next few days, Peter began to establish a routine of studying the flight exercise on the bus going to the airfield, studying the second lesson at lunchtime and reading the Law book on the way home to the crew house. He then changed and went for a run, followed by his evening meal—usually a take away or something from the local shop—and more study with the group before bedtime.

Friday came around quickly enough and after getting back to the house following the afternoon session, he was eager to grab his bag and make for the tube and commence the journey home. The tube and train to Westlea were packed with commuters, but Peter found a seat and tried his best to continue reading, but he was too excited to see his parents to take anything in. When the train pulled into Westlea station, he could see his mother anxiously waiting behind the ticket barrier.

As soon as she saw Peter, she ran towards him, throwing her arms around him and kissing him on the cheek. "How are you, sweetie—have you had a good week?" she asked breathlessly.

"I'm good, thanks and it's been a great week. I'll tell you all about it when we get home." They walked slowly towards the bus stop and Annie linked her arm through his, desperate not to let go.

The bus ride home seemed to take ages, but finally they were back indoors. Paul quickly came to meet them, hugging Peter quickly and then both parents began firing questions at him. Peter smiled and was then forced to say, "OK—one at a time please."

This made both Annie and Paul laugh and they settled down and Peter began to recount the first week, going into every detail and nuance of the flying and studying. "Wow—that's pretty intense," Paul remarked.

"Yes—it's been a busy week," Peter replied before enquiring about the evening meal.

"Ready shortly," Annie said, her eyes never leaving Peter and they were shining with pride. "Have you bought me any washing home?" Annie asked and Peter replied to the affirmative.

"Yes—and there are five new uniform shirts to wash and iron before Sunday afternoon if that's OK," he said. Annie smiled her agreement and was soon busying herself in the kitchen with the evening meal.

After dinner, Paul asked Peter what his plans were for the weekend. "Lots of study, I'm afraid," Peter replied, adding, "Air Law—and the exam is on Friday."

"Crikey, that's quick," Paul said, genuinely surprised.

"We have fourteen subjects to study for and they want the exams all passed within six months, along with the basic flying course," Peter explained.

Paul nodded. "Lots to do then?" he asked.

"Yeah—lots," Peter said quietly. "They're certainly going to work us hard."

Annie came in and sat down next to Peter. "What are your fellow students like?" she asked.

Peter thought for a moment and then began to tell them both about each of his colleagues. "There are five others—Sanjay or Sanj as we call him, Tom, Paula who is the first female cadet in the airline, Mark and Arnie. We're all about the same age with the exception of Tom, who is in his early twenties. It's his third attempt at getting on the course so he's pretty pleased to be there. Sanj is from an Indian family from south of London and his parents have allowed him to have his own career choice which is pretty unusual in their culture."

Paul and Annie listened with interest—they were still anxious about Peter fitting in and not feeling too isolated. "Well, they sound like a super bunch," Annie said and Peter agreed.

He wasn't sure about Tom, but decided to see how things panned out. Annie went on, "Tell me about the instructors—are they nice people?"

"Well," Peter started. "There's three flying instructors—Brian, Paul and Mike. They're all very experienced and easy to get on with so far. We swap around so we each fly with all of them and we pair up so we do a lesson in the left seat flying the aircraft with a co-student in the back and after the lesson we swap over and repeat the same lesson and that way we get a double shot at it.

"We get jumbled up each day so that we're not always flying with the same people which is great and in the evening we tend to get together and discuss the day's lessons and do some ground school study. So far it's been great fun."

"Have you had any problems fitting in?" Annie asked anxiously.

"No not really," Peter replied—he'd been half expecting the question. "Just keeping myself to myself and remembering to say nothing inappropriate."

Annie smiled answering "Good" very quietly, adding, "I hope that you're making friends."

"Yes, I think so—especially with Sanj—we get on really well," Peter replied.

A short while later, Peter made his way upstairs to his room. A quick look around showed that everything was in its place—it was good to be back in familiar territory, back in his own room with its familiar sights, smells and sounds—the loose floorboard by the window creaking a friendly greeting whenever Peter stood on it.

This was his safe haven—his happy place. He sat down on the bed and opened the law book at the marked page, but shortly found that his eyes were becoming heavy and the words were starting to swim around the page, so he closed the book and went to bed. He was asleep in an instant.

25

The following morning Peter was up early and was soon engrossed in his book and making notes. He stayed in his room, not wanting to wake his parents and he'd finished two further chapters before he heard movement. He made his way downstairs and saw Annie filling the kettle and he sat down at the table gratefully accepting the cup of coffee she placed in front of him.

"How are you today?" she asked.

"Mmm, OK, thanks—nice to be back in my own bed," Peter replied with a chuckle.

Annie smiled and sat beside him. "We've been very worried about you this week," Annie said, adding, "Just want you to settle into your new routine and enjoy the course."

"I know," Peter said. "But honestly you don't need to worry. I'm OK and I'm enjoying spreading my wings if you'll pardon the pun."

Annie laughed and said quickly, "Oh you're certainly spreading your wings. I can't believe that my boy—my little boy—has flown an aeroplane. Amazing. Do you always fly with the instructor?"

Peter thought for a moment as he knew that his mum would be anxious if she knew that one day he'd be flying on his own. "At this stage yes, but one day we have to fly what we call the first solo, which is a quick circuit of the airfield on your own. Don't worry though—that's ages off and we won't be sent on our own until we're ready."

He decided that he'd not tell Annie beforehand that he was coming to that stage. Afterwards would be best. Annie nodded with a frown on her face. "What are your plans for today?" she asked.

"Well, with the awful weather outside, I guess I'll be studying for most of the day. I may give Alex and Liam a ring if that's OK?"

"Yes, of course," Annie replied. "It's important to stay in touch with your friends."

Peter was quickly back in his room studying and a short while later Paul popped his head around his bedroom door. "Morning son," he said.

"Morning Dad—you OK?" Peter asked.

"Yes, good, thanks—what are you up to," Paul enquired, coming into the room.

Peter held the book up—"Studying," he laughed. "What else?"

Paul nodded, saying, "I guess with this fog we won't be going over to the airport to watch the aircraft?"

Peter smiled. "No—too much to do."

"Well, I'll leave you to it—I'll be in the garage later on if you fancy a break. I finished the bike frame by the way—it works a treat," Paul said and he turned to leave.

"Dad—before you go, can I ask you something? Do you think I'll make it through this course?" Peter asked anxiously.

Paul sat down on the bed, looking Peter straight in the eyes. "Yes, I do— you've a proven track record for studying and a good work ethic which I've seen first-hand. There is absolutely no reason that I can think of why you shouldn't make it through. I'm sure that you'll pick up the flying OK as you can turn your hand to most things and academically you should do well with the exams. Just remember what I've said before—with hard work and determination, you can achieve anything. Why?" Paul asked.

"Well, I've never really fitted in and you know I find groups of people and new situations difficult, but I really really want this," Peter said quietly.

Paul moved closer and put his arm around Peter's shoulders. "I know you do. You seem to have made a good start and the older you get the better you'll fit in and adapt I'm sure," Paul said reassuringly.

Peter slowly nodded his head. "Thanks, Dad, for everything. Best get some studying done," Peter said brightly and Paul stood up and left him alone.

After a welcome lunch, for which Annie had made hot sandwiches, Peter decided to join Paul in the garage for an hour. Paul had started reassembling the gearbox for the motorbike and he showed Peter how to put the various components together. Peter enjoyed getting his hands working on something mechanical and it reminded him of the pre-flight checks on the aircraft. After a short while, the gearbox was essentially complete.

"That's just about ready to go back into the frame when it comes back from the painters," Paul said. Peter nodded. "What are you going to do with it when you've finished it?" he asked.

Paul smiled. "Ride it, of course!" he said laughing.

Peter smiled again. "You should take it to shows—it'll look like a new bike when it's finished," he suggested.

"Yes—good idea. I might just do that," Paul said, adding, "but I'll not get your mother on the back—she hates bikes. Says they mess her hair up," Paul said with another laugh.

Peter laughed along with his dad. "Well, you can take me out on it if you want," he said. He rather fancied the idea of having a bike or his own car once he'd qualified.

"Sure—we can do that," Paul said.

They made their way back towards the house and Annie was pegging Peter's washing onto the washing line. The fog had finally cleared and there was now a stiff breeze and it was freezing cold. "There—all done," Annie said to Peter.

"Thanks, mum," he replied, hurrying inside. They quickly closed the back door and Peter went to wash his hands. "Can I ring Alex?" he asked.

"Yes, of course," Annie replied and Peter picked up the phone, dialling Alex's number.

After a short wait, Alex answered. "Hi, buddy—it's Peter," Peter said.

"Hi—how are you? How was your first week?" Alex replied.

"Great, thanks. Lots of studying to do and been doing some flying as well," and Peter went on to tell Alex about his first week and the adventures he'd been having. Alex listened intently, asking the occasional question, but happy to let Peter speak. He knew how much Peter could talk about his favourite subjects and he was happy to hear how Peter was getting on.

After some time, Peter asked Alex how he was getting on with his A Levels. "OK, I guess—early days, but doing alright. Just a bit boring—nothing as exciting as flying planes," Alex replied. They chatted for a while longer and arranged to meet up the following weekend.

Peter returned to his book and read non-stop until dinner time, after which he stayed downstairs with his parents. He was enjoying being home and was happy to be with them just to talk and catch up. "What time will you be setting off tomorrow?" Annie asked.

"I thought I'd get the 3 PM train, which will get me back to the house by about five-thirty," Peter replied.

"OK, I'll make dinner for early afternoon so you have a hot meal before you go," Annie replied. Peter nodded his thanks. "I'll get your uniform shirts ironed in the morning as well," she went on. "Did I tell you that we had a letter from Ben?" she asked.

Peter shook his head, disinterested. "Yes, he was telling us how warm it has been and that he's enjoying himself. He also said that he was thinking of starting some kind of business outside of the army, but he never said what it was. I didn't know that you could do that," she said.

"Oh, we had a bloke in our squadron who did something similar," Paul said. "Except, his idea of a business was buying stuff in the local shops and selling it to his squadron buddies at double the price. He nearly got kicked out for that," he added, shaking his head.

Annie smiled, saying, "Well, I'm sure whatever Ben's idea is it won't be anything like that."

Paul smiled to himself—*I wouldn't put it past him*, he thought, but decided not to say anything. Peter sat quietly in thought, wondering what on earth Ben was up to. He never thought Ben would have any kind of business acumen, so it was all somewhat of a mystery.

The following morning Peter returned to his law studies. He had just about finished the book and at the back of the book he found some practice tests and answers. He decided to sit a couple of these under self-imposed exam conditions just to see how he was getting on. He went through the first test within the time allowed and then he turned to the very back of the book for the answers. He'd scored ninety-two percent. *Not too bad*, he thought and sat down to complete the second one.

This time he scored ninety-three percent. He was happy with those results, so decided to pack up for the day and spend the rest of his time with his parents. Downstairs he found Annie just finishing the ironing and she'd folded his uniform shirts carefully. "Pack them at the top of your bag," she said, handing them over.

"Thanks, mum," Peter replied and he did as she suggested. "Can I help with dinner?" Peter asked and Annie asked him to begin preparing vegetables. Peter felt so good with the familiarity of the routine, which was something he'd missed over the previous week.

Paul came in from the garage and was assigned to lay the table—something he always did with great care and attention to detail. "It's the engineer in him," Annie whispered and this made Peter smile.

He knew where he got his love of routine and detail from and he hoped that it would stand him in good stead on the flightdeck. A short time later, Annie called them both in for dinner and Peter wolfed down every morsel—he'd missed his mum's cooking. A warm sausage roll from the corner shop just didn't fill him up in the same way.

Soon, it was time to leave and both Annie and Paul decided to accompany Peter to the station. Annie sat next to Peter on the bus, chatting non-stop, which Peter knew meant that she was nervous. When they arrived, the train was standing at the platform and Peter decided that as he didn't like saying goodbye, he'd just go straight for the train.

He gave Annie a quick cuddle and hugged Paul quickly before turning away. "See you next weekend," he shouted over his shoulder.

Both his parents waved as he got into a carriage. Peter waved back and settled down next to the window. He was once again excited at the prospect of the coming week. Annie watched tearfully as Peter closed the door and disappeared from view. Paul put his arm around her and squeezed her shoulders. "He'll be fine," he said quietly.

"I know—but you know how I worry," Annie replied.

"I know—but look at him—he's done really well in this first week, so I don't think that we've anything to worry about," Paul said reassuringly. Annie nodded, keeping her darkest fears to herself.

Within a short while, Peter arrived back at the crew house, where he found Paula and Arnie in the living room with their books and notepads. He quickly said hello and went upstairs to unpack and to hang his uniform shirts up. A few moments later there was a knock on the door. Paula was standing outside. "Hi," she said quietly.

"Have you a few minutes to spare? We've been on with this air law all weekend and there are parts that are making no sense whatsoever. Wondered if you could help?"

"Yes of course—I'll get my notes," Peter replied and shortly followed Paula down the stairs. Peter sat down, asking, "What's confusing you both?"

"It's these International Conventions they just don't make sense," Arnie said.

Peter nodded. "Yes—they are a bit confusing. I made a chart in my notes—you can see here how they connect each convention to each subject," Peter said, showing them both his notes and the chart he'd drawn.

Both Paula and Arnie leaned forwards and looked at Peter's chart. Slowly the frowns on their faces eased and Arnie suddenly said, "Brilliant. Can I copy that?"

"Of course," Peter replied. "Happy to help."

"Have you finished the book?" Paula asked.

"Yes, just about. Did you know that there are practice tests at the back of the book? I've done a couple of them and did OK. Do you want to try one?" Peter asked them both.

Both Paula and Arnie looked at each other and nodded in unison. Peter smiled and got them both to sit the first test. At the end of the allotted time he called, "Time's up" and told them to swap over their answers and to mark each other's paper. Both scored mid-eighties percent and seemed happy.

"I'm sure we can improve that before Friday," Peter said and both of them thanked Peter for his help.

"Do you find the studying easy?" Paula asked.

Peter thought for a moment. "Not easy, but it's all about having a methodical approach to each subject. I make my notes by writing down the keywords in each chapter and they serve as a reminder for me," he explained.

Paula nodded slowly. "I was never good at studying and I know that it's the exams that I'll fail on," she said.

"No, you won't—we'll see to that," Peter said. "All of us can work together—we'll support each other," he said with a determined closing of his notebook.

She looked up at Peter. "Thank you," she said, squeezing his arm lightly. Peter felt himself blushing and he turned and went back upstairs to his room.

Monday morning and Peter was up early as usual. Outside he could see that it was dark and blustery, but dry. He'd finished breakfast and was ready for the bus before his colleagues appeared. Eventually, they were all sat around waiting and Peter was becoming more impatient—he was eager to get started.

"Doesn't look very nice today," Tom said gloomily.

"It may be OK at the airfield," Sanj answered and Peter agreed. Just then, they heard the bus outside and they all rushed out, quickly getting to their usual seats. The bus started on its way, creaking and thumping over the potholes. It was soon on the main road and Peter watched as the now familiar landscape rushed by. Tom, as usual, had fallen asleep. The sky brightened as they left the city and soon they arrived at the airfield. Sanj slapped Tom on the back to waken him up amid much laughter from the rest of the group. They were soon inside and ready for the morning briefing.

Brian soon appeared and after a quick good morning, began to brief them on the morning lesson. "It's quite a blustery day as you've already seen, so it could be a fun morning, so make sure you know where the sick bags are," he ended cheerily.

Outside, the wind was winnowing its way across the field and the windsock was whipping around. Peter was with Tom and Tom elected to fly first. Peter strapped into the rear seat and they were soon bouncing down the runway. The lesson for the morning was recovering the aircraft from the stalled condition— where it stops flying and wants to descend rapidly. Tom was anxious about the lesson and was struggling to follow the instructor's commands, but eventually he seemed to be getting the hang of it. It was soon Peter's turn and he found that the aircraft was being bounced around quite a bit in the weather.

They levelled off and Peter began the exercise, allowing the aircraft to stall and recovering from the dive. All of a sudden Peter heard a loud exclamation in his headphones, quickly followed by the acrid smell of vomit. Brian the instructor turned around to see Tom being violently ill into a bag. He told Peter to level off and turn gently back towards the field.

"Are you OK," he said and Tom shook his head. "OK no worries, we'll get you down," and he gave Peter a heading to fly and told him to descend. Soon they were back on the ground and Brian opened the door to get some fresh air into the cabin. Peter taxied across the grass and shut down. Brian got out, quickly followed by Tom, who sank slowly to his knees onto the grass. After a few moments, Brian helped him to his feet and they walked towards the classrooms.

A few moments later Brian reappeared and jumped back into his seat. "Right, old boy—let's go finish the lesson."

Peter started the engine and they were soon climbing towards the cloud base. With the lesson soon completed, Peter began to fly back towards the field, descending to make his approach. He was waiting for Brian to take control, but a quick glance showed Peter that he was sitting with his hands in his lap and he had his eyes closed. Peter concentrated on the approach, adding flaps and reducing his speed and as they flew over the hedge at the end of the runway he felt a slight nudge on the control column and the aircraft settled onto the grass.

"Nice approach and landing—you had the speed nailed perfectly," Brian said.

Peter was speechless—he'd been allowed to fly the approach and landing without being briefed. "Thanks—I thought you had your eyes closed," Peter said.

"Only the one closest to you," Brian said and he let out a roar of laughter. "An old instructor's trick." Peter shook his head, smiling. "I think we'll get you onto take-offs and landings this afternoon," Brian said, climbing stiffly out onto the wing.

Peter smiled to himself—he finally felt like he was getting somewhere. Inside the classroom, Tom was feeling better, but was somewhat ashamed of his performance earlier. Peter shrugged it off. "I didn't have any breakfast and with the bumps it just came over me," he explained.

The whole group teased him throughout lunchtime until the afternoon briefing. Peter was once again paired with Sanj and they were to start the most difficult phase—landings. They were to be instructed by Paul, who tossed a coin and Sanj elected to go first. Over the grass they bumped, climbing away and turning immediately at right angles to the runway. Levelling off, they turned parallel with the runway and carried out the pre-landing checks.

Turning towards the runway, Sanj began a descent before turning onto final approach. Down they went, with Paul calling out the speeds and, as Sanj said afterwards, "I was always too damn fast or too slow."

After an hour and about ten circuits of the field, it was Peter's turn. Up they went and everything seemed to be happening so quickly. Climb, turn, level off, turn, checks, turn, descend, turn, line up and lower flaps, close the throttle, onto the ground, raise the flaps and off again. By the end of his hour, Peter was exhausted, but was getting the hand of holding the aircraft in the landing configuration until it decided when it would touch down.

"That's excellent, both of you. Holding the aircraft off is something I just can't teach—it's all in your fingertips," Paul said. "Same tomorrow, Mother Nature permitting," and they both sat down to fill in their logbooks.

Once back at the house, Peter quickly changed into his running gear and set off at a pace. It had been three days since his last run and he was desperate to get out. He's worked out a route through the streets which was about six miles and he wanted to improve his times as much as possible. He pounded his way around

184

the roads, making mental notes of their names and of any danger areas such as traffic lights, but it seemed to be fairly quiet and most of it was along leafy streets.

He soon arrived back at the house, exhausted but feeling elated. A very busy but rewarding day and he'd just run off all the adrenaline and it felt good. He made his way straight for the bathroom and after a long hot shower, went back downstairs. Mark, Arnie and Sanj were just about to head out to the shop, so Peter joined them. He was starving!

After they had all eaten, they got together in the living area to continue discussing the forthcoming exam. Peter was again thrust into the spotlight by Paula and he quickly went through his chart which he'd shown to them the day before. Soon, people were beginning to yawn and look at their watches and Peter took his leave and headed upstairs. He was quickly asleep.

26

The next few days followed the same pattern—drive to the airfield, wake Tom up (They were now taking it in turns to do this) attend the briefing and fly the lessons. Debrief, lunch and start again. Peter seemed to be making good progress and was soon landing the aircraft with minimal input from the instructors. Thursday was lost to the weather, so an intense day of ground school was undertaken and then on Friday morning, they arrived and were told that the exam would be sat first before any flying was done.

Nervous glances were exchanged and they were told to sit at desks well-spaced apart and they were given the exam paper and answer sheets. The exams were of the multi-choice type and soon they began. Peter sat down, writing his name carefully on the answer sheet, his hands clammy with sweat and his heart racing. He carefully read each question before putting a tick in the appropriate box on the answer sheet. He finished and read back through his answers. Satisfied, he put his pen down and sat quietly.

Shortly after, he heard one of the instructors call, "Time up" and everyone sat upright. Brian walked along the row of desks collecting the papers and answer sheets. Paul was at the front and he cleared his throat.

"Right, the exam will be marked over lunchtime and you'll get the results before this afternoon. In the meantime, we'll carry on with the lessons. The rota is on the board—be out at the aircraft in five minutes."

Peter was rostered with Mike and paired with Paula. She wanted to fly first, so Peter strapped himself in the back. They were soon climbing away from the grass and into the first left turn. Round and round they flew and Paula was making a decent fist of it, approaching and landing with minimal input from Mike. It was soon Peter's turn. He quickly settled into the routine and as there was little wind, flew the whole session with hardly any intervention.

At the end of the session, they taxied in and after Peter had shut down, Mike climbed out and let Paula out of the back seat. He then ducked his head back in and said to Peter, "Start up again and go and do one on your own if you want."

Peter was dumbfounded. "Are you sure?" he asked.

"Yes, go on, off you go," Mike replied, closing and locking the door and jumping down off the wing.

Peter read through his checklist, took a deep breath and started the engine. He called over the radio that he was taxiing to the runway and heard Mike's voice say, "All aircraft remain clear—first solo underway."

Peter lined up at the end of the runway, checking everything carefully. Once he was ready, he pushed the throttle lever forwards and the aeroplane leapt towards the horizon. At the correct speed Peter pulled back gently on the controls and the ground fell away. He immediately turned into the circuit—the aeroplane was climbing like a homesick angel without Paula and Mike's weight!

He levelled off, reducing the power and turned parallel to the runway. He looked across towards the runway to make his "Downwind" call and saw the empty seat next to him. "I'd better get this right," he said aloud to himself. In no time he'd turned and begun his descent. Finally, he turned towards the runway, lowering his flaps and hearing Mike's voice in his head saying, "Picture, airspeed, picture, airspeed."

Gradually, the threshold floated up towards him and as he crossed the hedge he closed the throttle. "Keep it flying," he again said out loud and the aircraft finally settled onto the grass. He'd done it! He slowly taxied in with real tears in his eyes—after all the years, the study, the waiting, the hopes and dreams, he'd finally flown an aircraft on his own.

He shut the engine down and slowly removed his headphones. He heard the door being opened and there was Mike with his hand extended. Peter shook the hand and Mike said, "Congratulations—you are now officially a pilot."

Peter couldn't quite believe it—he had just twelve hours in his logbook and he was the first of the group to solo. He clambered out of the aircraft, legs shaking and was met by Paula, Sanj and Arnie. They all offered their congratulations, shook hands and Paula gave him a hug. Tom and Mark were still flying. Slowly they walked towards the classroom building, with Peter's feet three inches above the ground.

He was uncomfortable with all the attention, but absolutely elated. He needed a drink and made his way towards the kitchen for a glass of water. He found it difficult to hold the glass steady as his hands were still shaking from the adrenaline and excitement. Finally he let out a long breath. "Wow—did I really just do that?" he asked of no-one in particular.

"Yes," came a chorus of voices—Peter hadn't realised that everyone had followed him into the kitchen. Everybody started asking him questions at once—what was it like, was it easy, were you scared? Whilst uncomfortable, Peter accepted everybody's congratulations and warm wishes.

Outside, Tom and Mark were taxying in and soon joined the group in the kitchen. Lunch was soon served and as they were getting their food, Brian called for them to bring their lunch into the classroom for the exam results. "Right gang, results time. We've put the results on the board, but I'm happy to tell you that you've all passed the Air Law exam. Your grades are on the board. Also, massive congratulations to Peter on completing his first solo. Peter, come and join me."

Peter stood up slowly, an cold feeling gripping his stomach. He hated this and really hoped that Brian wasn't going to ask him to speak or make an example of him. Peter needn't have worried. Brian shook his hand, saying, "Congratulations to Peter—first to solo," and he handed Peter a certificate.

All the group clapped, whooped and shouted their own congratulations. Peter mumbled his thanks and sat back down. On the certificate was the airline crest, Peter's name and the date and it signed by all three instructors. *One for the scrapbook,* Peter thought to himself.

Brian continued "OK—it's Friday afternoon, so a short session this afternoon and then an early bus home. You can hand in your law books and get out the next subject—Principles of Flight. Exam will be two weeks today. We'll meet out at the aircraft in thirty minutes."

Peter finished his lunch and his hands were still shaking. He went to the library getting a copy of the next book and looked at his results on the board. Ninety-six percent. One question wrong. Ahh well he thought—who cares? He then looked at the flying roster and noticed that he was back with Paula and Brian. Perfect. Before the afternoon flight, Peter asked Brian how to fill in the solo flight in his logbook.

Brian showed him and told him to log it under the "Pilot in command" column. Peter did so and sat and stared at the entry. In command. Wow. "Mum would be beside herself with worry if she knew," he mused with a smile.

Back in the aircraft with Paula, she continued to fly the circuit under Brian's careful tutelage and after an hour came in for her final landing of the session.

Peter was watching from the back seat and he could see that she had it well under control—and the final touchdown was as smooth as silk. They taxied in and Brian hopped out, motioning Peter to get out as well. Peter stood to one side and Brian jumped back into the aircraft before exiting once again.

He walked over to Peter and smiled, saying, "It's the day for first solos." As he did so, the engine barked into life and the aircraft slowly began to move forwards. Peter watched as it taxied towards the runway and it lined up. After a minute or so, the engine roared and the aircraft shot forwards and up into the sky. Both Peter and Brian watched in total silence as it climbed, turned and settled down, eventually turning back towards the runway.

Peter watched intently, seeing the flaps come down and the engine note died to a quiet whisper. Down it came, lower and lower, crossing the hedge and finally settling onto the ground. She's done it—down safe and sound. Peter again felt a tear pricking his eye and stood motionless as Paula taxied in and shut down. Brian hopped up onto the wing, wrenched the door open and stuck his head inside before exiting, closely followed by Paula.

She was wearing the biggest grin Peter had ever seen and jumped down onto the grass before shouting at the top of her voice, "Yes…yes." Peter walked over and offered his congratulations, giving her a hug. The other two aircraft were still airborne, but would be down soon and Paula, Brian and Peter made their way back to the classrooms. Once back inside, they were shortly followed by the others and again congratulations were given and Paula received her certificate.

Brian spoke, "OK team, a great end to a great week. Hopefully get the rest of you solo next week and then it's hour-building time. The bus has just arrived, so off you go and have a great weekend."

There was a general shout of "Thanks" and they trooped outside to get on the bus. Paula came and sat near to Peter. "What a day, eh?" she said.

"Yes, indeed," Peter answered. "I can't believe that we've soloed. I didn't know when it would happen or if you had to have a certain number of hours, but a great day indeed."

"I can't believe it either," Paula said. "I've waited so long for this day—I'm going to celebrate tonight. What will you be doing?"

"Well, I'm off home for the weekend just like everyone else and I'm meeting up with my old school buddies tomorrow, so hopefully it'll be a fun weekend," Peter replied.

"Can I also say thank you for the help you gave me for the Law exam—I don't think I'd have passed it without you," Paula said, putting her hand on Peter's arm.

"Of course you would," Peter said. "You're welcome."

Back at the house, Peter packed quickly before ringing his mother and running to the tube station. He wanted to try and make the earlier train if he could, as it would give him more time with his parents, who would no doubt want to know every little detail of his solo flight. When the tube arrived at the mainline station Peter ran up the stairs two at a time and just managed to catch his train.

It was packed and he was forced to stand in the aisle for three stops before a seat became vacant. He settled himself down for the journey home and thought about the day once again. He know that this day would stay with him for a very long time—he was so excited but he managed to stifle the urge to tell the total strangers on the train with him what he'd achieved that morning.

Eventually, the train pulled into Westlea station and Peter saw his mother behind the barrier. He called out and waved and ran over for a hug. "How are you? You look terribly excited," Annie said.

"Yes, I'm OK thanks. Passed the Law exam this morning, so it's been a good day."

"Oh, well done, sweetie, that's great news," Annie replied.

Peter wasn't going to say anything about the solo flight until after dinner—he wanted to see both their faces at once. They chatted on the bus and once inside the house, Annie asked Peter to get all his dirty washing out and that she'd do it straight away. A few minutes after they arrived, Paul came in through the back door.

"Hiya, Peter—home early," he said, giving Peter a hug.

"Yes, we got off a bit earlier today. Passed the law exam this morning as well, so it's been a good day," Peter said.

"Well done—not that I doubted you for a second," Paul replied.

"Thanks," Peter said quickly before adding, "Lots more study this weekend again, although I've arranged to meet up with Alex and Liam tomorrow."

"Good—what subject this time?" Paul asked.

"Principles of flight," Peter said.

"Pretty heavy going I think." Paul nodded.

Annie came in saying, "Right Peter, that's all in the wash," before turning to Paul and giving him a kiss on the cheek. "Has Peter told you about the exam?" she asked.

"Yes—great result," Paul replied.

Peter went upstairs to his room to unpack the rest of his things. At the bottom of his bag was the solo certificate which Peter fancied having framed. He looked around the room and everything was in place as usual. This pleased him and he began to look for a suitable place for the certificate to hang. Shortly, he heard Annie calling him down for dinner. *Great—home cooked food*, he thought before sprinting downstairs.

After dinner, Peter helped clear away as usual before both he and Annie joined Paul in the living room. "How has your week been?" Paul asked.

"Oh—hang on, something in my bag upstairs that I need," Peter said, running to his room and grabbing the certificate. He placed it face down on the sofa next to him before answering Paul's question.

"It's been a great week—managed four days of flying and we all passed the exam. I found myself helping the others with a few things, but we all got through which is the important thing. The flying has been awesome—I've something to show you both," he said before handing the certificate to Paul.

Paul put his reading glasses on before studying the certificate. He read and reread it a few times with his mouth agape before handing it to Annie. "Congratulations, son—does that mean that you flew the aeroplane on your own? With no instructor on board? Completely alone?"

Peter nodded his head. Annie read the certificate and let out a shriek—"On your own?" she asked with a tremble in her voice.

"Yes, mum—on my own," Peter replied.

His parents looked at each other for a long time before Annie broke the silence. "Our boy can fly an aeroplane. Do you realise what that means? All those so-called experts we saw during his childhood were wrong, the doctor was wrong, the primary school teachers were all wrong—all of them! I know we always believed in him, but he's proven himself to be more than capable."

Paul nodded and put his arm around Annie, tears in his eyes. Peter listened, but had no idea what they were talking about.

Eventually, he plucked up the courage to ask "What experts? What did my teachers say?"

Annie and Paul looked at each other uncomfortably before Annie spoke quietly. "Peter—we've always believed in you and thought that you'd achieve great things, but when you were small there were lots of—of difficulties. You didn't speak until much later than other children and we found you very difficult in situations where there were lots of people—especially strangers. You've always had very set routines and you used to have a meltdown if anything disrupted those routines or you couldn't achieve what you wanted. We saw the doctors, we spoke to education specialists, to your teachers and practically everyone agreed that you'd probably not do well in life.

"The teachers actually said that you'd never pass any exams, as they didn't think that you had the capacity for learning or study. We were amazed and so proud when you flew through the eleven plus exams and got your place at grammar school and we gradually began to realise that, far from being not very intelligent, that you were in fact extremely clever and your GCE results confirmed that. We're both so proud of what you've managed to achieve—especially in the last two weeks—and I still think that you'll achieve great things."

Peter sat quietly for a long time thinking over what Annie had just said. Slowly, it was as though he was suddenly growing up in the space of a few minutes and the childhood difficulties fell away.

Finally, he spoke, "I can vaguely remember being encouraged to talk, but I can also distinctly remember thinking to myself that whilst I knew the words, I could just get along by pointing and grunting and you and dad would do what I wanted. I understood every word. It was the same at school—I remember listening to the teachers and taking stuff on board, but I got so frustrated at the slower kids not understanding, that I almost used to rage inside, thinking "Why can't you understand—it's easy". I think the frustration led to some episodes and again I can remember being hauled off to the doctor when as far as I was concerned, I wasn't ill, so why were we going to the doctor?

"When we got to the eleven plus exams, I thought to myself that I now had a chance to be rid of the dunces in my year group and to get some proper learning done. I found the exams a doddle really. Same for my year end exams and the GCE's—yes, I had to study, but I worked out a method of study which makes it so easy. The biggest pain in my life has always been Ben—he obviously hates having a brother who he sees as needy, but to be honest I hate having a brother who is as thick as he is and a total under achiever."

There was a long silence before Paul finally spoke. "Listening to what you've just said, you seem to have a far greater awareness than we ever thought regarding your make up and personality. I've always found your ability to give an honest answer—a very honest answer—refreshing. I know some people can't deal with that, but your insight is quite remarkable."

Peter continued, "Thank you. I have been aware that I'm not wired up in the same way as other people, but there are a lot like me who, whilst we don't fit into the expected norm in our society, still have much to offer."

Annie was looking at Peter with piercing eyes and she finally stood up, came over to Peter and taking him by the hand, pulled him upright and put both her arms around him as far as they would go. Peter hung on to Annie as tightly as he dared and she refused to let go. Finally, they parted and sat back down and she said in a quiet trembling voice, "So you've always known that you'd be alright?" she asked.

Peter nodded his head, tears filling his eyes. Finally he spoke once more, "Sorry if that's been a revelation, but it's been difficult being under Ben's shadow and with his larger-than-life personality, it's been nearly impossible to get out from under that shadow. I've always wanted to show you both what I was capable of and now that Ben's left home, I've managed to do that—or at least go some way to doing so."

"Well, you've certainly done that," Paul said. "Learning to fly and land a plane in just two weeks is a remarkable achievement in my eyes."

"Thanks, dad," Peter mumbled.

Annie finally broke the spell. "I'm going to put the kettle on—anybody else like a drink?"

Paul shook his head and Peter asked for a glass of water. Annie left the room and Paul looked at Peter for a minute before saying, "I'm so proud of you, son. So proud. Not just for what you've achieved at work, but also for what you've told us tonight. Remarkable insight for such a young mind."

Peter smiled to himself, thinking, *If only you knew*—It had been a truly momentous day—and a perfect day for such an honest discussion with his parents. Peter went to sleep that night a very happy and fulfilled young man.

27

Saturday arrived angrily, with the rain lashing against Peter's bedroom window. Peter lay awhile, allowing his mind to wander and to relive the events of the day before. Eventually, a loud clap of thunder jolted him into full consciousness and he got slowly out of bed. The muscles in his shoulders ached—probably from the tension of flying landings for most of the week—but he felt satisfied. The talk with his parents the evening before had been a cathartic experience and he felt closer to them somehow. He allowed himself a smile—life was on track.

A knock at the door made him turn his head and there was Annie's face peeking around the edge of the door. She smiled and came into the room bearing coffee. Peter took the cup gratefully, saying, "Good morning, mum, thanks."

Annie smiled and sat down next to him. "How are you today?" she asked.

Peter turned to look her in the eyes, saying, "I'm fine. Really good in actual fact."

Annie gently squeezed his arm and stood up. "Good—see you downstairs," and she left the room.

After breakfast, Peter rang Alex and they arranged to meet at the coffee bar as usual. The rain was still falling so it was a quick dash to the bus stop and another dash to the coffee bar when the bus arrived. Alex and Anna were sitting over by the window and after Peter had got his coffee, he snuck up on them, making them both jump.

"Jeez man!" Alex exclaimed, which made Peter laugh. Anna scolded him gently and Peter sat down with his friends. Alex immediately began firing questions at Peter. "How's it been? Have you done any flying? What are your co-students like?"

Peter took a deep breath "Well—it's been great. There are six of us on the course—including a girl." This made Anna nod in approval. "The crew house is OK, but it's been a steep learning curve looking after myself, although mum is doing my washing at weekends as we've no facilities there. The first week was a bit slow, but this week has been awesome. I passed the first of fourteen exams yesterday and—"

Peter allowed himself to pause, enjoying the tension. "Yes and?" Alex asked.

Peter took a long drink of coffee. "Where was I?" he asked.

"The last thing you said was 'and'," Anna said.

"Ahh, yes," Peter continued. "And yesterday, I flew solo for the first time."

There was a pause whilst Anna and Alex stared at Peter and then Alex slapped him on the shoulder, saying, "That's awesome, buddy. Well done! How was it?"

Peter paused once again before replying, "It was incredible. Both harder and easier than I thought it was going to be, but so immensely satisfying."

Both Anna and Alex offered their own congratulations before Peter asked about Liam. "Oh, he's fine, I think," Alex replied. "Still seeing Sally I think, just that we haven't seen him for a couple of weeks. We've both been busy with these damn A Levels."

"How are they going?" Peter asked.

"Boring," Anna said quickly, with Alex nodding in agreement.

"Which subjects?" Peter asked.

"Biology, chemistry and physics," Alex answered, rolling his eyes.

"We do a lot of physics in our subjects, but I really enjoy it," Peter said.

"Yes, but your subjects relate to something tangible, whereas ours are just theory," Alex replied.

Anna finished her coffee and looking out of the window, said to Alex, "It's stopped raining—come on, let's go shopping."

"If we must—you coming?" he said to Peter. Peter nodded—it would be good just being around his friends again.

After wandering around the town centre for most of the day, with Anna dashing in and out of shops and dragging Alex along like a stubborn puppy, Peter suggested that they get something to eat as he was famished. They went to their favourite cafe and ordered hot food. Discussion quickly turned to Peter's ongoing training.

"How long until you're flying the big jets?" Alex asked.

"It depends. I can't get my commercial licence until I'm eighteen, so at least another eighteen months, but in the meantime there's lots to do. Once I finish the basic flying syllabus, we move onto advanced training, learning to fly with sole reference to the instruments and flying aircraft with more than one engine which prepares you for the airline flying," Peter explained.

Anna listened, but her mind was on other things. "So, the girl on your course—is she pretty?" she asked coyly.

"Anna!" Alex exclaimed and Peter smiled.

"Yes, I guess so, but no, I'm not interested," he quickly responded. "We've become friends, but I've become friends with all of them and there's certainly no room for anything else," Peter added.

Anna looked at Alex and smiled. "I thought you and Sally made a good couple," she said.

"So did I at first, but she got too pushy," Peter said quietly. "I'm sure she'll be OK with Liam—they both want the same thing," he added as the food arrived.

They all quickly attacked the food and when they finished, Peter said that he was going home as he had lots to study and so they walked back to the bus terminus together, chattering amicably as they did so. Peter could see his bus about to depart, so he quickly hugged Anna, shook Alex's hand and ran like fury, just hopping onto the rear platform just as the bus began to move.

Sunday was a blur of study, followed by hurried goodbyes and Peter soon found himself back at the crew house, bag bulging with clean laundry and food. Annie was going to make sure that he didn't starve. The house was quiet, with only Tom and Mark in the living area. Peter waved as he climbed the stairs and was shortly back down with his book and notepad, settling into a seat by the window.

Tom looked up from the magazine that he had been leafing through. "Don't you ever relax?" he asked.

Peter looked up. "Yes, of course—I find studying relaxing and I go for a run most days which relaxes and calms me," Peter replied.

"How's your studying going?" Tom screwed his face up.

"Not opened the new book—there's plenty of time," he said.

"I just want to concentrate on the flying."

"And how's that going?" Peter enquired.

"I've only just completed the stalling—ever since I threw up I've not enjoyed that particular exercise," he said.

Mark looked up and said, "Well, the exam is less than two weeks and it's not an easy subject so you'd better crack on."

Peter agreed and Tom just stared into the far distance. A short time later, they heard the door open and footsteps in the hallway, closely followed by Paula poking her head around the door. "Hi, gang," she said.

There was a murmur of greetings and she disappeared upstairs. Shortly afterwards, Mark stood up and left the room, but Peter took no notice and continued with his reading and note taking.

The group were soon back at the airfield, with Peter and Paula sharing an aircraft but flying circuits alone. Once Paula had completed her first hour, Peter climbed into the aircraft, adjusted his seat and belt and started the engine. A shimmy of excitement ran across his back and he put his headphones on, calling for taxy clearance. He was soon back up in his element, flying a left-hand pattern this morning. He flew for his allotted hour, landing just before lunch.

Brian met the aircraft, asking him how everything went. "OK, I think—one slightly heavy landing, but I'm pretty satisfied with the rest."

"They looked good from the classroom," Brian said as Peter jumped down from the wing.

As he did so, he heard an aircraft engine being revved and then going quiet before being revved again. He looked up to see an aircraft coming down the approach. At first it seemed too high, then too low and it finally thumped onto the ground, bouncing about six feet into the air before bouncing a second time. The engine then roared and it lifted shakily into the sky.

"Who's that?" Peter asked.

"Not sure—either Sanj or Tom," Brian replied. Peter nodded—*probably Tom*, he thought. After lunch, it was time for more solo time and Peter flew first. He could hear Tom's voice over the radio and he sounded pretty tense. Once Paula had replaced Peter, he went inside to continue his reading and before he knew it the whole group were back inside and Mike called for everyone's attention.

"More first solo congratulations today—Sanj up you get if you please." Sanj walked to the front to be presented with his certificate and everyone clapped. Mike then continued, "OK, gang. The weather looks reasonable tomorrow, so the plan is for one final hour of solo circuits for both Paula and Peter in the morning, solo circuits for Sanj and carry on for the rest of you. We'll decide about the afternoon roster in the morning."

Sanj sat back down next to Peter who whispered "Well done" to him. Sanj smiled saying thanks. Soon it was time for the bus and Peter took his usual seat. Paula came to sit be him. "What's next?" she asked.

"Not sure—navigation, I think," he said. Paula nodded and Peter fell silent for the rest of the journey.

Once back at the house, Peter was quickly into his running gear—it had been four days since his last run and he'd missed it. He was quickly out of the house, pounding the now familiar streets. He found that running helped clear his head and made him concentrate and for the whole time he was thinking about the Principles of Flight exam. Over and over he turned the subject before eventually arriving home. A quick glance at his watch showed that his times were about the same as the week before and he climbed into the shower, satisfied.

Once dressed, he went hunting for food. There were the pies that his mother had packed for him and he found them on his shelf in the fridge. Popping a couple into the oven, he sat down to wait. Tom wandered into the kitchen and seeing Peter sitting at the table, he asked, "Have you been out running again?" Peter nodded. "I don't know why you bother," Tom said scornfully.

"Because I enjoy it," Peter replied. "Was that you who bounced the aircraft this afternoon?"

Tom stayed silent for a few minutes before replying, "Yes, why?"

"Oh, I just wondered," Peter said.

"Got caught by a gust of wind," Tom explained.

Peter nodded, thinking, *I was stood watching and there wasn't any wind*, but he said nothing. He was soon tucking into his pies.

On Tuesday morning, Paula and Peter were taken into a separate classroom by Paul and he sat them down and began drawing on the board in front of them. "Right—you've done three hours solo each and you've learned to fly the aircraft, so time to teach you how to use it. Onto navigation," and he started explaining how the Earth was divided into so many degrees, how each degree was measured and how the wind affected their flight path.

Peter listened with huge interest. This was everything he'd been interested in since being small and the library books he'd read over the years were about to stand him in good stead. After the briefing, Paul sat down with them both to plan a flight to another airfield which was about an hour flying time. Peter would plan and fly outbound and Paula would plan and fly the return leg. They were shown where to get the weather and wind information from a special television terminal and after some struggles with an old-fashioned circular slide rule known affectionately as a "Whizz wheel" they were ready.

Once airborne, Peter settled into the flight with the map across his knees. He glanced at it occasionally, trying to match features outside on the ground to those marked on the map. Paul sat alongside, offering words of advice and encouragement and Peter concentrated on following his planned course, keeping an eye on the time elapsed which would tell him if he was early or late at a particular point, giving him information about the wind.

The flight went well and he spotted the destination airfield quite a few miles out—it was an ex RAF WW2 field with three huge runways, so it was hard to miss. Peter called the tower on the radio, getting his joining information and set up for a descent, turning onto final approach with room to spare. This was going to be his first landing on a tarmac runway, but once down he found it easier than the grass he'd got used to. He taxied in and shut down, breathing a sigh of relief.

"Well done—good flight," Paul said before jumping out and letting Paula out of the back. Peter was last to exit through the single door and he felt a sense of achievement as he stepped off the wing.

Following a quick break, they reboarded the aircraft, with Peter taking the back seat. They were soon on their way and Paula was holding a steady course. For Peter, it was nice to just be a passenger for once—he'd never flown in an airliner and he imagined that this was the sort of experience his future passengers would enjoy. In no time at all, the training field came into view and Paula landed the aircraft smoothly. Paul took them inside to debrief and he seemed pleased with their progress.

"OK, good flying both of you. No problems following your headings and holding altitude, which is exactly what we're expecting. For this afternoon's session, we'll repeat the exercise, but Paula can fly outbound and Peter can bring us home. Happy?" Both Paula and Peter nodded and they got up to get a late lunch.

The afternoon followed the same pattern as the morning, although on the return leg, Peter was forced to descend from his planned altitude because of cloud building up, but he took it in his stride and they were soon back safely on the ground. They found the rest of the group waiting for them—with both Mark and Arnie wearing big smiles and clutching their solo certificates. They were soon homeward bound, happily chatting and swapping stories of the day. Only Tom stayed quiet, sitting alone at the front of the bus.

The rest of the week followed the same pattern for Peter—navigation flights in the morning and afternoon and running before studying in the evening. It was becoming more intense and by the time Friday afternoon arrived, he felt ready for the weekend, although he knew it would be one of studying for the exam the following Friday.

After a busy weekend, in which Peter managed a quick visit to his Gran who was amazed at his progress, he was back at the crew house and planning for the morning's navigation trip. Brian had given them all—except Tom—routes to plan for the morning, with just the wind calculations to make when they arrived at the field. Tom was taken off by himself to continue take-off and landings and the rest were split over the remaining two aircraft for the training.

Peter was told to sit out the first session, which he did so by getting into his book once again, taking a practice test which he was pleased with. After lunch, he was again airborne at the controls, flying further afield this time and getting slightly off track.

"No worries," said Brian who was instructing. "It just shows that the wind is just a forecast and that sometimes it misbehaves itself."

Peter made corrections as suggested and they completed the flight without any further problems. As he was alone with Brian without another student, he quickly planned the return trip which went seamlessly and he was soon back in the classroom, completing his logbook. He'd completed just over twenty-five hours flying so far in four weeks.

Friday morning was soon upon them and when they arrived at the airfield, they were told that they would be sitting the exam before the flying programme commenced. As before, they took their seats and the papers and answer sheets were distributed. Peter read through the paper and then started marking his answers. Once he had finished and had checked his paper, he again sat quietly until "Time up" was called. Within a few minutes they were all at the noticeboard reading the schedule before making their way out to the waiting aircraft.

When lunchtime arrived, as they made their way back to the classroom in their pairs, they were told by Mike that the exam results were posted. Peter walked to the board with Sanj and he was pleased to see that he'd passed, again with a high score. Sanj had also passed. Soon they were sitting enjoying lunch along with the others—although Tom was absent. Peter hadn't really noticed until Tom walked in shortly afterwards looking crestfallen. He took a seat and began to eat but without joining in the general conversation.

Peter took no notice whatsoever as he was busy thinking about the afternoon exercise of planning airborne diversions and was eager to get started. Soon it was time and Peter walked out to their aircraft with Sanj. "You first or me?" Peter asked.

"Hey, I'm not bothered," Sanj replied, so Mike their instructor settled the argument and chose Peter to fly first. Once they had completed their flights, all of them were soon back on the bus with the usual Friday afternoon chatter and excitement. As soon as they got back to the house, Peter shot upstairs to grab his bag and run for the tube, but on the way down the stairs, he saw Tom at the bottom. "Could I ask you for a bit of help on Monday?" he asked.

Peter thought for a moment and then asked, "What with?"

"I failed the exam—only scored just over half the pass mark. I've two more attempts and if I fail, then I'm out," Tom replied.

Peter was momentarily shocked, but not at all surprised. "Err—yeah sure, I'll try and help, but I've my own study to do for the next subject," Peter replied.

"Thanks—yes I know and so have I—I don't get any leeway with the next one, I have to sit on the same day as the rest of you."

"OK—see you on Monday," Peter replied, running for the door. He just made the early train and sat looking out of the window, thinking about Tom and his predicament. Eventually, he just shrugged his shoulders thinking, *It's not my problem* and looked forward to being home.

28

Peter arrived back at the house late on Sunday afternoon. He was looking forward to a run and then some reading and he made his way upstairs thinking that the house was empty. He unpacked, carefully hanging his shirts in the wardrobe and began to change into his running gear when a sound from upstairs caught his attention. He paused, listening intently. He heard the sound again— unmistakably a girl laughing.

He looked out of his window, but saw nothing. He then heard male laughter and realised that Mark and Paula must already be upstairs. He thought for a moment, shrugged and took off for his run, arriving back in a new personal best time, exhausted, sweaty but satisfied. After showering, he settled down to read, but the noises from upstairs kept disturbing him. Eventually, he thought he might be better off downstairs, so he went to the living area and settled into a chair and was soon lost in the textbook.

Early in the evening, Sanj arrived and was soon busy in the kitchen. "Hey, Peter—have you eaten?" he called.

Peter got up and walked to the back of the house. "Hi, buddy—I ate before I left home. My mum won't send me off without a hot meal," he said, laughing.

"Well, my mother has sent me with lots of food—have you ever tried Indian cuisine?" Sanjay asked. Peter shook his head. There were warm, spicy and inviting smells coming from the cooker. "You must try some—come, sit," Sanjay said, motioning Peter to a chair.

Shortly he placed a bowl of what looked like stew in front of Peter, but it had a strange colour and smell. "Mild chicken curry," Sanj explained adding "And these are Naan breads—to mop up with."

Peter, taking his lead from Sanj, tore a piece of the bread, tentatively dipping it into the sauce. It was delicious. Soon, he was enjoying chunks of chicken and the sauce and before he knew he had finished. "Wow—that was amazing. Thanks," Peter said.

"You're welcome—have to broaden your education somehow," Sanj laughed.

Peter went to the sink and washed everything and then sat down to talk. "Did you know Tom failed the exam?" he asked. Sanj shook his head. "Yes—has to re-sit and still has to do the next exam on time. He's asked me for help and I will try to help him, but I'm busy with my own reading," Peter explained.

"Well, I could offer some help as well, but like you, I've lots to do," Sanj replied.

Peter nodded. "I'm all for supporting each other, but Tom really needs to put in a bit more effort," Peter said. Just then, they heard footsteps running down the stairs and lots of giggling.

Paula appeared in the doorway, closely followed my Mark. She stopped dead. She was wearing shorts and a thin shirt—very obviously with nothing underneath. "Oh—hi, guys. I didn't realise anybody else was here," she said, blushing furiously, drawing her arm across her breasts.

"Yep—here we are," Sanj replied, turning to Peter and winking. Peter didn't get the joke and he looked across to Paula but couldn't read her expression. He chose to say nothing and turned back to Sanj. After an awkward silence, Paula went to the fridge, removed a bottle of soft drink and she and Mark disappeared back upstairs.

"They seem to have become very good friends," Sanj said, emphasising the word "Very."

"Have they?" Peter asked. He hadn't considered the matter and thought it none of his business.

"Oh, yes—it's been going on for the past week or so," Sanj replied. Peter just shook his head. He really didn't understand people.

The following morning, they were all waiting for the bus early and the rain was lashing against the windows. "No flying today sadly," Arnie said gloomily.

"Oh, you never know—it may be lovely at the field," Sanj said cheerily.

Soon they were on the bus as it made its way slowly through the wind and rain, wipers furiously trying and failing to clear the water from the windscreen. It was the same when they arrived. Brian soon called them into the classroom.

"Right—as you probably have realised, the weather has cancelled flying, so we're taking to opportunity to get one aircraft serviced today and hopefully it'll be back online tomorrow. Who's for some ground school?" he asked jovially.

This was met with a collective groan. "Aww, come on—it'll be fun," he retorted, laughing. "OK—flight performance. Now, for this exam, we used to use old-fashioned slide rules or paper tables, but there is a new bit of kit on the market—an electronic calculator. The scientific version will do everything you need for this exam and couple of the others.

"The one we recommend is the Hastings 6401. It's not cheap at just under five pounds, but a worthy addition to your flight bags. We have one here which you can use and share, but when it comes to the exam, you'll need your own. Seeing as you've all just been paid, it may be a wise investment. We have an arrangement with a supplier and can get them slightly cheaper, so if you want one, let us know and we'll place an order."

Peter made a mental note to order one—his pay would have gone into his savings account by now, so he could easily afford it—he still hadn't touched the money from the engineering company.

The day wore on slowly, with Brian and then Mike guiding them expertly through calculating performance and fuel requirements, but Peter was finding all the different fuel calculations hard to follow. Eventually, he was thankful to be able to get up and stretch his legs. Soon, they were heading home. As they got inside the house, Tom again asked Peter for some help.

"Hmm OK—I'm going for a run first and then I'll eat, so maybe around seven?" he said. Tom muttered his thanks and Peter ran upstairs two at a time.

Once he had showered and eaten, Peter wandered back downstairs, finding Tom sitting at the kitchen table surrounded by papers and an assortment of pens. Peter sat down saying, "OK. How can I help?"

"It's these calculations for working out lift equations," Tom replied. "They make no sense at all and I just can't get my head around Bernoulli's theorem"

Peter leafed through his own notes, finding the relevant part. "OK," he started and began to help Tom through the complexities and physics of just how an aeroplane flew. After an hour or so, Tom seemed exhausted, but felt as though he was making some headway, so Peter left him to it, returning to his room to commence the next subject. After an hour, he felt tired, so switched the light off and was soon asleep.

The week went by quickly with Peter trying to help Tom with his re-sit and to get his own work done. Tom was still flying take-offs and landings with an instructor and hadn't yet gone solo and as Arnie commented in the living area one evenings, he didn't think he was going to make the grade. There was a general consensus that this may turn out to be the case and on Friday morning, Tom was called into the classroom for his re-sit exam whilst the rest continued with the flying programme.

Peter, Paula and Sanj were scheduled to be learning emergencies today— engine failures in flight. Peter had been quite excited by the prospect, but Paula was nervous.

Once airborne however, under Mike's expert hand, she made a good job of dealing with the situation and it was soon Peter's turn. He had great fun cutting the engine and selecting a field to pretend to land in and after his allotted hour, landed and taxied in quickly. Mike jumped out, followed by Paula and then Peter. "Great job guys—perfect. Qualifying cross country flights next week," he said and walked towards the classrooms.

Paula looked at Peter dumbfounded. "Qualifying flights—already?" she asked.

Peter shrugged his shoulders. "Guess so, if Mike says so," he replied, intrigued as to what the flights would entail.

Back inside, once lunch had been demolished, Brian called them all into the classroom and he handed out boxes to each of them. "These are the calculators we ordered for you all. The cost will be deducted from this month's wages. Read the instructions and learn how to use them—you won't be allowed the instructions in the exam."

Peter slid his into his jacket pocket. *More homework for the weekend*, he thought wryly to himself. Just as Peter was about to go out for the afternoon session, Tom came over to him. "I've done my re-sit. Scraped through with seventy-five percent. Thanks for your help."

Peter mumbled, "No problem," and walked outside. Wow. Seventy-five percent. That was poor by anybody's standards, but at least he was through. *A pass is a pass is what Mr Watkins my old maths teacher used to say*, he thought to himself. He then put Tom's problems out of his mind as he prepared for the afternoon session. Shortly, he was on the train back to Westlea.

Peter spent the weekend reading and getting to grips with the complexities of his new calculator. Helpfully, inside the slide-off front cover were formulae for the most common calculations and he soon found it easy to use. Paul was interested in how it worked and he said that if he had one at work, it would save lots of difficult head-scratching. A quick visit to Peter's Gran on Sunday morning and some time spent answering the inevitable questions and very shortly Peter was back on the train.

"Why does the week sometimes drag and yet the weekends go so quickly?" he mused to himself, watching the trees and countryside speed by. Once back at the house, he locked himself in his room to study, not wanting to see anyone.

When they arrived at the airfield on Monday morning, they were, as usual, split into three groups. However, as Tom was still flying dual circuits with Brian, Peter was left without an aircraft to fly.

Instead of having him do little else but read, Mike gave Peter the route for his cross country flight to plan for the following day. Once his colleagues were all out of his way, Peter sat down at a desk with the aeronautical chart, ruler, protractor and his whizz wheel. Carefully plotting the route on the chart, he measured distances, direction and also marked the location of nearby airfields in case of emergencies, just as he'd been shown.

After a couple of hours, he'd finished all the basic planning and just had the wind calculations to do on the day. He then turned back to his study book. He'd finished the final chapter by lunchtime and resolved to use the afternoon answering some of the practice tests, although he was still struggling with some of the different fuel requirements and was just reading the questions when Paula and Sanj walked in.

"Hi, buddy," Sanj called out.

"No aeroplane to fly?" Peter looked up and shook his head.

"No—Tom's still in the circuit, so I've been planning my cross country."

They both walked over to take a look. "Wow—that looks a long way," Paula said, eyes wide.

"You'll have to let me borrow your planning once you've flown it—save me doing it," Sanj said, laughing.

"No point," Peter quickly retorted. "We each get a different route so that there's no copying."

Sanj shook his head, looking deflated. "Oh, well—nice try," he said, following Paula and heading for the kitchen. Peter joined him and they were soon all engrossed in the day's most important lesson—lunch.

The afternoon session began as soon as lunch had been finished—the instructors were beginning to push them a bit harder and there was very little let-up. Peter spent the afternoon doing practice tests and then rereading his notes to see where he'd been wrong and to try to improve his score but without success.

After arriving home, he went out for his usual run and returned to find shouting going on in the kitchen. He looked into the doorway as he passed to see Mark, Arnie and Tom in heated discussion.

Peter paused just out of sight and heard Mark saying, "Oh come on, Tom—you've hardly put in much effort have you? You haven't even flown solo yet and you failed the last exam and had to re-sit and you're asking for help again, yet when I came in you were reading the newspaper."

Tom didn't reply and then Peter heard Arnie's voice, "There's no point asking us for more help—we've as much work to do as you and I'm finding it difficult enough. If it hadn't been for Peter helping you out, you'd not have passed your re-sit. You need to pull your finger out."

There was a pause before Tom replied, "I don't think I'm going to make it to solo standard—I just can't master it. Too tense I guess. As for the exams—I'm finding a lot of it irrelevant, so why bother with it?"

"Because as Captain Woods said to us—it's to learn and then we'll use about twenty percent of it once we're qualified, but you've still to pass—it's a rite of passage," Arnie replied.

"Yeah well, if I flunk this next exam I'll be out of here," Tom growled. Peter snuck upstairs, leaving them to it, showering and going straight back to his book.

The next morning dawned bright with light winds. Peter was excited about the prospect of the day's flying—from Longley to another small airfield on the South Coast, then on to an airport near the River Thames and return. Three separate flights with Mike, there and back again. Then if all went well, to do it again solo tomorrow. Once they had arrived, Peter made a bee line for the weather information, getting the wind and weather for the route. All looked favourable, although the wind was expected to increase later in the day and he sat down to finish his calculations and planning.

At about nine-thirty, Peter was just getting up and putting his chart and planning together when Mike walked in. "All good to go?" he asked.

Peter nodded and Mike walked over. "Let's have a look at your planning then," he said, taking the flight log from Peter and giving it a cursory glance. "That all looks good. We're in Oscar Romeo, so go and pre-flight her and I'll join you in five minutes."

Peter went outside to see the aircraft sitting waiting on the grass. He carefully put everything he needed inside and turned on the master switch to begin his checks. Once satisfied that everything was in order, he slid into the left hand seat, put on his belt and plugging in his headphones, waited for Mike to join him. Glancing over his shoulder, he saw Mike striding towards him, accompanied by another man in uniform, but he couldn't make out who it was.

Shortly, the door was pulled open and a familiar face appeared—it was Fozzy. Peter was surprised to see him. "Hello, dear boy—mind if I join you?" he asked.

"Err—of course not," Peter mumbled. He hadn't been expecting this. Fozzy jumped into the back seat and Mike sat down in the right hand seat.

Once they had put their headphones on, Mike said, "You may remember Captain Fosdyke from the interviews. He sometimes joins us to check on progress. I think he just likes to keep an eye on us instructors," he laughed and then Fozzy added, "Exactly right. Got to keep you guys on your toes."

Peter smiled and continued with his preparations. Once Peter was ready to depart, he heard Fozzy say, "Just forget I'm here. I just fancied a day out and a bimble in a light aircraft."

Peter said nothing and they were soon on their way, with Peter carefully following his log and flying his headings.

After an hour, Peter had his first destination in sight, so he commenced his descent, lined up on the runway and bought the aircraft down to a smooth landing. There was no comment from either of his passengers. Once they had shut down, Fozzy asked to be let out for a "comfort break" and he and Mike walked off, returning ten minutes later. There were quickly on their way and this leg of the journey was more complex for Peter, flying around controlled airspace near to large airports, but he managed to keep out of trouble and they were soon on the ground for a second time.

"No need to shut down—we'll taxy around and get straight off if that's OK," Mike said.

Peter nodded and taxied back down the runway, turning around and taking off immediately. Very soon, Longley hove into view and Peter called for the airfield information, noting down the runway in use and the wind information. "A bit of a crosswind," he said and Mike just nodded his head, adding, "No problem."

Peter turned onto final approach, wrestling the controls against the blustery wind blowing straight across the runway. Ahead, he could see the other two aircraft on the parking area. Over the hedge and Peter landed as smoothly as he could, taxying in and shutting down quickly. As the engine died, he pulled his headphones off and listened to the ticking of hot metal from the engine and the whine of the gyros running down and let out a long breath.

Mike unlocked the door, turning to Peter saying, "Well done—good flying. Solo tomorrow," and he stood up and clambered down off the wing, closely followed by Fozzy.

Peter soon joined them on the grass and Fozzy slapped him on the back, saying, "Well done, old boy—good effort. Hope you enjoyed that as much as I did?"

"I did, thank you, Sir," Peter replied quietly and he saw Fozzy wink at him.

When they arrived back in the classroom, Mike and Fozzy went into huddled conversation before Peter heard Fozzy say quietly, "Long haul." He had no idea what this meant, but Fozzy shortly turned to him and said, "OK—well done. I'm off—hope to see you soon," and he came over, shook Peter's hand and disappeared. Peter was exhausted but elated. What a great day's flying and so good to see Fozzy again.

The following day, Peter was scheduled to fly at eleven thirty, so he spent the morning carefully replanning the flight with regard to the prevailing winds and just before he was ready to set off, Mike came over to check his planning. In his hand was a sheet of paper.

"Right—when you land at both airfields, it's vital that you go to the Air Traffic unit and get this paper signed, so we know that you've actually landed there. Don't, whatever you do, forget. OK?" Peter nodded. "OK then—off you go," Mike said, shooing Peter out of the door.

Within the space of a few short minutes, Peter was once again airborne. Both legs passed without incident and Peter was soon turning towards the runway at Longley, landing and quickly taxying in and shutting down. He slowly climbed down off the wing, his muscles aching from the tension, but very pleased with himself. Inside, he found Mike in his office and handed the cross country confirmation over.

"All signed? Good. All go well?" Mike asked and Peter nodded. "Good— then it's more navigation solo time next to build your hours and keep you going until your birthday in a few months," Mike said, putting the piece of paper in a filing cabinet. Peter smiled, muttering his thanks and turned towards the door. "Captain Fosdyke was impressed," Mike continued. "He's now chief pilot, so he's a good man to get on your side."

Peter simply said, "Thanks" and went towards the kitchen. He needed a drink.

The next two days saw both Paula and Sanj complete their solo qualifying flights and by Friday morning they were in high spirits. Sitting down for the exam, Peter glanced across at Tom, who looked completely flustered. Peter, for the first time in his life, felt totally unprepared for this exam, despite all the studying and practice tests he'd done. Turning his attention to the exam paper, he ran his eyes down the list of questions and none of them made any sense.

His palms began to sweat and with his heart racing and a dry mouth, he filled in his name on the answer sheet and began to read. Peter slowly filled in his answers, carefully checking them over and over and making furtive glances at the clock on the wall. All too soon, time was called, just as Peter filled in the final answer. He let out a long-held breath and slowly rose to his feet.

He'd failed—no question of that. He knew somewhere along this journey, he'd mess up. Sighing and silently cursing his own stupidity, he joined Paula as they had been rostered together for a dual flight to another airfield, flying one leg each way. Once airborne, Paula chatted constantly about the exam and Peter listened politely, not wanting to jinx his chances.

When they landed back at Longley, the results were posted. Both had passed with good scores. Relief washed over him—how had he passed? No matter—it would remain a mystery. Looking closer at the results, Peter noticed the word "Review" next to Tom's name. He shook his head and put it out of his mind.

On the bus home, the conversation was kept to a minimum and Peter was planning his usual quick getaway to try and get the early train. When they arrived, he shot into the house, quickly changing out of his uniform and stuffing his clothes into his bag, he dashed downstairs to see Tom staring out of the window.

"I'll see you on Monday," Peter called and Tom turned around.

"I hate to ask, but I'll need your help again next week—I failed again today," Tom said quietly. Peter quickly nodded and ran for the door. By the time he was on the train, he'd forgotten all about it.

29

Monday morning saw all the students waiting for the bus as usual and everyone except Tom seemed to be in high spirits. Peter felt that he was making good progress and was happy with his achievements so far and this was generally reflected with the group. Soon, they were back at the airfield and Peter, who was paired with Sanj, was planning a route for the morning navigation exercise.

Tom had been taken to one side by Brian when they arrived, but Peter had taken no notice, his mind focused on the morning ahead. Soon he and Sanj were airborne, grinning and laughing like two small boys who had been given the keys to the best toy box in the world.

Outbound they flew and after about ninety minutes they saw their destination and Sanj—who was flying—lined up for landing. Once they had shut down, they went in search of coffee and after a short break, they were back in the air with Peter at the controls. It was an uneventful flight, but Sanj teased Peter all the way home, pointing out aircraft on a collision course that weren't really there, non-existent airspace and false problems with the aircraft. Peter was smiling to himself at Sanj's antics and thoroughly enjoyed the flight. All too soon they were back on home ground.

Over lunch, Brian called all of them together and cleared his throat. "Sadly, I have to tell you that Tom's training has been terminated, for reasons that I can't discuss. He's been sent back to the crew house in a taxi and will have cleared his room and probably have left by the time you get home this evening. At this point I want to reassure the rest of you that we're happy with everyone's progress and we want you to carry on as you have been doing."

He left the room to stunned silence. After a few nervous glances, the students began to speak. "I'm not really surprised—he was lazy," Arnie ventured to general agreement.

"I think he expected us all to pull him through, but I've enough on getting myself through," Mark added.

Everyone started to talk at once and Peter listened to the conversation without saying anything. He felt no regret for Tom—no sympathy. He was gone and that was it. Soon, it was time for the afternoon's flying and Peter was paired with Paula, who busied herself with route planning. After two enjoyable flights, they were soon on the bus back home and Peter was desperate for his evening run as he'd been cooped up in a small aircraft for about five hours.

Once Peter had returned, showered and eaten, he joined his colleagues in the living area. The mood was sombre, but the discussions of Tom's departure had ceased and everyone was looking ahead. There was simply nothing else for anyone to add.

The weeks turned into months and they flew and studied hard as spring turned into summer, with each of them achieving the goals set for them. In late August, Peter was on the train home back to Westlea and he was troubled by a phone call he'd had with his mother. She'd told him that "Something was up" but didn't elaborate. Peter thought at first that maybe his Gran was ill, but Annie had reassured him that it was nothing like that.

Dark thoughts filled his head—were his parents OK? Were they getting divorced? Had dad lost his job? If Gran was OK, then what could possibly be wrong? Finally, the train screeched to a halt and Peter jumped down onto the platform, seeing his dad behind the barrier. Strange—Paul didn't finish work at this time and he was always met by his mother. A quick hug and they were shortly on the bus towards home. Paul was saying nothing and Peter found the silence uncomfortable.

Once inside, Annie came rushing to the door, throwing her arms around Peter. He returned her embrace, setting his bag down onto the floor. Finally, she let go and Peter looked at them both before asking, "OK—what's going on?"

"Come and sit down, son," Paul said, opening the living room door.

Peter sat nervously in his usual place and Annie and Paul sat together. There was a tense silence, which was finally broken by Paul. "It's Ben," he began.

Peter thought for a moment before asking, "Is he OK? Has he been hurt or something?"

"No, it's nothing like that," Paul replied. "You remember your mother saying that he'd said that he was thinking of starting a business?" Peter nodded. "Well, we've had a letter from the ministry of defence—he certainly started a business. He's been buying and dealing drugs to his fellow squaddies and has been arrested. They are saying that it's a very serious offence and he's going to be facing a Court Martial—if guilty he could face time in Army detention."

Peter remained silent, but could see the tears filling Annie's eyes and the look of total loss on her face. Finally, Peter managed to speak. "Oh. That sounds bad—why would he do something so stupid?"

Paul shook his head. "Beats me—we always bought him up to be honest and to have nothing to do with that sort of thing. Anything like that in the RAF was dealt with harshly—although we didn't have drugs back in our day," Paul added.

"So what happens next?" Peter asked.

"There's a preliminary hearing in a couple of weeks and in the meantime he's been confined to barracks," Paul said quietly.

Peter sat quietly and then after a short while he got up and went to his room. Sitting down on the bed, all he could think was *What an idiot* and decided that Ben deserved all he got.

Later, he heard Annie calling him and he went downstairs finding her in the kitchen. He put his arm around her and she stood very still, her hand covering his. "You OK?" he asked.

"I guess so," she replied, her voice trembling. Peter stood and just held her, not releasing his grip. Finally, she lifted her head and said brightly "OK, young man—what do you want for dinner?"

Peter smiled—he hoped that she was going to be OK, but guessed that it must be an awful shock for them both.

After dinner, the conversation turned to Peter's progress as usual and Peter updated them with where he was and how he was doing. Paul asked his usual questions and Peter could see Annie looking at him with a slight smile on her face. *I won't let you down*, he thought to himself.

Eventually, Peter decided that it was bed time and he climbed the stairs.

Monday morning was a departure from the normal routine. The students were to attend the head offices for dress uniform fitting and there was an air of excitement amongst them all. Paula was first be called and she disappeared into a room with a female secretary who was acting as chaperone, emerging about twenty minutes later with a huge smile on her face.

"Well?" Mark asked.

"Perfect—I looked amazing," Paula replied, laughing.

One by one they were called, with Peter being last. Once inside, the tailor asked Peter to go into a makeshift changing room and he found a uniform hanging on a peg. Peter carefully put it on, noting that there were pins sticking out of the lapels. He slid into his shoes and pulled the curtain aside. The tailor came over, pulling and smoothing the jacket, adjusting some of the pins to suit. Looking down at the trouser cuffs, he said to Peter, "We'd better let these down a little, seeing as you've grown since last time."

Peter just nodded, embarrassed by the whole episode. He hated personal contact. On the shoulder of the jacket were epaulettes with one gold stripe. Peter glanced at these in the mirror, allowing himself a moment of reflection—at least he looked the part, even though there was a long way to go. "All the gear and no idea," he mused, smiling.

The following week, the instructors called them together for a briefing. Mike stood up. "OK—as you're now all at the same point, next week we'll be bringing in a twin engine aircraft to commence multi-engine training. You'll train as you have been doing, with one flying and one in the back seat, swapping over as usual. Seeing as we're now into long evening daylight, we plan to fly into the evenings. Any questions?"

Peter raised his hand. "How long is the multi-engine course for?" he asked.

"Good question," Mike replied. "Seven hours training and then a test. Once completed, we're going to start instrument training. Any more questions?"

There was silence, so Mike dismissed them all and left them to continue with their studies. On the bus home that evening, there was an air of excitement and anticipation and Peter was determined to finish his studies for what was the final written exam.

On Saturday morning, Peter was just getting up when he heard the phone ring. Shortly, Annie knocked on his door, telling him that Alex was on the phone. Peter rushed downstairs, grabbing the receiver. "Hi, buddy," he said, hearing Alex's voice.

"Hi—how are you?" Alex began. Soon they were chatting as though it had been just yesterday since they'd seen each other. In reality, it had been a couple of months. They arranged to meet in the afternoon and Peter put the phone down, excited to see his friend. After a leisurely breakfast and some time with his parents, Peter set off. He was soon in town, with its familiar sights and smells and he walked slowly towards their favourite coffee bar, arriving early.

He was soon sat by the window, watching the world go by and enjoying himself, when he heard his name being called. He looked up to see Alex and Anna approaching. He stood up, giving Anna a quick hug and clasping Alex's hand. Anna was first to speak. "Wow—have you grown again since we last saw you?"

Peter nodded, saying, "I think so. We had our uniform fitting and the guy said that he'd have to let the trousers down an inch or so, so guess I must have."

Anna nodded, adding, "and your beard is so dark—are you shaving every day?"

Again, Peter nodded. "Poor you," said Alex. "Being fair skinned, I've not really started shaving yet."

"That's because you're still a baby," Anna joked and they all laughed. Peter smiled to himself—it was so good to see his friends and be back to normality, if only for a weekend.

Soon, they were catching up with each other, swapping stories of what they'd been up to and how things were going. "How's the A-Levels going?" Peter asked.

Anna and Alex exchanged glances before saying in unison, "Boring."

Peter laughed. "Well, you must have finished for the summer, so guess you'll be in your final year soon?" he asked.

"Yes and we can apply for Med School around next April, as soon as we get our predicted grades," Anna said.

Peter nodded, saying "Confident?"

"No, not really," Alex replied, but Anna silenced him, saying, "Yes—and Alex is being modest. He'll do OK."

"I hope so or my dad will slaughter me," Alex said, looking across at Anna.

"You'll be OK—you seem to be taking it in your stride." Anna smiled, squeezing Alex's hand. "Let's get some sunshine," she said, standing up.

Outside, it was a hot still day and the Saturday crowds seemed to all be enjoying the weather. They strolled aimlessly along the high street, pausing every so often to glance in shop windows and buying ice creams to combat the heat.

Sitting down on a bench, they continued to chat and then a familiar face caught Peter's eye. Quickly he stood up, calling out, "Liam. Liam—over here."

He could see Liam and Sally in the crowd and saw him look over before turning away. Peter ran towards where Liam had been and quickly caught up. "Liam—hi, buddy," he said, grabbing Liam's arm.

Liam turned around, smiled and said, "Oh, hi, buddy. How are you?" Sally stayed facing the other way.

"I'm fine—how are you both?" Peter asked, glad to see them.

"Oh, OK, I guess," Liam responded and Peter said to Sally, "and how are you?"

For a moment there was no response, but finally she turned around, smiling and said, "Oh, hi, Peter. I'm fine, thanks."

As she turned, Peter noticed that she folded her arms across her tummy and that it was swollen to a considerable size. He didn't know how to react or what to say. Sally, seeing Peter looking at her said quietly, "Yes—I'm pregnant. It's due in December."

Peter stayed silent, desperately seeing the right response and finally said, "Oh. Err—congratulations."

"Thanks," Sally mumbled.

Liam said nothing, but looked uncomfortable. Soon, Alex and Anna had caught up and again there was a momentary silence before Anna gave Sally a hug, Alex slapped Liam's on the back and the girls walked off chatting furiously.

"Err—well done, old boy," Alex said to Liam. "When did this happen?"

Liam looked at Alex long and hard before replying, "It was an accident, but her parents wouldn't let us get rid of it, so I'm stuck with the situation. I'm only just halfway through my apprenticeship and my dad's furious."

"Well, I'm sure that you'll make best of it," Alex replied.

"I'm not so sure—it's the last thing I needed," Liam replied forlornly. They turned to follow the girls and the silence between then was deafening. Alex remained silent and Peter just didn't know what to say, but gradually Liam opened up. "We're going to rent a flat and when it arrives, Sally's mum is going to help out. My mum will as well, but she's not to enamoured with the prospect of being a granny. I've really made a mess of things," he sighed.

"I'm sure it will all work out," Alex said, trying to reassure his friend, but Liam just shook his head. All Peter could think was that Liam had been foolish and that he'd had a lucky escape. If he'd stayed with Sally, his aviation career would be finished before it had begun.

Eventually, Peter decided that it was time to head home, so he said farewell to his friends and headed off. He decided to walk as it was such a lovely warm day and he needed the fresh air. He hummed as he walked along the familiar streets, leaving the town centre behind and reaching open spaces with trees and flowers in full bloom, birdsong in the hedgerows and insects buzzing as they went about their busy lives. The heavy scent of honeysuckle filled the air and Peter felt at peace.

Finally, as he neared home, he heard the unmistakable sound of aero engines. Pausing to look towards the airport across the fields, he saw one of the old piston freighters climbing slowly towards the summer sky, engines straining at full power. He smiled, knowing the pilots would be squinting against the summer sun, watching their instruments carefully for any overheating.

He could also see the mound next to the runway—the mound where he'd spent so many days, watching, listening, noting down registrations and enjoying his hobby. Was it really a year ago when he'd sat beneath the lone tree in the wind and rain opening and reading his exam results? A year ago that Ben had screwed them up and thrown them in his face? A year ago that he'd slipped the note into Ben's rucksack? What a massive difference twelve short months had made—here he was in a far better place and where was Ben? Confined to his room in Cyprus, facing a very uncertain future, that's where.

Eventually, Peter walked the last half-mile towards home, where he found Annie sitting in the garden in her shorts and a bikini top. "Hi, sweetie," she said as Peter let himself through the gate. "How was Alex?" Peter sat down next to Annie asking where Paul was. Annie nodded towards the garage. "With his mistress," she whispered, laughing.

Peter smiled and said "Mum—do you remember when I was going out with Sally that we had a discussion about—you know—adult stuff. Physical stuff?"

Annie looked at him carefully, answering, "Yes—why?"

"Well, I met up with Alex and Anna, who are both fine. They've finished their first year of A-Levels and will be applying to Med School next year. I also saw Liam in the distance—I called his name and he turned and saw me, then walked off. I caught up with him and he was with Sally. He seemed very distant and when I said hello to Sally, she turned around—and she's pregnant. I didn't know what to say so I didn't really say anything."

Annie remained quiet for a few minutes before replying, "That's so sad and so unnecessary in this day and age. How is Liam about it?"

"Pretty fed up I think," Peter replied. "They are going to get a flat and Sally's mum is going to help out. I'm just so glad that I—I didn't do anything so stupid."

Annie put her hand on his arm. "So am I—you did the right thing. I think Sally would have walked all over you in the end."

Peter nodded an agreement, saying, "Yes—I think she was a bit wild for me—she seemed very pushy."

Annie squeezed his arm, saying, "there will be plenty of time for that—you get yourself qualified first," to which Peter just smiled in agreement.

Seeing Liam and Sally and with Paula and Mark upstairs at the house, it seemed that everybody was at it, but he wasn't interested. Flying was his mistress and she was an unpredictable one, with many moods and foibles and he loved her for it.

30

Arriving at Longley on Monday morning, Peter looked out across the airfield, but couldn't see any new aircraft. Inside, they were called straight into a briefing. Paul Woods stood in front of the board, chalk in hand. "Right boys and girls—multi engine theory," and he started to take the cadets through the physics and differences in flying an aircraft with two engines.

He drew complicated diagrams, charts and wrote a long checklist before finishing with, "This is your engine failure checklist. Learn it off by heart—it serves for any multi-engine aircraft, piston or jet. Things happen very quickly in one of these and you have to be on the ball. Failure to follow this quickly or mis-identifying the failed engine will result in death—simple as that, so learn it and learn it well."

There was a stunned silence before Arnie quipped, "What happens if both fail?" which bought a roar of laughter from everyone and Paul laughed before saying simply, "Pray, dear boy—pray hard."

Soon they broke for lunch and sitting outside Peter was chatting to Mark when they heard a new sound—more powerful engines and they turned to see a sleek new aircraft approach over the hedge and settle onto the runway before taxying in. It was white with a blue and gold flash along the fuselage and had an engine on each wing. Peter felt a shiver of excitement run through his veins—this looked so cool, so sexy and so sleek. He couldn't wait to be sat in the flightdeck.

It finally shut down and Brian appeared through the door, waving. As a group, they all walked over to take a look at their new toy. "Here we are—A Piper Twin Comanche," Brian said by way of introduction.

Soon, they were crawling all over their new aircraft, pointing out features in wonderment. Peter managed to be first through the door and into the left seat—where he saw a bewildering array of new instruments and three pairs of levers in place of the two single ones that he was used to, each pair a different colour. He sat trying to take it all in before Sanj tugged on his arm saying, "C'mon—let someone else have a look," and was pulled from the cockpit.

Everyone was chatting excitedly and Peter walked around the plane trying to take in all the features. Shortly, they were called back inside.

Paul spoke quickly, "Right—you've seen your new toy and the flight roster is on the board. It's different from the usual roster as we're pairing you up but you'll each do the whole course and test before someone else takes over. That usually means a whole week of intensive flying, although if the weather is kind, we may get a second course started this week. For those still on the single engine aircraft, navigation hour building as usual. Off we go," and with that he walked to the back of the room and out of the door.

Inside, there was a mad scramble to look at the roster—Paula and Arnie were first and Peter saw his name in the second set with Mark. Disappointed, he went to the planning room and sat down with his chart. He was shortly joined by Mark and they discussed a route for the afternoon and began to plan and were soon out at the aircraft.

Once they had landed back at Longley, they could see the twin in the circuit. It looked really fast compared to what they were used to flying and as they watched, it turned towards final approach, lowering its wheels and setting up for landing. Down it came to about two hundred feet and suddenly they heard the engines at full power and saw the nose rise.

Immediately the sound quickly diminished and the nose swung hard to the left. They continued to watch as the wheels were retracted and the nose continued to swing to and fro. Around it went for another try. Captivated, Mark and Peter continued to watch and they were treated to a repeat of the whole performance.

"That looks like a handful," Mark commented and Peter nodded in agreement. Handful or not, he was eager to try it out. Shortly, they were back on the bus, with Paula and Arnie regaling the rest of them with their versions of flying the twin.

"It's so hard—it all happens so quickly," Paula was saying. "The instructor tells you to go around and as you apply power and pitch up, he covers the throttles with his clipboard and pulls the power off of one engine. You have to work out which one whilst not letting the speed drop below the blue line and go through the shutdown checklist. I don't think that I'll ever get it right. My legs are killing me with the effort of applying full rudder to counter the asymmetric thrust."

Mark jokingly leant forward to rub her thigh but she slapped his hand away, much to everyone's amusement. Arnie then spoke, "My turn tomorrow—I was watching you and thinking how the hell are you managing to fly and control the aircraft. Your hands were a blur of motion, darting everywhere. Think I'll need a big breakfast in the morning."

Peter's afternoon with Mark seemed tame by comparison.

The week went by quickly and by Thursday evening, Paula had managed to complete her seven hours and was ready for test on Friday after the final exam. Hopefully Arnie would also finish and on Monday it would be Peter's turn with Mark. He was so excited and after studying for most of the evening, he went to bed early. The early sunrise work him and he was up and ready by seven thirty. Slowly his colleagues appeared and Paula looked nervous and flustered. Peter was trying to remain calm, but this final exam was known to be the hardest and he wanted to do well.

Everybody seemed a little subdued and the journey to the airfield was taken in silence. Once inside the classroom, they were quickly organised by Brian for the exam. "Have you all got your calculators?" he asked. There was a murmur of "Yes" and he handed out the exam papers and answer sheets, face down. "Right—you have ninety minutes for this exam—read the questions very carefully," he said and allowed them to start.

Peter turned the paper over, wrote his name on the answer sheet and began. He had to read the first question three times before he understood it, quickly calculating the answer and putting a tick in what he hoped was the correct box. Slowly, he worked his way through, leaving one question unanswered, which he planned to come back to at the end.

Eventually, he got to the end and returned to the one he'd left blank. Reading it through once again he understood it and quickly put the answer in before realising that he'd not left a space on the answer sheet. All of the subsequent answers would now be out of sync, so he furiously went through crossing out and rewriting the answers. He was so cross with himself for his stupidity, but he managed to complete rewriting the answer sheet just as Brian called out, "Time up—pencils down."

Phew—that had been a close call. As Brian came to Peter's desk, he explained what he'd done and apologised for all the crossing out. "Don't worry—we've all done it," Brian said helpfully, making Peter feel a whole lot better, although he was still cursing himself for being so stupid.

Once outside, they all watched as Paula was pre-flighting the twin, finally clambering aboard. She'd be on her own with just Paul for this flight as he was the multi-engine examiner. Soon she'd started up and was climbing furiously towards the heavens. Due to it being an exam day and also Paula's test, the rest of them hadn't been assigned anything and so they sat around chatting and drinking.

After an hour or so, they heard engines approaching and saw the twin on final approach, wheels down and looking good. Just like a few days earlier, as it crossed the hedge, it pitched up, engines at full power, quickly followed be the simulated loss of one engine. Wheels went up and the nose was lowered slightly, but it didn't swing like last time. Around it flew, setting up on approach a second time. This time it landed and slowed to a stop.

Peter turned to look at Arnie, saying, "Your turn," Arnie smiled thinly and disappeared back towards the classrooms.

Finally Paula appeared and jumped off the wing. She was holding a piece of paper and jumping up and down enthusiastically. "She passed is my guess," Mark said to Peter, who nodded his agreement.

She soon re-joined the group, laughing and chattering excitedly. Peter offered his congratulations and asked how it had gone. "Very quickly and bloody hard work," she replied, "but great fun."

Peter smiled—he was looking forward to Monday so much. Arnie reappeared and walked slowly to the aircraft, joining Paul next to the aircraft. Soon he climbed inside and off they went. Peter got up to stretch his legs and went back to the classroom, just in time to see Brian pinning the exam results to the board. Immediately, his heart began to beat hard in his chest and with a dry mouth he asked if he'd passed.

"Your paper was a bit of a mess but we worked out which answer was which," he said laughing.

"Thanks," Peter mumbled and he looked at the results. Passed—ninety-six percent. A wave of relief swept over him. *That's a big hurdle out of the way*, he thought before going back outside and telling everyone that the results had been posted. There was a charge of bodies towards the building and Peter sat back down in the sunshine, content. Shortly, his colleagues reappeared one by one, all wearing big smiles.

Sanj came and sat with Peter and said, "Well, that's it. All the theory passed. I'm so relieved to get it out of the way."

Peter nodded his agreement, saying quietly, "So am I—now we can concentrate on the fun stuff."

Soon, Arnie reappeared and just as Paula had done, he set up for approach before going around and "losing" an engine. It all looked very smooth and he was soon back on the ground and just like Paula, he'd passed. Everyone was so pleased for them both and soon after a debrief with the examiners, they were sent off early for the weekend.

Peter was anxious to get home, as this week should have been Ben's preliminary hearing and he was worried—not for Ben, about whom he cared not a damn, but for his parents. They had taken the news hard and even though Paul hadn't said much, Peter know that he was taking it all badly. It went against Paul's military background and every family member who had served throughout the ages had done so with distinction and this must be hard for Paul to deal with.

Being on the train gave Peter time for thought and reflection. He was anxious and excited all at the same time about the training on the twin, but had decided that if others could manage, then so could he. In no time at all, he was pulling into Westlea station. As soon as he jumped down from the train, he saw his mother waving enthusiastically and he strode towards the barrier as fast as he could. As used as he was getting to living independently, he relished the weekends, just to be back with the people that he loved and to be once again in that familiar environment.

Once through the barrier, Annie rushed up to him, giving him a great big hug. "How's my man?" she asked.

"Mmm, I'm great thanks—how are you both?" he asked.

"OK," Annie replied quietly, turning towards the bus stop. "How come you're so early this week?"

"We sat our final exam and for two of the others it was their multi-engine tests and we've all passed, so the instructors sent us home early," Peter explained.

"Oh that's good to hear," Annie replied. "So all your exams are finished?"

"All of the written ones, yes," Peter said, as they sat down to wait for the bus.

Annie nodded her head, saying, "Good," quietly. Once home, Peter quickly emptied his bag of washing for Annie to attend to and they sat down to talk. "So what's next?" she asked.

"Well, on Monday I start flying the aircraft with two engines, which is much more difficult, but great fun I expect," Peter began. "Once I've done that, we start learning how to fly the aircraft blind, using just the instruments. Remember I showed you some of them in the transport museum in town?"

Annie nodded her head. She was listening and taking it in, but it didn't make much sense to her. "Why do you have to do that—why can't you look out of the window?" she asked.

Peter smiled—it was a familiar question. "Imagine if we're flying in a cloud or if it's foggy on the ground. If it's foggy, we use a radio beam from the runway to keep the aircraft on the runway heading and at the correct height so that we don't just fly into the ground. All we do is follow the instruments and do as they tell us. It's very accurate and very reliable." Peter explained.

Annie listened quietly, just saying "Amazing" when Peter had finished explaining. Soon, they heard the door open and Paul's voice. "I'm home," he called, adding, "What time are you collecting Peter?"

Peter got up, held his finger to his lips and tiptoed to the door, which he opened slowly. He could see his dad, back towards him, removing his boots. "About now," Peter said and Paul spun around, a big smile crossing his face.

"Hello, son—you're home early," he said.

"Yes—they let us out early today as we've finished all the exams and we had nothing scheduled this afternoon," Peter explained once again.

"Good—great to see you home," Paul said, coming across the kitchen and giving Peter a hug.

"It's always good to be home," Peter replied, adding, "I wonder what's for dinner?"

This made Paul laugh out loud and he shouted to Annie, "Annie—we've a hungry young man here who wants to eat us out of house and home."

Annie quickly joined them, kissing Paul on the cheek and asking, "Well what do my two men fancy for dinner?"

Paul shrugged his shoulders and Peter told them about Sanj bringing chicken curry to the crew house and that it was delicious. "Well, I've nothing like that, but I could look at a recipe sometime if you want."

Peter shrugged, answering, "It's OK—no need. It was delicious though—you should try it sometime."

Paul nodded, saying, "We had an Indian lad in our unit during the war. He could whip us some fearsome curries—from mild to blow your head off. I did enjoy the mild ones though."

"Well, I've no curry, but let me get started—it's Annie's surprise for dinner this evening," Annie said, laughing and she shooed the boys out of the room.

Once sat comfortably, Peter asked—in his usual direct fashion—whether they had heard anything about Ben. Paul went quiet for a moment before answering.

"Yes. The ministry telephoned your mother yesterday. Ben's preliminary hearing was on Wednesday and he's been remanded to stand before a Court Martial on a few charges. There's bringing drugs onto Crown Property, supply of drugs, desertion as he was absent without leave for a week when all this kicked off and bringing his Regiment into disrepute. He's been remanded in custody until the Court Martial, which will be in a couple of months. He's been appointed a Lawyer Officer to defend him and so we'll have to wait and see what happens."

Peter listened quietly before asking, "How are you feeling about all this dad? You must be pretty disappointed."

Paul sat quietly, but Peter could see the tears welling up in his eyes. "Well," he began. "Not good, really. Never had to deal with anything like this before. Your mother's in pieces as you'd expect and to be honest, I'm ashamed of him. Never happened in our family before—no-one has ever been absent without leave. It's desertion and that's just not on."

Peter nodded but remained silent. He'd never seen his parents like this and we were at a loss of how to deal with it. He was lost in silent thought for a few minutes before Paul bought him back to reality. "So—you said you'd passed the final exam correct?"

"Yes," Peter replied. "I start training on a twin engine aircraft on Monday, then it's on to Instrument flight." Peter went on to explain once again about flying on instruments, but Paul understood immediately.

"Yes, we had those on Hurricanes in the war—it was called the blind flying panel," he explained.

Peter nodded saying, "Exactly the same I guess, although we have direction finding and approach instruments as well."

"Sounds very interesting if a little difficult," Paul replied.

"Yeah, guess so," Peter replied, hearing Annie's voice calling them for dinner. Peter was there in a flash.

31

Monday morning found Peter awake early as usual. He was excited and nervous all at the same time and had spent the weekend reading and rereading his checklist for the twin. He felt confident that he'd memorised the emergency drills, but it was now a case of getting used to the controls and switches. He'd been paired with Sanj, so it would be a week—or more—of flying and studying together. Peter had finally managed to come out of his shell a bit more with his colleagues and he got on well with Sanj, so didn't foresee any problems arising.

When they arrived at Longley, the cloud base was low but flyable and Peter and Sanj were taken immediately into a separate room by Paul, who began to take them through the complexities of flying an aircraft with retractable undercarriage and two engines. Once the briefing was over, they went out to the aircraft and Peter elected to fly first. He was soon strapped in next to Paul, who showed him the location of the important switches and levers and most importantly, a large wheel on the throttle pedestal for rudder trim—something that he'd not used before.

"You wind that thing like fury when one engine fails," Paul said with a grin. He then helped Peter through the engine start up and they taxied out for take-off. Lining up carefully, Peter shoved both throttles forward and the plane shot forwards like a racing car. They were almost instantly at take-off speed, so Peter pulled back on the controls and they shot up into the sky. This thing was fast! All the time, Paul was prompting him and they soon settled down and got the aeroplane stabilised.

This first hour was just a familiarisation flight and they were soon headed back to the field. Peter set up for the approach, put the wheels down and floated over the hedge to settle onto the grass this thing was a joy to fly! They were soon parked up, engines cooling and Peter and Sanj swapped places. Peter was going to enjoy watching his friend work hard!

Following Sanj's flight, they debriefed over lunch. "So how did you like a proper aeroplane?" Paul asked.

"I was amazed at how quickly things happen," Peter said. "I guess I'll get used to doing nearly twice the speed that I'm used to."

"You will—and it will become second nature to you," Paul replied. "Now this afternoon, we're going to see what happens when we fail an engine just after take-off. Whatever else, you must maintain your airspeed—never let the needle drop below the blue line. I'll obviously be helping at first, but your checklist actions must be quick, positive and concise—understand?" Both Sanj and Peter nodded. "Good—when you've finished lunch, we'll get going," Paul added, getting up to leave.

Soon, they were strapping in and Peter ran through his start up checks, bringing both engines online. They lined up and Peter shoved the levers forward. Off they shot and Peter pulled back on the controls and out of the corner of his eye he could see Paul covering the throttles with his clipboard.

All of a sudden, the engine note died and the aircraft swung hard to the left. Peter shoved the right pedal forwards, watching the airspeed indicator and Paul prompted him through the actions he needed to take—lower the nose, identify the failed engine, wind in right rudder trim, simulate closing the propellor control and throttle, switch off the magnetos and alternator, stabilise the aircraft. All of this was accomplished in seconds and Peter was shaking with concentration as they slowly climbed.

"Not too bad for a first effort. I'll give you the engine back, bring us round the circuit and we'll set up for a go-around and do it all again," Paul said quickly.

Peter did as requested and soon they were pointed at the runway, wheels down. Paul called, "Go around" and as Peter reapplied the power the same thing happened—only this time the nose swung right.

"Right failure," called Peter and he went through the actions once again, the nose swinging wildly left and right. For a whole hour, Peter was put through his paces, eventually getting the gist of what he was doing. He and Sanj then swapped places and Peter fell into the back seat, exhausted. He'd sleep well that night!

The rest of the week followed along the same lines and they explored the flight envelope of the twin, taking it up to ten thousand feet, stalling, doing steep turns and generally having fun. Peter loved flying it and very soon he'd done the required hours and was pronounced ready for his test, which would take place on Friday morning. The day dawned and Peter was up very early. He sat on the end of his bed, flying the aircraft around the circuit in his mind as he'd been shown by Paul.

Sitting with his eyes closed, he mimicked the actions, reaching out for invisible levers and switches until he was satisfied and decided that it was time for breakfast. On the way to the field, Peter stayed silent, his mind in a different place—this was his first real flight test and he wanted to do well and didn't really know what to expect. Once they had arrived, he was again briefed by Paul and was sent out to the aircraft alone to carry out his pre-flight checks. Soon he was strapped in and Paul joined him.

"OK—all ready?" Paul asked. Peter nodded in confirmation. "Right—start up and off we go. Take your time with everything and if you're unsure of what I've asked you to do, ask for clarification, understand?"

Peter just said "Yes" quietly and was soon lining up ready for take-off.

"OK—let's go," Paul said and Peter opened the throttles. The first part of the hour passed by in a blur as they rolled, swooped and stalled the aircraft. Peter knew the hard work was to come and very soon Paul told him to head back for the circuit. Peter shortly lined up on approach, lowering the wheels and stabilising his speed.

All of a sudden, Paul called "Go around" and Peter opened the throttles and lifted the nose, raising the wheels. Almost immediately the noise subsided and the nose swung to the left.

"Left failure," Peter called and commenced his failure actions, which he ran through in order as quickly as he could, saying his checks out loud. Eventually he stabilised the aircraft and Paul told him to set up for a second approach, but only using one engine. Remembering which way the nose would swing as he reduced the power, Peter eventually lined up and lowered the wheels, swooping low over the hedge and settling onto the grass.

"Good—taxy in and shut down please," Paul said quietly.

Peter shut down the engines, turning off the master switch and removed his headphones, letting out a very long breath. Paul turned towards him and smiled. "How do you think that went?" he asked.

Peter thought for a moment and replied, "OK, I hope."

Paul laughed saying, "Better than OK—that's a pass—and a good one at that." A huge wave of relief swept over him. Passed. He was now multi-engine qualified. Another step along the way accomplished. Slowly, he got his things together and joined Paul on the grass. Waving to his colleagues as tradition demanded, he walked with Paul towards the classroom building. He was soon amongst his colleagues, accepting their congratulations.

"How do you feel, buddy?" Sanj asked.

"Relieved—and hungry," Peter laughed and he headed towards the kitchen.

In the afternoon, Sanj sat and passed his test and the bus ride back to the house was one of high spirits and laughter. Mark would be starting in the twin on Monday all on his own, so was expected to complete the course by mid-week. The following week had been planned as hour building for the rest of the group and then they were scheduled for a week's holiday. As soon as they arrived, Peter as usual got changed, packed and made his way towards the tube as quickly as he could. Has was so looking forward to seeing his parents again and sharing his good news. He knew that they'd be delighted for him.

Once on the train homeward bound, Peter finally found time to relax. His shoulders ached from the effort of flying asymmetrically and he began to feel tired. No matter, he'd soon be home and that's all that counted. Annie was waiting for him at Westlea as usual and she smiled as soon as she saw Peter, rushing over and hugging him.

"How's this week gone?" she asked.

"Amazingly well," Peter replied. "I passed my multi-engine test this morning, so I'm now qualified on twins. A good feeling—I'm finally starting to believe that I might just make it through to the end."

"Oh, well done—I'm so proud and, of course, you will," Annie said, taking his arm. Shortly, they were sat on the bus as it creaked and swayed its way through the familiar streets and in no time, they were home. "Now then," said Annie as she unlocked the door, "I've a treat for us all this evening."

"Oh—what's that then?" Peter asked.

"Well, following you telling me all about your friend bringing food to the house, I got a recipe book from the library and tonight we're having a chicken curry," Annie said proudly.

"Oh, yum," Peter said, his mouth already watering in anticipation. "Look forward to that." As he took his bag into the kitchen to unload his washing, he could smell the spices and chicken cooking in the oven. "That smells amazing," he said, asking "Are we all having the same?"

"Well, I've made it for you two as I've never had curry before, but I'm going to try it and see," Annie said.

Reluctant to break the spell, but knowing he must, Peter asked "Have you heard from Ben at all?"

Annie looked down, replying, "No, not at all. I'm sure he'll write soon though."

"I hope so," Peter said, putting his arm around her. He didn't care if he never heard from Ben ever again, but he know how much his parents were worried.

Soon, Peter heard Paul's voice, so he ran down the stairs to see him. "Hi, son—how's it going?" he asked, playfully punching Peter on the arm.

"Great, thanks, Dad—I passed my multi-engine test this morning."

"Oh, that's brilliant—well done," Paul said. "So what's next—astronaut school?" he laughed.

"I wish. More hour building and then after our week off we start the instrument course," Peter replied.

Paul nodded, then asked "What's that smell? What are we having for dinner?"

"Annie's surprise," Annie said, winking at Peter, who grinned.

Soon the heard Annie calling them for dinner and they both wandered back into the kitchen. "What's this?" Paul asked.

"Annie's chicken curry," Annie said proudly. It smelled divine and Peter and his dad were soon tucking in. Annie had put herself a small bowl out to see if she liked it, but she was soon wolfing it down along with the boys, announcing that she thought it delicious.

Peter finally pushed his clean plate away, saying, "Thanks mum—that was awesome."

"Yep—gets my vote as well. What did you think?" Paul asked Annie.

"Lovely—smooth and creamy and not too spicy. Thanks for the suggestion, Peter."

Peter just smiled, saying, "Anytime," and he got up to start clearing the plates.

Saturday dawned bright and clear and amusingly, Peter found himself awake early listening for the morning departure. Sure enough, he shortly heard the sound of engines and as he'd done for the past few years, he jumped out of bed and grabbing his binoculars, he threw back the curtain. He saw the aircraft climbing as it passed over the house, like an old friend waving across a crowded room.

Automatically he read the registration and it was one he knew well. He smiled at himself, thinking, *Old habits die hard* and wondered if he'd ever grow tired of aviation. He threw on his dressing gown and made his way downstairs, flicking the kettle on and settling himself down in his usual chair. Soon he was sipping hot coffee and he heard footsteps upstairs. He knew that it would be his mother so he got up and made her coffee, setting it down on the table.

"Morning," he said as she appeared in the doorway.

"Morning—you're up early," she said, sitting down.

"Yes—couldn't sleep. For the first time since I started the course, I've actually nothing to study for this weekend. We're just going into the hardest part of the course, which is why we get next week off. Don't really know what to do with myself this weekend," Peter said.

"Well, why don't you see your friends—I'm sure that they'll be glad to see you?" Annie suggested.

"Yes I was planning to—maybe we should go and see Gran as well, as I haven't seen her in a while."

"Good idea," Annie said, getting up for a refill. "More coffee?"

Peter shook his head. "No thanks—I'll go and change—I fancy a bike ride," he said.

In the garage, Peter's bike sat forlornly in the corner, covered in dust and with flat tyres. He quickly grabbed a cloth and wiped it over and then got the foot pump and re-inflated the tyres. The rest of it looked OK and after applying oil to the chain he pushed it out into the sunshine. Like an old friend who's woken from a long sleep, it seemed to sit, leaning against the wall, blinking in the sunlight.

Peter couldn't believe that he'd not ridden in in nine months, but he was soon out on the country lanes, pushing himself as hard as he could. He rode around his usual route, enjoying the familiarity and was soon heading for home. As he arrived, he glanced at his watch, nothing the time. It had taken him longer than he expected, but he consoled himself with the fact that his seating position hadn't been right—the saddle was too low.

Grabbing a spanner, he loosened the bolt and raised the saddle by a couple of inches. *That'll do it*, he thought to himself and locking the garage door, he went back into the house, where he found Paul sitting at the kitchen table. "Good morning—good ride?" he asked.

"Mmm, yes, OK, but not a comfortable one—my saddle was too low," Peter explained.

"Have you sorted it out?" Paul asked and Peter nodded. "Good man," came the reply and Peter ran upstairs to the bathroom to shower.

After he'd made himself breakfast, Peter rang Alex and they arranged to meet at Alex's house. After a brisk walk, Peter knocked on the door, which was opened by Alex's mother. She smiled immediately, saying "Hello, stranger. Gosh—you've grown. Come on in—Alex is upstairs."

Mumbling his thanks, Peter kicked his shoes off and ran up the stairs two at a time, knocking on the bedroom door. He heard a muffled "Come in" and opened the door. The room was bathed in sunshine and Alex was standing by the window in his dressing gown. "Hiya," he said and Peter walked over to where he was standing.

"Hi, buddy—what are you looking at?" Peter asked.

"Oh just watching the birds," Alex said, adding, "Let's go and get a drink."

Soon, they were sat outside in the garden, listening to the birdsong and chatting about their days. Alex started by asking Peter how the course was going and Peter filled him in on where he'd got to, gaining his multi-engine qualification and told Alex about his forthcoming week off.

"Hmm, that's a shame—I'm in school all week," Alex said, disappointed.

"No worries. We could always meet up at the weekend and maybe go to the cinema," Peter suggested.

Alex nodded his head, then Peter asked about Liam. "I spoke to him last Saturday," he said. "He's pretty much down in the dumps. He feels that he's in a tight corner and can't see a way out."

"Well, there isn't a way out, is there?" Peter asked.

"Surely if he's made Sally pregnant, then he'll have to stand by her and make it right?"

"Well yes, you'd have thought so, but he's not keen. I think he was just after some fun when they got together and didn't anticipate this. I hope he does the right thing," he added, his voice training away. Peter said nothing, but hoped Alex was right. He still liked Sally and felt sorry for her predicament, but felt that she had no-one else to blame.

Anxious to break the sombre mood, Alex asked, "Shall we go into town? Anna's away today visiting her aunt, so we won't get dragged around all the clothes shops. I fancy a change."

Peter immediately agreed and after Alex had changed, they walked the two miles to Westlea centre.

The town centre was packed—far more than usual. Peter couldn't understand why and it was only when they'd got onto the high street that they realised that it was the day of the annual carnival. Finding a spot where they could sit and watch, they waited for the parade to begin. Shortly, they heard the sound of a marching band and this appeared at the top of the road, complete with girls dressed in Majorette costumes, twirling large pom-poms and dancing along to the tune.

One after another, floats of every description passed, some on foot, some on the back of highly-decorated lorries. There was a great air of excitement and people were clapping, cheering and singing. The whole town had been turned into a blur of noise and colour. Both Alex and Peter sat and watched the parade pass by and eventually it disappeared around a corner. They could still hear the bass drum of the band and people began to gradually disperse.

"Wow—that was colourful," Alex said.

Peter just nodded before saying, "Shall we get a drink—I think I need one after that."

They made their way towards the soft drinks bar and found a seat in the shade. "That was really good. I remember the carnivals from when I was small—although they seemed to go on for longer back then," Peter said.

"Yes, they did—perhaps it's just that our attention spans were shorter," Alex replied, laughing. Peter nodded his agreement and the two friends continued to chat and laugh for the rest of the afternoon before Alex decided that it was time to head home.

Peter agreed and they walked together to the bus terminus, going their separate ways.

As Peter walked through the door, Annie said, "I've arranged to go and see Gran in the morning. We can take your bag and you could go straight to the station from there if you want?"

"Sure," Peter replied, asking, "What's for dinner?"

Annie laughed out loud. "Is that all you think about—your stomach?" she said.

Paul looked up saying, "Of course, he does—he's still a growing lad."

"Well it's high time you stopped—you're probably taller than your dad now. In fact—Paul, stand up. Stand back to back," and with that she stood up on a kitchen chair and put her hand on Peter's head. "You're about an inch taller—and no doubt still growing," she said, climbing down.

"Exactly—which is why I need to eat," Peter said, letting out a bellow of laughter.

Paul laughed as well, saying, "For goodness sake, feed the boy," and Annie, shaking her head, began to prepare the evening meal.

In the morning, after a visit to Peter's Gran—who also commented on how grown up he was becoming—Peter was back on the train. He knew it was going to be a long week as they were just marking time and putting hours in their logbooks whilst Mark complete his multi engine training, but he was excited all the same. Flying was flying and he loved every moment aloft—he saw it as his own special place and constantly reminded himself just what a privilege it was to see the sights that Mother Nature treated them to and hid from lesser mortals.

32

The week of flying passed by with Peter following his usual daily routine. They decided, as a group, to all go out for a meal on the Thursday evening to celebrate getting through the first part of the course and also to mark the fact that they had all passed their Multi-engine tests. Paula and Mark had been to a small Italian restaurant a few streets away and suggested that they all went there and Peter was interested to see what Italian food was all about.

Once they arrived back at the crew house, Peter dashed upstairs to change into his casuals and they met downstairs. They strolled casually to the restaurant with Paula and Mike holding hands and Peter as usual bringing up the rear talking to Sanj. It was a warm sultry evening, with the sun high in the sky and birds still busy on the wing. For once, their conversation was not about flying, but about cuisine. Sanj was telling Peter that he'd tried many different national dishes and advising Peter on what he may like.

"If you like meat, then try either the meatballs or a lasagne—that's a type of pasta pie with layers of meat sauce and cheese. You'll love it I'm sure," he said.

"What's pasta?" Peter enquired, thinking to himself that he should really know.

"It's made from a special wheat and is lovely and soft to eat. It comes in different forms—sheets, shapes, as spaghetti which is like long strands and flat ribbons. All tastes pretty much the same though—lovely with a cream sauce and tomatoes and meat."

Peter was intrigued and couldn't wait to try it. "I told my mum about the curry you bought to the house and she made one from a recipe last weekend—it was lovely," Peter said, adding, "My dad loved it and so did she after being a bit tentative at first."

"Good for her—stick with me buddy and I'll show you lots of different stuff to eat. We eat all sorts of different stuff at home. Being Indian, people think that we eat curry all the time, but we don't—we try all sorts. Life is a culinary adventure—think of all the dishes we can try when we're staying at hotels on layover," Sanj said, laughing.

Soon they were seated and looking over the menu. With Sanj's help, Peter ordered a lasagne with salad—he was pretty hungry by now—the lunchtime sandwiches seemed so long ago. Both Arnie and Mark had ordered beer, but Peter stuck with soft drinks—he'd never tried beer and after seeing what it had done to his brother last time he was home, he had no intention of doing so and besides, he'd be up early in the morning ready for the last day of flying.

They'd decided before setting off that the subject of flying was banned as dinner conversation and Arnie was regaling them with tales of his prowess in the school and local cricket team, much to Mark and Sanj's amusement. Sanj followed test cricket avidly and began to tease Arnie about England's poor performance against India in the last test match and this provided for much amusement at Arnie's expense.

"What sports do you follow?" Mark asked Peter.

"None really, although I'm a keen cyclist at home and I do a lot of miles on my bike when I'm there, although it's obviously suffered since we started the course, which is why I go running," he replied.

"You enjoy keeping fit then?" Paula asked, suddenly squeezing Peter's thigh, which made him jump and they all roared with laughter.

Blushing furiously, Peter just said, "Yes," and Paula apologised for making him jump.

"I should keep an eye on you, touching other men's legs," Mark said with a huge smile on his face.

"Well, you've only got puny little legs," she replied, adding, "Perhaps you should start running with Peter and build some muscles."

Mark shook his head, saying "You wouldn't want me all muscle-bound," and Paula immediately responded, "Oh, wouldn't I?" and they all laughed out loud again at her riposte.

The food began to arrive and Peter stared at the creation before him. "Well don't just look at it—tuck in," Sanj said, prodding Peter in the ribs with his elbow. Peter cut a slice and slowly put it in his mouth—this was followed quickly by another and then another. "I think he likes it," Sanj said, pointing with his thumb, as they all fell quiet to enjoy the meal.

As they finished their meals, Paula began asking them about their family life and in particular if they had girlfriends. "Nope—not yet," Arnie answered first.

"Did have one at school, but we kind of agreed that whilst I was on this course we'd live our own lives. Just me, my parents and baby brother. Plenty of fish in the sea though," he said, winking at Paula.

"What about you Sanj?" she asked.

"Nope—never had one. Just have my folks and a little sister at home and Dad and mum run their own business. Often in our culture marriages are arranged between families, but my parents are pretty westernised and don't go in for that. I'm sure I'll meet someone one day."

Paula nodded before turning to Peter. "Come on, Mr Shy—what about you? Have you ever kissed a girl?" she asked.

"Yes, I had a girlfriend for a short while," he said. "She started getting a bit too serious for my liking and so we stopped seeing each other. She's seeing one of my long-term school buddies now, but she's in a spot of bother," he said, not wanting to say any more.

"Oh, wow, so you've actually had a girlfriend then?" Paula asked. Peter nodded. "What sort of bother is she in then?" she enquired.

"Erm well—I saw them the other weekend and she's pregnant," Peter said matter-of-factly.

Paula's hand shot up and covered her mouth, eyes wide, before she eventually said "No—really?"

This was scandalous! Peter again nodded, saying, "I'm just glad that it wasn't me."

"I bet," said Mark, looking at Paula, who returned his look with a thin smile.

"What about you guys?" Arnie asked.

"I'm an only child. My Dad died a couple of years ago so it's just me and my Mum at home," Mark said quietly.

"Sorry to hear that, buddy. Come on—what about your family, Paula?" Arnie pressed.

"I'm an only child as well. My Dad has a couple of businesses and Mum works part time for him. With me, they obviously stopped once they'd realised that they had achieved absolute perfection," she said, fluttering her eyelashes and laughing. This bought another roar of laughter. "They obviously didn't to upset the apple cart after that—although to be honest, having another one like me would have been a serious handful for them both," she laughed.

"Come on boys," she continued. "With that I think it's time to walk back home," and she stood up. After they'd paid the bill, they walked slowly back to the house in the cool evening air and as soon as they were home, Peter went straight upstairs to bed.

The following day passed quickly and by lunchtime the instructors had finished for the day and they were allowed to leave early. Peter was soon back on the train, filled with anticipation for the coming week and eager to see his parents as usual. Annie met him at the station and they were soon sat in the kitchen, drinks in hand and Peter was able to relax in the familiar atmosphere, allowing his mind to wander.

"Peter—Peter," Annie said, prodding him.

"Oh, sorry—I was miles away," Peter replied.

"That's OK—I was asking you about your birthday in a couple of weeks. Is there anything you need for your course or anything that you particularly want?" she asked.

Peter thought for a moment before replying, "No, not really. I have everything I need for the time being and the airline are providing everything thanks."

Annie nodded—he'd never been one for birthdays and didn't seem bothered by getting presents, especially now he was older. She'd have to put her thinking cap on. Peter shortly got up and after changing, got his bike out of the garage and set off on his usual route—he needed to stretch his legs.

The following morning, Peter had arranged to help Paul with the motorbike as it was nearly complete. He still enjoyed the feel of tools in his hands and the smell of oil, grease and petrol—the aircraft at the school had a similar odour. Paul had completed the engine rebuild and the frame had been delivered back from the painters in the last week, so Peter started carefully unwrapping the frame from the brown paper wrapping before carefully placing it on the workbench.

"Looks good—what do you think?" Paul asked.

Peter nodded in approval, saying, "Yeah—looks brilliant. Is it just painted?"

"No, it's been what they call stove—enamelled. It's sprayed with an enamel paint and then it's baked on. Makes for a very tough finish, which is good against stone chips and the like," Paul explained. "Come on, let's get the engine and put it in the frame."

Carefully, they wriggled the engine onto the mounts and finally after some minor adjustments, Paul slid the mounting bolts into place and Peter tightened them up. They stood back to admire their handiwork and just then Annie appeared with bacon rolls and coffee.

"Here we are, boys," she said, placing the tray next to the bike.

"Mmm, thanks, mum," Peter said, attacking the food.

Annie shook her head, smiling and asked, "Don't you eat all week before you come home?"

It was Peter's turn to shake his head and he said, "Nope—I save it all up for weekends," before stuffing more food into his mouth.

"So I see," Annie laughed and she left them to it.

By the end of the afternoon, they had reattached the front forks and both wheels and with both lifting the bike at each end, stood it on the floor. Paul cast a critical eye over their handiwork before saying, "Well, that's all we can do today. I've more parts on order, so we'll carry on when they arrive at the shop."

Peter felt a great sense of achievement and he'd had a great day.

Whilst Peter had some preliminary reading to commence the instrument course, he'd decided to try and relax during the week off. Sunday morning he was getting his bike out of the garage when Paul shouted to him from the back door. "Hang on—mind if I come with you?"

"Of course not," Peter called back—"I'll wait for you."

Soon, the pair of them were cycling out towards the country roads—Peter was keeping his speed down as he was aware that this wasn't a ride that Paul had attempted before. As they rode along, Paul was asking loads of questions about the next part of the course. "I understand what it's about," he began. "But what exactly do you have to know?"

Peter thought for a moment before replying, "We need to be able to fly the aircraft just like we do now, but without looking out of the window. Once we can keep level and straight and we can turn climb and descend accurately, we start to use radio beacons to get position information and eventually learn to make approaches using just the instruments.

"It's a bit like following two radio beacons—one in the horizontal plane to give us information about where the centreline of the runway is and another in the vertical plane to show us where the glideslope is—that's the vertical path to the runway which we use for our descent. If you keep the needles on the instrument in the right place, you'll arrive at the runway touchdown point."

Paul nodded saying, "Sounds scary."

Peter smiled and replied, "It does and I'm sure that until I get used to doing it, it will be."

"Is it a new system?" Paul asked.

"Nope—it was initially developed before the war, but adopted in 1947 to be the system that we use now. I'm sure that as new aircraft develop, there will be new and exciting things to use which will make our lives easier," Peter replied, pedalling harder. "Come on—I'll race you up this hill," he cried, setting off at a furious pace.

Paul did his best, but he was no match and arrived at the top of the hill breathlessly a few minutes later. Peter was sat on the grass waiting and Paul climbed off his bike to join him, collapsing beside his son.

"My fifty-year old legs can't keep up with you—especially with your exercise regime," he complained.

Peter laughed, punching him gently on the arm. "Nonsense—you've plenty left in the tank," he said, reaching for his water bottle.

"I wish," Paul replied, turning around and opening his rucksack. "Here you go—mother made us sandwiches," he said, passing Peter a package. Peter's eyes lit up and he ripped open the paper, taking a huge bite.

Between mouthfuls, he asked Paul, "Have you heard any more about Ben?"

A shadow passed across Paul's face before he replied, "No nothing. He's still in custody and I think they are aiming for a Court Martial in October or November. We'll no doubt be informed in due course."

Peter nodded before asking, "Is mum OK—she doesn't talk about it at all?"

Paul shook his head. "She's very disappointed—we both are. She doesn't mention it to me either, but no doubt when it's all sorted out she'll have something to say. I just hope that she doesn't take it too badly," Paul replied.

Peter sat quietly, saying nothing. He just didn't understand why or how Ben had got himself into so much trouble and inside he really didn't care. *Blood may be thicker than water*, he thought to himself, *but not in this instance*. Soon, they remounted their bikes and rode home at a brisk pace, with Peter darting ahead and then slowing, allowing Paul to catch up.

33

After a relaxing week spending time with his parents, seeing Alex in the evenings after school and doing some preparatory reading, it was soon time to head back to the crew house to begin the instrument course. In Peter's logbook there were now just over a hundred and fifty hours and he was keen to get started. Monday morning quickly arrived and he was soon back at the airfield with his colleagues.

Inside the classroom, the instructors had already prepared the briefing on the board and in no time they had commenced the lesson. "Good morning—I trust your week's holiday was relaxing and restful—it needed to be," Brian commenced, with an evil chuckle. "Today we begin the instrument rating, most of which will be flown in here or in the simulator at the offices. Only when we're happy with your progress will we transfer to the aircraft. OK, to begin—" and he began to explain the intricacies of flying solely on instruments.

Peter sat with rapt attention, not daring to allow his attention to wander—this was serious stuff and so outside his frame of reference that he needed to give it all he had. He scribbled notes and made quick crude diagrams—anything to help when it came to reread the briefing. Slowly the morning dragged on and fact upon fact was piled on top of each other.

Eventually, they were all allowed some relief and broke for lunch. Peter grabbed a sandwich and a cup of coffee and sat alone by the window. How was he ever going to understand all this? Would he simply just fly the aircraft into the ground? For the first time since the commencement of the course, he felt very alone. Glancing around the room, he could see his classmates looking very much the same—it had been a sobering morning and he was sure that there was worse to come.

In the afternoon, they were divided up into pairs, two per classroom and Peter joined Arnie with Paul instructing. On the board he drew a diagram of the basic instrument panel and began to explain how to read the instruments in a scan pattern.

"You must scan and scan again—and I'll know very quickly if you're concentrating too much on one instrument," Paul said, "as the other instruments will wander off and all of a sudden you'll notice and no doubt swear at me," he laughed. "Most important thing is to relax—remember, if you've set the aircraft up to fly straight and level properly, it doesn't know when it's in a cloud, only you know that. Best not to tell it I think," he said, winking at Arnie.

They continued throughout the afternoon with exercises on the board, flying a virtual aeroplane and with Paul giving them harder and harder tasks to accomplish. By the end of the session, Peter felt that his brain was dribbling out of his ears, although the logical part of his brain was finding the concept easy to assimilate—it appealed to Peter's need for logic and routine. Paul eventually closed the session and Peter heard Arnie mutter, "The defence rests," before they both got up to catch the crew bus.

The deflated mood was shared by everyone. "What the hell have we let ourselves in for?" Mark asked nobody in particular.

"I'll never get this," Sanj muttered, whilst Peter remained sitting on his own, silent for the whole journey.

Once home, Peter didn't really feel like doing much, but forced himself to go for a run—he'd been sat down the whole day and he know that it would make him feel better. On the way back he stopped at the corner shop to get a warm pie, which he ate quickly before showering and reading over his notes. He soon fell asleep, notes in hand, waking just before midnight when set his alarm and he crawled between the sheets.

For the rest of the week, each day followed the same pattern—board exercises, lunch, more exercises and finally home. By the end of the week, it was beginning to make some sense to Peter and he began to feel a little more confident. By Friday afternoon, the rest of the group all seemed a little more relaxed about this part of the course and they were told that the simulator training would begin at head offices on Monday.

Peter had decided not to go home that weekend, as he wanted to study and read his notes until it was second nature to him and his mother had understood on the phone. He knew that he'd be too busy to miss them and that the weekend would probably pass quickly. One thing that he hadn't counted on was having to wash and iron his own shirts—along with Paula and Arnie who had also stayed back for the weekend. He did his best and was happy that, whilst they didn't have Annie's perfectionist touch, at least they were clean.

Monday morning arrived far too quickly and it saw them in the reception area at the offices and Paul soon took them through a labyrinth of corridors to the simulator room. Inside, it was in use with one of the junior pilots flying approaches along with a training captain. They all stood at the back of the room in silence, not wanting to disturb anybody's concentration and shortly the session was ended.

The captain strode past Paul, saying "All yours" in a gruff voice and they were again split into pairs—one to "fly" and one to observe from the jump seat. The others watched from the back of the room. Peter stood, quietly petrified. He didn't want to mess up on his first session and he certainly didn't want his colleagues to see if he did so. His only consoling thought was that they were all in the same boat.

Eventually, he and Mark were called forward and Peter was directed to sit in the jump seat. Mark made himself comfortable and his session began. With gentle encouragement, Paul guided him from the left seat, gently nudging the controls to help him correct. After his allotted hour, they swapped over and Peter slid into the hot seat.

"Ready?" Paul asked. Peter nodded and he felt the controls come alive in his hands. Was it really such a short time ago that he'd sat here with Fozzy? It seemed like a lifetime. Paul started Peter off with very basic manoeuvres flying level, then moving on to climbing and descending and finally turning.

Peter stared at the instruments in furious concentration and Paul finally said quietly, "Relax—you're gripping the controls far too tightly. Don't forget—we fly with our fingertips. Try and think back to when you were learning to land the aircraft—remember that phrase "Squeezing the teddy bear" Try to do that now."

Peter relaxed and after a while his flying became more accurate and he began to put together a routine for his instrument scan. He saw the world through pictures and the scan routine appeared before his eyes as an image to follow. In no time, his hour was up.

Sweaty and exhausted, he pushed the seat back and climbed out—he needed a cold drink and to sit down. That was the hardest thing he'd had to do so far. Getting a drink from the fridge at the back of the room, he watched as Paula was put through her hour of torture. *At least she didn't do any better or worse than me*, he thought to himself.

This pattern followed for the rest of the day and got progressively harder during the week. By Friday lunchtime, Peter and the rest of the cadets had seen quite enough of the "Sweat box" as they had christened it. As a reward for their efforts, Friday afternoon was given over to final uniform fitting and soon Peter and his colleagues were walking the short distance back to the crew house carrying their new dress uniforms and Peter hung his proudly in his wardrobe. They had also been issued with name badges bearing the airline crest and Peter packed this in his bag to show to his parents, alongside his weekend reading.

The journey home passed in a blur and soon Peter was sitting on the sofa telling Annie about the past two weeks. She sat listening quietly, not asking any questions for fear of making herself sound stupid—she was struggling to understand the complexities of what Peter was talking about but being polite, she tried to think of something positive to say.

"How long is this part of the course?" she asked.

"We have to do a minimum of thirty hours in the sim and that's followed by at least twenty hours in the aircraft and if we're ready we have to sit a flight test with a staff examiner from the Civil Aviation Authority, which sounds pretty scary," Peter explained.

Annie nodded, asking, "How do you feel about that dear?"

"At the moment, nothing," Peter answered. "As I'm nowhere near that yet and haven't even begun to think about it."

Annie smiled, patting his hand and then thought to change the subject. "It's your birthday on Sunday—do you want to do anything special?"

Peter was dumbfounded—he'd completely forgotten. "Err—I don't think so. Maybe instead of buying presents, could we go out for a meal instead?"

Having tasted both Indian and Italian cuisine, he was keen to expand his palate. "Yes of course—I'll ask your dad," Annie answered, getting up to begin the evening meal.

Peter was up and out on his bike very early the next morning, as he'd not ridden for two weeks. He followed his usual route, enjoying its familiarity and it seemed like an old friend welcoming him back. He arrived home breathless and hot, but satisfied. He found his parents in the kitchen and flopped down into a chair. "You look worn out son—good ride?" Paul asked.

Peter just nodded, gratefully accepting a drink from Annie. "What have you got planned today?" Paul asked.

Peter paused before answering "Reading—lots of reading. We start following and intercepting radio beacons this week, so lots to read and try to understand," Peter replied, swallowing the last of his coffee.

Paul nodded, adding, "Well if you fancy a break, we can always head out for a walk to enjoy this September sunshine."

Peter got up to head up for a shower, replying, "Hmm maybe," and in no time he was standing beneath the hot water, the shower spray stinging his skin like hot needles.

Peter was soon engrossed in his book, making notes and drawing diagrams as best he could. It was confusing at first and every time he looked at a diagram he'd made, it always seemed to be backwards from what was shown in the book. He read and reread the chapter before finally a light bulb came on and he realised where he'd been going wrong. He continued to read until a knock on his bedroom door made him look up to see Annie's face peering round the edge.

"We're just going to book a table for a meal—would you like Alex and Anna to come?" she asked.

Peter got up, stretching and moving his head from side to side, answering, "Yes please if that's OK."

Annie nodded and walked into the room with an envelope in her hand. "For you," she said before turning and vanishing and Peter looked down at the letter. It bore the crest of Channel Ferry Airways. Tearing the top off the envelope, he unfolded the letter and began to read. Once he'd digested the contents, he picked up his book again before looking at his watch—he'd been sat reading for six hours. Time for a break he thought and went over to the open window.

Looking out, he could smell the garden flowers and the gentle breeze as it whispered its way through the trees at the bottom of the garden. Taking a deep breath, he smiled—he loved this place. It had been his home, his sanctuary, his place of safety for his whole life and apart from his room at the crew house, he knew little else. He wondered idly how he'd find hotels in foreign countries if he was ever lucky enough to fly long haul and to enjoy stopovers.

Annie interrupted his musings saying that Alex and Anna would be coming and that they were meeting at the restaurant at 7 o'clock.

After another hour of reading, Peter tired of the subject and wandered downstairs. At first he couldn't find his parents, but heard his father's voice coming from the garden, so he headed outside. Annie and Paul were sitting in the late afternoon sunshine and there were bags of leaves, grass cuttings and garden debris on the patio.

"Been busy?" Peter asked, looking around.

"Yes—doing some weeding and getting the garden ready for autumn," Annie replied, motioning Peter to sit beside her. "What was your letter all about?" she asked.

"It said that the cadet course will be delayed for another year due to budget cuts and that I should reapply next year if I'm interested," Peter replied.

"How's the reading going?" Paul asked.

Peter let out a loud "Harumph" before replying, "OK I guess, although how I'll ever intercept and track a Direction Finder I'll never know."

Paul nodded, saying, "Ahh yes—we had those fitted to aircraft in the war. One of our lads explained it to me once. Now then...how did he explain it?" Paul scratched his chin for a few moments before adding, "Ahh, yes—he said that you push the Head and tug the Tail of the needle whatever that means."

Peter stared at his dad for quite a few moments, digesting what he'd said. Suddenly it became clear—why hadn't he worked that out? Jumping up, he quickly said, "Thanks dad," before racing upstairs. He turned to one of his diagrams and by using Paul's words, he saw exactly how it worked. Eureka! He could now see that from wherever his aircraft was situated in relation to the beacon, he knew which way to turn to track it. He shook his head, reminding himself once again just what a clever guy his dad was.

Shortly afterwards, Peter began to get himself ready for the evening ahead. He went to the bathroom to shave—something that he was now having to do daily—and once finished he went back to his room, selecting his casual slacks, a shirt and a light jacket for the evening. He joined Annie in the kitchen—she was dressed in a light summer dress and white cardigan.

"You look lovely," he said simply—there seemed no need for further words.

She squeezed his arm, saying, "Thank you," before looking him over. "So do you—although those slacks are a bit short. Are those the ones I got you last year?" Peter nodded. "Well you've out grown them—you are going to have to stop growing," she said laughing.

Peter looked down at his trouser cuffs standing proud from his shoes. "I'll get some new ones one day," he said, not being really bothered.

Annie just smiled. They were shortly joined by Paul and they quickly set off for the twenty minute walk to the restaurant, where they found Alex and Anna waiting for them. Alex waved whilst Paul spoke to a waiter and they were shown to their table.

"How are you, buddy?" Alex asked.

"I'm good, thanks—tired at the moment though. This past two weeks has been pretty intense."

"Really?" Anna asked, asking why.

"We've just started the hardest part of the course—learning to fly solely on instruments," Peter began, going on to explain what that meant and about the training. Alex and Anna sat quietly listening—they knew from experience that Peter's ability to discourse about his favourite subject was endless and that if interrupted, he would simply carry on where he'd left off. Finally, Peter asked them about their studies and was met with the usual screwed up faces and comments of "It's boring."

"Have you sat your year-end tests yet?" Peter asked.

"Yes, we sat those in July," Alex answered.

Peter looked at him quizzically, asking "And?"

"Yep—all passed. Anna got much better grades than me, but we're both still on track. My dad won't let up with his chasing me to study," Alex added, laughing. Peter nodded, smiling. Just like the Alex he'd always known—modest and self-effacing.

Once they had ordered, Peter continued to quiz his friends about their medical studies. "It's a basic five-year course, followed by a year working as what they call a "Pre-registration" junior doctor," Anna explained. "Once you've completed that, you start moving up the ladder, eventually specialising into your chosen field."

"What do you fancy doing?" Annie asked.

"Children's medicine," Anna answered and Annie then asked Alex the same question.

"I've absolutely no idea," he replied with a smile. "Dad is a physician, but in reality I think I fancy some kind of surgical speciality, but I'm keeping my mind open," he added.

,Annie nodded and Paul then asked "Can you change specialities later on if you want?"

"Yes," Alex responded, adding, "But you often have to start at the bottom again."

Peter let out a short laugh, saying, "Ha! That's just like aviation. You can get to be a Captain in about six or seven years, but if you change airlines, it's back to being an FO."

Alex looked at Peter with a question on his face. "What's an FO?" he asked.

"Sorry—a First Officer—a junior pilot. We jokingly refer to FO as meaning Flap Operator—which with some captains, it's just about all you do," Peter said and everyone laughed. "I'm being serious," Peter went on. "With some of the older crusty ones they do all the flying and treat you like dirt, not letting you get any hands on flying and think that you're just there to raise and lower the flaps and wheels and do the paperwork. Hopefully that's all changing though," he added with a note of caution.

"Oh, I hope so, dear," Annie said, looking across at Peter. She so wanted him to not only succeed, but also to enjoy his new profession. Peter was about to answer when the food arrived and they all busied themselves with the task in hand.

After the plates had been cleared away, Alex asked what Peter wanted to fly—short haul daily hops or long haul. "Tricky question," Peter began. "With short haul you get more take-offs and landings, but as I said before, with some skippers you don't do any flying. With long haul you get less hands on time, but get to see the world and stay in some amazing places. The further you go, the more layover time you get—rest hours as opposed to duty hours. It would be nice to see the world and I do fancy flying a bigger jet if the opportunity arises," Peter said wistfully.

"I've read about flight crews staying in hotels and having parties in their rooms," Alex said, looking directly at Peter and winking.

Peter just shook his head. "I'm not sure about that and if I'm in a room on my own, that's what I'll be—on my own," he said emphatically.

"I'm sure you'll be fine and have a lovely time—you must send us postcards," Annie said, worried about Peter finding himself in situations that he couldn't cope with.

"I'll be fine, mum. I really will, San Francisco on Tuesday and home as usual by Friday evening," he laughed, hoping to put Annie's mind at rest. "How's Liam?" Peter asked and Alex and Anna exchanged glances.

"We haven't seen him for a week or so. Think they are still trying to get a flat somewhere—the baby will be here in a couple of months and they need to get settled. I don't think that Liam is coping to well really," Alex said quietly.

"Poor Liam and Sally," Annie said, looking knowingly across at Peter. Peter returned her glance, lowering his head. He'd had a narrow escape for sure.

34

Back at the simulator on Monday and the cadets were briefed on the Automatic Direction Finding and again, each took turns of one hour flying. Each day followed the same pattern, with each task being completed before moving on to the next. Gradually the days became shorter and towards the end of October, one of the instructors announced that as the clocks would be going back by one hour, then night flying would commence.

By this time, most of them had completed the required sim hours and would be moving onto training back in the aircraft, so it fitted in perfectly. On the very last day of the month, they were once more gathered back at the airfield, but starting slightly later in the day. Peter was paired with Sanj for his first instrument flight and after getting airborne, he settled quickly into his routine, scanning the instruments constantly and following the needles.

Once back on the ground, they swapped places and Peter watched with detached amusement as Sanj put on the "hood"—the device preventing the student from seeing out of the window—as it kept falling down around Sanj's neck and he was forced to tighten the straps to the maximum. Eventually, they got going and Peter watched from the backseat—each manoeuvre making more sense to Peter now that he could see ahead.

At the end of the afternoon, they were all gathered together and briefed for night flying and once again they set off in their pairs. As Peter levelled the aircraft he was treated to a spectacular sight with the black sky above studded with jewel-like stars, the crescent moon low on the horizon and the twinkling lights of the towns and major roads.

The air was smooth and they flew in almost total silence as if disturbing the night was an obscenity. Once again, Peter reminded himself just what a privileged view this occupation afforded him. By the end of that week, all the students had completed the required five hours and five night landings and so were signed off as competent.

Before they knew it, winter had once again set in and Christmas was almost upon them. As they were training for bad weather flight, the weather did little to interfere with the flying programme and the short days were maximised. It was anticipated that they would be ready around mid-January for test and were given just three days leave over the Christmas period, with another day for New Year. Peter was so heavily involved with his training that he nearly forgot to buy gifts for his parents and his Gran and he had to make a last minute dash to the shops nearby to make his purchases. He was soon joining the Christmas commuters on the train home, arriving mid-afternoon on Christmas Eve.

He was met by Paul, who had finished work the day before for two weeks—Peter was used to his dad taking long breaks over the holiday period, as it was traditional in the engineering industry. He soon realised that this might be his last Christmas holiday for a while, as by next year he may well be flying people home for their holidays. Paul was pleased to see Peter, but was subdued on the bus home. Peter thought that he must be tired and thought nothing of it.

As soon as he was through the door, Annie came running up to him, throwing her arms around him and squeezing him tightly. "Hi, mum—how are you?" he asked. Annie said nothing for a few moments before releasing her grasp and Peter could see that she'd been crying. "Are you OK?" he asked, suddenly concerned.

She nodded and taking Peter by the hand, led him into the lounge, sitting down on the sofa. Paul followed closely behind and Peter began to get a cold feeling inside. Was Gran ill? Had somebody died? He couldn't stand the tension, so in his usual blunt way he said, "What's wrong?"

Paul and Annie exchanged glances and Paul said "It's Ben. He's been to trial. We got a letter yesterday, which is probably somebody at the Ministry of Defence's idea of an Xmas joke."

Peter quickly looked at them both before taking a deep breath and asking, "What's happened?"

Paul looked at the floor and said quietly, "He was found guilty on all four charges. He's been sentenced to two years custody, the first year in Cyprus and the second year here in the UK at an Army detention centre, after which he's getting a dishonourable discharge."

Peter sat quietly absorbing the information, eventually saying, "I'm so sorry, I really am. I know that this must be hard to take."

Annie took his hand, hers trembling as she did so. "It is—my poor boy, my poor stupid boy," she said quietly.

Peter sat quietly, holding her hand and Paul eventually broke the silence. "I'm sorry that it's come to this, but he's put himself in this position. We've a long military tradition in our family and nothing like this has ever happened before. I'm sorry to say this, but he deserves all he's got. I'm just so ashamed," and he got up and left the room.

Peter went to stand up but Annie quickly said, "Leave him" and pulled Peter closer. After sitting for some time, Peter released Annie's hand and went into the kitchen. Paul was nowhere to be seen, but the light in the garage was on, so Peter guessed that's where he was. He'd come in eventually. It was the first time Peter had seen his parents in such a state and nothing like this in his short life had happened before.

He felt at a loss of what to do, but Annie shortly appeared and clapping her hands together said, "Right, young man—where's your washing?"

Peter lifted his bag onto a chair and Annie soon had his shirts and dirty laundry into the machine and it was switched on.

"What do you fancy for dinner?" she asked, turning towards the cooker. *She needs to keep busy I think*, Peter thought to himself and said, "Anything you've got. I'll go and ask dad," and before she could stop him, he was outside, pulling at the garage door.

Inside, Paul was looking over the motorcycle, picking things up from the bench and putting them down again. Peter stood for a minute before saying, "Are you OK?"

Paul looked him directly in the eye before replying, "No, not really, but I guess I'll get used to it. Mustn't be too glum though—it's Christmas and as you know, your mum loves this family time of year."

Peter nodded and spoke quietly, "What's done is done—you can't change that. Ben has to be accountable—that's what you always taught us and now he'll find out the hard way."

Paul nodded slowly before walking over and putting his arm around Peter's shoulders. "Yes—you're right. I just hope that you never let us down—and somehow I doubt that you will. You've made us so proud this year."

Peter placed his hand over Pauls and said "I won't, so don't worry. Mum wants to know what you want for dinner by the way."

Paul let out a short yelp of laughter and said, "C'mon, let's get back indoors," and he turned off the light and locked the door.

The next morning, Peter was awake early and after going downstairs, he made drinks and placed them on a tray. He carried this upstairs and knocking on his parent's bedroom door, pushed it slowly open. Annie was sitting up and Paul was just stirring.

"Happy Christmas—I made drinks," Peter said brightly, putting the cups down on the bedside tables.

"Happy Christmas, Peter—and thank you," Annie said, grasping Peter's hand.

"Happy Christmas, son" came Paul's gruff voice and he too sat slowly upright.

"Drink up—I'm going down to start breakfast. My treat this year," Peter said and he raced back downstairs, keen to show off his cooking skills. Over the past couple of weeks Sanj had been showing Peter the basics of cooking and he felt that his parents deserved a treat—he just hoped that he didn't poison them!

From above, Peter heard lots of movement and he arranged the various ingredients on the worktop in a line, slowest to cook first, quickest at the end and using the kitchen clock he began to cook, sliding sausages and rashers of bacon into a pan and breaking eggs into another. He'd already buttered some bread and sliced some tomatoes and was so focused on cooking that he didn't hear Annie come into the kitchen.

"Wow—what's all this," she said, making Peter jump.

"Sit down and take a rest—I've got this," he said, motioning Annie to the chair beside the kitchen table. Within a few minutes, he put plates laden with a traditional breakfast on the table, joining Annie and Paul. They ate in silence and once finished, Paul sat back, spreading his hands across his stomach.

"I don't know where you learned to cook, son, but that was lovely—thanks."

Annie nodded her agreement and said, "I've obviously no need to worry about you living in that house now—that truly was delicious."

Peter gathered the plates and began to clear up, refusing any help. Afterwards, they gathered in the lounge. Peter quickly raced upstairs to get his parents gifts from his bag, handing them over saying "Happy Christmas" once again. Annie and Paul tore the paper and opened the boxes that Peter had given them—he'd bought a gold brooch for Annie and a tiepin for Paul and they both proffered their thanks.

Then then handed Peter a box wrapped in traditional paper. Peter couldn't guess at what was inside—he was shy and usually felt awkward receiving presents and today was no exception. "Are you going to open it then?" Annie asked.

Peter tore the paper off to find a plain square black box. Opening the lid he saw inside a new wristwatch, with three buttons on the side and three small dials inside the main one. "It's a chronograph—a stopwatch," Paul explained. "We got the idea when you were explaining how you had to fly for certain times—was it called holding?" he asked. Peter nodded. "You'll be able to time it on there just by pushing a button," he explained.

Impressed, Peter pulled the watch from the box and taking off his old one, he slid it over his hand and fastened it to his wrist. "Wow—thank you so much. That's perfect—absolutely perfect," he said and getting up gave both of them a hug.

"You're welcome," Annie said quietly before asking if there was anything Peter would like to do that day.

"No not really—just happy to spend it with you. Will we see Gran over the holidays?" he asked.

"Yes, if you want," Annie replied.

"I'd like that," Peter said, looking again at his new watch. He loved it and it would be so much easier than using the stopwatch on the instrument panel—which frequently stopped mid-hold.

On Boxing day morning, Peter decided that he'd leave his books in his bag and have a day with the family, not thinking about flying, aeroplanes on instrument scans and with that in mind he was downstairs early, making coffee and trying to relax. Upstairs, he could hear Annie pottering around and she soon appeared in the kitchen doorway, dressing gown flapping behind her. She came straight across and kissed Peter of the forehead, murmuring, "Good morning."

"Morning—you OK?" Peter asked.

She looked at him before nodding her head. "I guess so," she said.

Peter nodded and got up to refill his cup, offering Annie the same. Soon, they were chatting about the day and planning to go and see Peter's Gran. Peter was looking forward to the visit—she was his only grandparent, as Paul's parents had died during the war and Annie's dad had died just after. She was a sharp old lady, but Peter knew that beneath that stern exterior there was a kind, butter-soft soul who loved her family dearly. She'd always watched out for Peter, especially during his younger years when his different personality and odd behaviour were giving concern to others and she often told Annie that he'd be fine—just different.

Due to the reduced bus service, they were on their way early in the afternoon and would have to be home before the last bus at six pm. As soon as they reached Gran's house, Peter ran ahead, knocking on the door and opening it slightly to call her name. "Come in," he heard her cry and kicking off his shoes, he went inside. As usual, she was sitting in her chair by the fireplace, legs covered in her favourite knitted shawl.

Looking up as Peter entered the room, she let out a gasp of amazement, "Is that you Peter? Gosh, how you've grown! You're quite a young man now," and Peter smiled, going over to kiss her cheek and sitting down beside her. "So, how are things with you?" she asked.

"OK, thanks—been very busy on my course but otherwise good. How are you?" Peter replied.

"Me? Oh, OK, I think—just getting old and probably grumpy," she said, letting out a laugh.

Just then Annie appeared in the doorway, laughing and saying "Grumpy? You? No, surely not," and coming inside she came over to her mother, kissing her and sitting down beside Peter.

Paul followed closely behind saying, "Happy Christmas, Mabel."

"Happy Christmas," she replied and she then turned back to Peter. "So young man, how is the world of flying aeroplanes? Can you actually fly one yet?"

Peter nodded, replying, "Oh yes—I've flown solo and am also qualified to fly aircraft with two engines. We're now learning blind flying."

Gran looked at him carefully before saying to Annie, "I said he'd do well, didn't I—it was just a matter of time."

Annie nodded in agreement, adding, "You did—and we listened. We're very proud of what he's achieved this year."

"Good," Gran answered before asking, "and how's Ben?"

Quick glances were exchanged before Paul spoke, "He's fine—still in Cyprus, We haven't heard from him over Christmas, but I'm sure he's having fun with his mates."

Gran nodded and getting slowly up out of the chair, she motioned for Peter to follow her. Into the back room they went and Gran asked Peter to pull a box out from under the sideboard. He opened the box and inside Gran rummaged around, pulling out three parcels. She stood back upright and went back towards the living room, asking Peter to replace the box. He did so and followed behind.

As she walked back into the room, she handed Paul a parcel saying, "This is for you," and Paul said, "Thanks very much" and she gave Annie a similar parcel, again offering her best wishes. "Thanks, mum," Annie said, kissing her on the cheek.

Slowly she sat back down in the chair before handing Peter his present. "Thanks, Gran," Peter said, holding it tightly on his lap.

"Well, don't just sit there the three of you—open them," Gran said, smiling.

Peter tore the paper open and inside there was a summer shirt with bright blue patterns on. Blue was Peter's favourite colour and he loved it. He leaned over, squeezing her hand and said, "Thanks—it's lovely."

She smiled and gripped his hand tightly. Paul had been given a blue tie and he said, "That's lovely—thank you," and Annie's parcel hid a new white cardigan. She said her thanks and turning to Paul she asked him to pass her bag over and she pulled out a couple of parcels.

"These are for you," she said, passing them to Gran. Gran's eyes lit up.

"Thanks," she said before ripping the paper off. Her face lit up "Humbugs—my favourite and bath salts too. Thank you both."

For the rest of the afternoon, Gran quizzed Peter closely about his course and the potentials of the career to follow and she seemed very interested in where his profession would lead him.

"Gosh—it's all so different now. Back in my day, aeroplanes were still new and experimental and nobody flew any distance. I've never been up in one and to be honest, I don't think I want to, but isn't it marvellous how the world is opening up and shrinking?" she said, adding, "and to think that you're going to be part of it and see places that I've only ever read about."

Peter nodded and smiled before answering, "Yes—that's why I've always wanted to fly. I can fly a big aeroplane, see far off places and get paid to do it. Perfect."

35

Christmas and the New Year celebrations passed in a flash and Peter and his colleagues were soon back in the aircraft, flying progressively more and more complex scenarios. They battled through winter weather before nature finally began to release her grip on winter and spring arrived. By this time they had all completed the required hours and were scheduled to sit mock tests with the instructors prior to the real thing.

Peter was rostered to be second behind Paula and he sat doing his planning as she was out flying. When she returned about two hours later, Peter was called straight out to the aircraft, where he quickly ran through his checklist and then began to set up the instruments in the order that he'd need them. Making sure that he had all the paper departure, holding and approach plates with him, he waited for Paul to join him and they were soon under way.

With the departure plate on his kneeboard, he took off and just flew the numbers as directed, levelling off at the indicated altitude. "OK, fly heading one four zero and we'll join the hold at Abingbourne," Paul said and Peter turned the dial to the heading and swapped his plates over for the next one.

Fortunately, it was a calm morning, although as he was wearing the hood, Peter had no idea of the conditions outside. He radioed ahead and entered the holding pattern, flying three times around the racetrack before breaking off for his first approach, which he completed without any difficulty. Going around, he suddenly felt the aircraft swing violently to the left and Peter called "Left engine failure" and quickly went through his engine failure checklist.

He then flew away from the airport to about twenty miles before setting up the next approach and swapping over plates, returning for his second approach using just the one engine. This was what was known as a precision approach and his leeway for error was just one degree, so he was concentrating furiously. Down the approach he flew, keeping the needles on the instrument in exactly the right position, until Paul called out "Minimum altitude—look up" and he peered up and could just see the runway and the approach lights above the instrument panel ahead of him.

"Go-around," Paul commanded and they then flew back to the base field for a normal visual approach and landing. As he shut down the engines, Paul turned to him and said, "Good job—that would easily have been a pass. You're ready for test."

Peter breathed a huge sigh of relief, answering, "That's easily the hardest thing I've ever done, not just in an aeroplane, but in everything else as well."

Paul chuckled, saying, "Maybe so and you did a good job, but remember, Mother Nature may not always treat you as kindly as she has today and there will be times I suspect when you have such a difficult time with her that you'll happily return your annual salary just for the privilege of being elsewhere on that day."

Peter nodded, the tension slowly easing from his muscles and he followed Paul out onto the grass.

The mock tests were completed over two days and on Wednesday the group were informed that the examiner would be there for the next two days, trying to get everyone completed. It was a sober journey home that evening and Peter went straight to his room to sit on the end of his bed and "Fly" the test in his head as he'd been shown. He felt tired and was asleep before ten.

The following morning, there was palpable tension as they rode the bus to the airfield. They were met my Mike and Paul and another short man was standing with them.

"Right, group," Mike began. "It's my pleasure to introduce Captain George Roberts who is the Civil Aviation Authority examiner and he'll be conducting your tests over the next two days."

The man cleared his throat and began, "Good morning. I've been looking at your training records with the instructors and I'm satisfied that you all meet the requirements. We'll be doing tests in the order on the roster on the wall there. My job is not to fail anybody, but to see that you not only understand what you're doing, but that you don't kill me in the process. Anybody who succeeds in killing me today will automatically fail."

The group laughed nervously. "You will fly the profiles that I give you exactly, as in this business there is no second best—and sloppy flying is not good enough when you've two hundred passengers down the back. If, at any stage, after I've given you an instruction that you do not understand—clarify it with me before acting. Understood?"

There was a murmur of "Yes sir" and he carried on. "Right. I think Paula is first, so if you'd like to join me in the other room, I'll give you a route to plan," and he strode off. Paula was up like a shot and closely followed him into the second classroom. After about thirty minutes, the examiner emerged and, after consulting the roster, called Peter's name. Peter stood up and moved to the front of the room.

"Follow me, lad and I'll give your route so you can get started."

Peter followed him into the third room and began to get his chart and plates out of his bag. The examiner looked at the chart for a moment and said, "Right. Standard instrument departure out of here, fly to Abingbourne airport at five thousand, into the hold followed by an NDB approach, then go-around to three thousand feet and return for the precision approach. I'll no doubt throw something at you at some point. Understood?"

Peter immediately responded, "Yes Sir," which caused the man to raise his eyebrows.

"It's George, dear boy—I prefer being informal."

"Err, OK, Sir—I mean George," Peter stuttered. His stomach was held in an icy grip and he was beginning to sweat, but knew that, despite only just meeting this stranger and having to work with him in such close confines, he'd have to do his best. On the other hand, Peter couldn't believe his luck, being given the same route that he'd got for his mock test. He sat down and started his planning.

A couple of hours later he heard the aircraft taxying in and looked out of the window. Sure enough, the twin was just turning onto its parking spot and Peter watched as the propellors finally slowed to a halt and the air was once again quiet. He'd completed his planning and had checked and rechecked it, but watching Paula walk towards the building, his nerves were doing somersaults. He knew he could do this and that he needed to concentrate, but he'd never done anything like this before.

Mike appeared in the room and said to him, "You OK? All ready?"

Peter just nodded—his mouth was too dry to speak. Mike came over and patted him on the back saying, "You'll be OK—it's just a formality. It's two hours that will change your life forever."

Peter again nodded and finally spoke in a quiet voice, asking, "Were you nervous?"

Mike nodded. "As nervous as a kitten, but to be honest once we were underway the concentration levels were so high I forgot all about it and just got on with the job. You'll be fine," he said walking away. Peter smiled a thin smile and awaited his fate.

The door opened and George popped his head around the frame. "If you're ready, they are just refuelling the aircraft, so if you want to go and pre-flight and then get yourself all set up, I'll be out in about ten minutes."

Peter nodded and gathering up everything he needed, he made his way outside. Instinctively he glanced at the windsock—it was hanging limp as he'd expected. Good. He threw his charts and plates into the aircraft and began his external checks and finally slid into the seat, arranging everything in the order that he needed it.

As he was checking everything for the third time, George appeared and sat down in the seat next to him with a thump. "Right, lad, when you're ready, start up and we'll get going."

Peter started the engines and gradually bought the systems online, checking everything carefully. When he was ready he said, "OK—I'm ready to taxy, so here's my departure brief," and he ran through his brief from memory with George nodding his head but saying nothing. Finally, Peter lined up on the runway.

"Just forget that I'm here," George said. *That's like the galley slaves forgetting about the man with the whip*, Peter thought as he shoved the throttles forwards. Levelling off at five thousand feet, Peter turned onto his planned heading and checked everything for the umpteenth time and swapping his plate over for the next one. He radioed ahead, remembering to use the "Exam" callsign and entered the hold, turning into the racetrack.

"We'll do two holds and then outbound for the procedure," George said quickly and Peter nodded. After the second time around he selected his outbound heading and began his initial descent. His hands were slippery with sweat on the controls and his stomach was still in a knot but he did his best to ignore it and he kept saying "Concentrate, concentrate" to himself. Round onto final approach he flew, carefully watching the needle and allowing for the changing wind.

Suddenly, George called "minimums" and Peter immediately responded with "Going around" and he shoved both throttles forwards. Almost at once, the aircraft swerved to the right and Peter called out "Right engine failure" before raising the gear and flaps and carrying out his failure checklist.

Eventually, he levelled off and George said, "Right—I'll give you the engine back for now, but once we position for the precision approach, I'll have it back."

Peter nodded and made the necessary adjustments. He turned back to commence the second approach and George said, "I'll take the engine now, but gently this time."

Peter smiled quickly, busy swapping his plates over. He flew round, was cleared to commence the approach and fixed his eyes on the one precision approach instrument waiting for the centreline needle to begin its movement across the dial. There it was—Peter waited until it was about halfway across and turned towards the runway, holding his course and keeping the needle central.

The second horizontal needle began to twitch and as it moved down, Peter lowered the landing gear and flaps, arresting the descent when the needles were in a perfect cross. Concentrating like fury, but hardly holding the controls, Peter kept the needles aligned, occasionally glancing quickly at the altimeter and waited—and waited.

"Minimums—look up," George called and Peter craned his neck up so he could see over the nose. There was the runway with two white and two red lights. Perfect. "Go around," George called and Peter pushed the single throttle forwards, arresting the swing as he did so. "Right, lad—back for a cuppa I think," George said, adding, "Would you like the second engine back?"

Peter laughed. "Yes please," he said and George let go of the throttle and Peter bought the engine up to speed. About thirty minutes later, he lined up for his approach, removing the hood and landed quietly, taxying back to the stand with minimum fuss. He ran through the shutdown checklist and as the engines died he let out a long sigh of relief. He felt as if he'd been holding that particular breath since he got into the aircraft two hours ago.

He turned to see George smiling with his hand outstretched. "That's a pass lad—very well done," he said, shaking Peter's hand. Peter mumbled his thanks, hardly daring to believe it. Instrument rating passed. Oh boy! Nearly there!! He climbed out of the aircraft onto jelly legs and walked with George back to the classroom. Once inside his colleagues all looked up quizzically.

"Well?" Paul asked. Peter just nodded and this was followed by whoops of delight and applause. "Well done," Paul said, coming over and shaking his hand, adding, "That's the easy bit done," and he winked at Peter, who slowly sank into a chair. After a couple of minutes, he gathered his thoughts and got up to find Paula who was in the kitchen.

"How did you get on?" he asked.

"Passed—what about you?" she asked.

"I passed as well," Peter replied.

"Brilliant," Paula said brightly, coming over and giving Peter a hug. "Two out of two so far," she said, asking, "Who is next?"

"I think Sanj is next, then Mark and Arnie tomorrow," Peter replied, switching the kettle on.

Waiting for Sanj to complete his test seemed like years, but finally Peter spotted the aircraft in the distance and within a few minutes it was safely back on the ground. Peter watched them both get out of the aircraft and then Sanj put his bag down, raised his arms and jumped up and down.

"I think he's passed as well," Paula said smiling. Peter was so happy for his friend. They were all so close now—within a hair's breadth of success and that coveted right-hand seat. There was joy and elation on the bus home that evening and Peter was desperate to get out for his run—his legs were still aching with the effort of holding the aircraft in the asymmetric configuration and he needed to burn off the adrenaline. As soon as they were home, he shot upstairs, changed and was out of the door in a flash, running as hard as he could.

The following morning, there was little for Paula, Sanj and Peter to do except to wish their colleagues the best of luck and to watch them disappear into the sky. Just after lunchtime, Arnie returned and both he and Mark had also been successful. They were called together into the classroom by the three instructors.

"Right—well done all of you," Brian began. "We obviously wouldn't have put any of you forward for test unless you were ready, but it's still an outstanding success. Over the summer we'll be completing the Commercial Pilot training, which is a bit like your basic training but souped up and with much tighter minimums. As the CAA can't issue Commercial licences until the age of eighteen, we plan to complete the training and get you tested and then as each of you reach that age—those who haven't already—we'll send off your applications.

"However, as a taster, next week you're all rostered for some jump seat flying, so report to the office at 09:00 on Monday in your best uniforms and we'll get you to the airport."

A shiver of excitement passed through the group. "You mean—in a real jet with passengers?" Arnie asked.

"Yep a real jet," Brian responded.

Arnie nodded his head, saying "Yes" out loud. Brian smiled, saying, "Right all done so you can buzz off home for the weekend and I'll see you on Monday."

For Peter, that couldn't come soon enough.

36

For Peter, the weekend went by in a blur of cycle rides, a visit to Alex and Anna and time with his parents, but in reality he was excited beyond measure about the coming week. He was soon back at the crew house on Sunday evening, making sure that his uniform was spotless, his shirts perfect and his shoes polished. He wanted to look his best and knew that first impressions were important—the Captains that he would be flying with this coming week would be his training Captains and he wanted to please them at this early stage so that he could learn as much as possible from them later on.

Along with his colleagues, he was up early on Monday, shaved and showered and dressed to perfection. Inside, he was in the usual turmoil of having to meet new people and situations and the cold feeling inside him persisted. Mike was there to meet them at the offices and after a quick chat, they were taken to a meeting room, where they were issued with their rosters for the week. They were all rostered on short-haul European flights and would be outbound and back in the same day.

Peter looked at his roster—Malaga today, Paris tomorrow, Nice on Wednesday, Rome on Thursday and Stockholm on Friday. He'd be flying in a Trident—the same aircraft he'd looked over at Westlea airport. He kept looking at the names of the cities—they were places that he'd heard about and studied in school, but here he was actually going there!

Before they set off to the airport, Mike issued them all with Passport application forms, saying, "Fill these in this evening and bring them in tomorrow. We'll do the photos here and get everything sent off. Your passport must be with you on the flight deck at all times along with your licence, so for this week you must not leave the aircraft at any time—understood?"

A murmur of "Yes" went around the room and then Mike said, "All ready? Good—let's get on the bus," and they trooped outside with the giddy air of a school geography trip. The bus drove through barriers and around buildings, eventually arriving at a door marked "Aircrew".

Once inside, Mike ran up a flight of stairs two at a time, pushing open a large door and they filed into a room—inside there were teleprinters spewing out reams of paper and large television set with weather information on and rows of desks. Crews were seated at some of the desks and Mike took each of the cadets over to a particular desk individually, introducing them to the crew.

Peter was last and Mike soon introduced his to a large jolly man with four gold bars on his shoulders. "Captain—this is Peter," he said.

Peter shook the proffered hand and the captain said, "So you're one of the newbies, are you?"

Peter replied quietly, "Yes, Sir."

"Good. I'm Bob Smith and this is my First Officer Alex—he'll be flying us down this morning. I'll let him take you through the proceedings" and with that he turned and walked towards a long table laden with cups and a teapot.

"Right," Alex said. "Whereabouts are you in your training?"

"Err, I've just passed my Instrument Rating and we start the Commercial course in a couple of weeks," Peter answered shyly.

"Good—and how many hours do you have?" Alex asked.

"About a hundred and eighty," Peter replied and Alex nodded his head.

"Not too scruffy then," he smiled, continuing, "What I've done here is got the en-route weather, which as you can see is pretty good today and I'm about to do the load sheet if you want to give me a hand."

Peter nodded and Alex pulled a printed form from a basket and began to fill in figures. "I'm starting with the number of passengers here and I multiply that by a standard weight for each one. I then put in this column their baggage weight and here I put in cargo weight," he explained. Peter managed to follow what he was doing. Alex continued, "I then work out our centre of gravity and ground speed based on the wind, just like you do and work out the flight time and then I do my fuel calculations here," he said, pointing.

Peter again nodded. "Then I give it all to the skipper and he decides how much fuel to uplift, bearing in mind diversion and holding fuel." Peter understood and Alex walked over and gave the paperwork to Captain Smith. He shortly returned, saying, "the skip wants to uplift seven tons of fuel, so I'll ring that through to the fuellers, then we'll meet the cabin crew for their briefing."

Peter again nodded—it seemed to be just like planning one of his navigation trips, but with bigger numbers. The Captain soon re-joined them and together they walked through a door marked "Briefing". There were groups of chairs arranged in clusters of six and each cluster had a sign beside them. Alex spotted the one marked Malaga and they strode across. Seated were four young women, all looking professional in their uniforms.

"Good morning, ladies," the Captain said. "Malaga today—any passengers with special needs?"

"No," said one of the crew.

"Good. We've only a little cargo and no dangerous goods today, so should be straightforward. Alex here is flying us down and I'll bring us home. We've also got Peter with us today—one of the pilot cadets," and Peter stepped out from behind Alex and raised his hand in greeting. Two of the women looked at each other and one leaned forward and whispered something and they both giggled.

Bob shook his head, saying, "Oh come on—it's his first day. Be nice," and laughed before saying, "Right—let's get on board and do our thing," and he turned and strode towards the far end of the room, exiting through a door marked "Airside". Peter followed Alex, his mind turning over and he felt that it was all going too quickly for him. The door led to some steps which they all descended and there was the waiting aircraft, gleaming in the sun.

Alex ran up the steps and Peter did the same, following him onto the flightdeck. The Captain was outside checking the aircraft. "Right—you can remove your jacket and hang it in that cupboard behind your seat," Alex explained, shoving his jacket to the back of the rail. Peter did the same and Alex then sat down and, using a large book kept next to him, began to tune in radio frequencies and navigation aids, explaining to Peter as he went on.

Soon, they were joined by the Captain and he took his seat and began to double check Alex's inputs. Peter sat quietly, trying to take it all in and people were coming and going on the flightdeck—fuellers to get the Captain to sign for fuel, baggage loaders reporting that the bags and cargo were loaded and the doors were closed and locked and the cabin supervisor asking if they could commence loading the passengers. Bob nodded in agreement and very shortly afterwards Peter heard voices behind him and the crew welcoming people of board.

In what seemed no time at all, Peter heard the doors close and Bob went on the radio asking for his clearance and to push back. Writing down his clearance, he passed it to Alex who got the appropriate departure plate and clipped it to his control column. Peter felt the aircraft judder and then it began to move backwards. In his headphones, Peter could hear the groundcrew asking permission to release the towbar and then Alex called for engine start.

Soon, with the faint whine of three jet engines in his ears, they began to move forwards. Following the airport map spread out on his lap, Bob taxied the Trident to the holding point and they waited for permission to line up. Shortly afterwards, they swung onto the runway and Peter could see the familiar long ribbon of black asphalt stretching out before him.

Peter heard the tower give permission for take-off and Bob looked across at Alex, saying, "Ready?"

"Yep," came the reply and Bob said, "OK—three, two, one, go," and Alex shoved the power levers forwards. Almost instantly Peter felt a shove in his back as the power from the engines shot the aircraft forwards. Bob was reading out the speeds and finally said, "Vee one—rotate," and Alex hauled back on the controls and the rumbling of the wheels ceased. Peter was flying in a jet! The wheels were quickly raised and Alex concentrated on following the numbers on the plate and he soon switched on the autopilot, releasing his grip slowly.

Up through the thin cloud they tore and Peter was amazed at the speeds on the indicator he'd never been at this speed in his life. Eventually, they levelled off at a dizzying height—or so it seemed. Everything had happened so quickly. Bob turned to him, smiling and said, "Well—how was that?"

Peter shook his head before replying, "Amazing—it all happened so quickly. I think my brain is still behind me on the tarmac," Bob laughed.

"Don't worry—you'll get used to it," he said and they settled into the flight. Thirty minutes later, they were over Northern France and Bob said to Alex "Why don't you let Peter have a seat at the top table for a while." Alex nodded and removing his headphones he stood up out of his seat and let Peter take his place.

Putting on the headphones, Peter looked all around him. This time, the instruments and dials made sense and the view from the flightdeck was amazing. "You like?" Bob asked.

"Yes, Sir, I do," Peter said emphatically. Bob allowed him to remain in the seat until it was time to start the descent and Peter and Alex again changed places. Through his headphones, Peter could hear Alex briefing the descent and approach and he'd already got the airfield information over the radio, so he'd got the correct approach plate set up. Alex then dialled in a lower altitude on the autopilot and Peter watched, fascinated, as the power levers came back on their own and they began to descend.

Lower and lower they flew and finally Peter saw the runway, about ten miles ahead. He shortly heard a voice with a heavy accent give them permission to land and Alex flipped the autopilot off and took the controls. Bob lowered the wheels and flaps and the runway sped towards them.

Finally, they shot over the threshold and Alex closed the power levers, settling the big heavy aircraft onto the ground. As they slowed, Bob took over and taxied the aircraft to the gate, carefully following the marshaller's commands. "Brakes on," he called and Alex flipped a lever and replied, "Brakes on," and then raised three small levers behind the power levers and all was suddenly quiet.

Peter removed his headphones, looking outside. Was he really in a foreign country? Alex turned to him and smiled, "How was that?" he enquired.

Peter sat silently for a few moments before replying, "Amazing—absolutely amazing."

"Ha! That's exactly what I said on my first trip," Alex said, laughing. Behind in the cabin, Peter could hear voices and doors being opened and out of the window watched the passengers walk in a line towards the airport building.

"Right—coffee time," Bob said and getting up he opened the cockpit door and asked one of the cabin crew, "Any chance of some coffee for three parched aviators?"

Shortly, one of the cabin crew appeared with three steaming cups. Turning to Peter she said, "Here you are. Gosh, you're a big lad—how old are you?"

Peter blushed furiously before muttering, "Err, I'm seventeen."

The woman shook her head, turning to Bob and saying, "Seventeen—he just a baby," and laughing, she left the cockpit. Peter started into the distance, not knowing how to respond.

"Ignore her—she's a frustrated spinster," Bob said, letting out a huge roar of laughter.

Alex laughed as well and said to Peter, "You'll get lots of that—lots of attention and lots of teasing. I hope that you can handle it."

Peter scoffed and said, "Well, I worked with my dad in an engineering factory before I was accepted for my training and believe me, those guys can tease and take the mickey big time."

"Just don't take it to heart," Alex said, adding, "A lot of cabin crew are desperate to seduce a pilot as they think we're all millionaires."

This made Peter smile and he then began to ask some technical questions about the flight. Shortly, the refuelling had been completed, baggage had been loaded and they were ready for the return trip. Again, Peter watched closely as Bob input the frequencies and they were soon taxying out for departure. The flight home passed as quickly as the outbound leg had done and they were soon back on the ground and getting their uniforms on and were ready to leave the aircraft.

"When we leave the aircraft for another crew, we reset everything back to zero so that there's no confusion with wrong frequencies," Alex explained and he then stood up and ran down the steps with Peter following closely. Soon, Peter was walking the familiar streets back to the house, but he noticed that his feet weren't actually touching the ground!

Peter's jump seat flights all passed way too quickly and he both enjoyed them, but also found he was retreating into himself with having to meet and work with new people. Potentially he realised that he may fly with a different Captain on each trip and he needed to get past his difficulties with strangers. In addition to watching the aircraft being operated, Peter managed to see some landmarks from the cockpit windows.

He saw the city of Rome spread out in the sunshine, the Eiffel Tower as they approached Paris airport from the south and the whole of Stockholm. Every evening, he almost had to pinch himself to realise that, not only was he seeing something of the world, but that he was being paid to do so. He couldn't wait to get home that weekend and tell his parents and Alex about his week.

Friday came around all too quickly and the trip to Stockholm was later in the day and it was early evening when they landed back at base. By the time Peter had got back to the house, had changed and hung up his uniform and got to the mainline station, it was already past eight o'clock. Fortunately, there was a fast train to Westlea and he was soon rattling through the countryside, eager to see his parents. Paul met him and Peter flopped into the seat next to him on the bus.

"So, tell me about your week," Paul began.

"Can I tell you when we get home?" Peter asked, not wanting to go over everything twice. Paul smiled and nodded in agreement. As soon as he walked through the door, Annie rushed up and threw herself at him in her usual fashion.

"How's my man?" she asked.

"Tired and hungry," Peter replied, which caused her to laugh and say, "What a surprise—come on, I've got a late dinner ready and you can tell us all about what you've been up to."

Peter attacked the meal and started to explain what he'd been doing between mouthfuls. "Well, I don't know where you guys have been this week," he started. "But I've been to Malaga in Spain, Nice in France, Paris, Rome and today to Stockholm."

Annie stared at Peter, her fork mid-way between her plate and her mouth and her eyes grew like saucers. "You've been where?" she asked incredulously.

Peter smiled and nodded. "Yep. We've all had a week of flying in the jet from the jump seat in the cockpit. It's been absolutely amazing. We flew right past the Eiffel Tower and I could see it clearly," he explained and carried on to tell them both about everything he'd seen.

Paul shook his head slowly, eventually saying, "Amazing. I've never been to any of those places and you've done all that in one week?"

"Yep. Such is the life of an airline pilot," Peter replied. Soon, both Annie and Paul were firing questions at him and asking for every detail. Eventually at nearly midnight, Peter fell into his bed and was asleep in an instant.

The next morning, Peter woke late and immediately telephoned Alex, arranging to meet that evening. He's bought some course reading home with him, but it didn't amount to much, just an explanation of the Commercial course which consisted of twenty hours in the single engine aircraft and ten hours in the twin, followed by a test. He ended up retelling his mum about his trips the previous week.

Annie had never left the country and had only taken holidays within England and these foreign places seemed rather exotic to her. Peter had to explain that if he was on the short-haul fleet, then he'd only get to see these places from the air, as they flew there and back in one day and he said, "To be honest, mum, one airport ramp looks exactly the same as any other. However, if I'm lucky enough to be selected for long haul, then we get what we call layovers, as our duty hours expire when we land and we have to have so many rest hours between duties, so we get put up in hotels and we can explore."

Annie thought that this was amazing and she again urged him to either send or bring home postcards so that she could build a scrapbook of all the places in the world that he'd visited. Peter made a solemn promise to do so before getting up to get himself ready. He was meeting Alex and Anna for a meal and he was already famished.

His friends were waiting at the Bistro where they'd decided to eat. They were soon seated and poring over the menu and quickly ordered. Anna began as usual, by asking Peter what he'd been up to since last time and Peter decided to play with his friends a little. "Oh, just flying," he began.

"What—just flying? Flying what?" Anna asked.

"Oh, you know—aeroplanes," Peter teased.

Alex remained quiet but was watching intently, his gaze going left to right as though he was watching a tennis match. "Yes, but your training aeroplanes or—" Anna tailed off.

"No, we've been allowed to look at the jets that we'll eventually be flying," Peter replied, enjoying himself. Anna was so easy to bait.

"Oh. You mean go inside them?" she replied.

"Well, yes," Peter replied, enjoying himself even more now.

"Did they let you sit at the controls?" she asked.

Peter could sense her impatience. "Yes—once we were over Northern France," he replied, taking a long pull at his soda.

"Northern France? What do you mean, Northern France?" Anna cried.

"Oh you know—that part of France that's in the north," Peter said, finally breaking down into laughter.

He suddenly felt a sharp pain in his ankle as Anna kicked him and she said, "Peter. Tell me."

Peter smiled and paused before beginning, "OK. I've had my fun. We've been riding in the spare seat in the cockpits all week. This week I've been to Malaga in Spain, Paris, Rome, Nice and Stockholm."

Anna's eyes grew large and she seemed lost for words. Alex finally broke the spell. "Wow, buddy, that's amazing. How was it?"

"Unbelievable," Peter replied and he then went on to tell them about each trip, what he'd seen and about the speeds and heights that he'd flown at. Just then, the food arrived and Peter continued to tell his friends about his adventures as they ate. He finally pushed his empty plate away and said, "That my friends is the life of a jet jockey."

"Gosh—it sounds so exciting," Anna said, turning to Alex and adding, "The inside of a hospital doesn't sound quite as romantic does it?"

Alex shook his head, answering, "Nope."

"Talking of hospitals—how are the studies going?" Peter asked.

"Hmm, OK, I think," Alex said, glancing at Anna. She shook her head. "What Mr Modest here is trying to say is, we've got our projected grades and we both look set to achieve what we need, so we're going to be applying to medical school in the next month."

Peter nodded his head, saying, "Good—well done."

He then looked at Alex and said, "Liam. Have you heard from him at all?"

Anna was first to speak. "Yes—we saw him last weekend. He and Sally got a small flat near the railway station and she had the baby in December, just after Christmas. Little girl, they've called her Samantha. She's really cute. I think they are both coping OK, but Liam's pretty fed up I think."

Peter nodded without saying anything. "I can give you their address if you want—I'm sure Liam would be pleased to see you," Anna said, but Peter shook his head.

"Thanks, but I've too much on at the moment and my weekends are usually crammed full with studying. I'll catch up with his at some point." Soon, it was time to part company and after saying his goodnights, Peter ran for the bus.

37

The following week all the cadets commenced the Commercial course. This was structured in exactly the same way as the initial flying course, with students paired and they started back in the single engine aircraft, flying an hour each. Monday morning as usual began with a briefing. Mike was in charge this morning.

"Right—we hope you enjoyed your adventures last week. We've heard no bad reports, so we're happy with that. Today, we start the Commercial course. This is like learning to fly all over again, but this time we will be far less tolerant of any sloppy flying and we'll teach you to think commercially—that is to say, how to fly the aircraft in the most cost-conscious way, bearing in mind fuel costs and getting passengers to destinations on time or even early. All happy?"

A murmur of "Yes" went around the room. "OK then—off we go," Mike said and started for the door.

The next two weeks passed in a blur of flying and having the instructors barking at them all, admonishing any flying which they didn't think was up to standard. Twice Peter was elbowed in the ribs for what Brian called "Sloppy flying". At the time he was a hundred feet too low and just five degrees off heading. He didn't realise just how strict it needed to be. His colleagues were pretty much in the same boat and Arnie found himself getting torn off a strip for suggesting that "Fifty feet is only fifty feet."

"One day, young man, fifty feet may be the difference between life and death," Paul had growled at him, adding, "And you certainly won't pass your commercial test flying like that."

The mood in the crew house was sombre, but they all knew that the instructors were trying to instil professionalism in them all and they rose to the challenge. Summer was getting itself established and they were flying into the evenings to make up the required hours. Finally, Peter had his necessary twenty hours, so he was moved onto the twin along with Sanj and Paula.

Peter loved this aeroplane—he loved the power, he loved how easy it was to fly and he loved how it handled. He was soon halfway towards achieving his twin hours when the weekend arrived and he decided to remain in London, to try and stay focussed. All through the following week they all followed the same pattern and eventually they each achieved the thirty hours required.

Friday afternoon, immediately after lunch, Paul gathered them all together. "Right, boys and girls. Well done—you're all ready for test. We're in the process of getting these arranged and in the meantime, we'll just keep ticking over, flying just an hour each per day to keep you sharp. We're hoping that the examiner can be here next week. Your test will each take about ninety minutes and we should get through you all in two days, but of course the weather may have other ideas.

"Over the weekend, I suggest you keep reading and rereading your test profiles, as you'll be expected to know them off by heart. This is what we've all spent the past eighteen months working towards, so we expect first time passes with no negative comments on your records—understood?" Heads were nodded and the atmosphere remained tense. Paul stood for a few moments looking over them all before saying, "Good—now get the hell out of here and we'll see you on Monday."

There was a rush for the door, but the emotion on the journey home was restrained. Nobody spoke until they were back in the crew house and it was Arnie who broke the spell.

"Why do I now feel like a condemned man awaiting my appointment with the executioner?" he asked. Nobody answered, but there was a general consensus that he was right. Peter remained his usual insular self on the journey home and all weekend. Annie tried to lift his mood, but he explained where he was and what he was about to undertake and she left him to himself.

On the following Wednesday morning, the instructors called them together. "Tests commence tomorrow. Rota on the board. Good luck," was all that Brian had to say. Nervous glances were exchanged and Peter—seeing his name first on the list—suddenly felt that cold grip on his stomach. This was it. Pass or fail—no other options available. He had to get through this—had to. He spent that evening "Flying" his bed again, going through the profile over and over. He was especially nervous being first to test.

After an almost sleepless night, Peter was up as soon as it was light, again reading his test profile. He couldn't stand the thought of breakfast, but know he'd have to have something, so forced himself to eat some cereal and toast. He then showered, shaved and pulled on his uniform, looking at himself in the mirror. "Come on, lad—you can do this," he said to himself and he then walked slowly downstairs, thinking, *Let's get this over with.*

At the airfield, as soon as they arrived, they were ushered into a classroom and there with the instructors was a familiar face—Captain George Roberts. Peter breathed a sigh of relief. At least he knew George from his Instrument rating test. Finally after introductions, Peter was called into a side room to begin his planning. George showed him which route he'd like Peter to fly and briefed him comprehensively on the test, finishing with "I'd also like to see your fuel planning and figures to include diversion and holding—OK?"

Peter nodded and stated work. After about an hour and after checking and rechecking everything carefully, Peter got up and walked into the instructor's office, knocking politely on the door. Paul looked up and said, "All ready?"

Peter nodded and George joined him to go over his planning and figures. Finally, he looked up and said, "Good—that all looks OK. So, I'm here to test you for your CPL—correct?" Peter nodded. "Good—well just like last time, I want you to act as pilot-in-command and take any decisions as required. My job is that of an interested passenger. I'll only intervene if I see danger which you may not see, such as another aircraft outside your field of view or to prevent you killing us both—understood?"

Again, Peter nodded. "Good man—so get yourself out to the aircraft. I'll give you fifteen minutes to get yourself set up and then I'll join you. I suggest a bathroom break before you go though," he added, smiling. Peter smiled and decided that was probably a good idea.

Once settled in the aircraft, Peter's nerves calmed just a little—he just wanted to get under way now and get it over with. Shortly, he felt the aircraft rock slightly as George climbed up the single step and sat down heavily in the seat. "You just get on with it, lad—ignore me," he said. Peter ran through his checklist, got the engines started and bought systems online. "Ready?" he said.

George nodded and Peter taxied out towards the runway. Within a few short minutes, he was climbing towards the thin cloud above. The next hour passed in a blur, with George giving him instructions, diversions and emergencies to cope with. Finally, George said, "OK—take me back to the field—I need a drink." *So do I—a stiff one,* Peter thought before quickly plotting a course and hauling the aircraft around the sky. "When we get back, I'd like you to fly three circuits," George said and Peter nodded.

He knew what was coming. Sure enough, after the first approach and landing, as Peter was climbing out, the aircraft swerved to the right. "Right engine failure," Peter called, quickly going through his mental checklist and saying them out loud. He flew slowly around the circuit and commenced his second approach, still on one engine.

"Do this one without flaps please," George said and Peter instinctively increased his approach speed. Down onto the grass they flew and off again. "OK—make this one to land," George said and he appeared disinterested, staring out of the window.

"Wilco," Peter said and he lined up carefully for the approach. He wanted this to be smooth—perfect if he could manage. As he crossed the hedge, he slowly closed the remaining throttle, using rudder to offset the thrust and worked the controls to keep her flying for as long as possible. Finally, he heard the wheels rumbling beneath him. Peter let out a long stale breath. As soon as he'd shut down, George jumped up saying, "I'll see you inside," and he jumped off the wing and strode towards the building. Peter was at a loss—had he passed or not? Was this a good sign?

Peter walked slowly back to the classrooms—he had a feeling of dread. His palms were once again slippery with sweat and his mouth was dry. He didn't think that he'd done too badly, but maybe the examiner thought otherwise. Inside, he dumped his flight bag on the table and as he did so, he heard his name being called. It was Mike. "Peter—come into the office please."

Peter's stomach was doing somersaults as he walked slowly to the instructors office. Inside, all three instructors were standing around the desk and George was standing to one side. Peter stood awkwardly, awaiting his fate, thinking, *Just tell me—get it over with.*

"Right, lad—I expect you want to know how you've got on?" George asked.

"Err, yes please," Peter replied. Momentarily, the sun stopped crossing the sky. Birds stopped singing. The Earth froze in its orbit. Time took a deep breath. George paused for a moment before a huge smile crossed his face.

"You passed lad and a very good pass as well. One of the best I've tested, so credit to you and these guys," he said. Peter's knees almost gave way and a huge wave of relief spread over him. One by one, the instructors shook him heartily by the hand, saying "Well done" in unison. Peter couldn't speak—his mouth was too dry and he just didn't know what to say.

275

Eventually after a few minutes he said, "Thank you—and thanks for everything you've all done for me. You've been amazing."

Brian said, "You're welcome—now I guess you'd better go and tell your colleagues."

Peter nodded and walked slowly to the kitchen where his buddies were having lunch. He slowly pushed the door open and four pairs of eyes swivelled around slowly, like the guns on a Destroyer, fixing him to the spot. Nothing was said. Peter paused for a moment, enjoying the tension before saying simply, "Passed."

The kitchen erupted. Everyone rushed over to shake his hand, Paula hugged him, people were slapping him on the back.

"Well done, buddy," Sanj said and finally they all wanted to know how it had gone. Peter walked to the kettle and switched it on before going over the whole test. His friends all listened intently—any clues that they could glean from Peter's success may help them.

Just then, Paula's name was called and she trotted quickly from the room. Her turn. Peter grabbed a couple of stale sandwiches and sat down. Stuffing the food into his mouth, he sat and just kept saying to himself, "That's it—I've done it. I'm a commercial pilot". Slowly it began to sink in and as the adrenaline subsided, he felt tired—tried but elated.

"Two years after leaving school and Eighteen months and three weeks," he thought—"eighteen months of hard work, hard study, sweat, disappointment and elation and here I am. Mission accomplished."

The next thing Peter knew, Sanj was shaking him gently, saying, "Peter— wake up. Paula has just landed and Arnie is next."

Peter shook his head—he'd never fallen asleep like that, although he'd hardly slept the night before. He got up to make more coffee and shortly Paula appeared with a huge smile on her face. "Yippee," she shouted, "I passed."

Once again, everyone hugged her and offered their congratulations. This was becoming a habit—and a very good one. As soon as the excitement subsided, Paula came to sit alongside Peter and they compared their tests. Both it seemed had gone flawlessly. Peter was happy to chat, but inside he desperately wanted to ring his parents. That would have to wait until he got home.

The phone call home that evening was a brief affair—Peter hardly had time to tell Annie that he'd completed his training and was now qualified before the phone receiver erupted into shouts and cheers. Briefly, Paul came online and had a quick chat, offering his own congratulations before Annie's voice reappeared, talking at full speed.

"We must go out to celebrate—I'll book a table at the same restaurant as last time—shall I invite your friends? Yes, I'll do that—oh and I'll bring your Nan as well, as she'll be thrilled."

Peter held the handset away from his ear until the excitement subsided before replying, "OK, Mum, but I'm tired and I just need to sleep."

"Of course you do sweetie, but won't it be fun?" Annie asked, not caring for Peter's reply.

Finally, Peter managed to end the call by saying, "OK, mum, I'll see you tomorrow evening. Love you—bye," and he hung up. All he felt like doing now was laying down on his bed, but he reasoned that he needed to burn off all that adrenaline, so he pulled on his running gear and was shortly pounding the streets.

The following morning, once Mark had set off for his test, the Instructors called Peter into the office. Peter immediately felt nervous and awkward, but Mike, sensing his nervousness, slapped him on the back and laughed. "Sit down, lad—nothing to worry about, we just want a chat."

Peter sat down in the chair across from the three instructors, eyeing them closely. What did they want? Brian cleared his throat and began, "Right, Peter— now that you're qualified, we have to decide what to do with you. Under normal circumstances, you would all start on the short-haul fleet to gain experience. However, we have a need for a couple of FO's to join long haul and seeing as both you and Paula have been the most outstanding of the group, we wondered if you'd like that?

"Of course, flying long haul means lots of time away from home, lots of living out of suitcases and actually getting less in terms of hands-on flying and take-offs and landings, but you'll travel to and stay in some amazing destinations. The downside is that it can be hard on family life, hard on relationships and quite disruptive. Have a think about it."

Immediately Peter asked, "What would I be flying?"

"You'd be on the Vickers VC-10," Brian replied.

A smile slowly crept across Peter's face. The VC-10—queen of the fleet. Yes please. "Hmm, OK—I think that I'd like that," Peter replied, hoping not to sound too excited.

Brian smiled. "OK—long-haul it is then. We can start the technical training in a couple of weeks as we've both of you plus another guy joining from another airline. Will you ask Paula to come in please?"

Peter stood up, muttering his thanks, his head in a whirl. Outside, he said quietly to Paula, "Brian wants a word" and he jerked his thumb towards the office before sinking into a chair. Long haul. All he'd ever dreamt about. He couldn't believe his luck.

Sanj came to sit beside him. "What was that all about, buddy?" he asked.

"Oh, they're deciding which fleet to put us on," Peter replied nonchalantly, not wanting to give up any clues.

"Oh, of course," Sanj replied before asking, "What have they offered you?"

Peter suddenly felt mischievous. "Oh, they've asked me not to say," he replied, winking broadly at his friend.

"Oh, come on—tell me," Sanj replied, punching Peter on the shoulder.

"No really—all our assignments are secret," Peter went on, enjoying himself.

"Secret? How can they be secret?" Sanj asked before continuing, "Come on, buddy—short-haul or long-haul?"

"Can't tell you," Peter said before losing his composure and letting out a loud guffaw.

Sanj smiled and shook his head before saying, "Are you happy with what you've been offered?"

Peter smiled and decided to put Sanj out of his misery. "Long haul, buddy—on the VC-10," he said simply.

"You jammy beggar," Sanj said, pleased for Peter. "When do you start?"

"In a couple of weeks for the technical training," Peter replied.

Sanj opened his mouth to say something but stopped. He didn't want to jinx his own chances. Just then, Paula reappeared and asked Sanj to go to the office. It was time for his test—the final one.

He was up like a shot and almost ran towards the instructors room. Paula looked at Peter. "Long-haul?" she asked.

Peter nodded his head. "You?"

Paula smiled. "Yep—long haul as well. I'm so excited," she added before sitting down. "What a journey this has been—the most amazing couple of years of my life."

Peter nodded in agreement. No words were needed.

On the bus home that afternoon, there was a real end-of-term atmosphere with lots of excited chatter and laughter. All of the cadets had qualified and Sanj, Mark and Arnie would be joining the short-haul fleet, with training commencing the following week. Both Paula and Peter had been given a short roster for jump-seating for the week, so there would be some flying to do, but had also been provided with a mountain of reading to complete before commencing the technical training.

Peter had quickly glanced through the books—electrical systems, hydraulics, engines, emergency systems. He knew that there would be exams in each subject to pass before he ever got near the aircraft and some Sim training thrown in for good measure, but he was so excited.

He decided to take the book on the hydraulic systems home with him that weekend, as his dad may be able to help with the study and in almost no time at all, he was on the train bound for home.

As soon as he and Paul hopped off the bus, they could see Annie standing beside the garden gate, waving. Peter strode quickly across, pushing the gate aside and hugging his mother. There were tears in her eyes and all she could say was, "Well done, Peter—well done."

Eventually, she relinquished her grip and taking Peter's hand, she led him towards the house and began to chatter at full speed. Peter smiled to himself—she was always the same when excited or nervous. Once inside, sitting on the sofa, Peter allowed her to run out of steam before attempting to answer the hundred or so questions she had fired at him.

"Have you had your final assignment?" she eventually asked.

Peter took a deep breath—he knew that this was going to cause some worry. "Yes—I've been offered long-haul," he said. There was a long silence whilst this sunk in.

"What does that mean?" Annie asked, her voice filled with concern.

"Oh—you know. Places like New York, Toronto, Cape Town," Peter replied before continuing, "We get to lay over and get a chance to have a look around. It'll be fun."

Annie looked at him with doubt filling her face. "Will you be OK with that—I mean meeting new people all the time and staying in strange places?"

"Well, I'm going to have to get used to it, mum—I am finding it a bit easier as I get older and I've got to get on with my life at some point. I know you and dad have always sheltered me from strangers and social situations, but I've got to find my feet and get on with it," Peter replied, hoping to convince her.

"Oh, I hope so," Annie replied, looking carefully at Peter.

"Mum—you've nothing to worry about. As a crew, we stay in the same hotel and usually eat together and I guess we'll become friends. It'll be nice to get to know people and see a bit of the world. Honestly, I'll be fine. I learned a long time ago to keep quiet, say as little as possible, to not say anything inappropriate and to just quietly fit in. I know I've always been a bit of a misfit and to use your phrase, a bit "Delicate" but I think I can cope."

Annie smiled thinly. He decided to change the subject. "Have you arranged anything for the weekend? I've lots of study to be getting on with."

"Ahh—yes. We've booked the restaurant, but Nan won't be coming as she's pretty tired at the moment and likes to be in bed early. Alex and Anna couldn't make it either as Alex has a family thing to attend, so it'll just be the three of us. Is that OK?"

Peter smiled and nodded, saying "Perfect."

After reading for most of the day and an enjoyable meal with his parents, on Sunday morning Peter asked if they could visit his Nan. They were soon knocking at the front door, pushing it open and kicking off their shoes. Peter heard his Nan's voice calling from the living room and he strode inside. She looked up at him quizzically for a moment before saying "Peter? Is that you?"

Peter laughed. "Of course, it's me," he said before going over and giving her a kiss on the cheek.

"Gosh lad—you're so tall and you're filling out massively. What a fine young man you're becoming," Nan said, taking Peter's hand. "Now sit down and tell me all about what you've been up to. Annie tells me that you have some news."

Peter sat beside her and began. "Well, I've just qualified as a Commercial Pilot and will shortly be flying passengers," he began.

Nan looked at him carefully. "How old are you now?" she asked.

"I'll be eighteen in a few weeks," he replied.

"Gosh—and they let you do that at your age?" she asked.

Peter laughed. "They sure do—although it will be about three months before I'm actually flying people around."

Nan smiled and nodded slowly. "This is all you've ever talked about and despite other people's doubts, I always had a hunch that you'd make it. Well done—I hope that it pays well and gives you the opportunity to meet lots of nice young ladies," she said, winking at Peter.

Peter blushed and replied, "Well, it pays well for one thing."

"Well, you need to meet a young lady soon enough—I can't wait forever to become a Great Grandmother," she said before laughing out loud.

Peter laughed with her before Annie said, "I don't think Peter's ready for all that yet, mum."

"A pity," Nan continued. "He's a fine specimen and if I was fifty years younger—"

"Mother!" Annie said, feigning shock.

Nan chuckled. "Those days are long gone," she said, her voice trailing away.

Annie immediately changed the subject, asking Nan about her medication and Peter soon lost interest in the conversation. He loved his Nan and she'd always had a wicked sense of humour which appealed to him. In no time at all it was time to leave.

Nan squeezed Peter's hand once again, saying, "You've done well. You always had a strong sense of purpose and determination and I'm glad that you've proved your doubters wrong. Come back and see me soon."

"I will, don't worry," Peter said, bending to kiss her. As they left the house, Peter was suddenly overtaken by a sense of loss. He knew these visits would become fewer in the future, but he was determined to still visit as often as possible.

38

Feeling refreshed after a great weekend with his family, Peter was scheduled to jump seat on the morning flight to Rome on Monday morning. He reported in plenty of time and introduced himself to the crew. They were friendly enough but busy with their planning, so Peter hung back until they had finished. The Captain then walked off without speaking a word, leaving the first officer John to talk to Peter. "Whereabouts are you now in the training?" he asked.

"I'm fully qualified, but can't get my licence through for another five weeks when I'm eighteen, but I'm just starting the technical course which looks pretty daunting," Peter replied.

John smiled and nodded. "Yes, I thought the same, but actually it's pretty easy. Once we get into the flightdeck I'll show you what I mean. Ignore the skipper—he's always like that with trainees," he said.

Shortly, they were climbing the aircraft steps and John quickly got busy inputting the route frequencies and navigation aids. Once he'd completed the task, the Captain joined them and began checking John's work, grunting his satisfaction. Shortly, they were climbing towards the high summer cloud and the autopilot was engaged. John turned to Peter and started to explain.

"See the overhead panel here it's arranged into sections. Each section is for a system—hydraulics, air conditioning and so on. You just have to memorise which area to look at and what each switch does—simple. You'll get the hang of it—the technical exams are just about normal operation of each system and what to do in the event of a failure, but most of it is automatic."

Peter nodded—he was beginning to understand. "Easier than in my day— you had to know the position and function of every bloody knob and switch," the Captain grumbled. John smiled and said, "Yeah—we're spoilt nowadays," and he turned to wink at Peter. Peter smiled quietly to himself. He had so much to learn.

After an uneventful but enjoyable trip, Peter was soon back in his room, studying hard. He made his usual copious notes and was struggling to remember the formula for Pressure times Force times Horsepower for the hydraulics systems. Arnie, Mark and Sanj were at the airfield and Paula was presumably flying as she wasn't about. Peter felt suddenly very lonely—in his own world, lost in his studies and another step nearer his goal—and he found it most agreeable.

Eventually, he glanced at his watch. It was nearly eight o'clock. He suddenly felt hungry. He walked downstairs, where to his surprise he found the rest of the group. He hadn't heard any of them return. He quickly made himself something to eat and went back to his book, reading until his eyes grew heavy. In no time he was fast asleep.

For the rest of the week and all through the following week, Peter applied himself to studying, often joining Paula to work together. Between them, they began to understand the mysteries of the systems on board the aircraft, until it was finally time to commence the official course. They were joined by an experienced first officer who was new to the company Andy. He had a couple of thousand hours flying short-haul for a competitor airline and had finally got a long-haul position.

They were being trained by a senior training captain who had many years on the actual aircraft and he slowly led them through the different subjects. After the first three days it was exam time. Hydraulics was the first subject and Peter passed without any difficulties. It was far easier than he'd expected and John's advice had come in handy. Soon, they were taken through electrical systems, engines and emergencies. By the end of the three week course, Peter was exhausted but satisfied. He'd passed all the exams easily, as had Paula and Andy.

On the final Friday, Fozzy appeared in his capacity as Chief Pilot and Fleet Captain for the VC-10 to talk to them. Seeing Peter, Fozzy came over and had a quiet word, congratulating him on getting through the course. "All thanks to you," Peter said and Fozzy just smiled before addressing them.

"Right—well done on getting through the tech course," he began. "Next stage is Simulator and base training—you'll need to make three take-offs and landings each before we allow you near passengers. We'll be doing that next week. Well, take off from the main airport and fly to Bristol where it's much quieter and we'll see how you get on. I'll be conducting the training and please treat me kindly—I'm not getting any younger," he pleaded.

There was a murmur of laughter before he continued, "Once base training is complete, you'll get your rosters for line training. You'll fly sectors with training skippers like myself and with a fully qualified FO in the jump seat just in case you forget how to fly. You need to complete forty sectors before you're released as fully-fledged FO's. Understood?"

Heads were nodded. "Some points to remember—firstly, you must always— and I mean always—have both your licence and passport with you. Keep them both in your flight bags. Always carry spare clothing and an extra set just in case of delays. Always have some local currency in your flight bag for use when on layover. Please report for duty punctually and ready for a long day. Any questions?"

They remained silent, so Fozzy dismissed them all, before walking over to Peter once again. "How's you, Dad?" he asked.

"He's fine thanks—still working hard and enjoying life I think," Peter replied.

"Good—do give him my best wishes when you see him," Peter said that he would and Fozzy left the classroom.

Peter decided to stay in the crew house for the weekend, but telephoned his mother on Friday evening for his usual chat. Once the usual pleasantries were over, Annie asked about the technical course and the exams. "All done and I passed all the exams," Peter replied.

"Good lad—what's next?" she asked.

"Oh, we get to fly the jet next week—we have to do three take-offs and landings by ourselves before we can carry passengers," Peter explained.

There was a short silence before he heard his mother say, "By yourself? What—you mean all alone in the aircraft?"

Peter laughed. "No—we'll be with a training Captain—I'll be with Fozzy," he said.

There was a high sigh of relief from Annie. "Thank goodness—I thought you meant you'd be all alone," she laughed. This made Peter smile to himself for the rest of the evening.

The base training was scheduled for Tuesday and Peter reported in plenty of time, getting the weather briefing and aircraft Technical log before Fozzy arrived. Fozzy quickly glanced at the information and, turning to the FO beside him, said, "Right—let's get on with it." They were soon climbing towards the clouds. En-route, Fozzy made Paula take the right-hand seat for her first landing, which she completed with only a small amount of assistance.

Just like during basic training, they flew around the airport in a circuit, setting up for each landing. After Paula's third landing, they taxied onto the taxiway where they stopped and Paula and Andy swapped places. Peter was sitting in the first-class cabin at the front of the aircraft, playing with the seat buttons and enjoying the view from the window. Andy, who had been flying a smaller aircraft, made a fairly firm landing on his first attempt, shaking Peter in his seat.

Paula, who was sitting across the aisle from Peter screwed her face up, saying, "I hope mine were better than that."

Peter reassured her, growing more tense with each landing. Finally, they again taxied in and stopped. Peter stood up and with a "Good luck" from Paula, he settled himself into the right seat, adjusting it to make himself comfortable. Fozzy looked across, saying, "Right, young Marham. I'll taxy us out and you can take over when we're lined up—OK? Remember—this is just another aeroplane, just a bigger one than anything that you've flown before. Remember your landings in the sim at your interview—it's exactly the same."

Peter smiled and nodded and he tried to ignore the cold leaden feeling in his stomach as they taxied along. Fozzy swung the aircraft onto the runway and turning to Peter, said, "You have control—in your own time, when you're ready, off we go."

Peter smiled thinly and taking a deep breath, he said, "Ready."

"OK—off you go," Fozzy said and Peter pushed all four throttle levers forwards. Unseen, Fozzy slowly slid his hands forwards towards the control column whilst calling out the speeds. He finally called "V-one—rotate" and Peter pulled back on the controls. The nose came up and the rumbling of the wheels stopped. "Positive rate—gear up please," Peter called out and Fozzy reached across to raise the landing gear.

Levelling off at just two thousand feet, Peter pulled the throttles almost all the way back whilst simultaneously rolling the aircraft around the circuit. As quickly as Peter could think, they were cleared onto final approach and Peter rolled the aircraft around, watching his speed and calling for flaps and landing gear. He aligned the aircraft with the runway, which he could see clearly ahead, but he double-checked his instruments as well.

Down they flew and Fozzy prompted him to raise the nose and cut the power—to Peter he seemed very high and the runway was about thirty feet beneath the nose, but he soon felt a bump as the main wheels touched. He lowered the nosewheel onto the runway and Fozzy's hands were a blur of lightning-fast movements as he re-configured the aircraft for take-off. He quickly called "Off you go" and Peter again slammed the throttles forwards, quickly lifting off.

Round they came for the second time and Peter again settled the aircraft onto the runway, lifting off quickly afterwards. This time, Fozzy said, "Right, old boy—climb straight ahead to ten thousand."

Peter acknowledged the command, thinking to himself, "I've only done two landings," but Fozzy soon explained what was happening.

"You can fly us back to Heathrow and make your third landing there—I'll show you the way," Peter smiled and settled into the seat. At last—he was flying a passenger jet and was going to put London Heathrow in his logbook. Fozzy made Peter hand-fly without the autopilot all the way back and they eventually joined the landing pattern, taking their turn on final approach.

Peter could see the layout of the airport in front of him just like he had from the jump seat a short while ago. Down he flew, finally settling the huge aircraft down with hardly a bump. Fozzy took over to taxy in and Peter felt a great sense of relief. He'd done it—surely he'd passed his base training. Once on stand, Fozzy set the parking brake and shut all four engines down before wearily climbing out of his seat, motioning Peter to follow him. He flopped down into a seat in First Class alongside Paula and Andy.

"Right—all passed—good flying. Line training next, so expect your rosters to appear in your pigeon holes in the crew room—any questions?"

Peter spoke quietly, "Err yes—I still don't have my licence as I'm not eighteen for a couple of weeks. What do I do in the meantime?"

Fozzy scratched his chin and said, "We'll roster you for a couple of jump seat flights—pack your bag and don't forget your passport."

Peter nodded his thanks and they all stood up and disembarked.

Once back in the crew house, Peter was giddy with excitement. He could hardly believe that he'd not only flown a passenger jet, but that he'd actually landed the aircraft at one or the world's busiest airports. He was buzzing so much that he found it difficult to keep still, so in an effort to calm himself down, he put on his running gear and set off at a furious pace. Whilst he'd been at home last time he'd treated himself to some weights so he could improve his upper body strength.

Once back inside the house, he ran up the stairs and began to lift the weights in the privacy of his room, carefully following a routine he'd set out for himself and he eventually fell exhausted on the bed. He loved the high he got from exercise and it suited his personality to be out on his own, not having to interact with the world.

Eventually, he got up to get some food and to ring his parents—he knew his mum was worried about the base training. He dialled the number, pushing pennies into the slot as soon as he heard his mother's voice. "Hi mum—base training completed so you can relax."

He heard Annie shriek down the phone. "Oh well done—how did it go?" she asked.

"Great—I was last so Fozzy let me fly back from Bristol to Heathrow. I've done my first landing at Heathrow—so cool," he said.

Annie was delighted for him and began to bombard him with questions in her usual way. Eventually, Annie's questions dried up and she asked Peter what was the next stage.

"Well, I don't get my licence until my eighteenth, so it's jump seat flights until then," he said. Annie immediately began to ask more questions about where he'd be going, which Peter couldn't answer and finally he hung up, returning to his room. He slept very well that night.

Peter didn't receive his roster for a couple of days, during which time he continued to read the aircraft technical manual to try and learn as much as he could. Eventually his roster appeared and he sat down in the crew room to read it. He was stunned by what he saw. On Friday he was scheduled to be on the morning flight to New York, returning on Sunday evening. He was excited and nervous at the same time.

Whilst he flown on the jump seat on short-haul, he'd never left the aircraft, so had never set foot on foreign soil and had not technically entered another country, yet here he was about to fly to another continent! His mind was almost instantly in a fluster—what clothing should he take? Where could he buy dollars? He walked through into the briefing room, where he saw a crew sitting at the New York desk, so he walked over to ask some questions.

The cabin crew were friendly—almost too friendly at first and Peter enquired about the hotel and what clothing to take with him. One lady who was about his mother's age, came over and stroked his arm before saying, "If you were on my flight honey, I wouldn't bother taking any clothes."

This was met with a roar of laughter from all the girls and Peter blushed furiously. Finally one of them said, "Take a couple of casual shirts, some slacks, a clean uniform shirt and some comfortable shoes along with two changes of undies and ignore her, she's recently divorced."

The first woman, who was still stroking his arm, winked at Peter before letting go. Peter mumbled his thanks and left the room in a hurry, listening to the laughter following him. He'd been warned about this, but had been caught unprepared. Walking back to the crew house, he mused that it may not just be his aviation education that was about to be expanded.

On Friday morning, Peter arrived at the airport in plenty of time, quickly making his way to the crew room. There he saw Fozzy and he walked over to say hello. "Ahh, young Peter—all set for today's adventures?" he asked.

Peter nodded and Fozzy introduced him to the first officer who was calculating the load sheet. "Dale—this is Peter who I told you about. Ready to commence line training but still a baby, so no licence for another couple of weeks. I think we can look after him."

Peter shook the outstretched hand and he asked Dale about the load sheet, so Dale took him through it. "It's just like planning for your CPL flights, except the numbers are much much bigger," Dale said, continuing, "For fuel, we don't calculate gallons per hour, we work in tons per hour. Apart from the distances and speeds, it's pretty much the same."

Peter nodded in understanding and eventually after Fozzy had checked everything, they walked through to briefing. Fozzy introduced Peter to the cabin crew and there was a buzz of excitement and a few giggles, which Fozzy ignored.

"Right, anything I need to know?" he asked.

A lady spoke up, "Just one wheelchair user, but nothing else of note," she said.

"Good—let's get going then," Fozzy said, striding for the door.

Outside, they climbed onto a bus which drove them to the waiting aircraft, which stood gleaming blue and white in the sunshine. Peter, as always, tried to keep as much distance from everyone else as he could, his mind working overtime with what lay ahead. He overheard one of the women whisper "He's such a big lad" as the bus stopped, but he ignored it. He followed Fozzy and Dale up the steps, turning left onto the flightdeck.

Fozzy showed him where to hang his uniform jacket and stow his overnight bag and Peter sat down on one of the spare seats, watching Dale input the route and asking questions as he went along. Fuellers, ramp agents and baggage loaders came and went and finally Fozzy called for the passengers to be allowed on board. Peter could hear the footsteps and the cabin crew greeting each one of them, but was lost in a world of watching and learning.

Finally, one of the cabin crew appeared and said, "All on board."

Fozzy called for the doors to be closed and asked Dale to get the departure information and get clearance to push back and start. This was all done quickly and soon Peter watched as Fozzy and Dale went through the engine start procedures. His stomach was full of butterflies and he found he had sweaty palms, but he was desperate to learn as much as he could.

Eventually, they called for taxy and the big jet rolled slowly forwards under Fozzy's expert hands. They soon joined a queue of aircraft, eventually lining up on the runway. "All set?" Fozzy asked. Peter nodded and he heard Dale say "All set" through his headphones. Fozzy advanced the throttles and the jet rolled forwards, gathering speed. In less than a minute they were climbing towards the clear blue sky.

Soon, they were settled in the cruise some seven miles above the ground and Fozzy was flying on autopilot. Eventually he pressed a button on the overhead panel and a crew member appeared. "Any chance of some refreshment?" he asked.

"Sure," she said, disappearing again, before returning a few moments later with three cups of very welcome coffee.

Sipping his coffee, Fozzy turned to Peter saying, "You OK there?"

Peter smiled and answered that he was just fine and happy to be watching and learning. "Good man—there's lots to learn. I'm still learning and I've been doing it for years. It this game, we don't take anything for granted and every day is a school day—am I right Dale?"

Dale raised his thumb, smiling at Peter. "Don't forget, there's lots to learn from the skipper, but ask your questions at the right time, that's my advice."

Peter nodded, looking out of the window at the ocean so far below. It seemed so unreal, like watching a movie slowly being played. After a couple of hours, Dale got up to visit the bathroom and Fozzy told Peter to take the right-hand seat, which he did immediately. He could still hardly believe it—here he was, sitting seven miles high in a modern passenger jet—and he was being paid for the privilege! Dale returned and Peter started to get up but Fozzy told him to stay where he was and Dale gratefully accepted the jump seat.

"We'll swap you over when we start the descent," Fozzy said and Peter nodded. Peter started questioning Fozzy about the aircraft systems, as he still had lots of questions unanswered. Fozzy patiently explained things in a more realistic fashion and things became clearer for Peter. Eventually, a thin ribbon of coastline appeared ahead and Peter asked where it was.

"North East Canada," Fozzy replied. "Shortest ocean crossing and from there we fly south towards the USA and New York." Peter nodded. This was the first time he'd seen anything else other that Europe and his excitement grew as the coastline got closer.

Finally, they crossed the coast into Canadian airspace and the aircraft rolled onto a southerly heading, following the planned route in the autopilot. In the distance from his window, Peter could see mountains and there were lakes spread beneath the aircraft. Onwards they flew, eventually reaching American airspace. Fozzy was dealing with the radio—Dale would normally be doing this but Fozzy didn't expect Peter to be ready at this stage.

Finally, Fozzy said that they were approaching top of descent, so Peter and Dale swapped places and shortly afterwards the throttles retarded themselves and the aircraft began to descend. Fozzy put his seatbelts back on and Peter did the same and he watched intently as Fozzy followed the commands of Air Traffic, who guided them towards the airport.

Fozzy picked up the internal microphone, saying, "Cabin crew—five minutes to landing."

Finally, Peter watched as the autopilot rolled the aircraft onto final approach and Fozzy flicked it off, taking manual control, calling for flaps and for the landing gear to be lowered. Peter could see the runway ahead and Fozzy guided them down to a smooth landing. As they slowed down, Dale placed the airfield map on Fozzy's lap so he could navigate the myriad of taxiways to the allocated stand. Very soon, they were on stand and Peter could hear the doors being opened and the sound of the passengers disembarking.

On the flightdeck, Fozzy was tidying away his paperwork and Dale was recording the fuel figures before resetting the radios and navigation aids for the next crew. Finally, Fozzy stood up, pulling on his uniform jacket and peered out of the cockpit into the cabin. The last passengers were just leaving, so he said "Come on lad" to Peter, who jumped up, donning his jacket and collecting his bag.

"A note of caution," Fozzy began. "Just watch yourself with the cabin crew—often there are some of them whose only purpose in life is to snare themselves a pilot, as they think we're all paid loads. I'm not sure of your experiences with women, but just be careful in the hotel." Peter nodded his agreement, but he was looking forward to the experience of actually being in another country.

Finally the cabin supervisor appeared and said that they were all ready and they all left the aircraft together. They made their way into the arrivals area and Peter took his passport from his bag for inspection, holding it open for the officer as Fozzy had shown him. Within a few minutes, they were being driven into the city in a minibus. A short time later, they arrived at the hotel and Peter found himself in a lift with the rest of the crew before hunting for his room.

Before they all disappeared into their rooms, Fozzy said, "In reception in one hour if that's OK," and there was a general murmur of "Yes" before Peter unlocked his door. Once inside, Peter quickly took his uniform off, hanging it carefully before changing into his casuals. He unpacked the rest of his things and then went over to the window to look out.

All he could see were other skyscrapers in every direction and he heard the constant hooting of car horns, of whistles being blown and some music being played somewhere. So this was America—he loved it so far. Glancing at his watch, he quickly grabbed his wallet, room key and his jacket and he made his way downstairs. In the lobby he found Dale and a couple of the cabin crew. Soon, everyone else joined them and Fozzy suggested the "usual" restaurant and off they walked.

The restaurant was only a block away and Peter walked behind the group, taking in the sounds and smells of the city. This was one lively place! They shortly arrived and Fozzy was met by somebody that he obviously knew and they were shown to a large table at the back of the room. Peter found himself being shoved and pushed to a seat which—unsurprisingly—was between two of the younger women.

"I'm Linda," said one of the girls, adding, "and this is Abbie. What's your name again?"

"Err—Peter," Peter said quietly, feeling himself retreating inside.

"So you're one of the new pilots?" Linda asked.

"Yes," Peter said in a matter-of-fact way.

"Is this your first trip abroad?" Abbie asked him, looking directly into his eyes.

Peter felt himself blushing. "Erm—yes," he replied.

"Oh wow," Abbie adding. "How old are you?"

"Erm—I'll be eighteen in two weeks," Peter stammered.

The two girls exchanged glances before Linda asked, "Eighteen—and do you have a girlfriend?"

Peter stayed quiet for a few moments before replying, "No." He began to feel decidedly uncomfortable before he heard Fozzy say, "Right—what are we having?"

Everyone suddenly began to talk at once, but Peter stayed quiet. "Peter—what are you having to drink?" Fozzy asked.

"Orange juice, please," Peter answered, trying to remember his manners.

"Orange juice," Linda said. "Don't you want anything stronger?"

Peter shook his head, adding, "I don't drink alcohol."

"Jeez—we've got our work cut out with this one," Abbie said, laughing. Linda agreed and they began to tease and giggle at Peters expense, but he managed to deal with it and kept quiet. Eventually the drinks arrived and the waiter began to take people's orders for food. Peter asked for a burger, as he'd had one at the new place in town a couple of weeks ago. He was quite unprepared however for the monster that arrived.

Soon, everyone was getting stuck in to the food and the chatter diminished whilst they ate. The girls ordered more wine but Peter stuck with his orange juice. He'd never tried alcohol and he certainly didn't want to make a fool of himself on his first trip out. Soon the meal was finished and Peter began to relax—even the teasing had ceased. Even though it was early in the evening, the crew's body clocks were five hours ahead and people began to yawn and stretch.

Peter felt tired, but was beginning to enjoy himself. So this was the life he'd trained for. He could see the potential for lots of fun ahead. A short time later, they all made their way back to the hotel for a well-earned rest and Peter went back to his room alone. Shortly after he closed the door, he heard a knock. Opening the door slightly he saw Linda.

"Can I come in for a few moments?" she asked. Peter hesitated before opening the door fully. She strode past him and sat down on the end of the bed. "I thought that it would be nice to get to know each other a little more," she said, kicking her shoes off. Peter's sense of self-survival hit alarm mode.

"In what way?" he asked.

"Oh you know, just a little better—why don't you come and sit with me," Linda said, patting the bed.

Peter stood where he was, his mind thinking furiously. "Look, I'm sure that you're a very nice person, but I'm really tired and it's a bit soon for me to get to know you a bit better," Peter said, struggling with keeping his voice as calm as possible.

"Are you sure?" Linda asked, patting the bed again. Peter walked over and taking her hand, pulled her upright.

"Maybe next time when I'm not as shy," he said.

Linda looked at him carefully before saying, "OK—your loss," and she slipped her shoes on and left the room. Peter breathed a huge sigh of relief. As attractive as she was, he wasn't ready for this—not on his first trip.

39

Peter woke early—his body clock and watch were still on UK time. Outside, it was still dark and the traffic was muted but the city was still very much alive. He looked at the clock on the wall—4 AM. Oh dear—he thought that he must try to get more rest, but inside his body was raring to go. After a feeble attempt to get back to sleep, Peter showered, shaved and got dressed.

He'd decided to go for a walk as it was now getting light. Remembering his wallet and room key, he took the stairs down to the lobby and he walked out into the street. It was warm for the time of day and he looked up at a cloudless sky. The doorman greeted him with a "Good morning" before asking where he was going. Peter, of course, had no idea, so the doorman told him where it would be safe to walk and where to avoid.

Peter set off, strolling along and taking in the sights and sounds of the city waking up. To his amazement, there were already places open to get breakfast and everywhere there seemed to be coffee shops already doing business. He decided to get breakfast back at the hotel, where it would be paid for by the airline, but he was amazed by the different fare on offer. Turning a corner he came across a barber's shop already busy. It was so outside his normal frame of reference that he could hardly believe what he was seeing. This just wasn't like sleepy Westlea at all.

Eventually, he made his way back to the hotel and he spotted Abbie just going in for breakfast, so he followed her inside where he found most of the crew already busy eating. He got some coffee and took a seat next to Dale and they were soon chatting about where Peter had been for his walk. "I got up and came straight here," Dale explained, "On account of being absolutely famished."

Peter was hungry, but his meal the evening before had filled him well, so he went to the buffet and got a small helping of cereal. Just as he was sitting back down, Linda walked in and spotting the empty seat beside him, came and sat down. "Good morning," she began. "How are you today?"

"I'm OK, thank you—how are you?" Peter replied.

"Oh, I'm OK—just spent a lonely night in my room, but other than that I'm just fine thank you," she replied before squeezing Peter's thigh and getting up to get some food.

"What was that comment all about?" Dale whispered.

"Oh, she came to my room last night and wanted me to get to know her a bit better," Peter explained innocently.

Dale smiled. "She's got a bit of a reputation that one—she was just trying to get laid," he said. "A good looking young lad like you will soon have them queueing up at the door," he chuckled quietly, looking quickly away as Linda returned.

This comment put Peter's head into a spin—was this really what happened on layovers? Perhaps that's why they were called "Lay over" he thought with some amusement. "Is that quite normal?" he asked Dale.

Dale smiled. "Listen, buddy, you'll get more offers for sex doing this job than any other that I can think of. Don't forget, we live in the so-called permissive society and everyone's at it. It wouldn't surprise me if old Fozzy wasn't at it."

Peter was shocked. "Really—doesn't he have a wife at home?" he asked.

Dale shrugged his shoulders. "Probably, but who cares these days?" he said.

Peter finished his breakfast in silence, his mind working overtime. He was nearly eighteen and he'd had that discussion about Sally with his mother some time ago. Perhaps, now that he'd qualified, he could finally start to think about a serious girlfriend. He'd want a long-term relationship though he mused, not a single sordid night in a hotel somewhere.

After breakfast, he found Fozzy in the lobby, deep in the morning newspaper. "Good morning, Sir," he said quietly. Fozzy's face appeared over the top of the paper.

"Ahh—good morning, young Marham. How are you today?" he enquired.

"I'm good thank you. Can I just ask you—what do we do on these layovers?"

Fozzy smiled. "Well, I've no doubt that the girls will want to go to Bloomingdales—the large department store up town. They'll no doubt be starting to buy Christmas presents. What we traditionally do is to have a look around the city and take in some of the sights. All old hat to me now of course, but happy to show you youngsters around," he said.

"That would be awesome, thank you," Peter replied, excited by the prospect.

"Well, let's wait for the others and draw up a battle plan," Fozzy said before returning to the news. Peter got up and looked around the lobby area—there were pamphlets advertising theatres, music venues and places to visit and postcards for sale. On a whim, he purchased a postcard, quickly scribbling "Hi mum" on the back and addressing it to his home address, buying a stamp from the receptionist, who put it the mail.

Collecting some pamphlets, Peter took them back to his room, stashing them safely in his bag. *Mum will enjoy seeing those,* he thought. After looking out of the window some more, he wandered back downstairs to fine most of the crew ready to set out. Fozzy was in command.

"Right team—what's on the agenda for today?" he asked. A chorus of "Shopping" came from most of the girls, but Dale and Peter kept quiet. Fozzy turned to them. "What about you chaps?" he asked.

"I'd like to see Times Square and the Empire State building," Dale answered and Peter nodded his head.

"OK—we have a plan. Shall we meet back late afternoon so we can get dinner early?" Fozzy asked and heads were nodded. "Right," he continued, "We'll see you later," and he set off for the door with Dale, Peter and a girl called Mary.

"It's my first trip as well," she explained to Peter as they walked along, "and I don't want to go shopping. I can do that at home."

Fozzy strode briskly along, seemingly knowing where he was and where he was headed and Peter, Mary and Dale walked quickly behind. You could tell that Fozzy was ex-military by the way he was almost marching down Broadway. Soon they arrived at a huge junction, with flashing lights and electronic notice boards attached to the buildings. There was traffic everywhere, with yellow taxis zooming in every direction. Peter found the noise, the bustle and the electronic signs fascinating.

"Times Square, ladies and gentlemen," Fozzy said with a large sweeping gesture of his hand. Peter had read about this place once in a book, but had never imagined that he'd be standing here—here in New York. He kept having to remind himself that this was really happening he wasn't dreaming it. He was craning his neck to look upwards at the buildings that seemed to rise forever and the different architecture caught his eye.

There was everything from modern glass and concrete buildings to delicate stone structures designed in the Art Deco style. Mary was as silent as Peter, standing and taking it all in. After a short while, Fozzy broke the spell. "The Empire State building is just a few blocks down this way and we can ride the elevator to the top if you like—we'll get a grandstand view."

The three of them nodded their heads and Fozzy was off like a shot, taking great strides towards their next goal. They quickly arrived at a beautiful building and Fozzy pushed open a door. Inside there was a short queue of people and they joined the back of the line. When they got to the front, Fozzy said politely to the young lady behind the counter, "Four adults to the top please."

The lady handed over tickets and they were let through a barrier, joining another queue for the lift—or "Elevator" as Fozzy described it. All around the lobby area there was polished wood panelling with gold leaf detail and the marble floor was spotless. Soon, the elevator doors opened with a hiss and they joined people and squeezed themselves inside. The doors then closed and Peter felt the lift jerk and it began to rise—and rise.

It seemed to go on forever, but eventually it slowed and the doors opened. Peter was surprised to see the display in the elevator show the number 102—the Hundred and Second floor! The air was a lot fresher here and Fozzy led them outside. Peter stopped dead in his tracks, mouth agape—there was the whole city spread all around him, looking just like it had the day before when they were approaching the airport.

Peter walked cautiously to the edge, gingerly peering over. Incredibly, even at this height, they could still hear the traffic and the general noise from below. He stood motionless for ages, taking it all in. He didn't hear Fozzy walk up to him and he jumped when Fozzy said, "Pretty amazing eh?"

"Yes—I've never seen anything like this in my life before," Peter replied, still struggling to take it all in.

"You'll get used to it lad—one of the privileges of our profession," Fozzy said before walking away. After a while, Peter began to walk around the building, seeing the city from different angles. He saw the two rivers, Central Park and the island of Manhattan narrowing to a point. He could see ferry boats crossing the river and could also see aircraft taking off from two different airports.

He turned another corner to see Fozzy with Mary—he was pointing out sights and details for her, with his left hand in the small of her back. She looked as excited as Peter felt—he was doing his best to drink it all in slowly. *I must buy a camera and learn how to use it properly,* he thought to himself, thinking that he would build a scrapbook of his travels.

Finally, after a couple of hours, Fozzy announced that it must be lunchtime and they took the elevator back to street level. "There's a lovely little diner just around the corner," Fozzy said, striding off.

Once seated, Peter asked Fozzy how much he owed for his ticket to the building. "First trip to the top?" Fozzy asked them all. They all nodded. "My treat then, although I'll let you buy me lunch as a thank you." Soon, they were tucking into eggs, pancakes, bacon and really hot, strong coffee.

After lunch, which cost the three of them just a couple of dollars each, they began to stroll along the streets, listening to the sounds and taking in the sights. Some shops had elaborate displays in the windows and Peter was amazed at the range of things on offer. *Mum would love this,* he thought to himself with a smile.

Fozzy kept pointing out certain sights and was telling them some of the history of the city. He told them that he'd first flown here some twenty years before and that the journey back then had taken twelve hours with two refuelling stops. He said that he knew the city really well and had his favourite places to visit and to eat.

"I used to take my wife small presents home from each city I visited, but stopped that some time ago," he said, adding, "The house was beginning to fill with ornaments and knick-knacks and she had so many clothes she didn't know what to do with them. However, there are some great shops around the next corner if you're looking for something to take back home. Cheaper here as well," he added.

Peter immediately thought of his parents. He'd look for small gifts for them, just to mark his first flight. As they turned the next corner, Peter stopped dead. There was a wide avenue with huge shops down each side. Taxis were shooting up and down like bumper cars at a fairground and horns were constantly sounding.

"Welcome to Fifth Avenue—the world's greatest shopping street," Fozzy said grandly. Peter could hardly take in what he was seeing—he'd never seen anything like this in his life before. "Right, chaps," Fozzy said. "I'll leave you to browse or whatever you'd like to do—shall we meet in an hour's time? There's a little coffee place called Franco's about halfway down on this side. I'll see you in there," and with that, he strode off.

Dale, Mary and Peter looked at each other. "I might get something for my girlfriend," Dale said, adding, "but I've no idea what."

Peter nodded saying he wanted to do the same for his parents. They both looked at Mary, who smiled before saying, "Oh, so now I'm suddenly your personal shopper, is that it?"

Dale and Peter both nodded and Dale laughed. Mary snorted, "Men! Come on then—let's go," and she walked into a large department store. Once inside, Peter felt like a child in a toyshop. He had no idea where to begin, but Mary was soon asking his questions about his parents, what they liked and the type of things that they might enjoy. Dale disappeared towards the ladies section and Mary eventually found a scarf—or Pashmina—for Peter's mum and some leather gloves for his dad. Both were marked with "Bloomingdale's. Fifth Avenue, New York" on the labels, so there could be no doubt as to their provenance.

Peter paid for them and the assistant also gift wrapped them to save Peter the trouble. He was delighted. They met up with Fozzy shortly after, strolling back to the hotel.

That evening, Fozzy suggested a local steak house to eat at and they enjoyed a filling meal together. Peter had never seen a steak as huge and he struggled to finish, finally admitting defeat and pushing his plate away, which caused Dale some amusement. "I thought that you'd have managed that easily at your age," he said, teasing Peter gently.

"I would, but I haven't been running or exercising since we got here, so I'm feeling a bit bloated," Peter replied, adding, "I may pack my running gear next time so I can keep up with it."

Dale laughed out loud. "Running? Exercise? The only exercise I get—apart from sex—is lifting pints in my local back home."

Abbie looked across at him and laughed. "Well, I can tell with that belly of yours you can't be getting much sex," which bought a roar of laughter from them all.

Dale laughed as well, saying, "Well, what time are you free," and he winked at Abbie.

Abbie immediately replied, "Ha! You've no chance," and chuckled. Peter sat, taking it all in and he tried to relax, but he still felt isolated and alone at times, deciding to keep his comments to himself. He just hoped that there wouldn't be any knocks on his door that evening. He really couldn't stand the thought of a one-night stand—it all seemed so vulgar to him.

Once back at the hotel, they all went to the bar and Peter got himself a soda before sitting over by the window. Outside, the streetlights cast an eerie glow and the headlights of the cars and taxis sent shadows dancing across the buildings. He felt somebody sit down next to him and turned to see Linda getting comfortable.

"Had a good day?" she asked.

"Yes thanks—what about you?" he replied.

"We went shopping and as usual I spent too much money. Do you like my new blouse?" she asked, opening her cardigan to reveal a thin white blouse which was unbuttoned almost to her waist and clearly showing her cleavage.

Peter looked and then immediately looked away. She out her hand on his thigh, saying, "You shouldn't be so shy—it's the 1970's. Everybody's doing it."

Peter smiled thinly and finally said, "Yes I guess so, but I'd like to get to know somebody a bit better first."

Linda smiled, pulling her cardigan closed. "OK I get it. You're shy—have you done it yet?"

Peter shook his head. Linda looked at him kindly before saying, "OK—I'll not frighten you off—at least not on your first trip."

She then got up and went over to talk with some of the other cabin crew. A short while later, Peter stood up and, saying goodnight, went up to his room.

The following morning, Peter was awake early and he began to read the technical manual for the return trip home. They were due to set off at 10 o'clock local time, arriving around nine pm that evening London time. After a while, he decided to go down for breakfast and as he was locking his door, he heard a door open further down the corridor. He looked up to see Mary leaving Fozzy's room, so he quickly turned away and headed for the stairs.

He didn't know why, but that had surprised him. He'd assumed that as Fozzy was married, he wouldn't be taking part in the fun and games, but reasoned that it was none of his business anyway, so put it out of his mind.

Downstairs, he found some of the cabin crew and Dale, who was already attacking a huge plate of food. "I'd suggest a generous breakfast, as we'll only get the airline food on the trip home and I'm normally starving by the time we're mid-Atlantic," he suggested to Peter.

Peter took his advice and loaded his plate high, enjoying every scrap. They were soon joined by Fozzy and he told them to be ready to be collected by the crew bus at half past eight. This gave Peter half an hour to get his uniform on and throw everything into his bag. His parents presents were safely in the bottom of the bag so wouldn't get creased and he folded the rest of his clothes, looking carefully around so he didn't leave anything. He finally pulled his jacket on, checked his appearance in the mirror and went downstairs.

Soon, they were in the bus on the way to the airport. As soon as they arrived, Fozzy, Dale and Peter went to the flight planning office to get the weather and passenger information. Fozzy asked Peter to do the load sheet calculations and some help from Dale he finally presented Fozzy with the final figures. Fozzy glanced down the sheet, nodding his approval and they then went to brief the crew.

"Anything to report?" Fozzy asked.

"Nothing really," said Linda, who was the cabin supervisor. "We're pretty full, but no passengers with special needs," she said.

Fozzy nodded and, looking at his watch, said, "We'll get out to the aircraft in ten minutes, as we'll need a bit more set up time on the flight deck."

As soon as they got onto the aircraft, Fozzy said, "Right—I want Peter to input the frequencies and Nav aids. Dale—only help if he's struggling and I'll check everything over when you've finished." Peter hung his jacket in the cupboard and taking the airway manual, he sat down, turned to the correct page and began.

After about half an hour and with almost no assistance, Peter said that he'd finished. Fozzy then took the manual and began double checking Peter's work, announcing that he was satisfied.

There was only one small error, but Fozzy said that it was of no consequence. He then instructed Peter to call the tower to get their departure information. Peter did this as quickly as possible, then he selected the correct departure sheet from the book and clipped it to Fozzy's control column. Fozzy called for the passengers to be allowed to board and soon they were ready. "Right swap seats," Fozzy said and Peter took his place on the jump seat. Within minutes, they were climbing towards a cloudless sky.

The flight home was uneventful. Their routing took advantage of the jet stream and this cut almost an hour off their flying time. Peter was amazed by the difference and realised that by capturing the jet stream, this could save the airline a great deal of money in fuel savings over the year. About halfway across the ocean, Linda came into the cockpit and asked if they were ready for their meals.

Fozzy nodded enthusiastically and after choosing different meals as the regulations required, she soon reappeared with trays laden with standard airline food. She offered Peter his tray and winked at him as he took it. He smiled back at her, realising that she was just being friendly and that his rejection of her advances hadn't caused any friction between them. He didn't want to start his career by making enemies.

Gradually, as they flew towards dusk, they saw the lights of towns and cities before them on the horizon. "Ireland," Fozzy pointed out in response to Peter's question. The vantage point from seven miles up was huge. Slowly, they changed course directly for London and things began to get busy. Dale, who was flying, began to input the instrument approach frequencies for the autopilot and he and Fozzy adjusted their seats and fastened their belts.

Finally, Dale called "Cabin crew—ten minutes to landing" over the intercom and Peter watched and followed his every move, eventually letting the autopilot capture the approach. Cancelling the autopilot, he called for flap and then landing gear before setting the aircraft gently onto the western runway. Fozzy taxied them to the gate with little delay, shutting the engines down and letting out a sigh.

"Home again," he said wearily. Peter stood up slowly, stiff after sitting for so long. They heard the passengers leaving and once they had all disembarked, Fozzy and Dale pulled on their jackets and as a crew they all left the aircraft together. Once through immigration, Fozzy bade them farewell and he bent to whisper something to Mary, who giggled. Linda came over and said goodbye to Peter, asking when was next flying.

"In four days—to Toronto," he replied.

She screwed her face up saying, "I'm not on that flight. Hope to see you again soon," and she quickly kissed him on the cheek before walking away.

Dale looked at him quizzically. "Did you—?" he asked.

Peter laughed and shook his head. "Nope," he said emphatically.

"Ha! You will someday," Dale replied before saying, "Good to have you along—you're going to do well," and he walked off with Peter's thanks. Peter walked slowly back to the crew house—he was on cloud nine.

40

The following morning, Peter set off early for the train—he wanted to be back home in time for his mother coming home from work. He was dying to tell both his parents about his adventures and to give them the gifts he'd bought home with him. He arrived back at Westlea station late morning and as it was a fine September day, decided to walk home.

Throwing his rucksack over his shoulder, he walked the familiar streets, whistling and recalling the past three days of his young life. He still couldn't believe what he just accomplished. He unlocked the front door, going inside and immediately switched the kettle on. Making coffee, he sat on the sofa, stretching his long legs across the carpet and closed his eyes. All he could see in his mind's eye was Times Square and the view from the Empire State building. How could he possibly describe that in detail to his parents?

A short while later, he heard the front door open and his mother's voice calling, "Peter—where are you?"

He jumped up, calling out and rushed out of the room throwing his arms around Annie's waist and lifting her off the floor, kissing her on the cheek. "Put me down, you daft idiot," she laughed, holding him tightly. She looked up at him, eyes shining brightly and asked, "Well—where have you been and how was it?"

Peter smiled and waited a few moments. He loved these times with his mother—she was his world in many respects. "We flew out to New York last Friday, layover on Saturday and flew back yesterday," he said as calmly as he dared.

Annie's eyes grew as big as saucers. "New York? New York as in America?" she asked.

Peter laughed. "No silly—New York just five miles up the road. Of course, New York in America," he replied. "Is there another one?" Annie slowly walked into the living room and sat down. "You mean to tell me that over a short weekend, you've crossed the Atlantic twice and stayed over?" she asked.

"Yep," Peter replied flippantly. "Great fun and what an amazing place—you should go sometime, you'd love it," he said, sitting down beside her.

"I can't believe it," Annie went on. "My boy has flown to New York. I've never been much further than the South Coast when we had our honeymoon in Eastbourne and I thought that was exotic, but New York—" her voice trailed away.

"That's nothing—I'm flying to Toronto in Canada on Thursday, coming back on Saturday," Peter said.

Annie looked at him, slowly shaking her head. "You've already seen more of the world in your eighteen years that I have in my nearly fifty," she said, quite disbelievingly.

Peter got up saying, "I think I need to make you a drink," and he walked into the kitchen. Annie followed and immediately started firing questions at him, scatter-gun style. Peter held both his hands up saying, "Whoa! I'm going to tell you both all about it after dinner this evening—I've so much to tell you."

Annie laughed—"OK—but I want to know everything, understood."

"Yes, mother," Peter said dryly and they both burst out laughing.

Peter helped Annie prepare dinner, enjoying her company as always. When everything was ready and pans on the cooker were bubbling away happily, Peter decided to grasp the nettle and ask Annie about relationships again. "Mum, I want to ask you something, but I don't want you to be worried," he began.

Annie looked at him closely and said "Go on—"

"Well, remember we had a conversation when I was seeing Sally and she was getting—you know—physical. Well, when I was at the hotel, one of the cabin crew wanted to—how did she put it? Ahh yes, she said she wanted to get to know me better. I know we live in a more permissive society nowadays and I'm sure that there a lot of affairs which go on, but was I right in saying no?"

Annie thought for a moment before saying, "If that's what you felt, then yes, you were right."

"The thing is, a couple of the other pilots have said that some of the cabin crew throw themselves at pilots as they think that we're big earners and are good prospects for the future, but I feel that the more somebody tries it on and throws themselves at me, the less likely I am to get involved. I'd rather find somebody by myself—does that make sense?"

"Absolutely," Annie said emphatically. "You'll know when the right person comes along and I'd hate to think of you being taken advantage of just because you're a big strapping good looking lad."

Peter nodded his head slowly. "I just don't want to make enemies that's all," he said.

Annie immediately said, "I think that if you had sex with one girl one trip and another on a different trip, you'd get an awful reputation and cause fights between the women concerned. You stick to your principles and you'll be fine."

Again Peter nodded, saying, "thanks, mum. You know how difficult I find it to relate to people and how hard I find it to read their expressions and body language. I just want to be myself."

Annie stood up, kissed him on the forehead and said, "You do what you think is best—just don't get caught out like Sally did."

Peter nodded his head again, muttering "Couldn't do with that."

A short time later, Peter heard Paul putting his bike away in the garage and rushed to the back door to greet him. Paul saw Peter and a huge smile crossed his face. "Hi, son—how are you?" he asked, coming inside and kicking his boots off.

"Hi, dad—I'm great, thanks—how are you?" Peter replied.

"Oh—the usual," Paul laughed, giving Peter a quick hug. "What have you been up to then? Been anywhere nice?" Paul said, taking his seat at the kitchen table.

"I'll tell you both all about it after dinner," Peter replied. For the moment he just wanted to enjoy this family normality—he was back in his happy place.

"Look forward to that," Paul said, as Annie put dinner plates in front of them and they began to eat.

After dinner, Peter cleared away and quickly washed the dishes before joining his parents in the living room. Paul looked at him and said, "Come on then—I can see that you're dying to tell us."

Peter laughed and took a deep breath. "I flew with Fozzy last Friday to New York. We stayed over on Saturday and we flew home on Sunday. Fozzy is great—he knows the place really well and he's so much fun to be with and is a great teacher," Peter began.

Paul nodded, saying, "He always was a great guy. I feel good knowing that you've flown with his as I trust him implicitly."

Peter then began to tell them both all about New York, about Times Square and going up the Empire State building, about shopping of Fifth Avenue and of the noise and bustle. Both Annie and Paul sat silently listening, unable to believe that this was their boy—their special, delicate boy who was telling them about his adventures half a world away.

Suddenly, Peter jumped up saying, "Won't be a sec," and he rushed upstairs, grabbing the presents and pamphlets. He came back into the room and said to Annie, "I picked these up at the hotel—thought you'd enjoy reading them," and he handed her the pamphlets.

"Thanks," she said, opening them out and glancing at them.

"There's more," Peter said. "We went down Fifth Avenue, which is supposed to be the best shopping street in the world. I went into a store called Bloomingdale's, which is a huge department store and it sells everything. To celebrate my first trip abroad and to say thank you for everything you've both done to help me, I got you both a little something," and he handed the gifts to Annie and Paul.

Annie needed no prompting, ripping the wrapping paper off and unfolding the scarf. "Oh, Peter, thank you—it's beautiful," she said, getting up and giving Peter a kiss.

Paul looked across and smiled. "Something else to wear," he laughed and Annie poked her tongue out at him.

"Aren't you going to open yours?" she said.

Paul carefully unpeeled the paper from his parcel, his eyes lighting up when he saw the gloves. "Oh boy, thanks, Peter, they are beautiful," he said, trying them on. "Such soft leather. Thanks—I needed a new pair for this winter as it happens."

"Yes I know," Peter replied, adding, "You can see from the label that it says Bloomingdale's New York on," Paul nodded, a big smile on his face.

"So it does. Just to think that you've flown to New York, stayed over, been shopping and flown back all in three days and the most exciting thing I did all weekend was to finally finish the bike," he said, shaking his head.

"Oh, have you—I'll have a look at it," Peter said with some excitement.

Paul nodded, saying, "It's turned out nice. I'm really pleased with it."

It was Peter's turn to smile and he said, "Dad. Do you know anything about photography? I want to get a decent camera so I can photograph some of the places I get to and make a scrapbook."

Paul thought for a moment before saying, "Hmmmm. I did a bit during the war, but cameras are so much more sophisticated nowadays. Why don't you buy a magazine and see what they say?"

"Good idea," Peter replied. "I may buy a camera next time I'm in New York as they are so much cheaper there for the same thing."

Paul nodded. "Much less tax to pay and you'll get it tax free if you show them your passport."

They continued to talk about Peter's flying and his next destination and before long, it was late and getting towards bedtime. Paul was first up. "Right—bedtime for me as I've work tomorrow. When are you going back?" he asked Peter.

"On Wednesday—have a really early start on Thursday so want to be back in plenty of time," Peter explained, adding, "See you tomorrow. G'night."

Peter was woken by the closing of the back door the following morning. "Dad getting off to work," he thought, stretching out and enjoying being back in his own bed once again. He closed his eyes and drifted for a while, his mind empty and no thoughts filling his head. Finally, Annie's voice calling up the stairs jerked him fully awake.

"I'm off Peter—half day today so I'll see you at lunchtime," she called, softly closing the door. Peter got up, showered and dressed. He wanted to ring Alex and catch up with things, so he wandered downstairs and after getting himself some coffee, dialled Alex's number. A very sleepy voice answered and Peter nearly didn't recognise Alex at first.

"Hi, buddy—it's me—Peter," he began.

Eventually, Alex began to speak in a recognisable voice as he cleared his head. "Oh, hi, buddy—how are you?" he asked.

"I'm good," Peter replied before continuing. "How's the study—are you going to Med school or what?"

There was a laugh down the telephone line, "Yes—we both start next week. We got into the same University, so Anna is going to have to put up with me a while longer," Alex joked before asking "What are you up to now. Are you fully qualified yet?"

"Yes, fully qualified and I've just got back from New York," Peter said as casually as he could manage.

"What?" Came Alex's reply. "New York—boy, that's so cool. How long were you there?"

"Oh, just three days—flew out on Friday, layover on Saturday and back on Sunday," Peter replied.

"That sounds awesome—so you're becoming a world traveller by the sounds of it," Alex replied.

This made Peter laugh out loud. "Hardly—although I'm off to Toronto on Thursday," he said.

It was Alex's turn to laugh. "Oh—only Toronto. Is that all?" he asked with a smile in his voice, adding, "Listen, we'll have to have a proper catch up when you're next home. Let's go out together and do something—I'll have to let you know when I'm home from Uni."

"Yeah, sure—I'd like that," Peter replied before ending the call. Alex had sounded awful on the phone—Peter wondered if he was OK.

Peter wanted to get a photography magazine to help him choose a camera, so he scribbled a quick note to Annie saying he'd be back mid-afternoon and he locked the house and ran for the bus, getting to the stop just in time. Once in Westlea town centre, he walked to the newsagents to enquire about the best magazine to get and the man behind the counter recommended one, which Peter paid for and took outside to begin reading.

Leafing through, there was articles on both colour and black and white photography and there was also a field test of portable cameras exactly what Peter was looking for. He decided to take it home and read it there before making a decision. He then walked to the bank to purchase some Canadian dollars for his next trip before walking to the coffee bar—the scene of so many teenage exploits with his friends—and got a drink, sitting down in the usual place by the window.

The town was quiet and there was hardly anybody walking around—a huge difference from the weekend before. Looking out whilst nursing his coffee cup, he saw a familiar face pushing a buggy along. Sally with the baby. He half stood up to go outside and say hello, but then sat down quickly. He actually didn't really have anything to say to her and he still felt a pang of guilt about letting her go. He felt guilty for her current predicament, as he would never have been so stupid as to have unprotected sex, let along father a child and he wondered how much it had altered her life.

Finally, he thought to himself that if he'd stayed with her, he'd never have got to New York last week and would probably have stayed at the engineering company with his dad. "It's amazing how small decisions can have such a huge impact on your life" he thought. This led him to think about Ben. He'd made a decision and was now paying the consequences, just like Sally and Liam. In turn, this made him think about the cabin crew, some of whom seemed to want to seduce a pilot at any cost and it strengthened his resolve to not get caught out.

Back at home, he found Annie pottering around the garden and they were soon sat together chatting amiably. "You are going to be eighteen next week—what are your plans?" she asked.

"I've a trip next week, but can't remember offhand which days, so I'll have to fit in around that," Peter replied. "I also have to go to the Civil Aviation offices in central London on my birthday to collect my licence, so I can start properly flying," he explained.

Annie nodded before saying, "So shall we do something when you're home after that?"

"Hmm if you want, but don't make a fuss as you know I'm not too bothered," Peter said, adding, "I just want to start line training properly."

Annie nodded—she knew Peter didn't like being the centre of attention and certainly didn't like any fuss, so she left the subject for the moment. When Paul arrived home, Peter showed him the magazine and they looked at the cameras together. Peter thought one with interchangeable lenses would be a good idea as it would allow him to slowly build his equipment up as time and money allowed and it would be more versatile.

"I've been speaking to a chap at work who is a mad keen photographer and he suggested one of the Japanese single lens reflex cameras would be a good place to start," Paul said.

"Yes, I was reading about those—they look OK," Peter replied, noting that they were nearly a hundred pounds in the UK, but probably a lot cheaper in the USA. "I think I'll have a look next time I'm in New York as there is a big camera store there I'm told," Peter said, putting the magazine down.

"Good plan—but don't be spending a fortune," Paul said.

Peter smiled, "Well, no, but I'll shortly be on full salary plus flight pay, so I should be able to afford it."

After a pleasant evening, Peter was early to bed. He wanted to be back at the crew house by lunchtime the following day to give himself time to press his uniform and read about the Toronto trip. He was asleep quickly and up early in the morning to say goodbye to his parents as they set off for work. After a quick shower and breakfast, he grabbed his rucksack, locked the door and waited for the bus. He was soon speeding through the countryside, excited at the prospect of his next flight.

Once back at the crew house, Peter unlocked his door to find an envelope on the carpet. Addressed formally to "First Officer Marham" he wondered what it could be. Setting his rucksack down, he tore open the letter and began to read.

"Dear Peter—as the crew house is for use by trainees, we have to inform you that the next intake of Cadets will be on 2 January and therefore require you to vacate the accommodation before Mid-December. We are able to offer assistance in helping you find suitable accommodation near to the airport and would ask that you contact the Personnel Department as soon as convenient."

Oh—he hadn't seen that coming, but realised that he'd known all along that it was really the "Cadet" house. He resolved to get in touch with Personnel in due course, but right now he had other things on his mind. Pulling his best uniform out of the wardrobe, he took it downstairs and wetting a handkerchief, he carefully pressed sharp creases into the trousers. He checked his uniform shirts were ironed to perfection and that his tie and epaulettes were presentable. He then polished his uniform shoes before packing his overnight bag with his casuals and toiletries.

He'd actually written himself a pre-trip checklist to follow and he ticked off each item individually, just like pre-flighting the aircraft. This had caused much amusement amongst his colleagues in the house, but he didn't care. At least he'd never forget something vital. Satisfied that he was ready, he turned his attention to the tech manual, reading the routing and approach procedures for Toronto. He was buried in the book when there was a knock on the door and Sanj looked around the corner.

"Hi, buddy—haven't seen you for a few days. How's things?" he asked.

Peter smiled at his friend. "Great, thanks—what have you been up to?" he asked.

"Oh, busy flying and trying to get to grips with the aeroplane. The Trident can be a tricky beast when it has a mind to be so," Sanj answered before asking, "How's the VC-10?"

"I don't really know as I'm still jump seating—not my birthday until next week," Peter replied.

"Ahh, of course—you were the baby of the group," Sanj replied, laughing. "Anyway—have you had a letter from Personnel?" he asked.

"One about being kicked out of the house?" Peter asked. Sanj nodded. "Yeah, just got it. I'll go to Personnel next week," he said.

"I've had an idea—let's get a flat together," Sanj suggested. "It'll be fun. We can share the rent and look after our own food seeing as you'll often be away for days at a time. My folks have said that they will help with a deposit."

Peter thought for a moment before saying, "That sounds like a really good idea—let's look into it."

Sanj raised his thumb and said, "I'll do the same. I can see you're busy with the tech manual, so I'll leave you to it," and he disappeared from view. Peter set his alarm for 4 o'clock in the morning and then put his running gear on and headed out. It had been a few days and he needed the release. As he was pounding along, he thought to pack the running gear as well, as he was sure he'd find opportunity in Toronto. He had a clean pair of shorts and a clean vest, so he was not concerned about getting all sweaty this evening.

41

The alarm intruded rudely on Peter's sleep, but he quickly silenced it and was soon showering and shaving. A quick breakfast of cereal and he then donned his uniform, checked his appearance and after checking that his passport was secure in his flight bag, he let himself out of the house. The morning was cooler and it was still dark with only the first tentacles of light appearing on the horizon. As usual, as soon as he arrived he went straight to flight planning, printing the weather and route information on the newly-installed computer system. Shortly a man a few years senior to Peter came over and asked if he was the new FO jump seating that day.

Peter said that he was and the man introduced himself as Ted. "I'm a senior First Officer, so I'll be helping you out and no doubt be jump seating for you in time."

Peter smiled—this guy seemed like a nice chap. "Who is the Captain today?" Peter asked.

Ted looked at Peter for a moment before saying, "Captain Denson. He's old school and probably approaching retirement. A good skipper, but not very good with trainees. Best advice I can give is don't speak until you're spoken to, but don't let me put you off either. He's very fair, he's one of the few who lets you fly half of the sectors and his experience is massive."

Peter nodded before saying, "Would you like me to start the load sheet?"

"Yes please, but I'll fill in the boxes, as he'll recognise my writing. I'll give you a hand," and they both sat down and Peter began to input the numbers on a scrap of paper, completing the numbers on his calculator. When he'd finished, Ted checked it and told him that it was correct and he then completed the official form. Peter looked up to see a short grey-haired man approaching.

"Morning, Ted," he growled.

"Good morning, Sir," Ted responded and before he could introduce Peter the man said, "You must be the new trainee—correct?"

"Yes, Sir," Peter replied. The man shook his head, muttering "They're now sending me children to fly the bloody aeroplane," before he asked Peter his name.

"Peter Marham, Sir," Peter said. The Captain grunted, took the load sheet and walked away. Peter's heart sank. He found it exceptionally difficult to deal with people like this and he was now dreading the next eight hours.

Finally, the man reappeared saying, "I've done the fuel figures. How much shall we take boy?" he asked, looking directly at Peter.

"I estimated fifty-two tons, Sir," he said.

"Hmm not too bad—I've asked for fifty six." And with that he walked towards the briefing room. Ted and Peter quickly gathered their flight bags and overnight cases and almost ran after him. Inside the briefing area, they saw the sign for Toronto and a crew of eight girls were sitting around. The Captain strode over.

"Morning, Alice—anything I need to know?" he asked one of the women.

A lady in her forties stood up. "Just two with wheelchairs today, Sir," she said before sitting down. The Captain again just grunted a reply. Peter stood behind Ted, waiting for the ground to swallow him up. "We've got Ted flying us out today and we've also a new trainee, Peter, who will no doubt get to know you all in due course. Come on, let's get going," he said, striding towards the airside door.

Peter waited politely for the cabin crew to walk ahead of him. One young woman was quite a bit taller than the rest—at least six foot tall. In her early twenties with raven-coloured hair neatly pulled back into the regulation bun and with makeup expertly applied Peter noted. *Very nice too*, he thought as he followed her through the door and outside. She didn't speak at all and Peter sat on the opposite side of the bus as it drove them to the waiting aircraft.

In the flightdeck, Peter followed Ted through setting up the route and the Captain watched from his side of the cockpit, saying nothing. Peter could almost feel the disapproval seeping out of him. They were soon set up and Ted asked him to check everything, which he did without saying a word. Finally he grunted his approval before getting up and leaving the cockpit for a few moments. Peter said nothing, but looked at Ted trying to judge the mood.

"He'll be OK once we're aloft," he whispered. Peter seriously hoped so. Peter was soon lost in the flurry of activity on the flightdeck and it came as a relief at the Captain called for departure clearance and permission to push and start. They were soon rumbling down the taxiway and taking their place in the queue.

The Captain was silently drumming his fingers on the controls, obviously impatient to get off. Eventually, they swung onto the runway and Peter heard the take-off clearance from the tower. Ted called "Ready" and this was acknowledged—the first words the Captain had spoken since getting the clearance. Ted shoved the throttles forwards and the Captain again called out the speeds. In less than a minute, they were climbing away, airborne once more.

The first few minutes were busy, but Ted soon had the aircraft on course and he engaged the autopilot. The Captain nodded and turning to Peter asked, "How was that then lad? Enjoyable?"

Peter nodded his head saying, "Yes, Sir, very much."

"Good," came the reply. "Welcome to my personal office—my home-from-home." Peter smiled—the Captain seemed to be relaxing. They were soon at their cruising altitude and the Captain said, "Ted—move over and let the lad show us what he can do." Ted obligingly moved out of his seat and Peter slid behind the controls.

As soon as he settled down, the Captain began firing questions at him. "What's our magnetic heading?"

"Err two-eight-seven degrees, Sir."

"Good—and our altitude?"

"Thirty-seven thousand feet, Sir."

"What beacon are we using and what radial are we on?"

"We're on the Compton, Sir, tracking the two eighty radial."

Peter felt two eyes boring into his skull before the Captain said, "Excellent—somebody who can read the instruments. Right, lad, you sit there and monitor our progress and tell me if anything is wrong and keep me updated on the fuel burn."

"Yes, Sir," Peter said, relaxing a little.

Turning to Ted, he said, "Sorry if I was a little grumpy earlier—I hate early starts and all that faffing around on the ground. Good to be finally under way."

"I think we all hate early starts, Sir," Ted replied before turning to look out of the window. After an hour or so, the Captain pressed the crew call button and the tall dark-haired girl appeared. "You're new, aren't you?" he asked.

"Yes," she replied.

"What's your name?"

"Amanda."

"Well, Amanda—welcome on board and could I possibly trouble you for some coffee?"

"Yes, of course, Sir," she replied and she disappeared, shortly returning with three cups on a tray. She handed the Captain a cup, Ted took one off the tray and she turned to Peter, offering him a cup.

Peter took it and said, "Thanks," and she smiled, looking him directly in the eyes as she did so.

"You're welcome," she said softly. Peter found himself blushing, at which the Captain burst out laughing.

"I think she's got a soft spot for you, lad," he said, sipping his drink. Peter just shook his head. He was warming to this man and reasoned that Captains like him were still a valuable source of information and training.

Onward they flew, the morning sun following them westwards. The air at this altitude was smooth and although the wind outside was blowing straight towards them, they made good progress.

Eventually, in the far distance, Peter saw a dark line appear on the horizon. The Canadian coast. "Ahh at last—dry land," he Captain said. "Let's get the airfield information," he said, dialling a frequency into one of the radios. Instantly, Peter heard a recorded broadcast telling them what runway was in use and the wind and pressure setting. "Did you get all that?" he asked Peter.

Peter said that he had and he'd written it down as he'd been shown. "Good lad," came the Captain's reply. After another hour, Peter was told to change places with Ted and he reluctantly gave up his seat. *Only another week*, he thought to himself.

Shortly, Ted briefed the approach and selected the correct approach sheet, clipping it to his controls. They started to descend and Peter watched in fascination as they were vectored in towards the airport, finally making a long sweeping right turn. Peter instantly spotted the airport ahead, glistening in the sun. Down the approach they flew and in no time, they were rolling off the runway towards the terminal building. The engines were shut down and Peter removed his headphones, listening to the dying whine of the gyros.

"Welcome to Canada, lad," the Captain said, now cheerful and much more awake.

"Thank you," Peter replied, standing up and stretching. He watched intently as Ted deselected all the frequencies before he too stood up.

"It'll be good to stretch my legs," he said.

Peter nodded—"It sure will," he replied. Soon, they were through immigration and on their way to the hotel. As soon as they arrived, the Captain said, "I'll see you all down here at 6 o'clock local for a meal—I need some sleep," and he walked off towards the elevators. Peter soon opened his room door and immediately took off his uniform, hanging it carefully in the closet. He then went straight to the window to look outside. It was busy with traffic, but nowhere near as crazy as New York had been.

He dressed in his casuals, thinking of asking at reception if there was anywhere suitable for going for a run. Running down the stairs two at a time, he arrived breathlessly at the reception desk. Pausing to catch his breath, he asked about an area that may be what he needed. "There is a park two blocks straight up the street. It's about three miles around so that may be OK," the receptionist said.

Peter thanked her and turning around he saw Amanda approaching. "Hi," she said.

"Hello," Peter replied.

"You look nice," she said before adding, "I was going to go for a walk—would you like to join me?"

"Yes, that would be fun," Peter said at once. "There's a park just up the street—shall we head up that way?"

Amanda nodded and they set off together. They strolled up a broad avenue with tall buildings and trees lining the way. Eventually, they reached the park and they meandered around the pathways, arriving at a lake. Amanda found a bench and they sat down. "How long have you been with the airline?" she asked.

"It'll be two years in January," Peter replied. "What about you?"

"Just two months, so I'm fresh out of training," she said.

"Same as me then," Peter said, going on to explain whereabouts he was and that after his birthday he'd be flying properly. Amanda nodded and reaching up, she pulled hair grips from her hair and shook her head. Her hair tumbled down over her shoulders and stopped about halfway down her back.

"I hate having my hair scraped all the way back, but it's regulations," she said, closing her eyes and sniffing the late summer air. "Isn't this a beautiful place?" Peter agreed that it was and he asked her whereabouts was she from. "I live in South London with my mother," she explained.

"How about you?"

"I'm from a small town near the east coast called Westlea," Peter said, adding "I live there—or I did—with my parents. I have a brother in the army, but he's away in Cyprus right now. I'm currently staying in the trainee crew house near Heathrow, but that's about to change."

Amanda nodded slowly. "Isn't it amazing that we get to do a job where this morning we were in London and here we are in a park in Toronto?"

Peter chuckled. "It sure is—and I get to fly a modern jet—and we get paid on top of it all!"

Amanda laughed lightly and agreed. "What do we do this evening?" she asked.

"I'm guessing that we go out together for a meal and then go for drinks—that's what we did last week in new York," Peter said. "Trouble is, I don't drink and I was getting seriously teased about it. I'm just not really interested," he said.

Amanda smiled, saying, "I know what you mean. I don't drink either, although I'll occasionally have a small glass of wine. It just makes me feel fuzzy and un-coordinated."

"Yes, some of the girls last week were drinking like their lives depended on it—but I guess when somebody else is paying, that's what you'll end up doing."

Amanda nodded again and she got up saying, "Come on—let's walk around the lake."

Peter got to his feet and they strolled along together, hardly speaking but enjoying each other's company. Eventually, she broke the silence. "Do you like sports?"

Peter thought for a moment before replying, "I enjoy running and lifting weights to keep fit. In fact, I was asking the receptionist where I could go running and she told me about this place. I also cycle when I'm at home—there are some great roads nearby. What about you?"

"I like doing yoga and I also run—not seriously, but I love the adrenaline buzz I get. Do you bring your running gear with you?"

"I have done this time," Peter explained. "It's only my second trip so I'm still finding my feet."

"I may do the same next time," she said. They reached a low wall with three steps going across. Peter jumped to the top and he turned around and offered Amanda his hand, which she took. She paused on the top step, but held on to Peter's hand for a few moments before jumping down. Peter's head was instantly in a whirl. He'd looked into her silken dark brown eyes and noticed her nearly perfect skin. *What a stunner*, he thought quickly to himself.

They walked on, going all the way around the lake. They spotted geese, ducks, cormorants, moorhens and swans. Amanda stopped once more to take in the view. "Isn't this idyllic?" she asked.

Peter agreed and then glanced at his watch. "Jeeps—we need to be back by six and I distinctly got the impression that the skipper doesn't like being kept waiting."

"What time is it?" Amanda asked.

"Five-thirty," Peter said, adding, "and I need to go to my room and get my wallet, just in case."

They set off back at a brisk pace, arriving with five minutes to spare. Some of Amanda's colleagues were already waiting in reception. "Oh hello—I see you've stolen this hunk of a man already," one said and they all burst out laughing.

"No—not at all. We bumped into each other so went for a walk," Amanda explained.

"Oh really," said another of the girls. "I can see we're going to have to keep an eye on you," and they all laughed once again.

Peter ran up to his room, grabbed his wallet and ran back down, arriving just as the Captain was getting out of the lift. "Right," he said. "Everyone here?" He quickly counted heads. "Yep—where do you fancy to eat?" he asked.

"How about the steakhouse around the corner?" one of the girls suggested.

"If everybody's happy with that, then off we go" the Captain replied and they set off.

Once inside the restaurant, there was a scramble for seats and Peter found himself between Amanda and another girl, Pauline. Pauline was very chatty, asking Peter about himself, where he was from, what kind of things he liked. Peter politely answered most of her questions and there then came the question that Peter was finding almost repetitive, "Have you got a girlfriend?"

Peter smiled—what was this obsession with people and relationships? "No, I haven't," he said truthfully, adding, "And I'm hoping to complete my line training before I think about having one."

The Captain, who had been listening intently, said, "Stay away from girls, lad—they're nothing but trouble," and he let out a roar of laughter. Peter laughed and the girls immediately started attacking the Captain for his joke.

Peter did his best to settle down and relax and turning to Amanda he said, "This seems pretty normal behaviour for crews on lay over from what I've seen."

She smiled and said, "It's good for everyone to let their hair down and relax and I enjoy a bit of banter." Peter agreed and the waiter arrived to take their orders.

After the meal, the Captain suggested going back to the hotel bar for drinks. They were all soon Settled in large comfy chairs and the banter continued. "What in God's name are you drinking, lad?" The Captain called across to Peter.

"Orange juice, Sir," he replied.

The man snorted. "It's John—Sir or Captain whilst on duty, John off duty. Orange juice? Are you teetotal?"

"Yes," Peter replied. "I've never been a drinker and to be honest I don't like the smell or taste."

"I can see that we need to repair a gaping hole in your education at some point," he laughed, calling the waiter over and ordering another round. Peter smiled again—he was beginning to enjoy long-haul life.

Soon, he was engrossed in conversation with Amanda about their school days and they discovered that they had achieved almost identical exam results. They continued to talk about sport, flying and their families. Amanda said that her parents had divorced when she was young and had been bought up solely by her mother and that her dad had died two years before in an accident at work.

She asked Peter about his parents, his brother—which Peter glossed over—and life in a small town. They were so focused on each other that they didn't realise that John and most of the cabin crew had left and gone to bed. Ted was still chatting with one of Amanda's colleagues, surreptitiously holding hands beneath the table and Peter soon realised that it was late in the evening and about three am in his body clock.

"Time for bed for me I think," he said, stretching his legs and getting up. Amanda agreed and they walked towards the stairs together.

"What floor are you on?" she asked.

"The sixth," Peter replied.

"Same as me," she said, as they walked upstairs slowly. Finally, they turned down the corridor and Amanda stopped outside her room. "This is mine," she said.

"Next door to me—I'll try to not keep you awake," Peter joked.

She then took both of Peter's hands, kissed him lightly on the cheek and said, "Thanks for looking after me—see you at breakfast," and she turned and unlocked her door, quickly shutting it behind her.

Peter stood motionless for a few moments. "Wow" was all he could think.

After breakfast the following morning, a group of the crew decided that they wanted to explore, so they enquired with reception and were told where to wait for a bus into the city centre. Soon, Peter, Amanda, Ted and two others were on their way, chatting excitedly like small children on a school outing. They quickly arrived and began to explore.

Peter thought that it looked a bit like New York or London, but cleaner, quieter and the people were very friendly and helpful. They were soon in the shopping district and Amanda was looking at autumn fashion. Peter stood alongside, politely giving his opinion when asked and he did his best to not look too bored. Ted was doing the same with his companion Sandra.

Eventually, laden with bags, they all headed for coffee. They chose to sit outside as it was still warm enough and quiet. Amanda sat with Peter, not saying much, but obviously enjoying the sunshine and the experience. "This beats rainy, dirty, noisy Croydon," she said.

"Westlea is cleaner and quieter, but so dull," Peter said. "I find it amazing that some people spend their whole lives there."

Amanda nodded. "That's why I wanted to do this for a living—so I could travel to places like this and see lots of the world," she said.

"You'll certainly do that," Ted said. "I've flown to most continents, been all over the northern hemisphere and all in four years of flying. I want to go to the southern hemisphere next—mainly Australia and New Zealand."

"The Australia trip is so long," Sandra said, rolling her eyes. "London to Singapore. Lay over, then Singapore to Sydney or Perth. Three days usually in sweltering heat and then do it all again on the way home. Ten days away from home and it takes three to recover. The only upside is that you get ten days off between trips."

"Sounds like fun," Ted said before saying, "Shall we continue?"

They all nodded in agreement and decided to look around the old part of the city.

Peter bought another postcard and quickly wrote it to his mother. He'd decided that it might be a fun thing to do to send her one from each destination he went to. As they were strolling along, Peter felt Amanda's hand slip into his.

He turned to her and she just smiled. His heart did a few somersaults, but he kept quiet. As both Sandra and Ted had done this trip a few times before, they acted as tour guides, showing Amanda and Peter most of the tourist sights and finally, exhausted, they headed back towards the bus station and the hotel.

Peter wanted to freshen up and change, so he walked upstairs with Amanda, stopping outside her room. "What are we doing now?" she asked.

"I just want to freshen up and change for dinner," Peter said.

"Good idea," she replied and said, "well you can't get changed there."

Peter smiled and unlocked his door—and he felt her follow him inside, closing the door behind her. Peter's heart began to thump loudly in his chest. What was she doing?? He turned to her and she took his hands and said, "Do you like me?"

"Yes, I do," he replied quietly.

"Good," she said, sliding her arms around his neck and holding him tightly. He responded with firm pressure, allowing his hands to stroke her back. Finally she broke away, saying, "I think that you're really nice, but very shy," she said quietly. Peter said nothing, having just enjoyed her embrace. "I don't want you to think of me like some of the others," she said. "I know some of them can be very forward and I'm just not like that."

"I don't," Peter whispered. "You're somehow different."

"I am," she said, looking up at him. "I'm glad we've got that out of the way," and she kissed Peter lightly on the cheek. When they broke apart, Peter was breathless and clearly aroused. She stroked his chest saying "Let's leave this for later on shall we?" and she turned and walked towards the door, saying "See you downstairs in twenty minutes."

Peter let out a long breath. Wow—she was beautiful, educated and classy, unlike some of the others. Suddenly he panicked—he'd need to find some protection if things went any further. He quickly washed, changed and then ran downstairs to the rest room, where he'd seen a machine on the wall. Fumbling for change, he inserted coins into the slot, pushed a button and retrieved a packet from the chute at the bottom. He put this carefully in his wallet. *Something else for my trip bag*, he thought.

Dinner that evening was a fairly wild affair. They'd decided on an Italian restaurant and the wine was flowing freely. However, despite John and Ted's best efforts, Peter stuck to his soft drinks. "Can't make a proper airline jockey out of you if you don't drink," John said in an exasperated way.

Peter just smiled, held his glass up and said, "Cheers." John snorted and returned to the conversation he was having with one of the crew. Amanda sat quietly next to Peter, occasionally stroking his arm under the table and they joined in the conversation when they could.

Eventually, they made their way back to the hotel, with John leading the way, weaving across the pavement from side to side. "I hope he's OK for tomorrow," Peter whispered to Amanda, concerned.

"Well, if he's not, he can snooze in First Class and Ted and you can fly us home," she giggled. Peter smiled he was beginning to enjoy having her around.

After a final drink at the hotel, people began to disappear to bed. Ted and Sandra were first, too much amusement and heckling from the rest of the crew. Amanda and Peter waited until they were on their own before climbing the stairs. Stopping outside her room, she unlocked the door, saying, "You can come in for a short while, but I'm not ready for anything more just yet."

Peter nodded and followed her inside. She slipped her cardigan off and immediately turned to Peter, throwing her arms around his neck and kissing him deeply. Between kisses, she whispered "How old are you?"

"I'm eighteen next week," Peter replied, holding her tightly.

She nodded, slowly toying with the buttons on Peter's shirt. "OK—next week then," she said, stroking his chest and kissing him again. Finally she broke away, holding him loosely and said, "Will this be your first time?"

Peter paused—not wanting to appear naive or foolish before saying "Yes" quietly.

"I see," she whispered before kissing him again. She then let go, stood back and said, "Right, buddy—back to your room. We'll sort this out another time."

Peter kissed her quickly and let himself out, quickly going into his own room, where he undressed. He was excited and aroused, but terrified at the same time. What had she meant? Another time? When? He fell into bed and did his best to sleep, eventually dozing off.

The return flight was perfectly normal, with Peter again allowed into the right-hand seat for most of the Atlantic crossing. After landing and leaving the aircraft, he caught up with Amanda in the arrivals area, getting her phone number. He promised to ring the next day and kissed her quickly before dashing off. He was soon back in the crew house, where he found a note from Sanj.

Opening it, he read, "May have found a two bed flat—I'll catch up with you on Monday."

He smiled, carefully refolding the note and putting it in his flight bag. He was looking forward to the weekend and maybe meeting up with Amanda.

42

As soon as Amanda arrived home, her mother came rushing out to meet her. "Hello, darling," she cried. "How was your trip?"

"Oh, mum, it was amazing," she said, so excited to tell her mother everything. "The flight was busy and we hardly had time to rest between services and being a long flight, we were serving meals and drinks most of the time. Once we got to the hotel, I met one of the pilots—oh, mum, he's gorgeous," she said. "He's only young, still in training, but what a hunk! About six foot four, muscular, very shy and so good looking.

"Anyway, we went for a walk around a park and sat in the sunshine for ages. The next day some of us went looking around—Toronto is such a beautiful city and the people are lovely. We did some shopping, had coffee and just enjoyed ourselves. In the evening, we all went to a restaurant and what a riot! I'd heard stories of wild times and room parties, but everyone was so funny and Peter— the pilot—just sat and watched everything going on. I'm hoping he's going to call me—I gave him our number."

Her mother, who was very liberal and a fully-paid up member of the permissive society, smiled saying, "I'm so glad you had a good time. I was so worried about it being your first time abroad and I'm pleased that your colleagues looked after you. If this young man is so good looking, you'll have to bring him round to meet me," she said, stroking her waist and thighs, laughing.

"Mother!" exclaimed Amanda. "You're too late—he's mine, all mine," she said with a giggle.

This made Amanda's mother raise an eyebrow. "Have you been to bed with him?" she asked coyly.

"No, not yet," Amanda replied, adding, "But it's his birthday this week, so who knows, he may get a very special present," and she winked at her mother before collapsing into a chair.

Peter stayed in London for the next few days and he rang Amanda the next day as promised. She was pleased to hear from him and once he'd got over his initial nerves, he was able to hold a normal conversation. It happened that their rosters coincided for the following Wednesday Chicago flight and Peter was due at the Civil Aviation offices the day before to collect his licence, so they looked forward to seeing each other again.

On Monday, Sanj was back from home, prior to a four-sector day on Tuesday and he bought with him details of the flat just three miles from the airport. It had two bedrooms, a lounge, bathroom with shower and a kitchen. Ideal for what they wanted. He'd been to see it over the weekend with his parents and was full of enthusiasm for it. The rent was about the same as the deductions from Peter's salary for the crew house and he'd now be earning flight pay, so he'd be far better off.

Tuesday morning, after speaking to Annie on the phone and opening his birthday card, he got ready for the trip to the Civil Aviation offices. The airline had made him an appointment for midday and he was outside by eleven-thirty. Eventually, he went in and spoke to the receptionist. "Ahh yes, please take a seat," she said.

A few moments a man appeared, asking Peter his name. "I'm Mr Adams. Please follow me," he said, returning the way he'd come. Peter was led to a desk and asked to sit down. "Do you have your passport please?" the man asked. Peter pulled it from his jacket pocket and handed it over. Mr Adams opened it and looked at Peter. "Perfect—thank you," he said returning it and opening a drawer.

He pulled out a sheaf of papers, each set marked with a yellow card. Leafing through, he pulled out a set, checking the name. Clipped to the papers was a small blue booklet, which he opened, checked and handed to Peter. "There we are young man—your Commercial Licence. Congratulations."

Peter opened the booklet—there was a sheet of paper at the front with his name on and underneath was the title "Commercial Pilot's Licence" A huge wave of relief swept over him. Finally he had it in his hand. He stood up, pocketing the licence and his passport, shook the man's hand, thanking him and he was shown out to the front door. *That was painless*, he thought before walking to the tube station to return to the Airline offices.

After getting his licence checked at the main office, Peter returned home, immediately ringing Amanda. After saying hello, he said simply, "I've got it."

"Happy birthday—got what?" she said.

"Thank you. My licence—I'm official," he said excitedly. "Ahh, of course—congratulations. I'm so pleased for you," Amanda said. "Does that mean you'll be flying us tomorrow?"

"I hope so" Peter said, "But it depends on the skipper. I now have to do about forty sectors before I'm released to fly without another FO on the jump seat."

"I still have to do ten trips before I'm signed off," Amanda said, "but I'm hopeful that it won't take too long." After chatting for a while and arranging to meet in the crew room, Peter dialled his home number.

"Hi, mum," he began, "I've been to the aviation offices and I've got it in my hand."

"Oh, Peter, well done," she replied. "Your dad and I are so proud of what you've achieved. So proud. When are you next home?"

"I'm flying to Chicago tomorrow, so will be back on Friday, but it'll be late, so I'll probably come home on Saturday morning," he said.

"Who are you flying with tomorrow?" she asked. "It's my first sector so I'll be with Fozzy according to my roster," he replied. He knew that this would satisfy his mother, as she felt like that she knew Fozzy through Paul. She wished him happy birthday once more and finished with "Safe flight—love you."

"Thanks—love you too, mum," he said, replacing the receiver.

Upstairs in his room, he carefully prepared for the trip. Making sure his licence and passport were in his flight bag, he packed his overnight bag, but also included a jumper and a jacket. Chicago's reputation as "The windy city" was well known amongst the crews and he'd been warned. He was beyond excited, yet full of apprehension at the thought of handling the aircraft for the first time with passengers on board. He know that Fozzy would look after him, as he seemed to have done so far.

He was up as soon as his alarm had shaken him awake and he quickly got ready. Satisfied, he decided to set off a little earlier to make sure he had enough time in flight planning to make amends for any errors he made. He soon arrived and went straight to the weather information, looking at the swirls and lines on the chart. It was looking stormy over the northern tracks, so he'd need to get a more southerly routing if required.

He was shortly joined by Ted, who was going to be his jump seat FO. Peter was relieved as he'd been apprehensive that he'd be with a stranger and didn't want to make a complete fool of himself. They sat down together with Ted checking his figures and they were finally joined by Fozzy. "Ahh young Marham—your first trip in the hot seat eh? Ready for some fun?"

"Yes, Sir," Peter replied nervously.

"Jolly good—we shall see what we shall see," Fozzy replied enigmatically before taking the load sheet and wandering off. He shortly returned, asking Peter for his fuel calculations.

"I've estimated seventy-two tons," Peter said.

Fozzy nodded. "I thought about the same," he said before getting up and saying, "Come on, let's go and meet the ladies." The three of them went through into Briefing and Peter spotted Amanda with her colleagues sitting around a table. Fozzy strode across and made his usual greeting of "Good morning. Anything of note?"

An older lady looked up and replied, "No, not today. About three quarters full so hopefully an easy ride."

"Good," Fozzy replied, adding, "It's looking a bit stormy to the North, so we may have to get a more southerly track if needs be. Stand by with the sick bags," he laughed and invited the cabin crew to join him on the aircraft.

Once on board, Peter went straight to the right-hand seat, taking the frequencies book and began to set his systems up. With Ted watching over him, he took his time, aware that trying to rush things was a precursor to trouble. Finally he finished and asked Fozzy to check everything. Fozzy announced that he was satisfied and then called the cabin crew to see if all the passengers were on board.

"Another five minutes," the supervisor Pauline said. Fozzy nodded, saying "Let me know."

Within a few minutes, the doors were closed and Fozzy was on the radio asking for departure clearance and pushback. As they were pushed slowly backwards, Fozzy said, "I do believe there are some people waving at you on the observation deck, old boy," Peter looked up at the top of the building—there were his parents, both waving enthusiastically. What a lovely surprise. Peter waved back before getting back to the job in hand.

Peter took the checklist and opened it at the "Engine start" page. As soon as the tug driver said that the towbar had been detached, Fozzy called for engine start and Peter read through the items, bringing all four engines on line. Another quick wave and they were soon gliding their way down the taxiway towards the runway. Bringing the aircraft to a halt, Fozzy said, "Right—take-off brief please,

Peter," and Peter went through his **pre-prepared** brief, hopefully covering all eventualities.

"OK—jolly good," Fozzy said, **finally steering** the aircraft on to the runway. Ahead of Peter was a long ribbon of **black, some** two miles in length. Beyond that—infinity. Peter checked everything for the millionth time and announced that he was ready. "OK—off we go," Fozzy said and Peter advanced the throttles. Using his feet on the rudder pedals **to stay straight**, they were soon at take-off speed and Peter pulled back on the **controls**.

The nose slowly came up and Peter **re-checked** his speed. Perfect. She hadn't felt as heavy as this during base training. "**Positive** rate of climb," Fozzy called and Peter replied, "Gear up." They **were airborne**. He was flying a passenger jet, with passengers, out of one of the **world's busiest** airports. He couldn't resist a smile as he concentrated furiously on **the instruments** before him.

Finally, he engaged the autopilot **and slowly released** his grip on the controls. "Well done—nice take-off," Fozzy **said, adding**, "Remember scant knowledge can be a deadly friend. In this **business we play** for keeps." Peter nodded, thinking, *Right—in that case, let's get about Fozzy's business*.

The flight passed uneventfully **until mid-way** across the ocean. Ahead of them they saw the storm system, **dark, ugly and** dangerous, the thunderclouds rising like huge black gothic spires **reaching to** the heavens, with turrets and ramparts rolling and tumbling—an **invitation for** fools and the unwary. Fozzy immediately asked for a turn away to **the left by** twenty degrees to avoid it. "Turn left twenty degrees and establish on **track six whisky**," came the response.

Peter turned the heading knob on **the autopilot** and the aircraft immediately rolled in accordance with his commands. **Fozzy flicked** on the "Fasten Seal Belt" signs, just in case. The air became **bumpy, but not** uncomfortable and within an hour they were past it and flying **smoothly once** more. They were soon inside American airspace and after an hour **or so, were reaching** the top of descent point.

Peter pulled his seatbelts on and **opened the** instrument book, selecting the correct approach plates before **giving his** briefing. Fozzy just nodded his agreement and as they descended, **Peter was kept** busy being vectored towards the runway. Eventually the airport **came into view** and Peter deselected the autopilot. *Here we go—the biggest test so far*, he thought to himself. He heard their landing clearance, called for **flaps and landing** gear and kept a close eye on the instruments, never letting the needles **wander**.

Unseen by Peter, Fozzy slowly slid his hands along his thighs until they were millimetres from the controls, just in case. The airport fence slid beneath the nose and Peter raised the nose, closing the throttles and waited. Finally, a bump announced that the main gear had landed and he slowly lowered the nosewheel. The auto brakes came on and the aircraft slowed. As they reached the runway exit, Fozzy said, "I have control," and Peter released his grip. He'd done it—relief washed over him.

"Nice landing, old boy—well done," Fozzy said.

"Thanks," Peter said, letting out a very long breath. Fozzy expertly parked the aircraft on stand, shutting the engines down and turning to Peter. "Well—how was that?" he asked.

"OK, I hope," Peter replied, wary of appearing too confident.

"Well, I'm very happy with that performance," Fozzy said, getting out of his seat and slapping Peter on the back. Peter allowed himself a smile of self-congratulation. He knew that sterner tests were yet to come as the winter approached and gave them the back of its hand, but for now he was content.

Once checked in at the hotel, Peter unlocked his door, immediately removing his uniform, which he carefully hung in the closet and he collapsed on the bed. Slowly the tension eased from his muscles and as it was still only mid-afternoon local time, he thought to himself about going for a run to unwind. Pulling his tracksuit on, he was about to leave his room when the phone rang. He picked it up tentatively, saying "Hello?"

"Hi—it's Amanda," said the voice on the other end.

"Oh, hi, I was just thinking of going for a run. Fancy joining me?" he asked.

"Mmm OK—I'll meet you downstairs in five minutes," she said and the receiver went dead. Peter waited anxiously in the lobby and Amanda shortly appeared in a grey tracksuit. "Come on then—I'll race you," she laughed.

"Err—where shall we go?" Peter asked.

"Oh, I don't know—let's just follow our noses," she said playfully, setting off. Soon, they were pounding along, chatting breathlessly. "Did you fly us over?" she asked.

"Yes—was it OK?" Peter replied.

"Yes, it was fine—I just wondered," she said, speeding up.

Round the city blocks they ran and after about thirty minutes Amanda flopped down onto a wooden bench, catching her breath. Peter sat down beside her. "You OK?" he asked. She just nodded and squeezed his hand. He smiled and tried to relax.

"Did you have a nice birthday yesterday?" she asked.

"Well—yes and no. A bit of a non-event as I was on my own but a great day as I got my Commercial licence," Peter replied.

She smiled and leaned across, kissing him full on the lips. "Well, that's from me—happy birthday for yesterday," she said.

"Thank you," Peter whispered.

"Now, where in heaven's name are we and how do we get back?" she asked.

"Let's just reverse our route," Peter suggested and jumping up, he set off at a furious pace. She quickly caught up and they were soon back at the hotel. Stumbling breathlessly into the lobby, Amanda almost crashed into Fozzy, who was holding a cup of coffee and reading a notice on the wall.

"Oops, sorry," she said blushing.

Fozzy looked at the pair of them, smiled and said, "Not my sort of exercise, but whatever floats your boat."

Amanda smiled and asked what time they were meeting for dinner. "Oh I don't know—how about 6 o'clock local?" Fozzy suggested.

"Perfect—gives me time for a shower," Peter said and they ran upstairs together. Amanda was staying one floor above Peter, so she ran up the extra flight of stairs shouting, "See you at Six."

Peter was downstairs earlier than planned and he looked through and purchased the now obligatory postcard for his mother. Scribbling the usual "Hi mum" on the back, he wrote the address carefully before handing it to the receptionist.

"Where can I pay for postage?" he asked.

"It comes postage-paid," the lady answered, taking it from him. "It'll go out this evening," she added with a smile. Peter thanked her and went to join his colleagues waiting for the skipper.

Shortly, Fozzy strode into the lobby and in his usual military way asked, "Who likes French food?"

Nobody protested, so he marched them all out of the hotel to a restaurant a few blocks away. After a quiet discussion with the Maître, they were asked to wait whilst tables were rearranged and finally they took their seats. Ted found a seat amongst some of the younger women and Fozzy took up his customary position at the head of the table.

Drinks were ordered and served and after taking a large gulp of wine, Fozzy cleared his throat and said, "Right, you lot. I'll be keeping an eye on your behaviour this evening. Anybody not behaving badly will be forced to undertake a penance. Anybody staying in the shadows or keeping themselves to themselves will also be punished by being made to recite Homer's "Odyssey" whilst standing on one leg. Good behaviour will NOT be tolerated. Have I made myself clear?"

"Yes, skipper," came a loud chorus of voices.

"Jolly good—let the mischief commence," Fozzy said laughing.

Amanda squeezed Peter's hand, saying, "I think he means you."

"I don't know, Homer," Peter said seriously before Amanda burst out laughing, punching him playfully.

"Silly boy—time to let your hair down," she said. Peter smiled—she was right, although he stuck to his orange juice and Amanda drank soda all evening. Peter experimented with the food and found that he was very much a fan of French cuisine. He loved the various sauces which accompanied the courses and by the time it came to the dessert, he was stuffed.

By this time, Ted was regaling them with tales of his days at boarding school and he had the girls in stitches with his brazen and youthful exploits. Fozzy then joined in, telling tales of his time in the fighter squadron in the war, living each day as though it would be his last, of flying and fighting and of getting uproariously drunk every evening, of chasing the local girls and generally having a wild time. Peter listened intently, his admiration for the man going up tenfold.

After dinner, people began to make their excuses and disappear back to the hotel as their body clocks dictated. "Shall we go for a stroll?" Amanda asked. Peter quickly nodded and they walked outside. It was a clear night with a bright half-moon, but it was chilly. Amanda took Peter's arm and snuggled up to him. They strolled along the Chicago River loop, listening to the sounds of the city. "I love all this," she said quietly.

"Mmm, so do I—it's what I've worked towards all my life," Peter replied.

They sat down on a bench next to the river. "Would you like to see me at home?" Amanda asked tentatively.

"Yes, I would—very much so," Peter replied. "I'd love to get to know you a whole lot better."

Amanda smiled at him. "Oh, I'm sure we can arrange that," she whispered.

Peter's stomach somersaulted. Did she mean what he thought she'd meant? *Time will tell*, he thought to himself. Finally she yawned, saying, "Sorry—but I really need to get some sleep."

"So do I," he replied and they made their way back to the hotel before kissing goodnight. Peter was asleep in an instant.

43

Peter went down for breakfast early—he'd woken at some ungodly hour, but with his body clock still in UK time, he'd enjoyed a full night's sleep. To his surprise, he found most of the crew sitting at tables enjoying their morning coffee and he spotted Fozzy at the buffet, loading his plate. Peter joined his colleagues, getting his coffee and food and enjoying their company.

Amanda shortly appeared, joining Peter and her friends and they began to discuss plans for the day. "I'd like to see the city centre," Amanda said, looking at Peter.

"Fine with me," he said, adding, "I spotted a camera shop yesterday whilst we were out running and I'd like to go there if that's OK."

Amanda nodded and one of the others said, "As long as it's near some other shops that's fine with me." Eventually, they arranged to meet after breakfast as the shops weren't yet open.

As soon as they all met up in the lobby, they headed out into the autumn sunshine. They walked—with directions from the hotel staff—towards the city, enjoying the views and the place coming to life. Onwards they strolled and finally Peter found the shop he was looking for. "I may be some time," he said to Amanda.

"No problem," she replied. "We'll wait in that coffee shop just down the road there," and she pointed towards a sign advertising "The finest coffee in Chicago".

Peter nodded and went into the shop. "Hi," said a man behind the counter.

"Oh, hello," Peter replied before going on, "I'm looking for an entry-level SLR camera which I can change lenses on. I've been looking at Nikon and Pentax. What can you advise?"

The man thought for a moment before asking, "How much do you want to spend?"

"Up to a hundred dollars," Peter replied.

"Well, for that we can do a Nikon camera and with this particular one we're doing a special—get a second lens half price," he said, taking a camera out of the display case behind him and handing it to Peter. "It has through-the-lens metering so doesn't need an exposure meter and it takes any lens in the Nikon range," he said.

Peter held it up to his eye turning the lens to bring the shop into focus. He then started asking all the questions that his magazine had suggested and tried to haggle the price down. "Tell you what," the salesman said, "Take the second lens at half price and I'll throw in a leather case for free."

Peter thought for a moment before saying "Done" and shaking the man's hand. He carefully counted out ninety-five dollars and left the shop with a large bag containing his booty. He was pleased with himself, as the same camera in the UK was over one hundred pounds and with the exchange rate, he'd just paid fifty pounds.

He walked briskly to the coffee shop where he found Amanda, Ted and the girls. "I see you bought something," Amanda said.

"Yes, I've bought a camera," Peter explained. "No point visiting these amazing places and seeing the world from seven miles up and not keeping memories."

"Absolutely," she agreed, saying, "C'mon, let's get going. I'm dying to explore." Back out into the sunshine they went and she slipped her hand into Peter's as they strolled along, much to the amusement of the others.

Lunchtime came and went, with the group enjoying an al fresco meal at a large diner and then it was back to the matter in hand. Amanda bought some autumn clothing and a present for her mother and finally Ted pleaded to be allowed to take them back to the hotel. "My feet are killing me and I need a beer," he said in an exasperated fashion.

Eventually they arrived back and found Fozzy—as usual—reading the paper. "Ahh—returning travellers," he exclaimed. "I trust all is well with my crew and that you're now all skint?"

"Peter is," Ted said. "He's been buying expensive toys."

"Oh really—what have you been buying, young Marham?" Fozzy enquired.

"I bought a camera, a second lens and a case," Peter explained.

"Oh good man," Fozzy said. "Should have done the same years ago I suppose, but somehow never got round it. Anyway, I thought we'd eat here this evening if that's OK, chaps?" he asked, not really caring about the answer. There

334

was a general nodding of heads and he jumped up saying, "Shall we say meet at seven?" Again, heads were nodded and Peter and Amanda walked back up the stairs.

"I'll see you back downstairs," she said, kissing him quickly and with that, she vanished.

Sitting down and glancing at the menu, Peter was somehow disinterested in food. His mind was preoccupied with Amanda and he was beginning to wonder how he could persuade her to stay in his room overnight, but he just had no idea of how to go about it. As it turned out, he needn't have worried. After another fairly crazy evening, which left Peter wondering if all lay overs were like this and if all crews acted the same, people started to drift off to their rooms.

Amanda took Peter by the hand and they walked slowly upstairs and when Peter turned towards his room, she tugged at his hand, saying, "Oh no, you don't—you're coming with me," and they climbed a further flight of stairs, arriving at her room. Peter's heart was pounding in his chest—he had an idea of what was happening, but began to feel his usual panic. Amanda put her fingers across her lips to indicate for Peter to be quiet and she unlocked the door, pulling him inside. She immediately put her arms around his neck and kissed him long and hard.

Eventually, Peter broke free and she turned away, saying, "I got you something for your birthday."

Bemused, Peter asked what it was. She turned to face him—Peter saw that she'd undone all the buttons on her blouse and that her ample cleavage was clearly visible nestling within her bra. "It's me," she whispered pulling him close and kissing him again. She took his hand and placed it on her breast and Peter squeezed gently. "That's the idea," she whispered and she began to unbutton Peter's shirt, pulling it quickly from his body. She took her blouse off and stood back. "Like what you see?" she asked.

"Oh, yes," Peter replied. He was so anxious but eager—he'd never seen a woman's body before and he was excited and aroused. Slowly, Amanda undressed them both and she led Peter to the bed, pulling him down beside her. "Just relax," she said softly. Over the next couple of hours, Amanda showed Peter what to do and they made love slowly and carefully, finally collapsing together, wrapped around each other, breathless and sweaty. Peter finally found his voice.

"That was the most amazing thing that's ever happened to me," he said quietly.

"Me too," Amanda replied, adding, "You're such a big man—in every department. That was wonderful."

Peter wrapped his arms around her a little tighter—"I never thought I'd find someone like you," he said, kissing her again.

"I didn't think I'd find someone like you. You're different from the other guys—even older skippers like Fozzy are still after one-night stands, yet you're not. You seem so private, so wrapped up in your own world, but you're a wonderful warm human being," she said. Peter lay quietly, stroking her beautiful soft smooth skin and eventually they drifted off to sleep together, curled up tightly.

Peter woke once during the night and he lay still listening to Amanda's soft, regular breathing. Not wanting to disturb her, he didn't move or change position and he slowly went back to sleep. In no time, the morning sun was playing through the curtains and Amanda started to wake.

Opening her eyes, she looked at Peter before saying, "Good morning, lover."

Peter replied with "Good morning gorgeous" and they kissed and cuddled for the next thirty minutes before Peter noticed the time. "Hell—it's breakfast in ten minutes and then I've got to get into the tech manual for the flight home," he said, leaping out of bed.

"No problem—you'd best get back to your own room," Amanda said, getting out of bed and walking past him, totally naked. Peter couldn't take his eyes off her.

"Err—yes, OK, I guess so," he mumbled before pulling his clothes on and making for the door. "See you downstairs," he said and she stood in front of him and said, "Don't I get a kiss?"

Peter immediately put his arms around her, kissing her deeply and said, "Sorry, but got to rush."

"I'm only teasing," she laughed. "Off you go," and Peter shot downstairs, diving into the shower and then shaving as quickly as he dared. Once downstairs, Fozzy was onto the business of the day.

"You fly us back, as it'll be good practice and I'll play monitoring pilot," he said to Peter, who nodded his agreement between mouthfuls. "We've a couple of hours until the crew bus arrives, so if you've any questions or queries, now's the time," Fozzy said.

"I think I'm OK—I just need to read the tech manual again for the return flight," Peter said and Fozzy nodded.

The bus arrived in good time and there was the usual flurry of activity at the airport, with Peter and Ted getting the weather information and the passenger and cargo details and Peter began to do his calculations, finally arriving at a figure which Fozzy seemed happy with. From the flight planning room they could see the aircraft land and taxy in. It was so graceful and Peter silently compared it to Amanda's beautiful body—so long, so sleek and elegant.

Finally, they took over from the inbound crew and Peter began his preparations. They were soon starting engines and taxiing towards the departure runway. Fozzy turned to him and smiled, saying, "After last night I hope you've got the energy to fly us home," and he let out a huge guffaw. Peter blushed furiously but said nothing and they were soon climbing into the early afternoon sky.

On this leg, Fozzy began to question Peter more about the aircraft, it's systems and performance. He seemed satisfied with Peter's answers and they flew along towards dusk with Peter enjoying the commanding view. This would be his first night landing in the jet and he was looking forward to it. As they crossed the English coast, Fozzy dialled up the information broadcast for Heathrow and Peter did not like what he heard. Fozzy looked across at him saying, "You're going to earn your pay tonight, lad. Two hundred meters in fog. This is going to be fun. If you're getting outside your comfort zone, say so and I'll take over."

Peter got the appropriate approach plate and clipped it to his control column and as they started the descent, he asked Fozzy to turn the cockpit lights all the way down to improve his night vision. He could see nothing outside and was flying purely on instruments. Following the vectors from Air Traffic control, Peter finally positioned the aircraft towards final approach. Watching his instruments carefully, he saw the needle that gave him the runway centreline begin to twitch, then move inwards.

Instantly he turned the big aircraft capturing the runway heading. Forcing himself to ignore everything else, he was fixed to the instruments. Slowly the horizontal needle showing the glideslope began to move downwards and Peter waited until the two needles made a cross, like the crosshairs in a rifle scope. Reducing the power, he felt the trim wheel next to his left thigh move to compensate and he called for flap then landing gear. Lower and lower they came with Fozzy calling out the heights and distance from the threshold.

"Concentrate, concentrate. Localizer, glideslope, speed" was all that Peter was thinking. Finally, Fozzy called "Minimums" and Peter looked up. He could just make out the runway lights in the gloom ahead. "Visual—landing," he replied and bought the aircraft down for a smooth landing. There was silence as they slowed to a near stop and then Fozzy took over and taxied the aircraft towards the terminal gate, finally applying the parking brake and shutting the engines down.

Peter let out a long breath. "Jeez, that was—interesting," he said, finally regaining his composure.

Fozzy laughed out loud. "It certainly was. I was watching you focused on the instruments. Very good approach and landing. Another twenty feet of fog and we'd now be flying to our alternate. Well done, lad," he said.

"Thanks, boss," Peter replied, adding, "and thanks for everything."

Fozzy stood up slowly—in the dim lights of the flight deck he looked suddenly weary, like the oldest professional in the world. "As I said before, in this business, we play for keeps. I think we might just make a pilot out of you yet," and he squeezed Peter's shoulder gently before pulling on his jacket.

Peter met up with Amanda in the cabin and they joined the crew to walk through immigration and they then left the crew and stood for a while talking. "Shell we see each other tomorrow?" Amanda asked, holding Peter's hand.

"Yes please, I'd love that," he said before remembering that he was due to go home for the weekend. "I'll speak to my mother in the morning and then ring you—is that OK," he asked.

Amanda nodded her head, gave him a quick kiss and ran towards where her taxi would be waiting. Peter walked out into the dank, dark night and wandered slowly back to the crew house. He was exhausted, but elated.

44

Peter rang his parents late on Saturday morning, arranging to be home the day after. Trembling with anticipation, he then dialled Amanda's number. After his initial nerves, they were soon chatting away quite happily and Amanda said, "Would you like to come over today? I'm not rostered again until Monday for an early New York, so we could spend the day together."

Peter immediately agreed, scribbling her address quickly in his diary and asking about the tube and buses. He was soon on his way, enjoying the late September sun as the bus rolled and creaked it's way along. He's asked the conductor to put him off at the right stop and as he jumped down, he saw Amanda waiting with a big smile. He strode over quickly, grasping her around the waist and kissing her.

"You sleep OK?" she asked.

"Yes—like a top, thanks. After the fog last night I was exhausted."

"I bet," she said, continuing, "come on—it's just around the corner. My mum is in if that's OK, but she goes out dancing on Saturday afternoon, so we'll have the house to ourselves."

Peter felt the usual chill of dread at meeting someone new, but he hoped that he'd have to get used to seeing Amanda's mother. They were soon inside the small terraced house, which was clean, bright and decorated in a bohemian style. Looking around, Peter liked what he saw. "We're here," Amanda called out and from afar, Peter heard a voice. Very quickly Amanda's mother appeared—about the same height as Amanda, with dark hair tied with a blue ribbon and dressed in jeans and a shirt.

Extending her hand she said, "Hi—I'm Annabel."

"Hi—Peter," Peter replied, sitting down next to Amanda.

"Gosh Amanda, you said he was tall and muscular, but you've under-sold him," Annabel laughed, adding, "If you don't want him, can I have him?"

"Mother," Amanda admonished. "You'll have to forgive her, she's a bit daft," she said to Peter, who was blushing quietly.

"So, tell me a bit about yourself then," Annabel said, settling back in the chair.

"Not much to tell really," Peter replied. "I'm a junior pilot with the airline, my parents live in a little town near the East Coast called Westlea. Mum's a receptionist and secretary at the local GP's surgery and Dad's an engineer. I have a brother in the army—and that's about it," he said, running out of things to say.

Annabel nodded, looking at him carefully. "I guess that flying is your career then?" she asked and Peter nodded. "Is it a good job?" she enquired.

"Yes—and great fun as well. I'm still in training, but the prospects are good and the whole world wants to travel these days, so it should be a job for life," he said.

"Indeed," Annabel said. "I'm hoping to use some of Amanda's staff discount to go places. I love travelling and flying seems so much more agreeable than traipsing around in an old camper van, don't you agree? What about you two then? Are you serious?"

"I think so," Amanda said, looking at Peter, who nodded his agreement.

"Good. I just needed to see if you were a suitable suitor for my girl," Annabel laughed and Amanda sighed.

"Mother—please."

"Sorry, just kidding, but you're my only and I need to know that you're going to be OK," she said.

Amanda shook her head, saying, "Will you ever grow up?"

"Nope—I intend to grow old disgracefully," Annabel laughed before glancing at the clock on the wall. "Gotta run—my feet need some dancing," she said, jumping up. "Lovely to meet you, Peter—I'm sure we'll meet again," she said.

"I hope so," Peter replied and she shot out of the room, calling "Bye" before slamming the front door. Amanda let out a huge sigh of relief.

"Sorry about that," she began, but Peter held his hand up, saying, "Not a problem. She certainly seems full of life and quite a character."

"You can say that again," Amanda replied, standing up and taking Peter's hand. "Come on," she said, leading him up the stairs. He was instantly back in the Chicago hotel room, trembling with anticipation.

Amanda's bedroom was decorated tastefully, with a double bed and windows which looked over the back gardens. She spun Peter around, pushing him backwards onto the bed and pounced on top of him. They were soon lost in their lovemaking, with clothes being torn from bodies and the urgency of the afternoon driving them onwards. As soon as they were both naked, Peter pushed Amanda off and she lay down beside him.

He turned to admire her body, saying, "You are stunning—just beautiful," his eyes greedily taking in the view.

She smiled and replied, "and you're such a big muscular guy—a perfect specimen," and closing her mouth over his, she kissed him for a long time.

Afterwards, they lay in almost total silence, holding each other tightly and listening to the sounds of the afternoon. Peter finally asked what time Annabel would be home, but Amanda said that they still had a couple of hours on their own. This prompted Peter to begin kissing and stroking her again and before they knew it, they were making love once more, this time with Amanda taking the lead.

After they had finished, Peter said, "You're going to wear me out at this rate."

She laughed, saying, "Well, it's more fun than going out for a run," and Peter was forced to agree. They lay for what seemed like hours, talking and laughing and never letting go of each other. Finally, Amanda said, "OK—Mum will be home soon, so I guess we'd better get dressed."

Peter nodded and following Amanda to the bathroom, he washed and returned to the bedroom to get dressed. Soon, they were back downstairs. "What are you doing tomorrow?" she asked.

"Going home for a couple of days to see my folks," Peter said.

She nodded and then asked, "Does this mean we're a couple? I don't relish the prospect of this just being another airline romance—you know, just crew sex like a lot of the girls and pilots."

"I'd like it to be serious," Peter replied. "I'm not into being propositioned by cabin crew who are only after one thing. Not my scene at all and I really like you a lot. I'll be a good boy on lay overs I promise," he said, laughing.

"So will I," Amanda replied, squeezing his hand.

"Good," Peter said quietly. "One of my school friends ended up going out with a girl I'd been seeing. She'd wanted to have sex but I never wanted it with her and I thought she'd be a hinderance to my flight training. Anyway, my buddy

Liam, who was desperate for a girlfriend who'd do it went out with her and ended up making her pregnant—at seventeen. He's in a real jam now, poor lad and so is she."

Amanda shook her head. "I've only ever had one boyfriend and we never really got around to having full sex, so you're really my first," she said, adding, "and I'm yours—right?"

"Yep—the one and only," Peter said smiling at her.

"Good," she said, almost in a whisper, before perking up and asking, "Are you hungry?"

"Starving," Peter replied.

"There's a little Italian place near here—fancy it?" she asked and Peter nodded vigorously. "Good—I'll get our jackets," she said, scribbling a note for her mother and they were soon strolling along in the cool autumn air. Peter had never felt as happy and content as he did right now.

Peter called Amanda the following morning and after a lengthy phone call, he rushed for the train. He was soon back home answering all of Annie's questions about his latest trip. "It was lovely seeing you in the cockpit at the airport. Did you see us?"

"Yes—thanks for coming. It was a lovely surprise," Peter replied.

"Was it you that did the take off?" Annie continued, obviously excited.

"Yes, mum, it was me."

"Amazing. Thank you for the postcards you've been sending," she said. "It's lovely knowing what you're up to and I like to show them to the people at the surgery."

Peter smiled, saying that it was no problem. He enjoyed keeping his parents informed of his movements they'd been so key to keeping him safe when he was younger. He'd bought his new camera to show Paul and the two of the sat discussing it and photography in general. Paul turned it over in his hands, saying "This is a well-engineered piece of kit. Have you taken any pictures yet?"

"No, but I will do before my next flight," Peter replied. He wanted to get comfortable with it to lessen any expensive mistakes or missed opportunities.

Before long, Annie called them in for dinner and she continued her interrogation. "Have you met anyone nice on your trips?" she asked innocently, an inquisitive look in her eyes.

Immediately, Peter knew what she was asking, so decided to play her along. "Yes—lots of people," he said.

Paul looked at him carefully, the faintest hint of a smile playing over his face. "Oh, anyone in particular?" Annie went on.

"Well, there's my training captains, who have been great and the FO's have all been brilliant," Peter replied. He was beginning to enjoy himself.

"And what about the cabin crew?" she asked.

"Oh yes, them as well. All been great—helpful when they bring you coffee mid-Atlantic," he said.

"What do you do when you're staying in the hotels?" Annie pressed on.

"Ahh—we meet up, go to restaurants, go out and see the sights, shop—you know, all the usual stuff," Peter said in a matter-of-fact way. Annie was now looking at him unwaveringly.

"Do you—I mean, do any of you, you know, pair up?" Annie finally asked.

"Oh I wouldn't know. You know me—teetotal and shy and living in my own dark world, so I take no notice," he said before bursting out laughing. He'd been doing his best to keep it in, but—

"Peter Marham, you know exactly what I'm asking," Annie said sternly, a huge smile on her face.

Peter finished his meal and pushed his plate away, saying, "Mother, I haven't the faintest idea."

Annie regarded him for a few long moments before saying, "Fine. Didn't really want to know anyway," and she got up to gather the plates.

"Liar," said Paul, laughing.

"I'm not so," she said immediately. "Just curious that's all."

Peter got up, taking the plates and pushing her back down into her chair. "OK. Her name's Amanda and she's cabin crew just out of training. She doesn't like the carefree attitude some of the crews have towards—you know—interpersonal relationships. We've been seeing each other since the Toronto trip, but nothing else to report." This was like a pressure cooker overflowing.

"What? Amanda—who is she? Where does she live? Does she have another boyfriend? How old is she?" Peter roared with laughter and sat back down.

"OK, OK—I plead the fifth amendment," he said laughing. "Where shall I start? She's single, an only child, early twenties, about six feet tall, her mum is really nice—she's called Annabel and they live in South London. She loves travelling, is quiet and well educated, smart and absolutely gorgeous," he said, adding "OK?"

"Oh is that all?" Annie asked with a laugh and a playful swipe at Peter. "Of course, you were going to tell your mummy everything in the fullness of time, no?"

"Of course," Peter replied, feigning shock at the suggestion.

"Well, when do we get to meet her?" Annie demanded.

"Soon, I promise," Peter replied and Paul said, "Give the lad some time love—let him take it at his own pace."

Annie nodded, a smirk on her face. "Good for you, Peter," she said quietly. Inside, she was delighted. The right person giving him some stability and watching out for him was just what he needed.

Shortly, Peter was back at work preparing for his next trip. Amanda wasn't rostered, so he'd miss her, but his line training was paramount. Over the next month or so, he flew with many different training captains and FO's on the jump seat, occasionally meeting his old training colleagues in Flight Planning. Paula was at about the same stage as he was and Sanj, Arnie and Mark were making better progress towards finishing line training due to their shorter sectors and busier rosters. He and Amanda managed to be on the same flight in November, flying to Vancouver with a fuel stop in Calgary on the way over and had an enjoyable few days—and nights—together.

Between rosters, they continued seeing each other and Peter finally took the plunge and moved in with Sanj in the new flat. Peter had his own spacious room, a shared bathroom, kitchen and living area and he and Amanda spent many energetic nights together there. As his and Sanj's rosters were so completely different, they sometimes didn't see each other for days.

Around this time, Sanj introduced his new girlfriend Suzi—a girl from the flight planning office and she quickly moved into the flat as well. He also managed to persuade Amanda to accompany him back home for a weekend after getting the OK with his parents.

"I hope you don't mind a single bed for the weekend," he'd asked and Amanda said that it'd be fine. She and Peter's parents got on really well and made her promise to return for another visit soon. Finally, early in December, Peter had just two line training trips to complete when he was approached by Fozzy.

"Bit of an unusual one if you're interested old boy. We've been chartered by the Ministry of Defence to fly a load of squaddies out to Cyprus for deployment and bring some back. They need the bigger aircraft, so we've copped for it on the VC-10 fleet. It'll be extra to your roster, so double pay, there and back in a day. Let me know if you fancy it."

"Will it count towards my line training?" Peter asked.

"Yes, of course," Fozzy replied.

"OK then—count me in," Peter said.

A few days later, Peter reported for duty and with it being an unusual route, the airline had also rostered in a Captain from the European fleet onto the second jump seat to help. He helped Peter with setting the frequencies and bought a European Airfield book with him for the departure and approach plates. Once completed, inside the briefing area, Peter was surprised to see an all-male crew.

"Lots of trouble on one trip, with drunken squaddies terrorising the girls," Fozzy explained.

"So it's all men today," Peter smiled and they were soon underway. Peter flew the aircraft down route, landing on time. In a break from normal practice, Fozzy asked Peter and the jump seat FO Gary, to go outside and check the aircraft prior to the return trip. "Too damn hot out there for me," he grumbled. Outside, it was unbearably hot and Gary and Peter walked around the aircraft in their shirtsleeves, checking it for serviceability. Peter could hear male voices barking out commands as the soldiers disembarked, but he took little notice.

Waiting on the ramp were a number of army trucks, with soldiers jumping out and forming a line. Something then caught Peter's eye. There was a line of twenty or so soldiers dressed in orange jumpsuits, each handcuffed to a military policeman.

"Naughty boys—probably been in detention. We load them first so there's no escapees," Gary explained.

Whilst checking the landing gear closest to the detainees, Peter heard his name being called and he looked up. There, in the middle of the line watching him closely was Ben, in a jumpsuit and handcuffed. Peter just stood and returned his gaze. Ben looked thin and scruffy, but his eyes were as defiant as always. Peter smiled to himself. *Well well—giving my big brother a lift home for the second year of his detention. What a pleasure that'll be*, he thought. Finally, the line of detainees began to climb the rear steps and Ben nodded his head in Peter's direction, but Peter ignored him.

He re-joined the team on the flightdeck and soon they were underway. Once in the cruise, Peter asked Fozzy about the soldiers in orange jumpsuits and he scoffed. "Probably deserters or people who have broken the military code—no time for 'em," he said firmly.

Peter just smiled—at the end of this sector, his line training would be finished and he'd be released on full pay to begin building his experience and knowledge, knowing that he'd be away from Ben's disruptive influence forever. What a great sector this was going to be—he was going to enjoy this flight enormously.

END

Ingram Content Group UK Ltd.
Milton Keynes UK
UKHW020354210623
423772UK00005B/103